The Dreamer

STORY AND ART BY LORA INNES

COLORS BY MICHAEL MOTTER,
TINA MCGIVERN, AND ALAN EVANS
ORIGINAL SERIES EDITS BY TOM WALTZ
COLLECTION EDITS BY JUSTIN EISINGER
COLLECTION DESIGN BY AMAURI OSORIO

COVER BY LORA & MICHAEL INNES

IDW Publishing
Operations:
Ted Adams, Chief Executive Officer
Greg Goldstein, Chief Operating Officer
Matthew Ruzicka, CPA, Chief Financial Officer
Alan Payne, VP of Sales
Lorelei Bunjes, Dir. of Digital Services
AnnaMaria White, Marketing & PR Manager
Marci Hubbard, Executive Assistant
Alonzo Simon, Shipping Manager

Editorial:
Chris Ryall, Publisher/Editor-in-Chief
Scott Dunbier, Editor, Special Projects
Andy Schmidt, Senior Editor
Justin Eisinger, Editor
Kris Oprisko, Editor/Foreign Lic.
Denton J. Tipton, Editor
Tom Waltz, Editor
Mariah Huehner, Associate Editor

Design:
Robbie Robbins, EVP/Sr. Graphic Artist
Ben Templesmith, Artist/Designer
Neil Uyetake, Art Director
Chris Mowry, Graphic Artist
Amauri Osorio, Graphic Artist
Gilberto Lazcano, Production Assistant

ISBN 978-1-60010-465-7
12 11 10 09   1 2 3 4

SEVERAL PEOPLE WERE PIVOTAL IN THE CREATION OF THIS BOOK:

MY PARENTS, WHO LET ME FOLLOW MY PASSIONS,
EVEN WHEN THEY WERE NON-CONVENTIONAL.

BEAU SMITH, WHO SAW HIDDEN POTENTIAL IN A SHY, AWKWARD TEENAGER
AND TOOK TIME TO INVEST IN ME THROUGHOUT THE YEARS.

AND THE DREAMER WILL ALWAYS BE FOR THE MAN WHO
REARRANGED OUR LIVES TO MAKE MY DREAM A REALITY-
MY BEST FRIEND AND TEAMMATE, MY HUSBAND MIKE.

THIS VOLUME OF THE DREAMER IS IN LOVING MEMORY OF THE MAN FROM WHOM
I GET MY REVOLUTIONARY ANCESTRY. YOU ALWAYS MADE ME FEEL LIKE THE MOST
IMPORTANT PERSON IN ANY ROOM. I'LL MISS YOU, FAVORITE MAN.

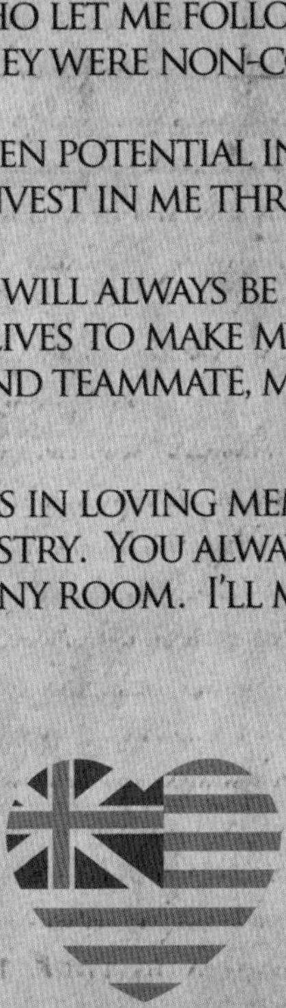

FOR MY GRANDFATHER,
DELWYN FRY
1930 - 2009

START HERE

1763, the end of the French & Indian War, where the British Army & American Colonists fought side by side to defend territorial claims in North America.

But wars cost money, and King George III and Parliament agree that the American Colonies should help pay the bill.

But the Americans have no representatives in Parliament, thus the cry "No taxation without representation!"

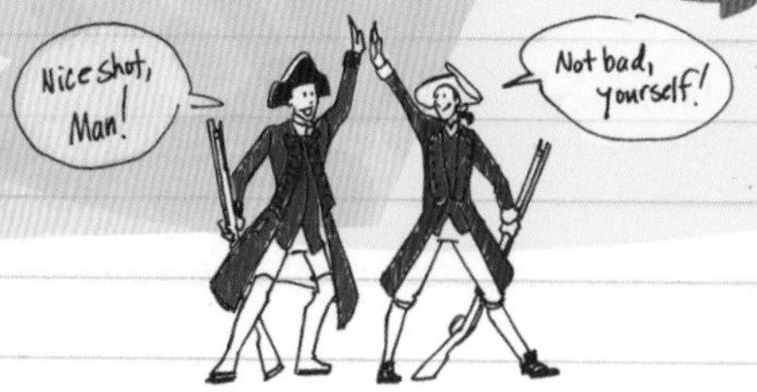
Nice shot, Man!
Not bad, yourself!

March 1770, on a dark, icy night, a rabble of Bostonian boys pick a fight with the British Regulars. Shots are fired into the crowd. Five peole die, and Paul Revere creates a grossly inaccurate drawing of the "Bloody Massacre" which inflames the American populace.

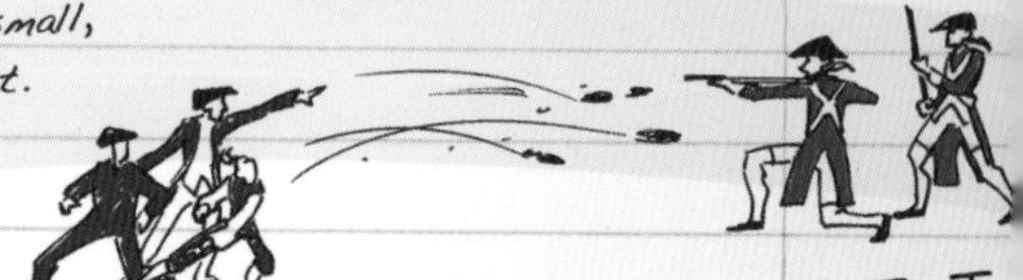

British Merchants, hurting from the boycotts, pressure Parliament to repeal the taxes. Again they do, except for the small, harmless Tea Act.

The Americans still object and throw the tea into Boston Harbor to make their point.

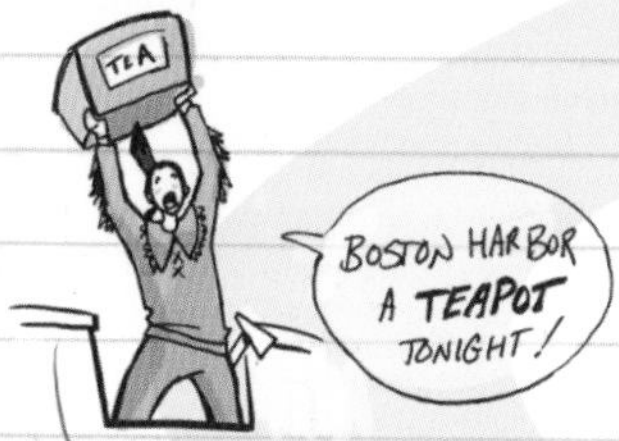
TEA
BOSTON HARBOR A TEAPOT TONIGHT!

King George has had enough. He puts a blockade around Boston to keep supplies from coming in- to starve them into submission. Instead, relief is sent from each of the other 13 Colonies. Boston groans but Unity grows...

THE AMERICAN (in just

All over, Colonial-appointed legislatures are being shut down by the Crown. So in 1774 the Colonists elect their own representatives and send them to Philadelphia for the 1st Continental Congress. The meeting is, of course, treason.

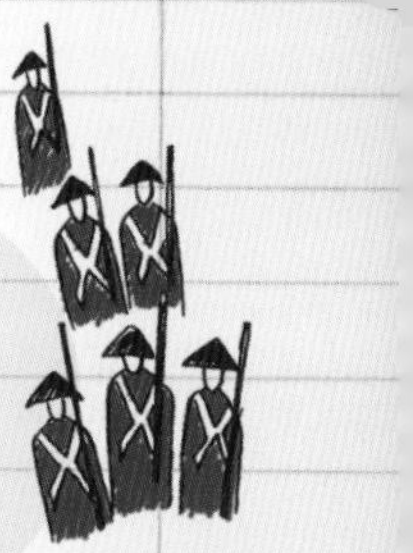

April 1775, Patriots in Boston learn that the British Army plans to remove their gunpowder stores to keep it out of the local militia's hands. The powder is hidden, the militia readied and when the Regulars arrive, someone fires the "Shot Heard Round the World" at Lexington Green.

The war has begun.

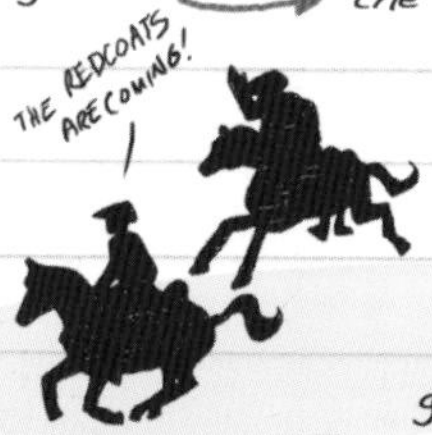
THE REDCOATS ARE COMING!

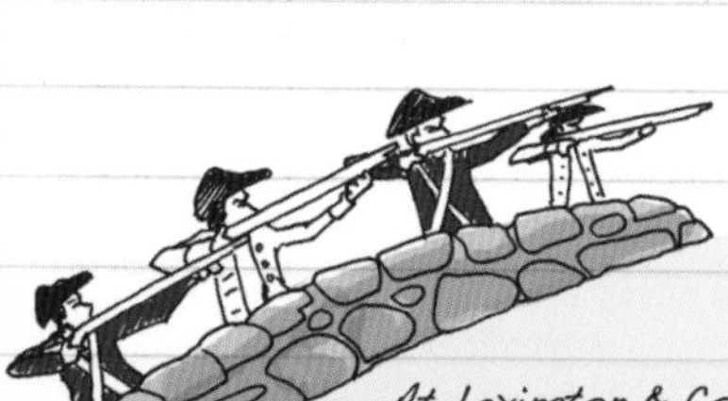

At Lexington & Concord the militia miraculously pushes the British army back to Boston where they lay siege on the city, trapping the soldiers inside.

Though Congress is outraged over the fighting, all 13 Colonies cannot come to a consensus on what should be done.

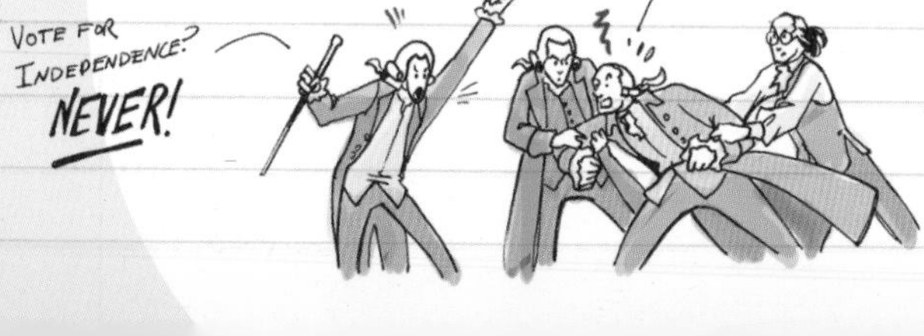
VOTE FOR INDEPENDENCE? NEVER!
YOU MINDLESS, SPINELESS, HEARTLESS, BRAINLESS —

While still waiting for Congress to send military supplies, the New Englanders secretly fortify Breed's Hill (across from Boston) in the middle of the night, June 1775. The British Regulars set fire to the city of Charlestown and then try to take Breed's hill.

In 1765, Parliament passes the Stamp Act anyway, taxing printed papers in the Colonies. The Liberty Boys are too busy burning tax collectors in effigy to actually *pay* the tax.

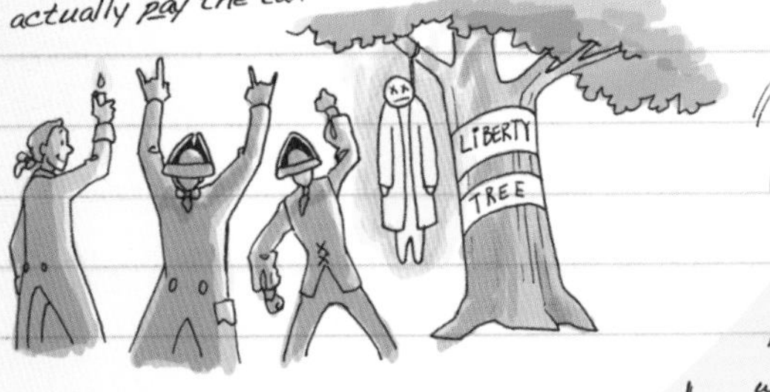

LIBERTY
TREE

Protests and boycotts work. The Stamp Act is repealed. But the repeal is accompanied by the Declaratory Act which is King George's way of saying:

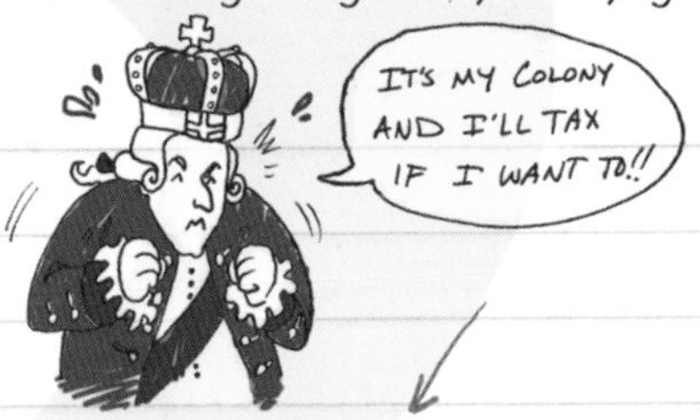

IT'S MY COLONY AND I'LL TAX IF I WANT TO!!

Parliament tries taxing the Colonies again with the Townshend Acts. The Colonists boycott again. They begin creating their own goods rather then import from England. Homespun cloth becomes fashionable, and the once derogatory term "American" is now worn as a badge of honor.

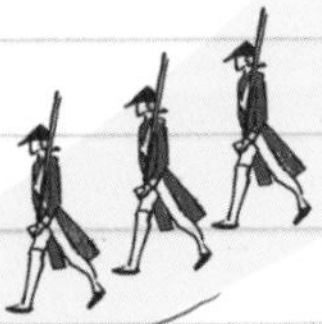

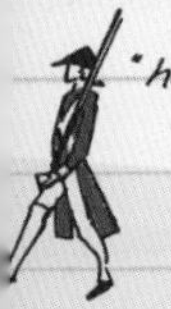

By 1768, King George decides the "hands-off" parenting techinque just isn't working with the Colonists anymore. British troops arrive to "babysit" Boston.

REVOLUTION
2 pages!)

But the Americans have the better position and retreat only after running out of "ammunition."

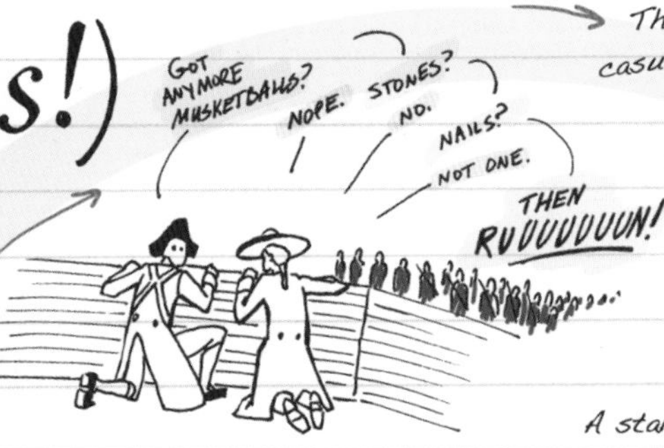

GOT ANYMORE MUSKETBALLS?
NOPE.
STONES?
NO.
NAILS?
NOT ONE.
THEN RUUUUUUUN!

The British suffer over 1,000 casualties, nearly half their force.

(The battle comes to be known as the Battle of Bunker Hill after Breed's taller neighbor.)

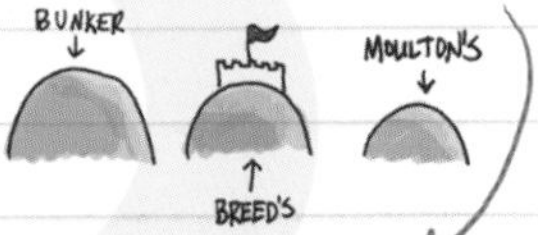

BUNKER
MOULTON'S
BREED'S

A stalemate continues for a year in both Boston <u>and</u> Congress. Congress agrees long enough to appoint George Washington as Commander of the yet-to-be-formed Continental Army.

March 1776, Henry Knox brings 50 cannons from Fort Ticonderoga on sleds, through the snowy mountains of New York to Boston.

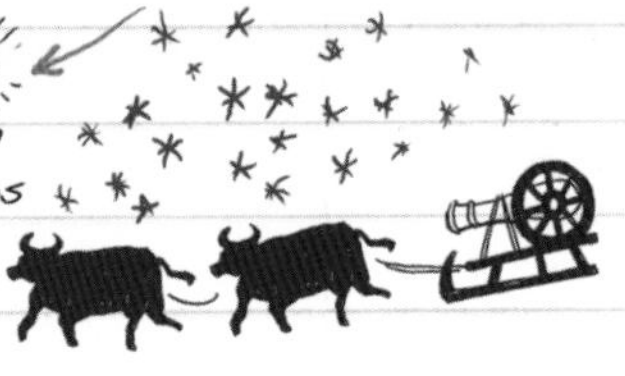

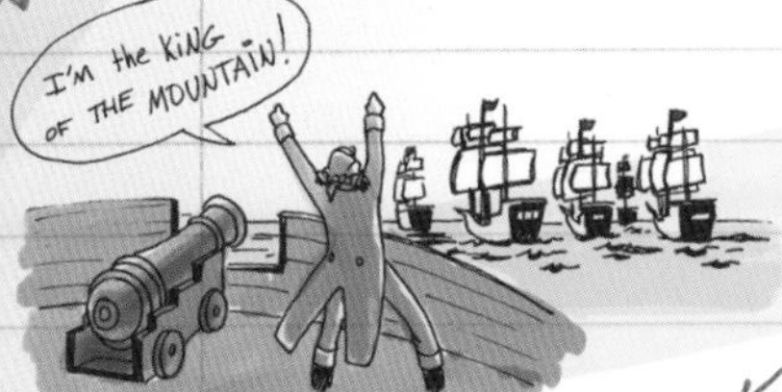

I'M the KING of THE MOUNTAIN!

Washington then wastes no time. He uses the cannons to secretly fortify Dorchester Heights, an adventageous position outside of Boston, much like they did at Breed's Hill. It works: The British leave Boston for good.

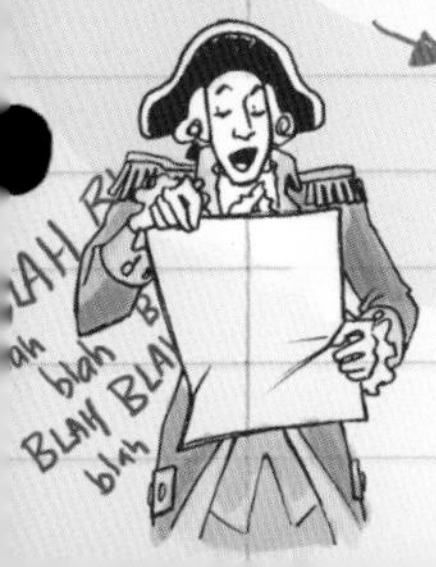

blah
BLAH BLAH
blah

July 1776, the Declaration of Independence is finally passed by Congress, severing all ties to England. George Washington reads it to his army assembled in New York City. It is met with tears, cheers and of course, <u>riots</u>.

August 1776, both Armies are assembled in New York City, as well as the most impressive show of British Naval power in history. The Americans have fortified Manhattan and Long Island. Both sides sit, watching one another and waiting for the inevitable battle to begin...

Which brings us to the events described in the following pages...

Chapter One

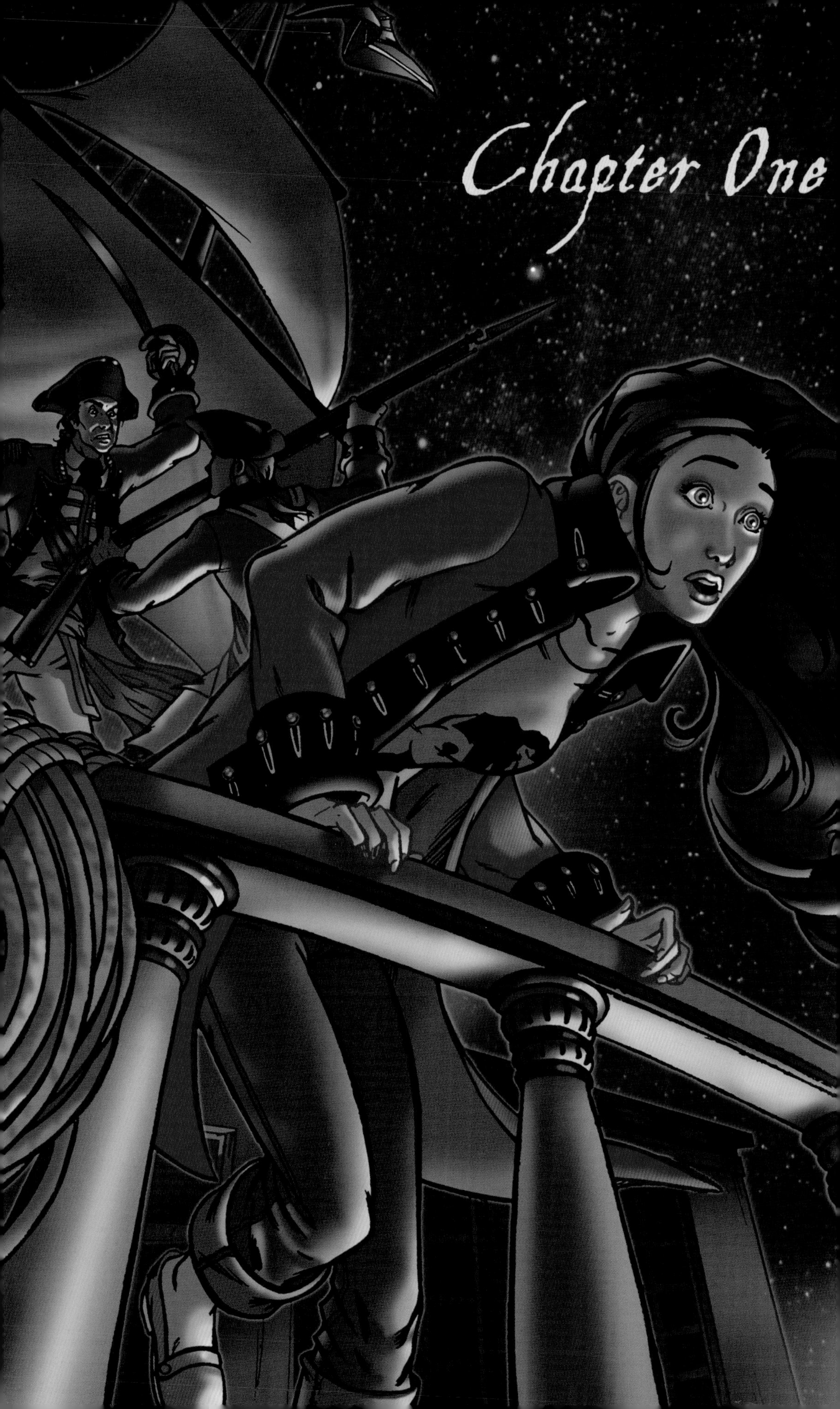

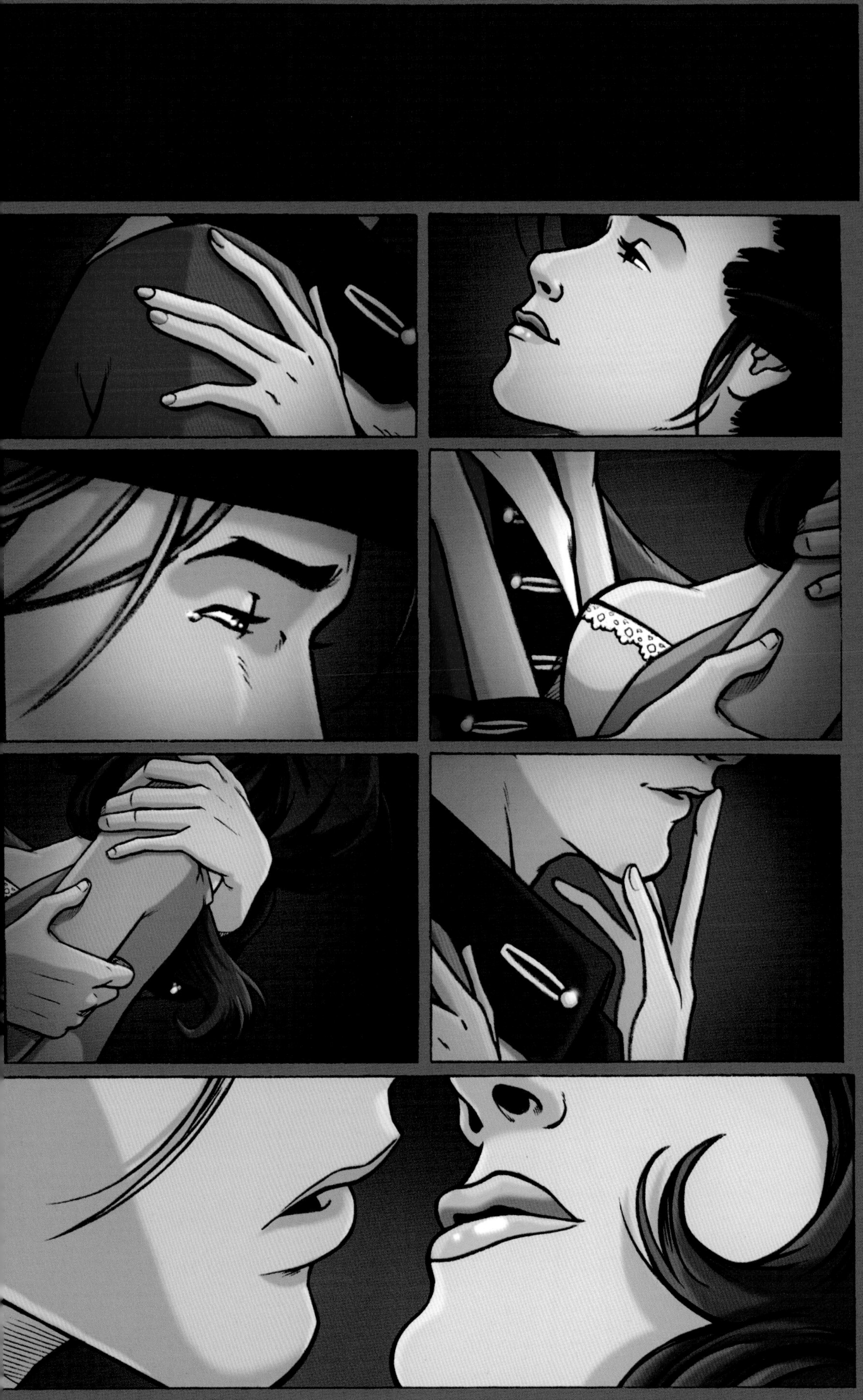

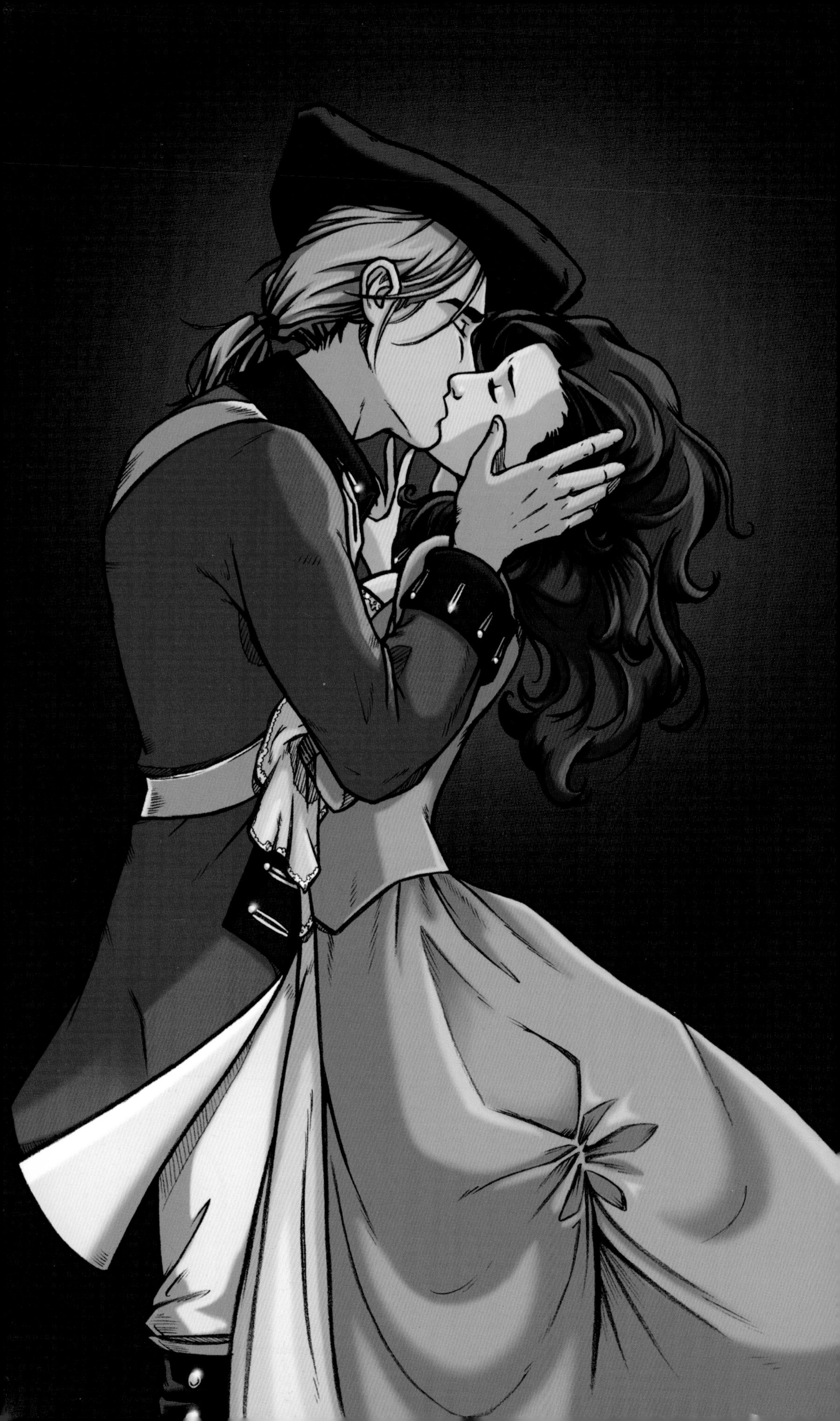

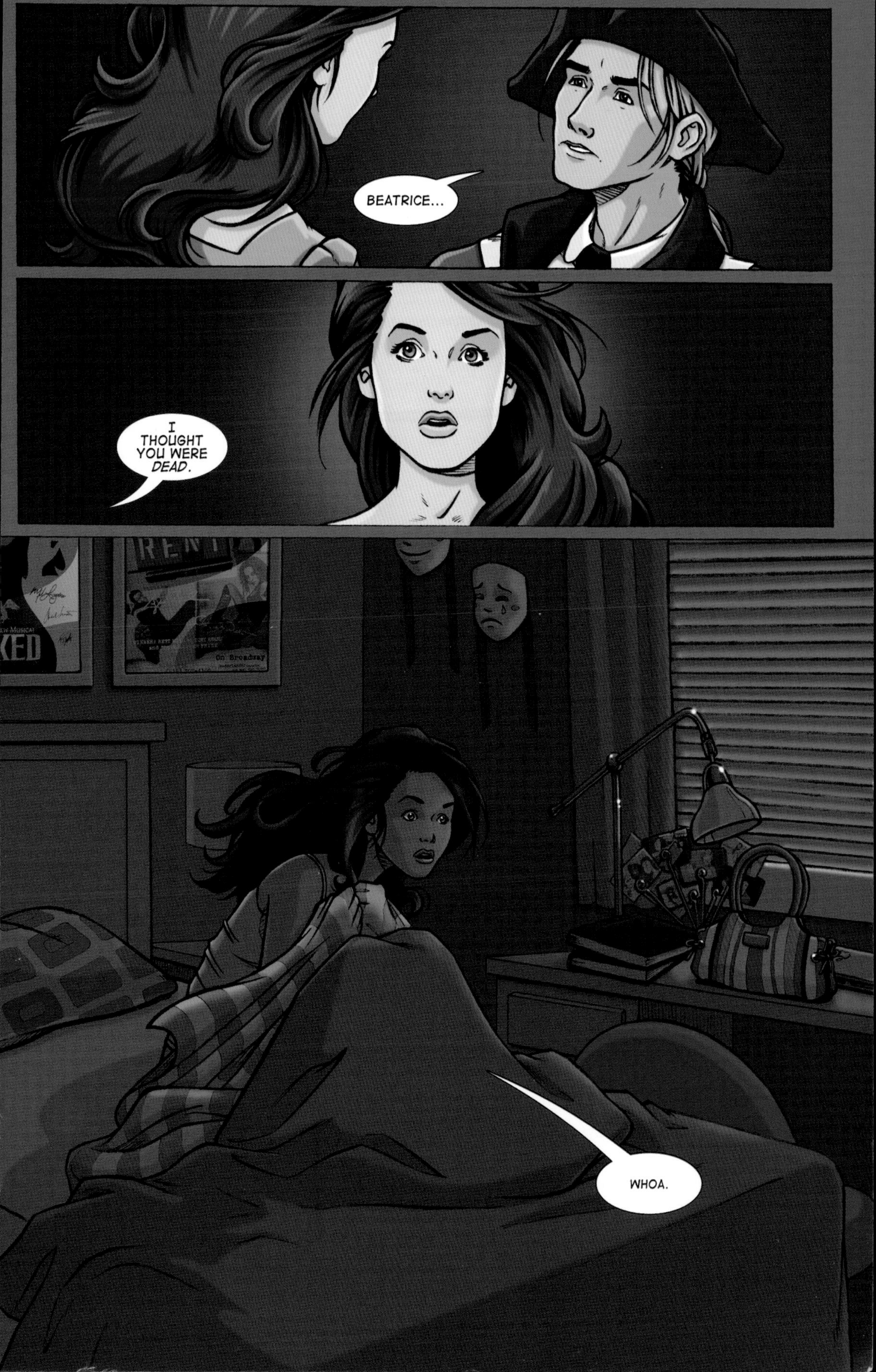
BEATRICE...
I THOUGHT YOU WERE *DEAD*.
WHOA.

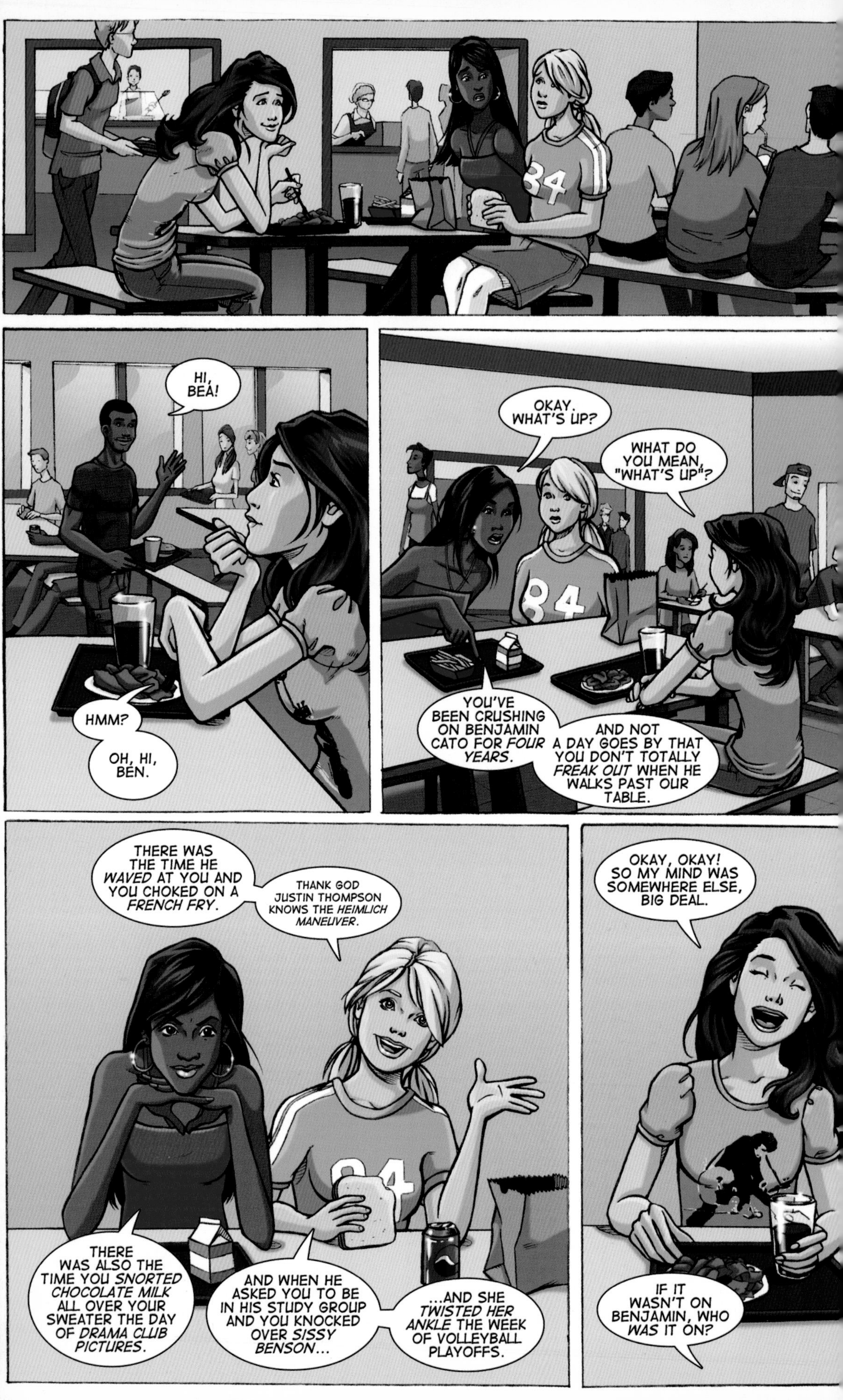
HI, BEA!
HMM?
OH, HI, BEN.
OKAY. WHAT'S UP?
WHAT DO YOU MEAN, "WHAT'S UP"?
YOU'VE BEEN CRUSHING ON BENJAMIN CATO FOR *FOUR YEARS*.
AND NOT A DAY GOES BY THAT YOU DON'T TOTALLY *FREAK OUT* WHEN HE WALKS PAST OUR TABLE.
THERE WAS THE TIME HE *WAVED* AT YOU AND YOU CHOKED ON A *FRENCH FRY*.
THANK GOD JUSTIN THOMPSON KNOWS THE *HEIMLICH MANEUVER*.
THERE WAS ALSO THE TIME YOU *SNORTED CHOCOLATE MILK* ALL OVER YOUR SWEATER THE DAY OF *DRAMA CLUB PICTURES*.
AND WHEN HE ASKED YOU TO BE IN HIS STUDY GROUP AND YOU KNOCKED OVER *SISSY BENSON*...
...AND SHE *TWISTED HER ANKLE* THE WEEK OF VOLLEYBALL PLAYOFFS.
OKAY, OKAY! SO MY MIND WAS SOMEWHERE ELSE, BIG DEAL.
IF IT WASN'T ON BENJAMIN, WHO *WAS* IT ON?

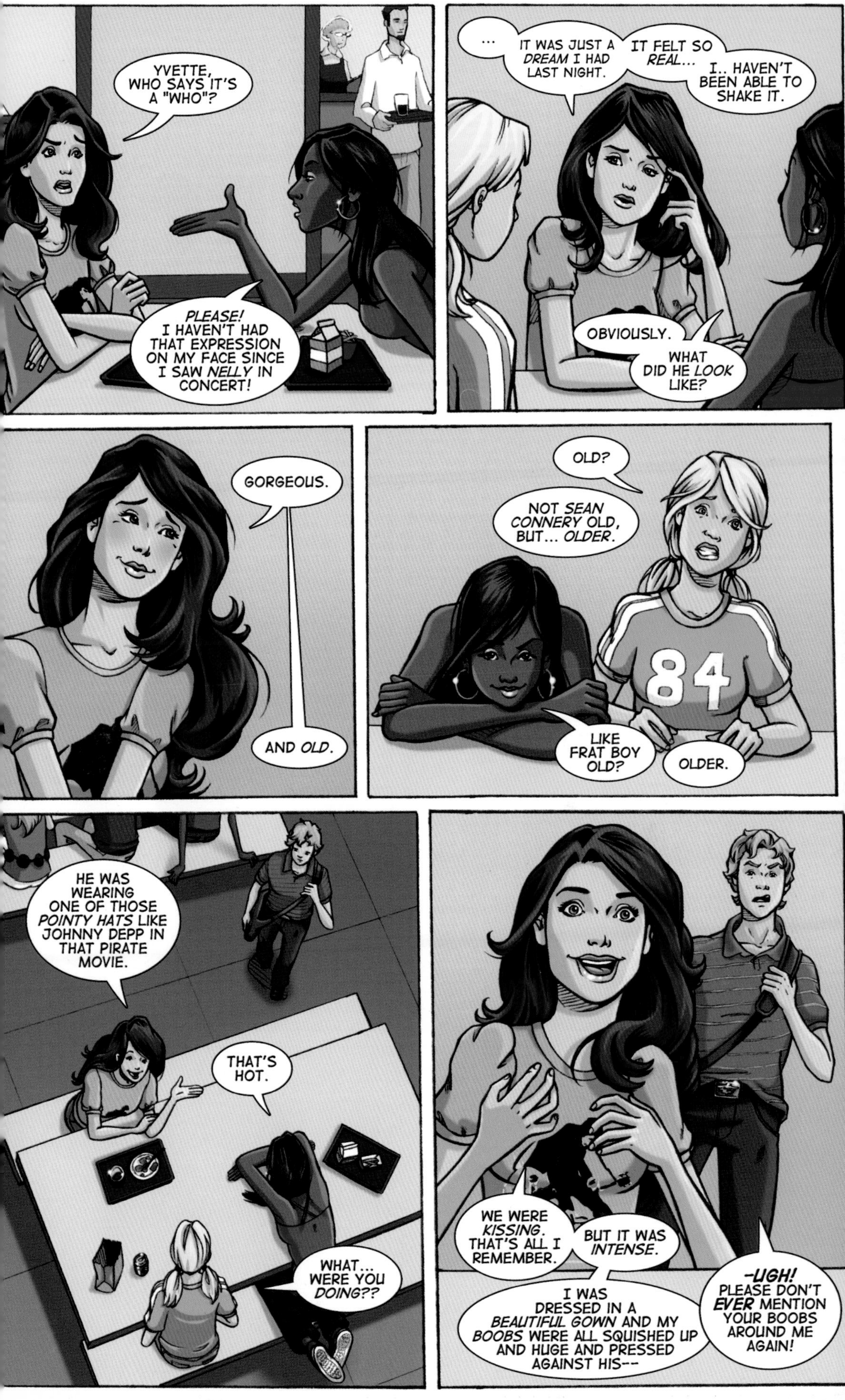
YVETTE, WHO SAYS IT'S A "WHO"?
PLEASE! I HAVEN'T HAD THAT EXPRESSION ON MY FACE SINCE I SAW NELLY IN CONCERT!
...
IT WAS JUST A DREAM I HAD LAST NIGHT.
IT FELT SO REAL...
I.. HAVEN'T BEEN ABLE TO SHAKE IT.
OBVIOUSLY.
WHAT DID HE LOOK LIKE?
GORGEOUS.
AND OLD.
OLD?
NOT SEAN CONNERY OLD, BUT... OLDER.
84
LIKE FRAT BOY OLD?
OLDER.
HE WAS WEARING ONE OF THOSE POINTY HATS LIKE JOHNNY DEPP IN THAT PIRATE MOVIE.
THAT'S HOT.
WHAT... WERE YOU DOING??
WE WERE KISSING. THAT'S ALL I REMEMBER.
BUT IT WAS INTENSE.
I WAS DRESSED IN A BEAUTIFUL GOWN AND MY BOOBS WERE ALL SQUISHED UP AND HUGE AND PRESSED AGAINST HIS--
-UGH! PLEASE DON'T EVER MENTION YOUR BOOBS AROUND ME AGAIN!

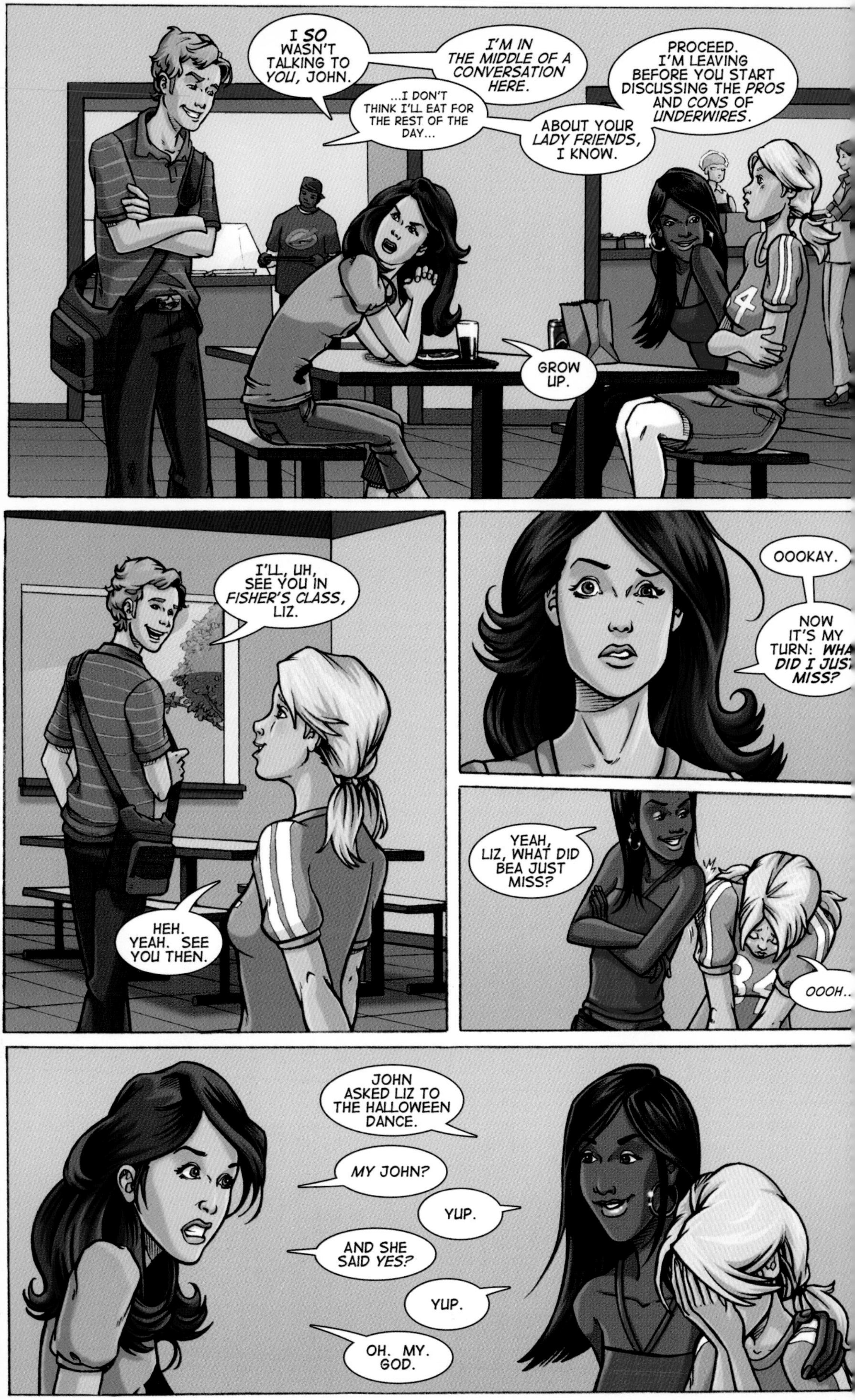
I *SO* WASN'T TALKING TO *YOU*, JOHN.
I'M IN THE MIDDLE OF A CONVERSATION HERE.
...I DON'T THINK I'LL EAT FOR THE REST OF THE DAY...
ABOUT YOUR *LADY FRIENDS*, I KNOW.
PROCEED. I'M LEAVING BEFORE YOU START DISCUSSING THE *PROS* AND *CONS* OF *UNDERWIRES*.
GROW UP.
I'LL, UH, SEE YOU IN *FISHER'S CLASS*, LIZ.
HEH. YEAH. SEE YOU THEN.
OOOKAY.
NOW IT'S MY TURN: *WHA DID I JUS MISS?*
YEAH, LIZ, WHAT DID BEA JUST MISS?
OOOH..
JOHN ASKED LIZ TO THE HALLOWEEN DANCE.
MY JOHN?
YUP.
AND SHE SAID *YES?*
YUP.
OH. MY. GOD.

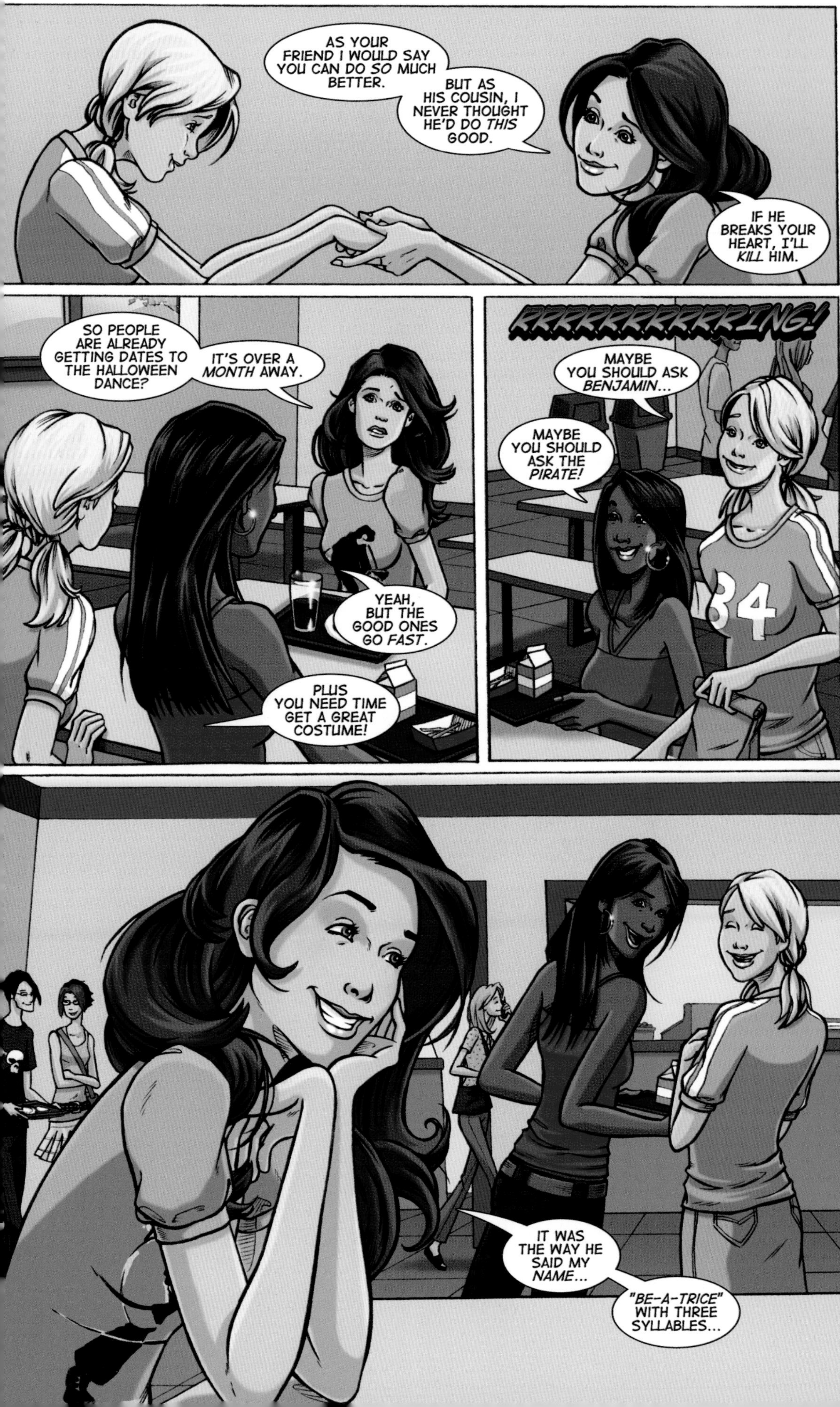
AS YOUR FRIEND I WOULD SAY YOU CAN DO *SO* MUCH BETTER.
BUT AS HIS COUSIN, I NEVER THOUGHT HE'D DO *THIS* GOOD.
IF HE BREAKS YOUR HEART, I'LL *KILL* HIM.
SO PEOPLE ARE ALREADY GETTING DATES TO THE HALLOWEEN DANCE?
IT'S OVER A *MONTH* AWAY.
YEAH, BUT THE GOOD ONES GO *FAST*.
PLUS YOU NEED TIME GET A GREAT COSTUME!
RRRRRRRRRRRRING!
MAYBE YOU SHOULD ASK *BENJAMIN*...
MAYBE YOU SHOULD ASK THE *PIRATE!*
IT WAS THE WAY HE SAID MY *NAME*...
"BE-A-TRICE" WITH THREE SYLLABLES...

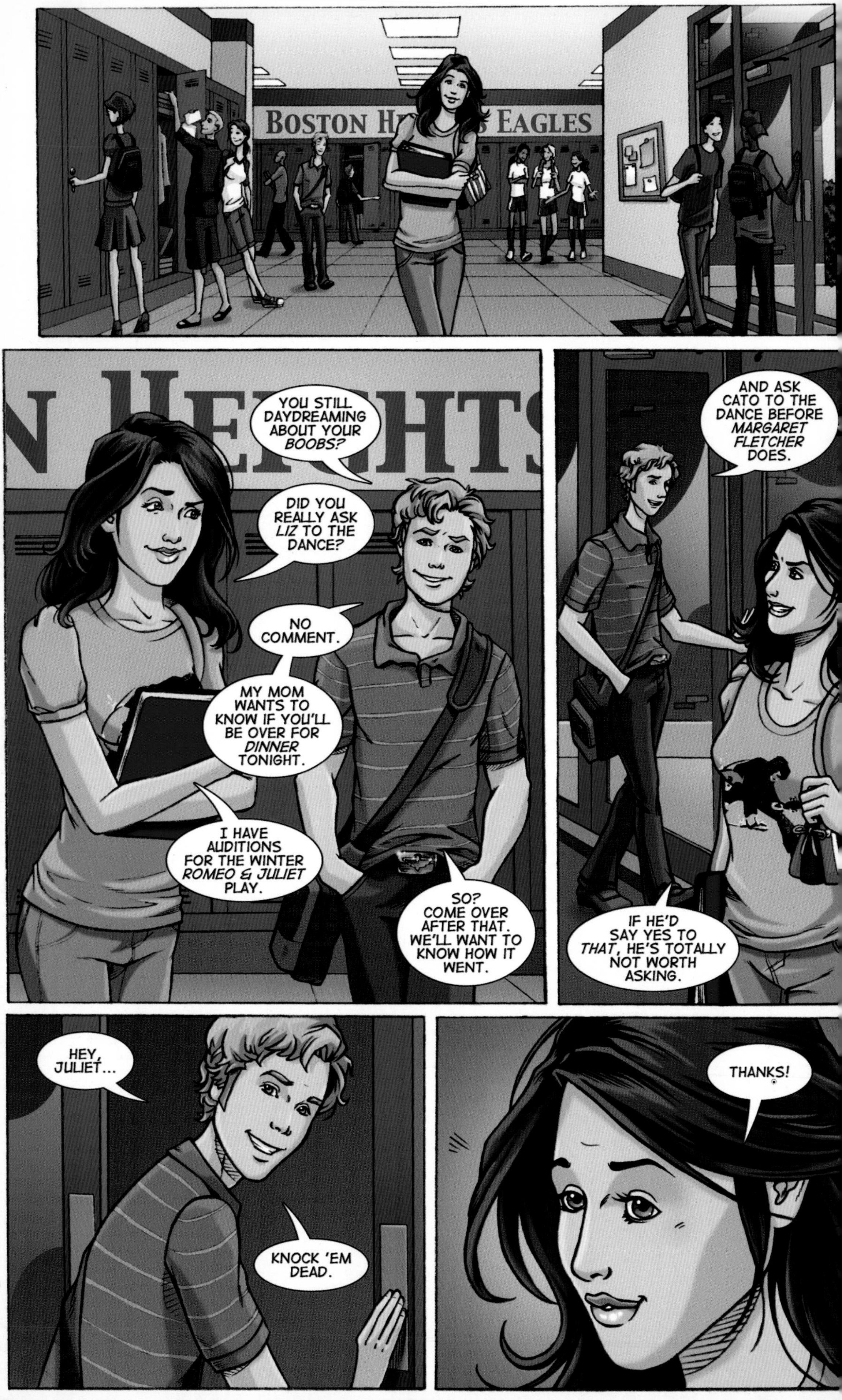
BOSTON H S EAGLES
YOU STILL DAYDREAMING ABOUT YOUR *BOOBS?*
DID YOU REALLY ASK *LIZ* TO THE DANCE?
NO COMMENT.
MY MOM WANTS TO KNOW IF YOU'LL BE OVER FOR *DINNER* TONIGHT.
I HAVE AUDITIONS FOR THE WINTER *ROMEO & JULIET* PLAY.
SO? COME OVER AFTER THAT. WE'LL WANT TO KNOW HOW IT WENT.
AND ASK CATO TO THE DANCE BEFORE *MARGARET FLETCHER* DOES.
IF HE'D SAY YES TO *THAT*, HE'S TOTALLY NOT WORTH ASKING.
HEY, JULIET...
KNOCK 'EM DEAD.
THANKS!

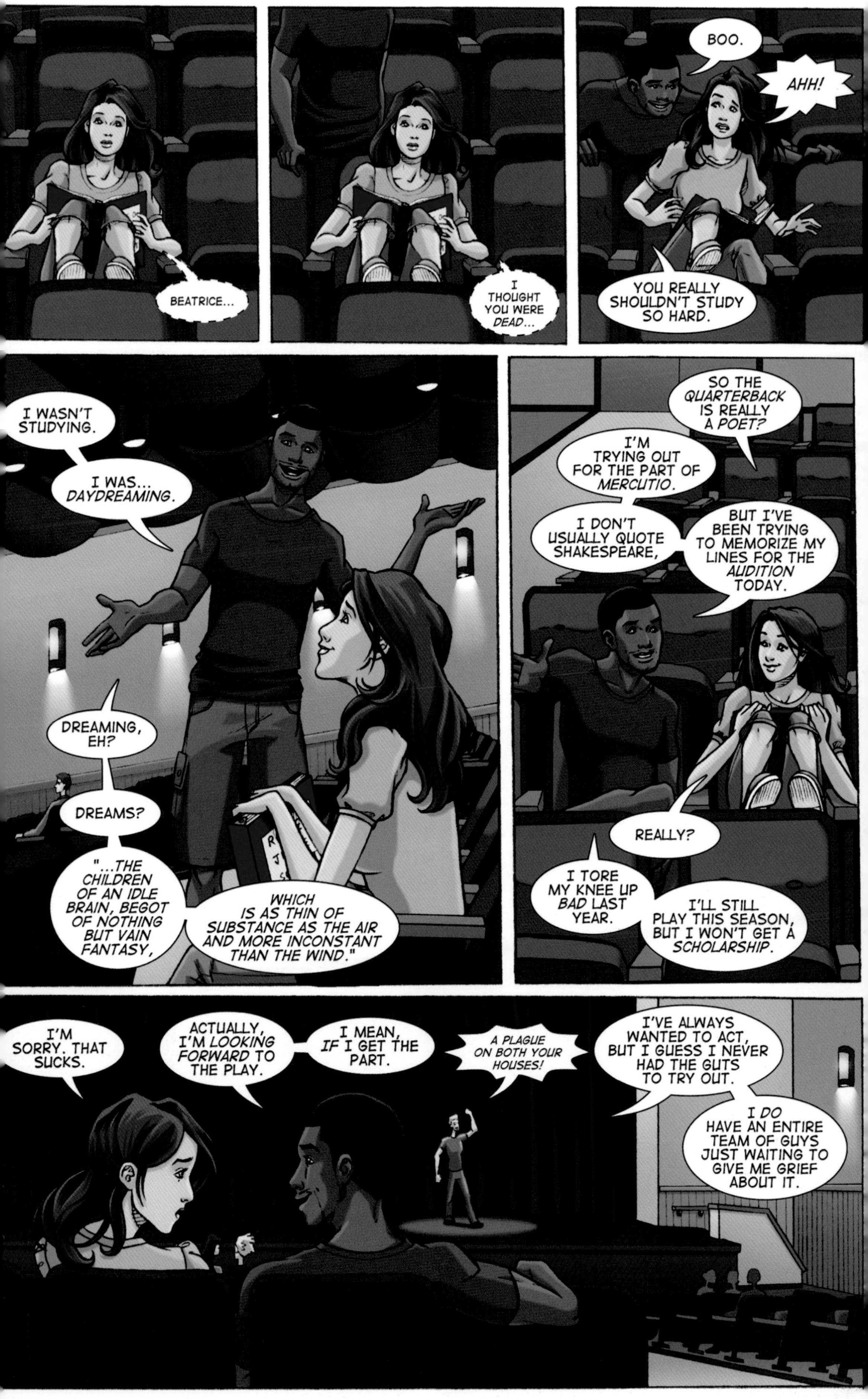
BEATRICE...
I THOUGHT YOU WERE *DEAD*...
BOO.
AHH!
YOU REALLY SHOULDN'T STUDY SO HARD.
I WASN'T STUDYING.
I WAS... *DAYDREAMING*.
DREAMING, EH?
DREAMS?
"...THE CHILDREN OF AN IDLE BRAIN, BEGOT OF NOTHING BUT VAIN FANTASY,
WHICH IS AS THIN OF SUBSTANCE AS THE AIR AND MORE INCONSTANT THAN THE WIND."
SO THE *QUARTERBACK* IS REALLY A *POET?*
I'M TRYING OUT FOR THE PART OF *MERCUTIO*.
I DON'T USUALLY QUOTE SHAKESPEARE,
BUT I'VE BEEN TRYING TO MEMORIZE MY LINES FOR THE *AUDITION* TODAY.
REALLY?
I TORE MY KNEE UP *BAD* LAST YEAR.
I'LL STILL PLAY THIS SEASON, BUT I WON'T GET A *SCHOLARSHIP*.
I'M SORRY. THAT SUCKS.
ACTUALLY, I'M *LOOKING FORWARD* TO THE PLAY.
I MEAN, *IF* I GET THE PART.
A PLAGUE ON BOTH YOUR HOUSES!
I'VE ALWAYS WANTED TO ACT, BUT I GUESS I NEVER HAD THE GUTS TO TRY OUT.
I *DO* HAVE AN ENTIRE TEAM OF GUYS JUST WAITING TO GIVE ME GRIEF ABOUT IT.

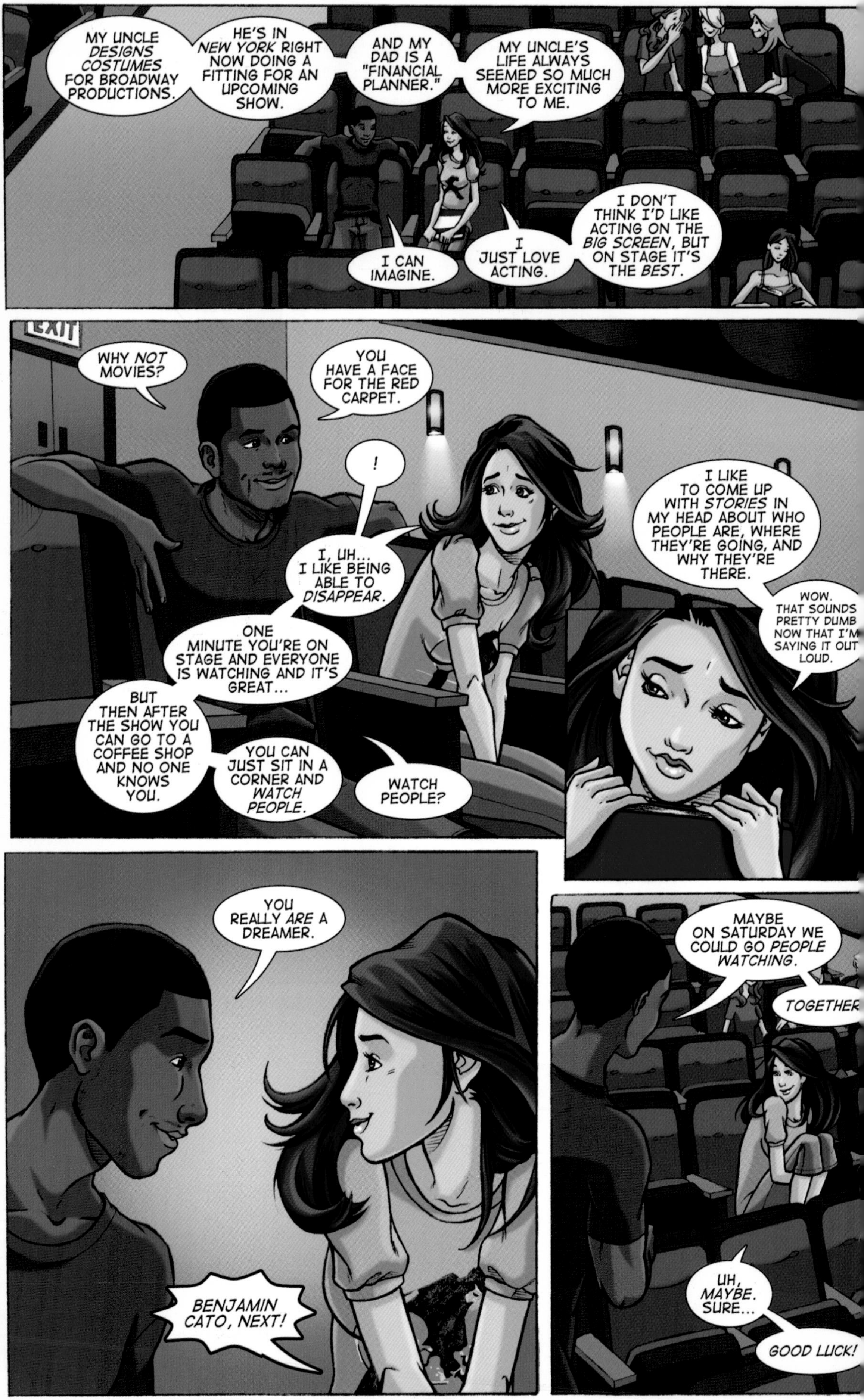
MY UNCLE DESIGNS COSTUMES FOR BROADWAY PRODUCTIONS.
HE'S IN NEW YORK RIGHT NOW DOING A FITTING FOR AN UPCOMING SHOW.
AND MY DAD IS A "FINANCIAL PLANNER."
MY UNCLE'S LIFE ALWAYS SEEMED SO MUCH MORE EXCITING TO ME.
I CAN IMAGINE.
I JUST LOVE ACTING.
I DON'T THINK I'D LIKE ACTING ON THE BIG SCREEN, BUT ON STAGE IT'S THE BEST.
WHY NOT MOVIES?
YOU HAVE A FACE FOR THE RED CARPET.
!
I, UH... I LIKE BEING ABLE TO DISAPPEAR.
ONE MINUTE YOU'RE ON STAGE AND EVERYONE IS WATCHING AND IT'S GREAT...
BUT THEN AFTER THE SHOW YOU CAN GO TO A COFFEE SHOP AND NO ONE KNOWS YOU.
YOU CAN JUST SIT IN A CORNER AND WATCH PEOPLE.
WATCH PEOPLE?
I LIKE TO COME UP WITH STORIES IN MY HEAD ABOUT WHO PEOPLE ARE, WHERE THEY'RE GOING, AND WHY THEY'RE THERE.
WOW. THAT SOUNDS PRETTY DUMB NOW THAT I'M SAYING IT OUT LOUD.
YOU REALLY ARE A DREAMER.
BENJAMIN CATO, NEXT!
MAYBE ON SATURDAY WE COULD GO PEOPLE WATCHING.
TOGETHER
UH, MAYBE. SURE...
GOOD LUCK!

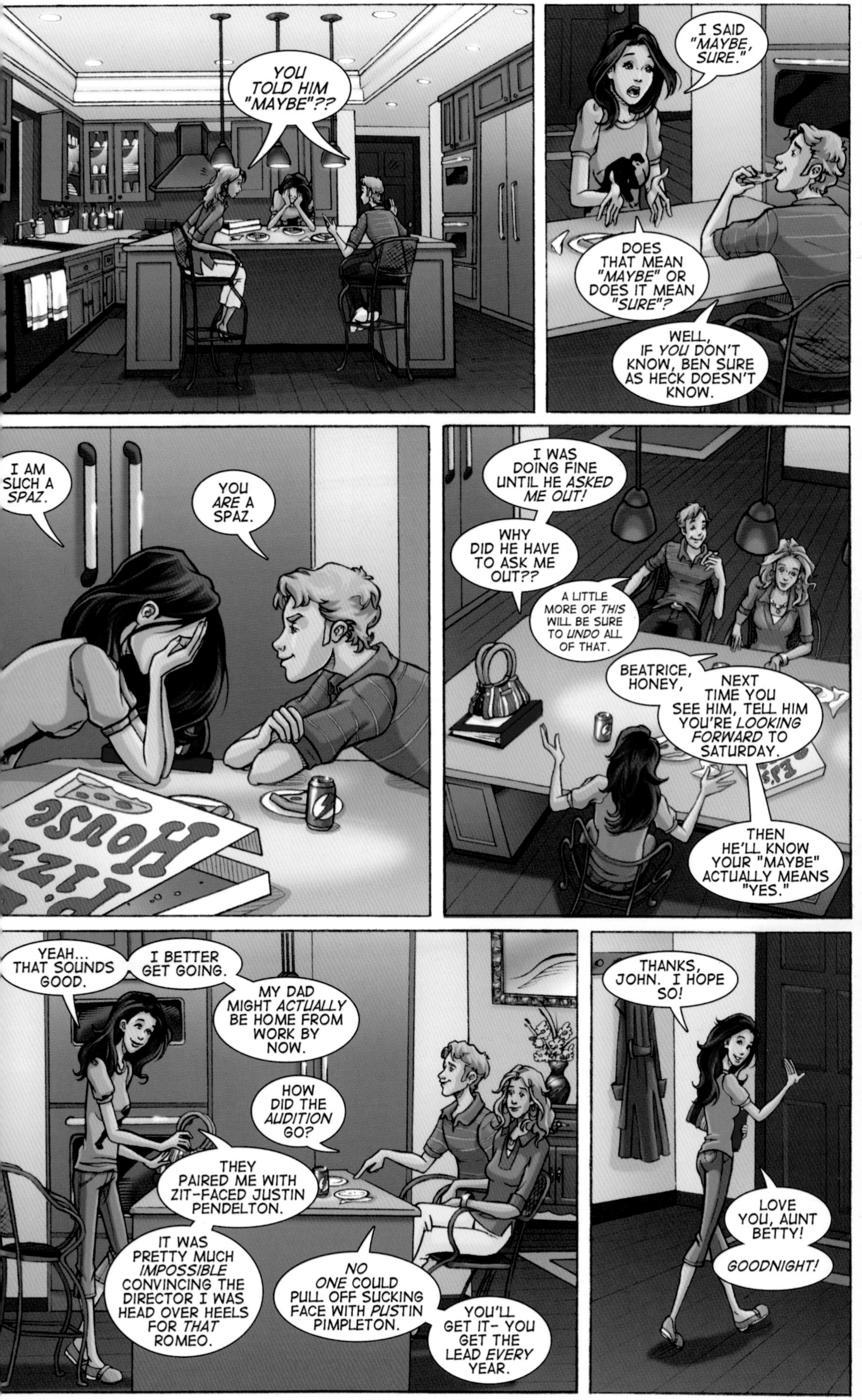
YOU TOLD HIM "MAYBE"??
I SAID "MAYBE, SURE."
DOES THAT MEAN "MAYBE" OR DOES IT MEAN "SURE"?
WELL, IF YOU DON'T KNOW, BEN SURE AS HECK DOESN'T KNOW.
I AM SUCH A SPAZ.
YOU ARE A SPAZ.
Pizza House
I WAS DOING FINE UNTIL HE ASKED ME OUT!
WHY DID HE HAVE TO ASK ME OUT??
A LITTLE MORE OF THIS WILL BE SURE TO UNDO ALL OF THAT.
BEATRICE, HONEY,
NEXT TIME YOU SEE HIM, TELL HIM YOU'RE LOOKING FORWARD TO SATURDAY.
THEN HE'LL KNOW YOUR "MAYBE" ACTUALLY MEANS "YES."
YEAH... THAT SOUNDS GOOD.
I BETTER GET GOING.
MY DAD MIGHT ACTUALLY BE HOME FROM WORK BY NOW.
HOW DID THE AUDITION GO?
THEY PAIRED ME WITH ZIT-FACED JUSTIN PENDELTON.
IT WAS PRETTY MUCH IMPOSSIBLE CONVINCING THE DIRECTOR I WAS HEAD OVER HEELS FOR THAT ROMEO.
NO ONE COULD PULL OFF SUCKING FACE WITH PUSTIN PIMPLETON.
YOU'LL GET IT- YOU GET THE LEAD EVERY YEAR.
THANKS, JOHN. I HOPE SO!
LOVE YOU, AUNT BETTY!
GOODNIGHT!

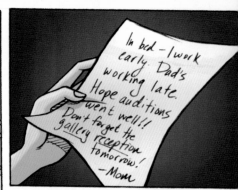

In bed — I work early. Dad's working late. Hope auditions went well!! Don't forget the gallery reception tomorrow! — Mom

click!

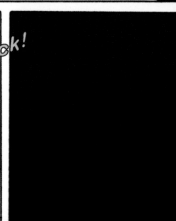

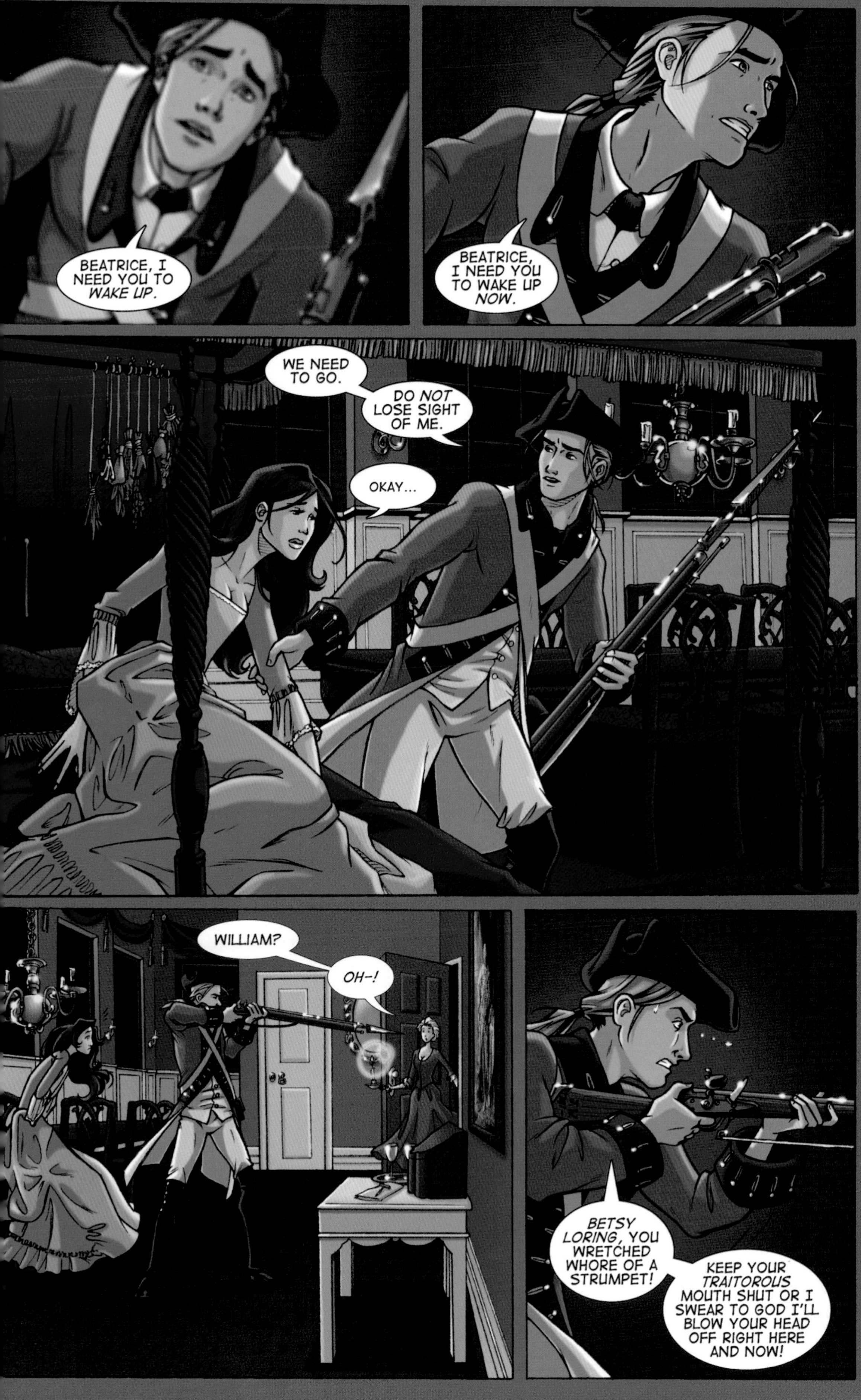
BEATRICE, I NEED YOU TO *WAKE UP*.
BEATRICE, I NEED YOU TO WAKE UP *NOW*.
WE NEED TO GO.
DO *NOT* LOSE SIGHT OF ME.
OKAY...
WILLIAM?
OH-!
BETSY LORING, YOU WRETCHED WHORE OF A STRUMPET!
KEEP YOUR *TRAITOROUS* MOUTH SHUT OR I SWEAR TO GOD I'LL BLOW YOUR HEAD OFF RIGHT HERE AND NOW!

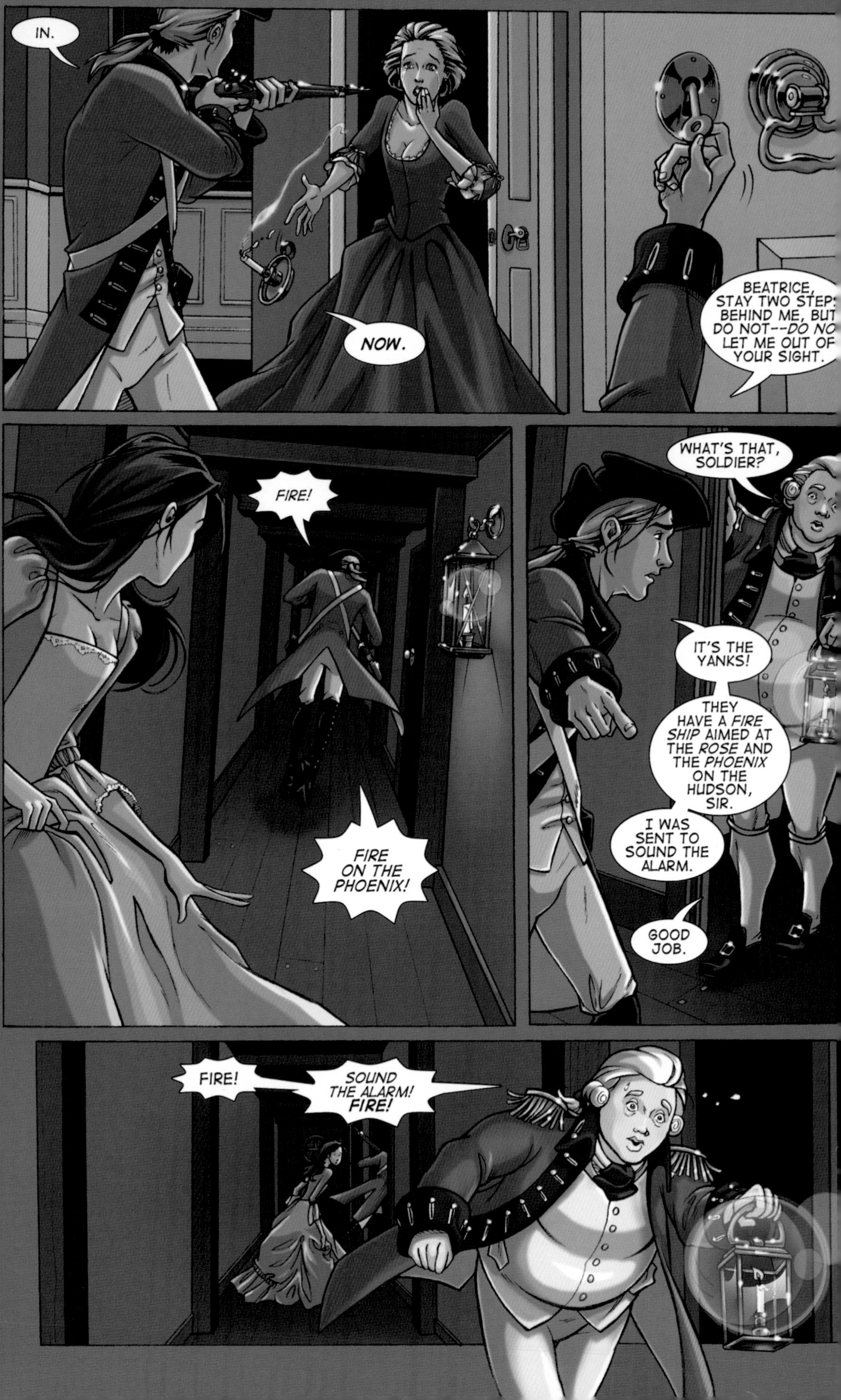
IN.
NOW.
BEATRICE, STAY TWO STEPS BEHIND ME, BUT DO NOT--DO NOT LET ME OUT OF YOUR SIGHT.
FIRE!
FIRE ON THE PHOENIX!
WHAT'S THAT, SOLDIER?
IT'S THE YANKS!
THEY HAVE A FIRE SHIP AIMED AT THE ROSE AND THE PHOENIX ON THE HUDSON, SIR.
I WAS SENT TO SOUND THE ALARM.
GOOD JOB.
FIRE!
SOUND THE ALARM! FIRE!

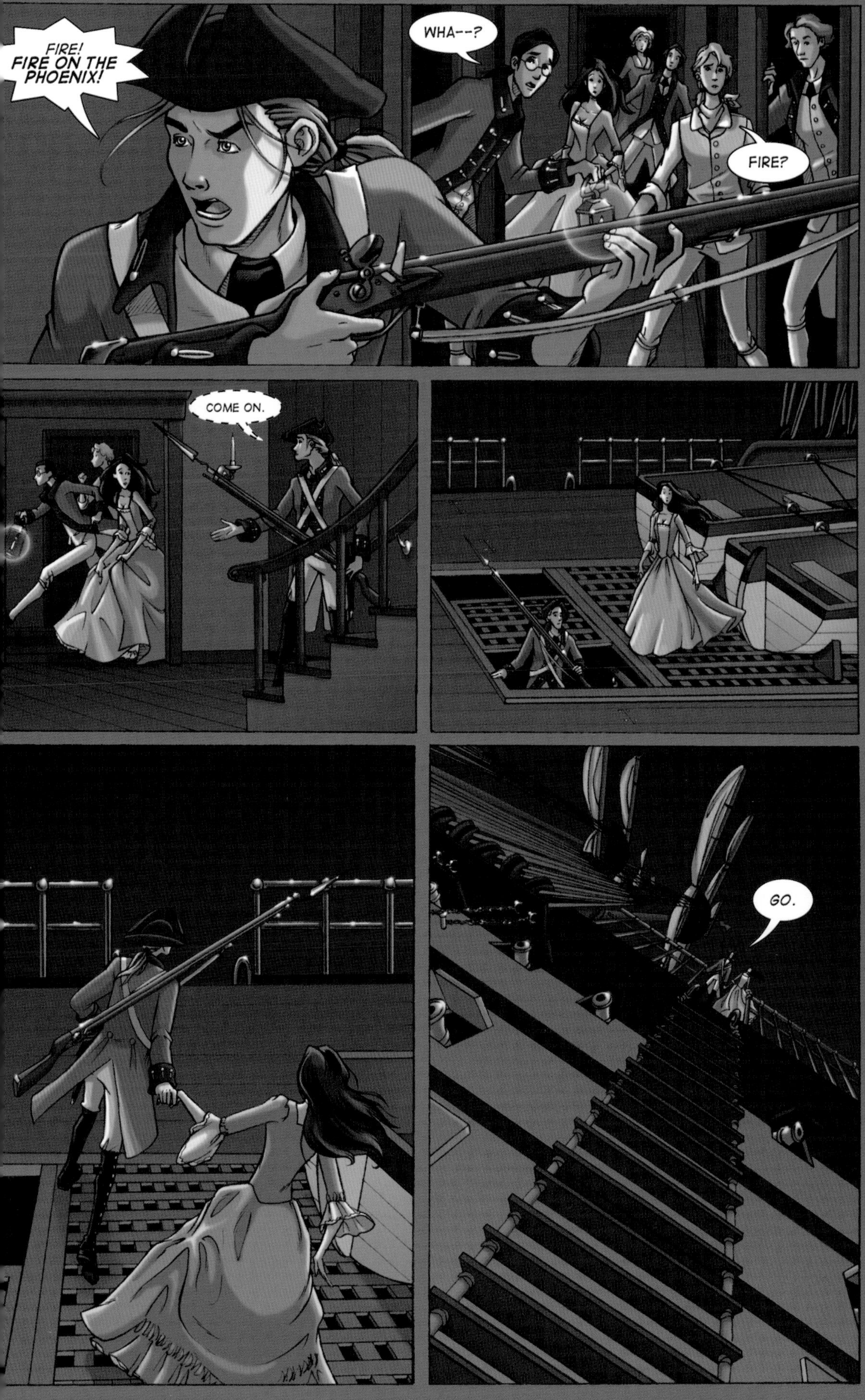
FIRE!
FIRE ON THE PHOENIX!
WHA--?
FIRE?
COME ON.
GO.

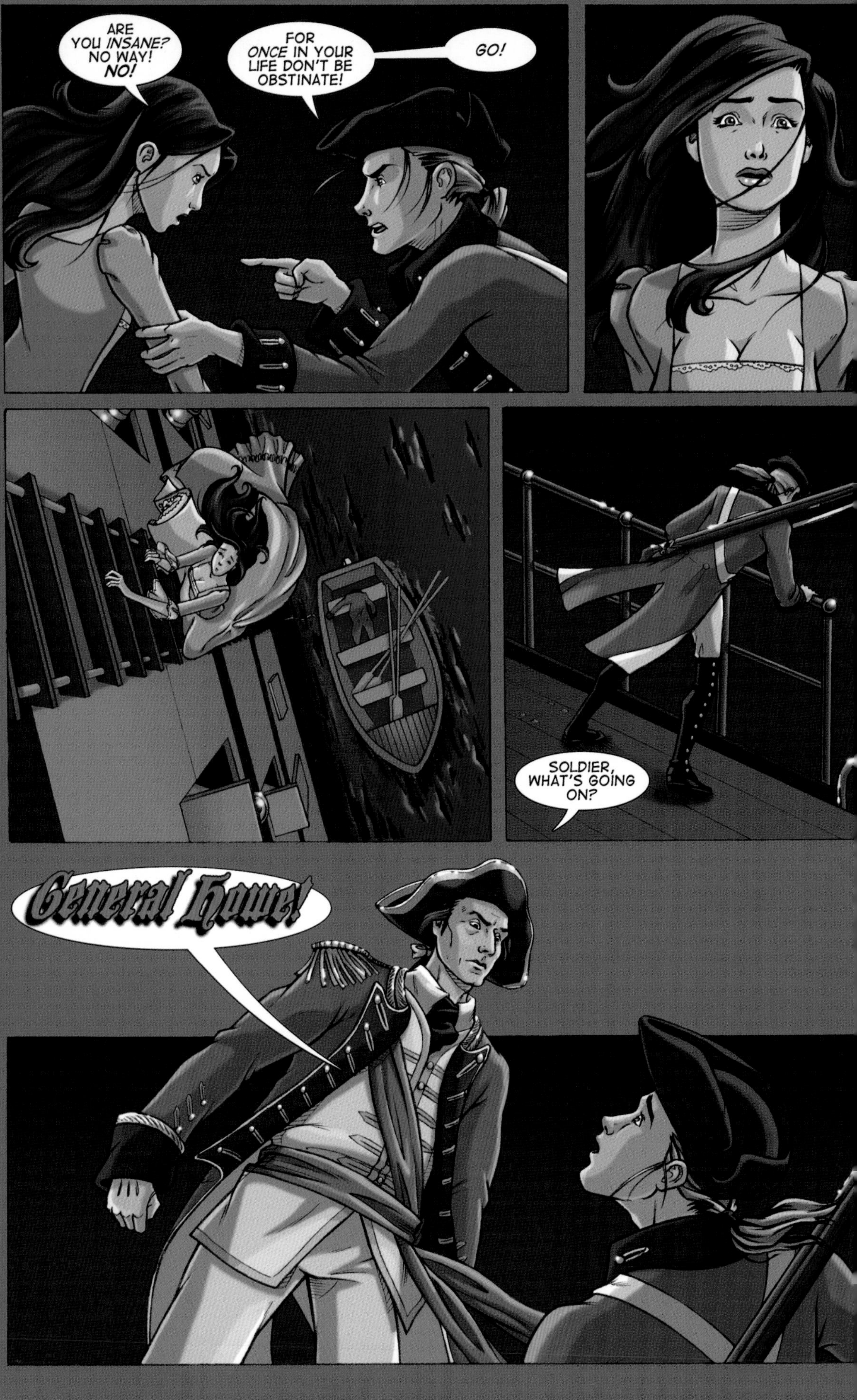
ARE YOU INSANE? NO WAY! NO!
FOR ONCE IN YOUR LIFE DON'T BE OBSTINATE!
GO!
SOLDIER, WHAT'S GOING ON?
General Howe!

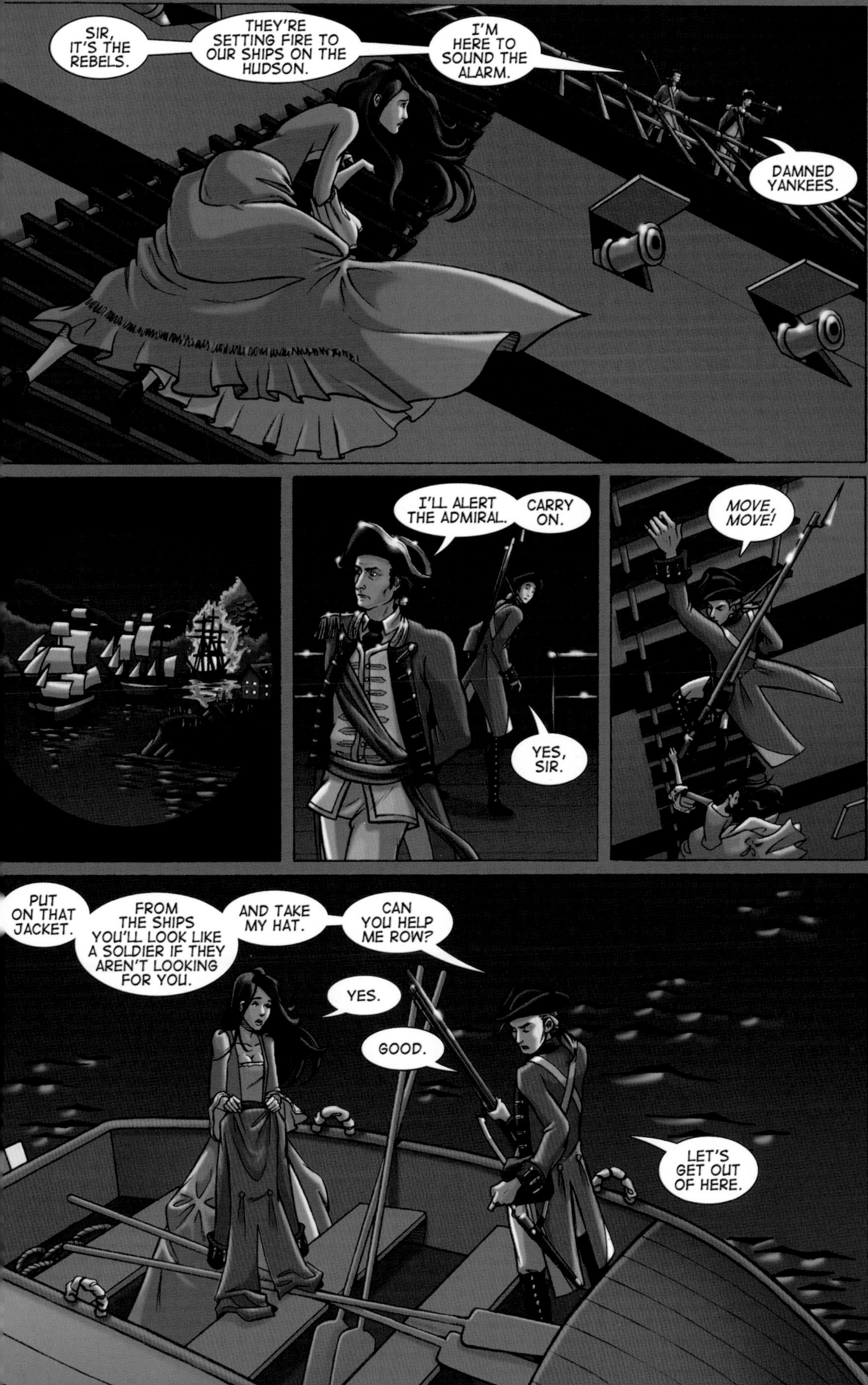
SIR, IT'S THE REBELS.
THEY'RE SETTING FIRE TO OUR SHIPS ON THE HUDSON.
I'M HERE TO SOUND THE ALARM.
DAMNED YANKEES.
I'LL ALERT THE ADMIRAL.
CARRY ON.
YES, SIR.
MOVE, MOVE!
PUT ON THAT JACKET.
FROM THE SHIPS YOU'LL LOOK LIKE A SOLDIER IF THEY AREN'T LOOKING FOR YOU.
AND TAKE MY HAT.
CAN YOU HELP ME ROW?
YES.
GOOD.
LET'S GET OUT OF HERE.

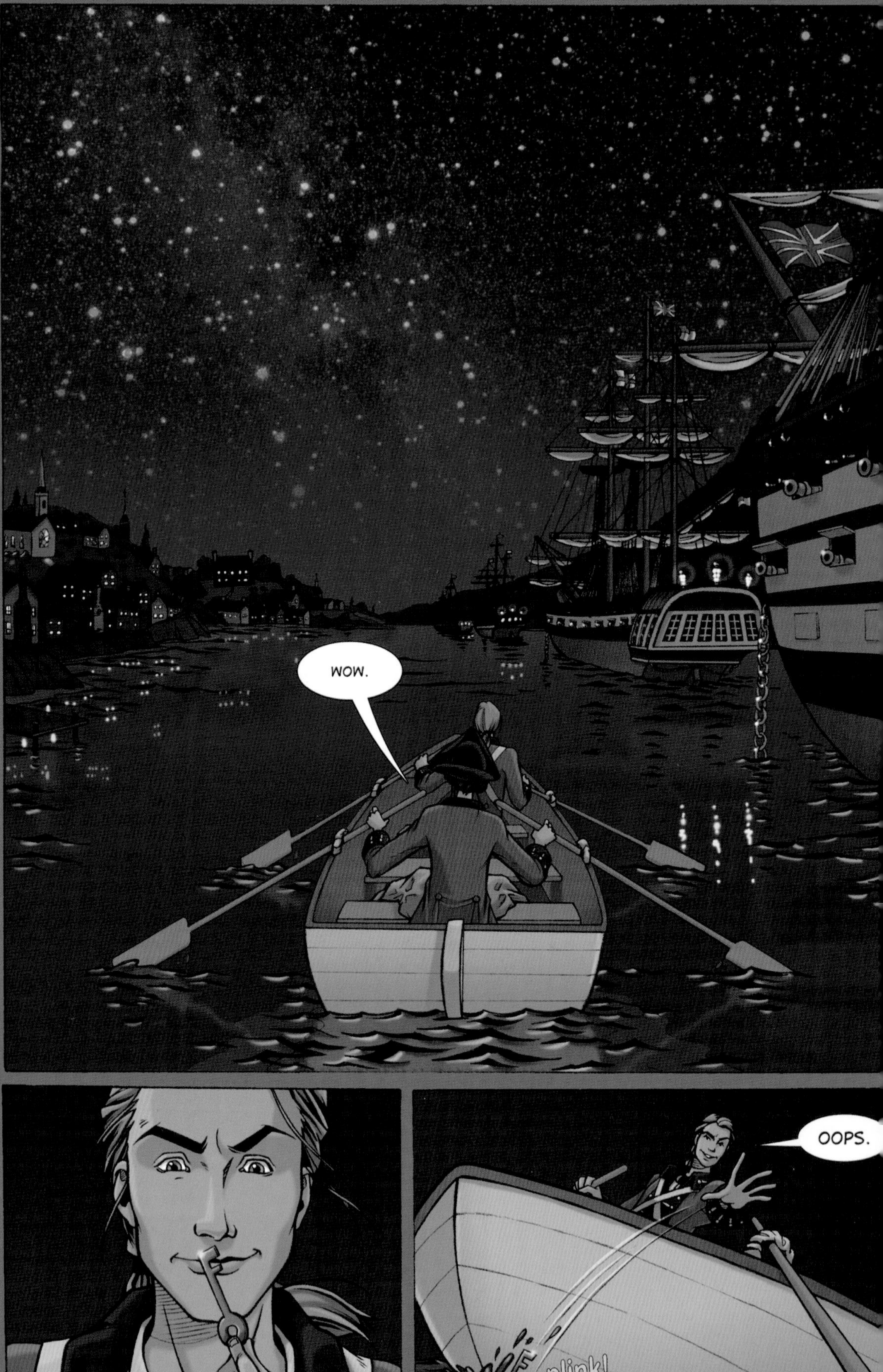
WOW.
OOPS.
plink!

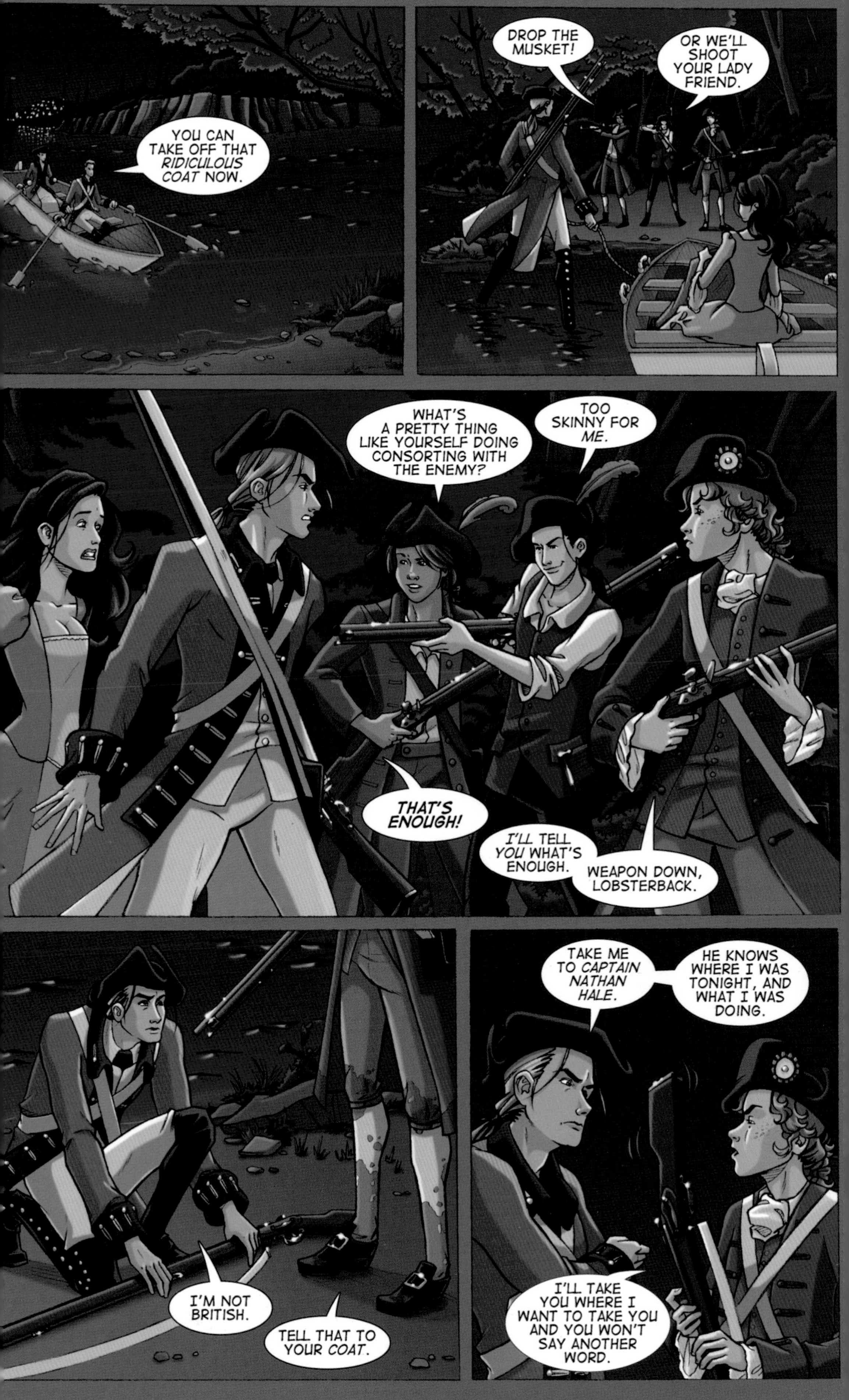
YOU CAN TAKE OFF THAT *RIDICULOUS COAT* NOW.
DROP THE MUSKET!
OR WE'LL SHOOT YOUR LADY FRIEND.
WHAT'S A PRETTY THING LIKE YOURSELF DOING CONSORTING WITH THE ENEMY?
TOO SKINNY FOR *ME*.
THAT'S ENOUGH!
I'LL TELL *YOU* WHAT'S ENOUGH.
WEAPON DOWN, LOBSTERBACK.
I'M NOT BRITISH.
TELL THAT TO YOUR *COAT*.
TAKE ME TO *CAPTAIN NATHAN HALE*.
HE KNOWS WHERE I WAS TONIGHT, AND WHAT I WAS DOING.
I'LL TAKE YOU WHERE I WANT TO TAKE YOU AND YOU WON'T SAY ANOTHER WORD.

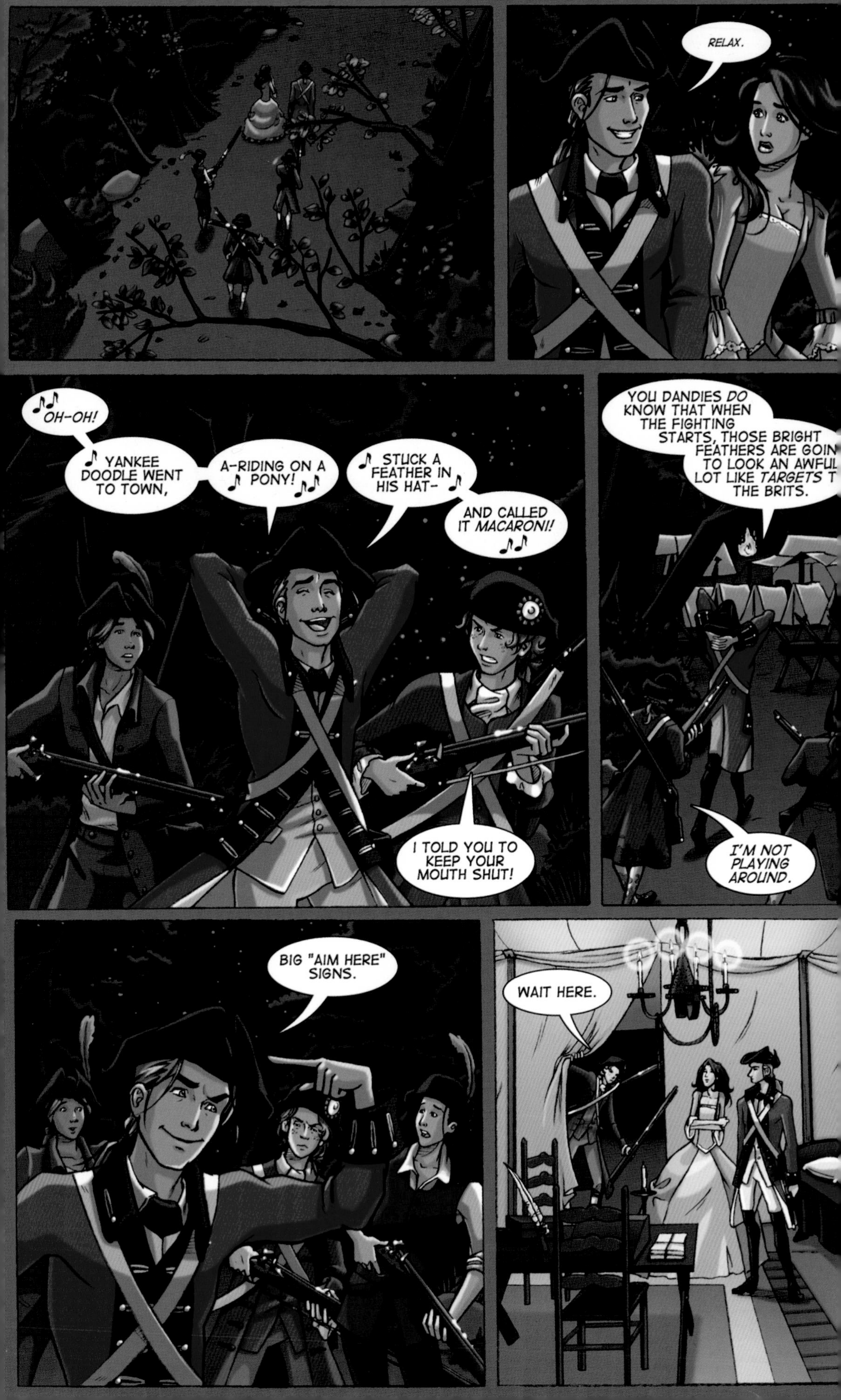
RELAX.
♪♪ OH-OH!
♪ YANKEE DOODLE WENT TO TOWN,
A-RIDING ON A ♪ PONY! ♪♪
♪ STUCK A FEATHER IN HIS HAT- ♪
AND CALLED IT *MACARONI!* ♪♪
I TOLD YOU TO KEEP YOUR MOUTH SHUT!
YOU DANDIES *DO* KNOW THAT WHEN THE FIGHTING STARTS, THOSE BRIGHT FEATHERS ARE GOIN TO LOOK AN AWFUL LOT LIKE *TARGETS* T THE BRITS.
I'M NOT PLAYING AROUND.
BIG "AIM HERE" SIGNS.
WAIT HERE.

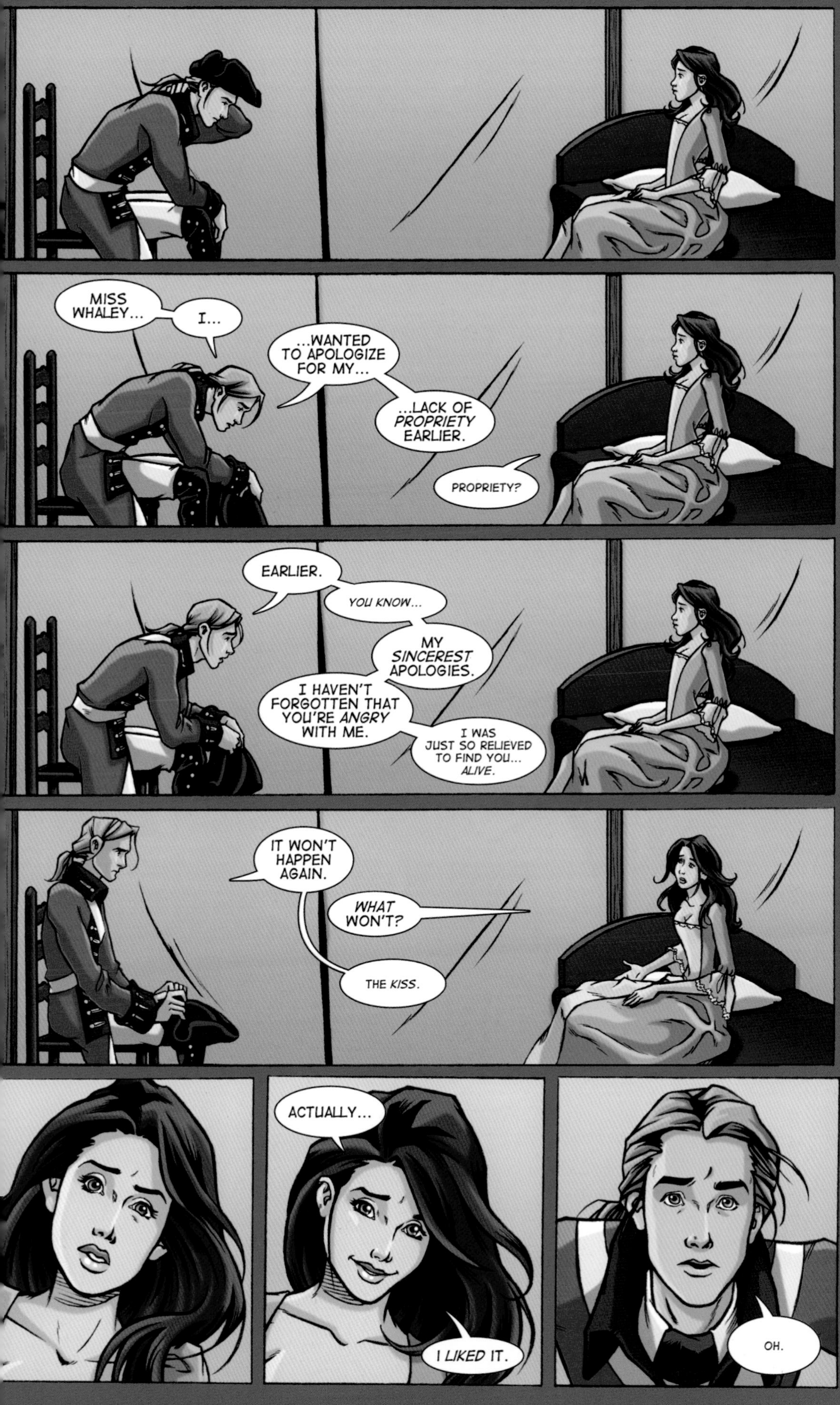
MISS WHALEY...
I...
...WANTED TO APOLOGIZE FOR MY...
...LACK OF *PROPRIETY* EARLIER.
PROPRIETY?
EARLIER.
YOU KNOW...
MY *SINCEREST* APOLOGIES.
I HAVEN'T FORGOTTEN THAT YOU'RE *ANGRY* WITH ME.
I WAS JUST SO RELIEVED TO FIND YOU... *ALIVE*.
IT WON'T HAPPEN AGAIN.
WHAT WON'T?
THE *KISS*.
ACTUALLY...
I *LIKED* IT.
OH.

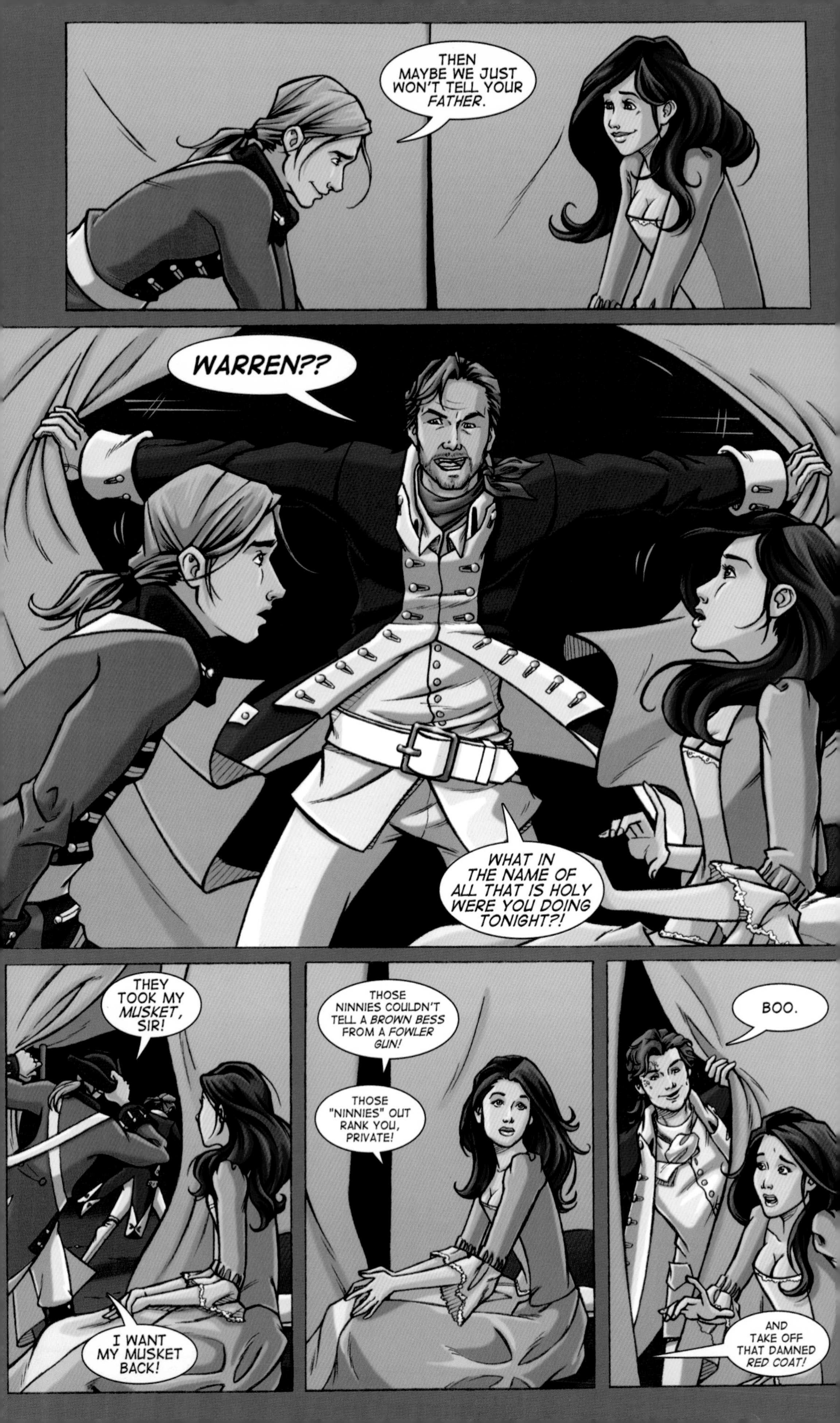
THEN MAYBE WE JUST WON'T TELL YOUR *FATHER*.
WARREN??
WHAT IN THE NAME OF ALL THAT IS HOLY WERE YOU DOING TONIGHT?!
THEY TOOK MY *MUSKET*, SIR!
I WANT MY MUSKET BACK!
THOSE NINNIES COULDN'T TELL A *BROWN BESS* FROM A *FOWLER GUN!*
THOSE "NINNIES" OUT RANK YOU, PRIVATE!
BOO.
AND TAKE OFF THAT DAMNED *RED COAT!*

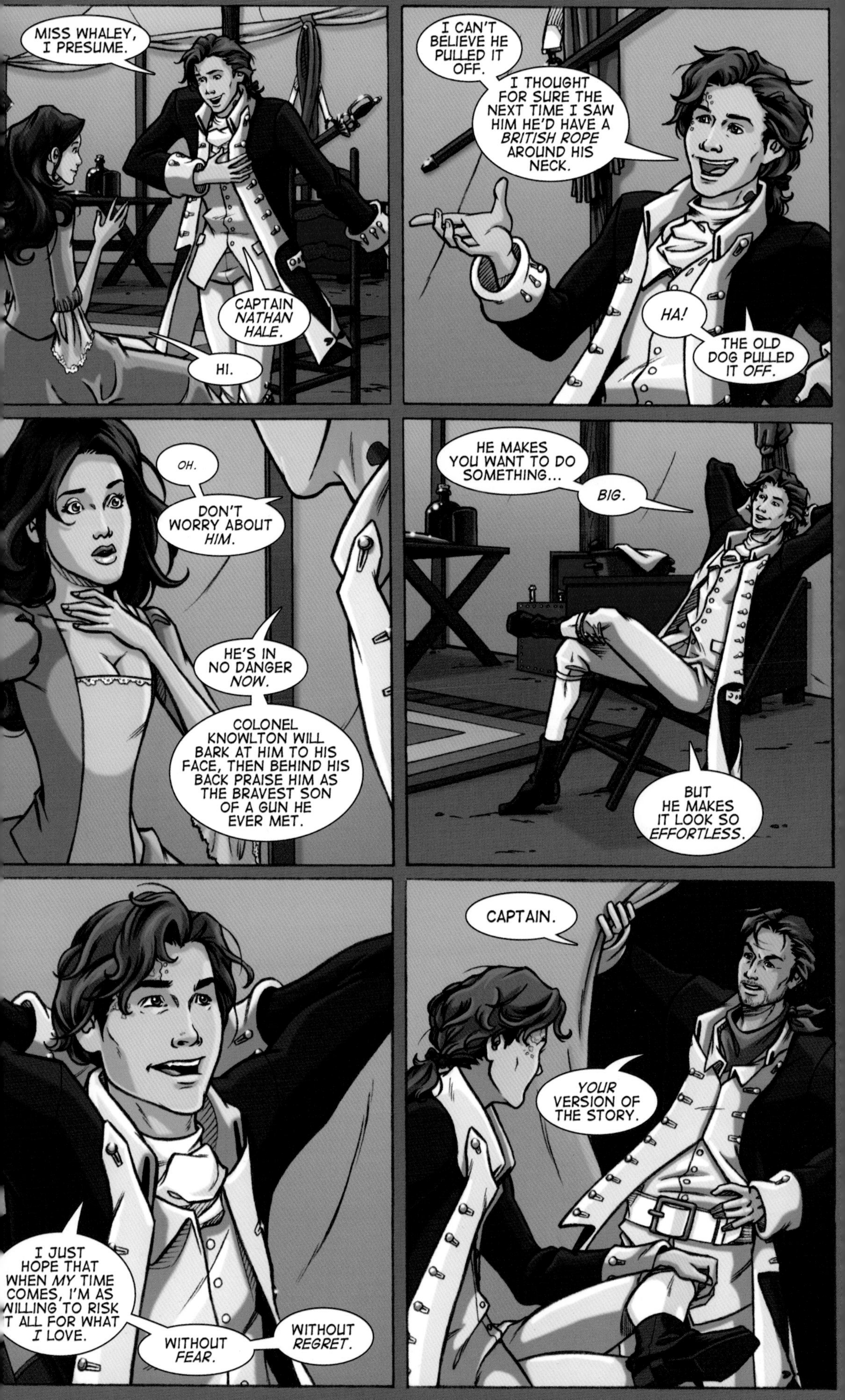
MISS WHALEY, I PRESUME.
CAPTAIN NATHAN HALE.
HI.
I CAN'T BELIEVE HE PULLED IT OFF.
I THOUGHT FOR SURE THE NEXT TIME I SAW HIM HE'D HAVE A BRITISH ROPE AROUND HIS NECK.
HA!
THE OLD DOG PULLED IT OFF.
OH.
DON'T WORRY ABOUT HIM.
HE'S IN NO DANGER NOW.
COLONEL KNOWLTON WILL BARK AT HIM TO HIS FACE, THEN BEHIND HIS BACK PRAISE HIM AS THE BRAVEST SON OF A GUN HE EVER MET.
HE MAKES YOU WANT TO DO SOMETHING...
BIG.
BUT HE MAKES IT LOOK SO EFFORTLESS.
I JUST HOPE THAT WHEN MY TIME COMES, I'M AS WILLING TO RISK IT ALL FOR WHAT I LOVE.
WITHOUT FEAR.
WITHOUT REGRET.
CAPTAIN.
YOUR VERSION OF THE STORY.

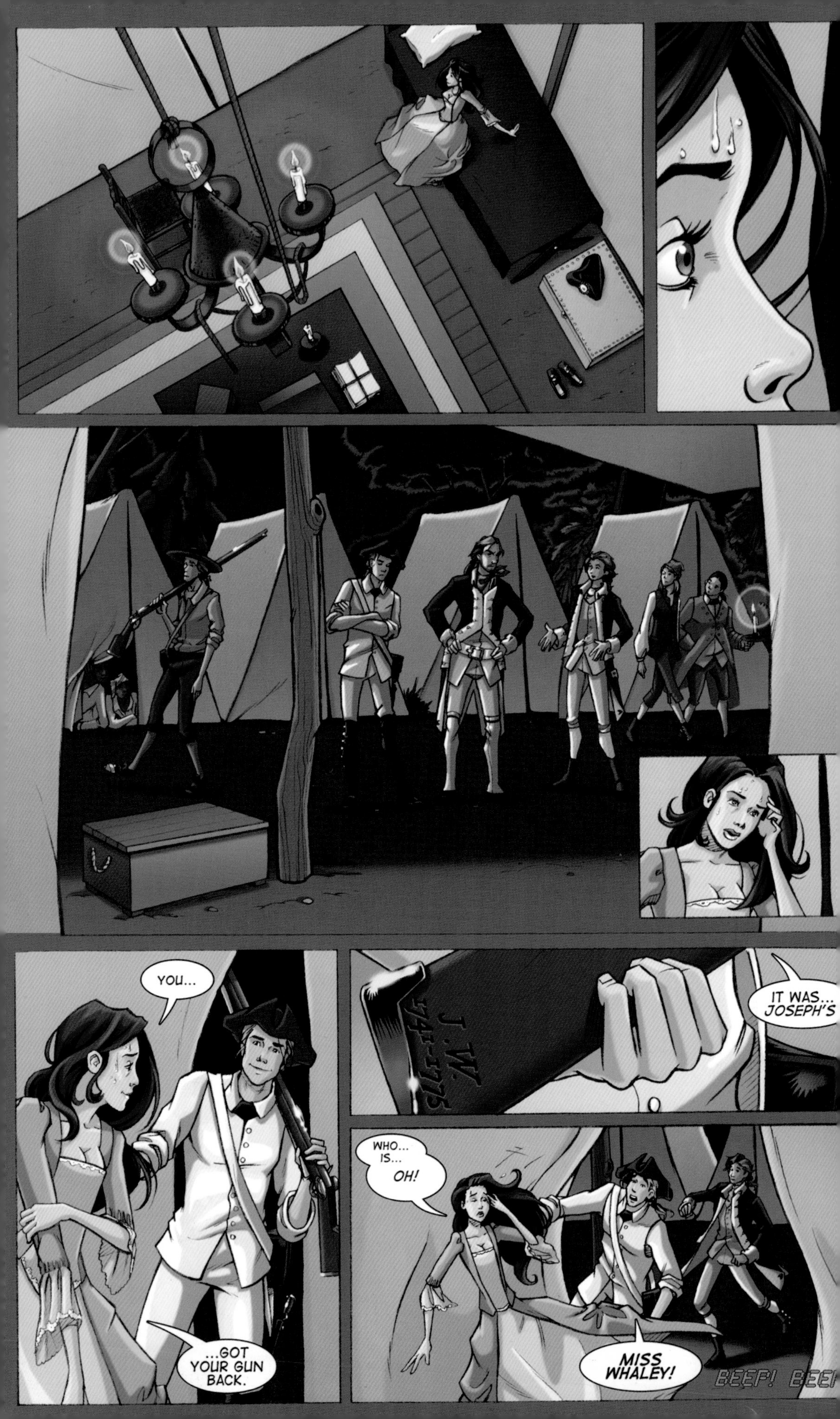
YOU...
...GOT YOUR GUN BACK.
J. W.
1741-1775
IT WAS... JOSEPH'S
WHO... IS... OH!
MISS WHALEY!
BEEP! BEE

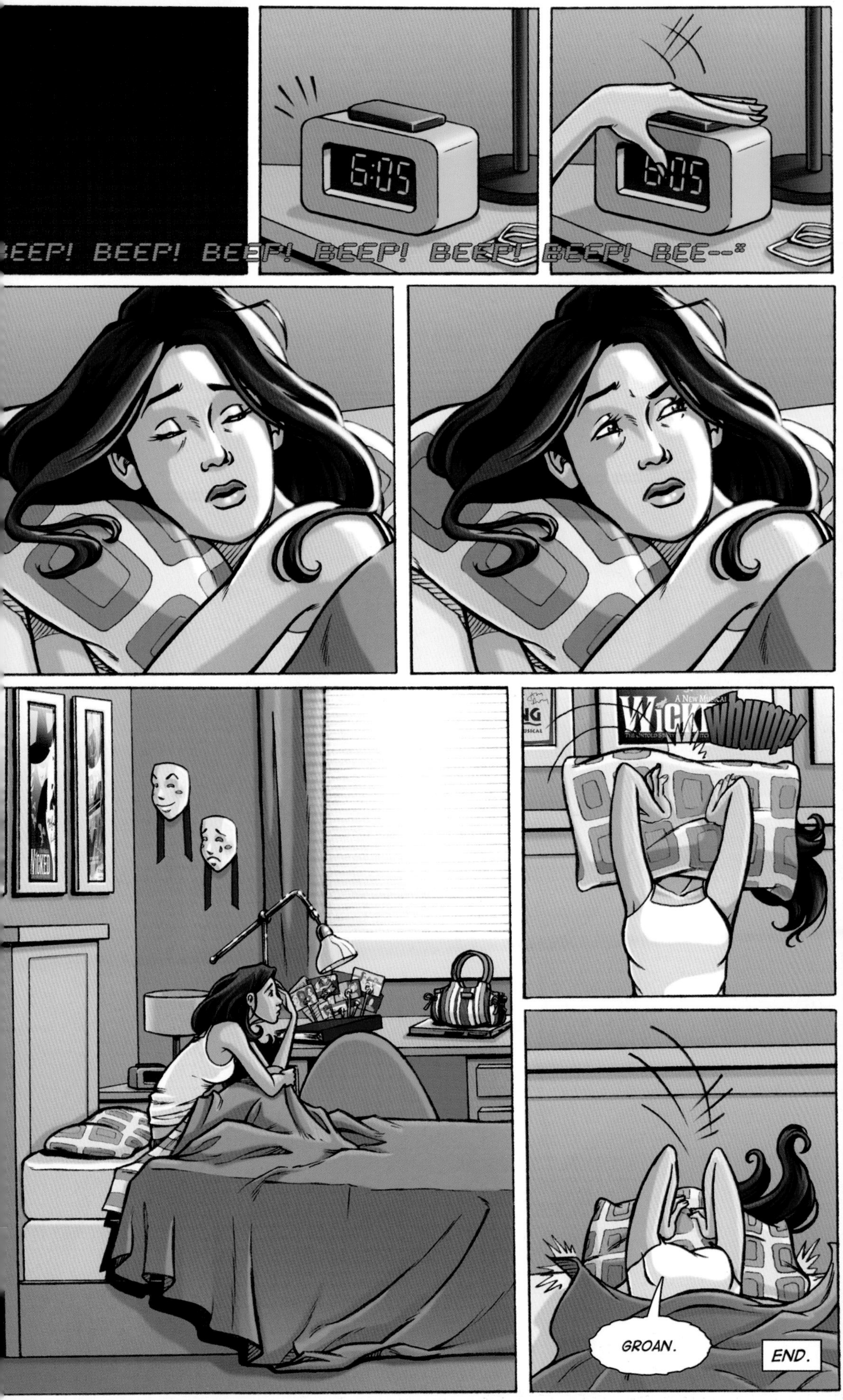
BEEP! BEEP! BEEP! BEEP! BEEP! BEEP! BEE--*
6:05
WICKED
A NEW MUSICAL
whump!
GROAN.
END.

Chapter Two

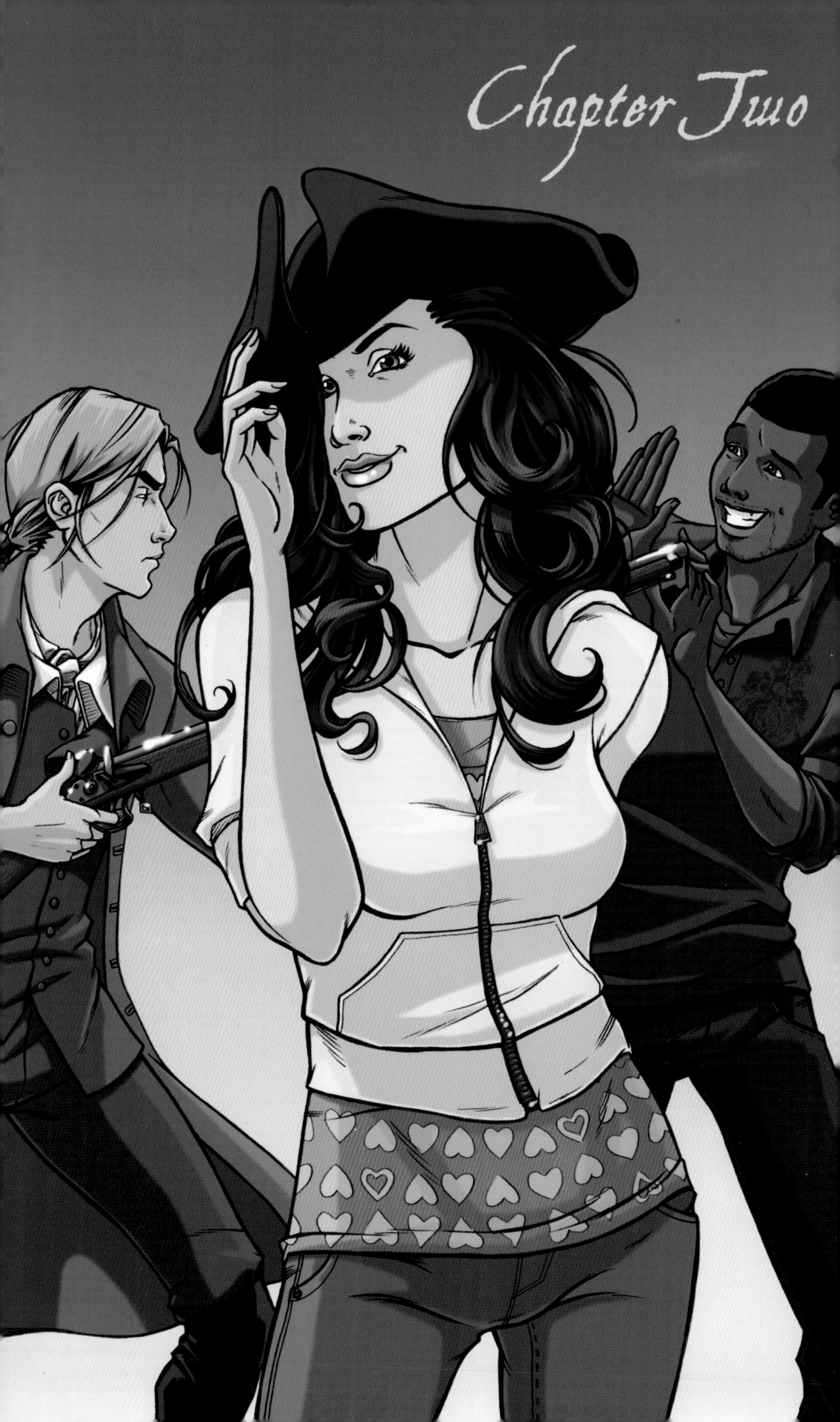

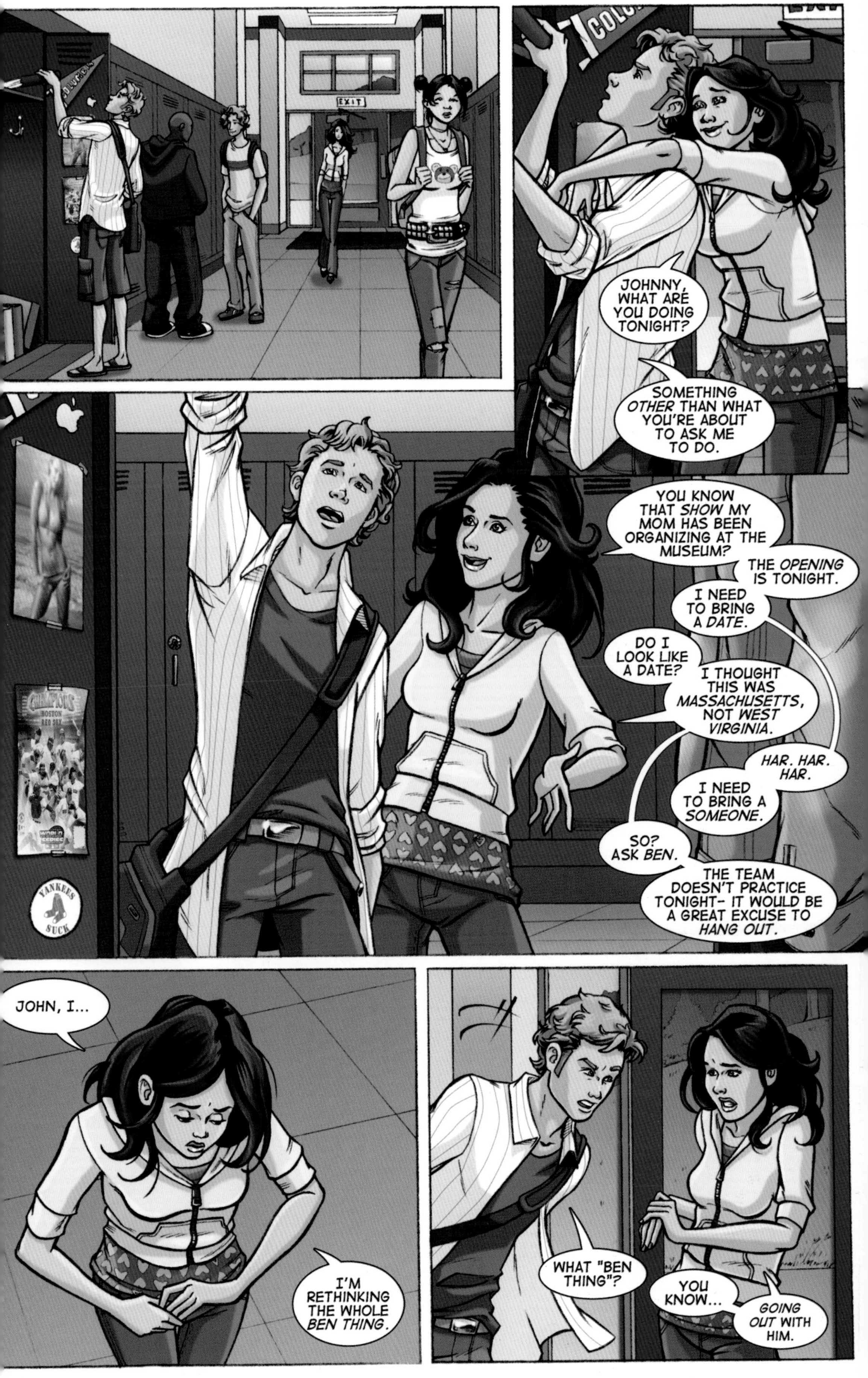
EXIT
JOHNNY, WHAT ARE YOU DOING TONIGHT?
SOMETHING OTHER THAN WHAT YOU'RE ABOUT TO ASK ME TO DO.
YOU KNOW THAT SHOW MY MOM HAS BEEN ORGANIZING AT THE MUSEUM?
THE OPENING IS TONIGHT.
I NEED TO BRING A DATE.
DO I LOOK LIKE A DATE?
I THOUGHT THIS WAS MASSACHUSETTS, NOT WEST VIRGINIA.
HAR. HAR. HAR.
I NEED TO BRING A SOMEONE.
SO? ASK BEN.
THE TEAM DOESN'T PRACTICE TONIGHT- IT WOULD BE A GREAT EXCUSE TO HANG OUT.
YANKEES SUCK
JOHN, I...
I'M RETHINKING THE WHOLE BEN THING.
WHAT "BEN THING"?
YOU KNOW...
GOING OUT WITH HIM.

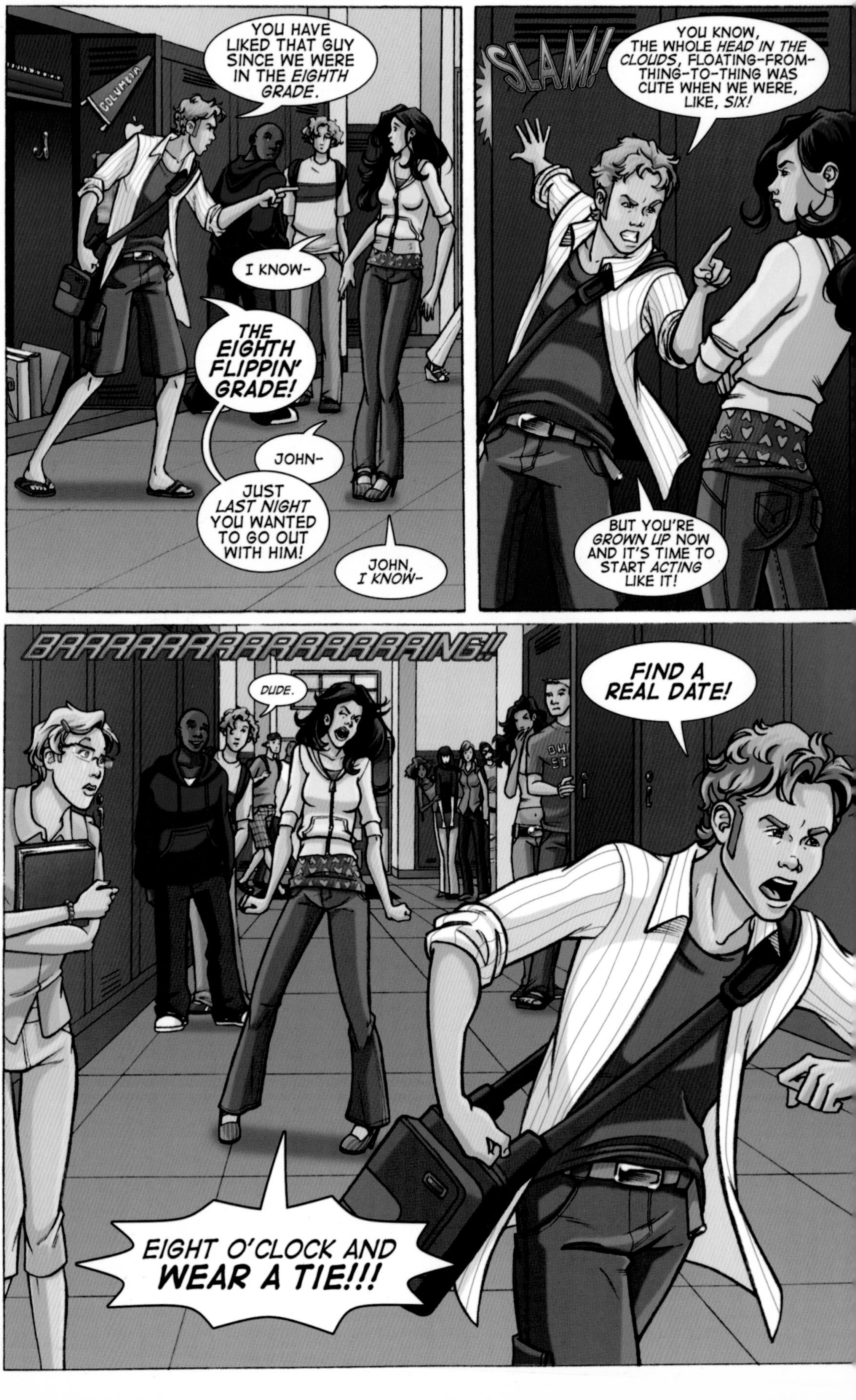
YOU HAVE LIKED THAT GUY SINCE WE WERE IN THE *EIGHTH GRADE*.
COLUMBIA
I KNOW-
THE EIGHTH FLIPPIN' GRADE!
JOHN-
JUST *LAST NIGHT* YOU WANTED TO GO OUT WITH HIM!
JOHN, I KNOW-
SLAM!
YOU KNOW, THE WHOLE *HEAD IN THE CLOUDS*, FLOATING-FROM-THING-TO-THING WAS CUTE WHEN WE WERE, LIKE, *SIX!*
BUT YOU'RE *GROWN UP* NOW AND IT'S TIME TO START *ACTING* LIKE IT!
BRRRRRRRRRRRRRRRRING!!
DUDE.
FIND A REAL DATE!
EIGHT O'CLOCK AND **WEAR A TIE!!!**

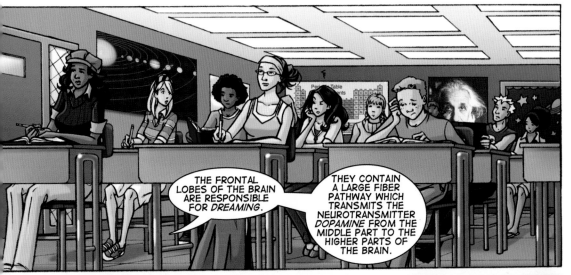

THE FRONTAL LOBES OF THE BRAIN ARE RESPONSIBLE FOR *DREAMING*.

THEY CONTAIN A LARGE FIBER PATHWAY WHICH TRANSMITS THE NEUROTRANSMITTER *DOPAMINE* FROM THE MIDDLE PART TO THE HIGHER PARTS OF THE BRAIN.

SINCE THE FRONTAL AND LIMBIC AREAS OF THE BRAIN ARE CONCERNED WITH EMOTION, MEMORY AND...

AHEM

AROUSAL...

...THESE BEHAVIORS MIGHT BE MORE PREVALENT IN OUR DREAMS SIMPLY BECAUSE OF THE LOCATION IN THE BRAIN THEY ORIGINATE FROM...

...IT HAS TO BE *DEEP* AND *PERSONAL*.

IT HAS TO FILL HER UP ON THE *INSIDE*...

FIGHT, BEATRICE, FIGHT.

I CAN'T LOSE YOU.

NOT A *THIRD* TIME.

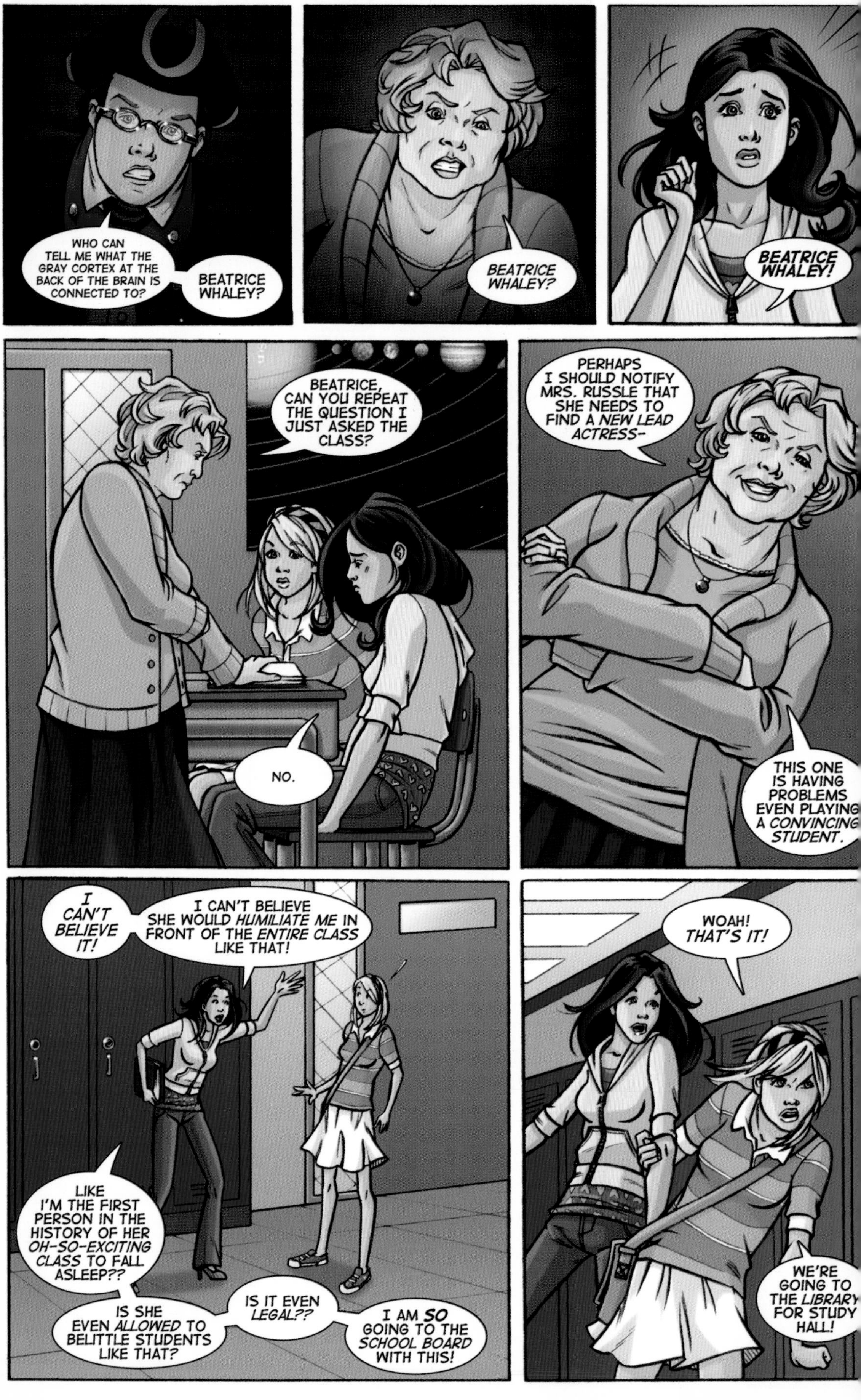

WHO CAN TELL ME WHAT THE GRAY CORTEX AT THE BACK OF THE BRAIN IS CONNECTED TO?
BEATRICE WHALEY?
BEATRICE WHALEY?
BEATRICE WHALEY!
BEATRICE, CAN YOU REPEAT THE QUESTION I JUST ASKED THE CLASS?
NO.
PERHAPS I SHOULD NOTIFY MRS. RUSSLE THAT SHE NEEDS TO FIND A *NEW LEAD ACTRESS*-
THIS ONE IS HAVING PROBLEMS EVEN PLAYING A *CONVINCING STUDENT*.
I CAN'T BELIEVE IT!
I CAN'T BELIEVE SHE WOULD *HUMILIATE ME* IN FRONT OF THE *ENTIRE CLASS* LIKE THAT!
LIKE I'M THE FIRST PERSON IN THE HISTORY OF HER *OH-SO-EXCITING CLASS* TO FALL ASLEEP??
IS SHE EVEN *ALLOWED* TO BELITTLE STUDENTS LIKE THAT?
IS IT EVEN *LEGAL??*
I AM **SO** GOING TO THE *SCHOOL BOARD* WITH THIS!
WOAH! *THAT'S IT!*
WE'RE GOING TO THE *LIBRARY* FOR STUDY HALL!

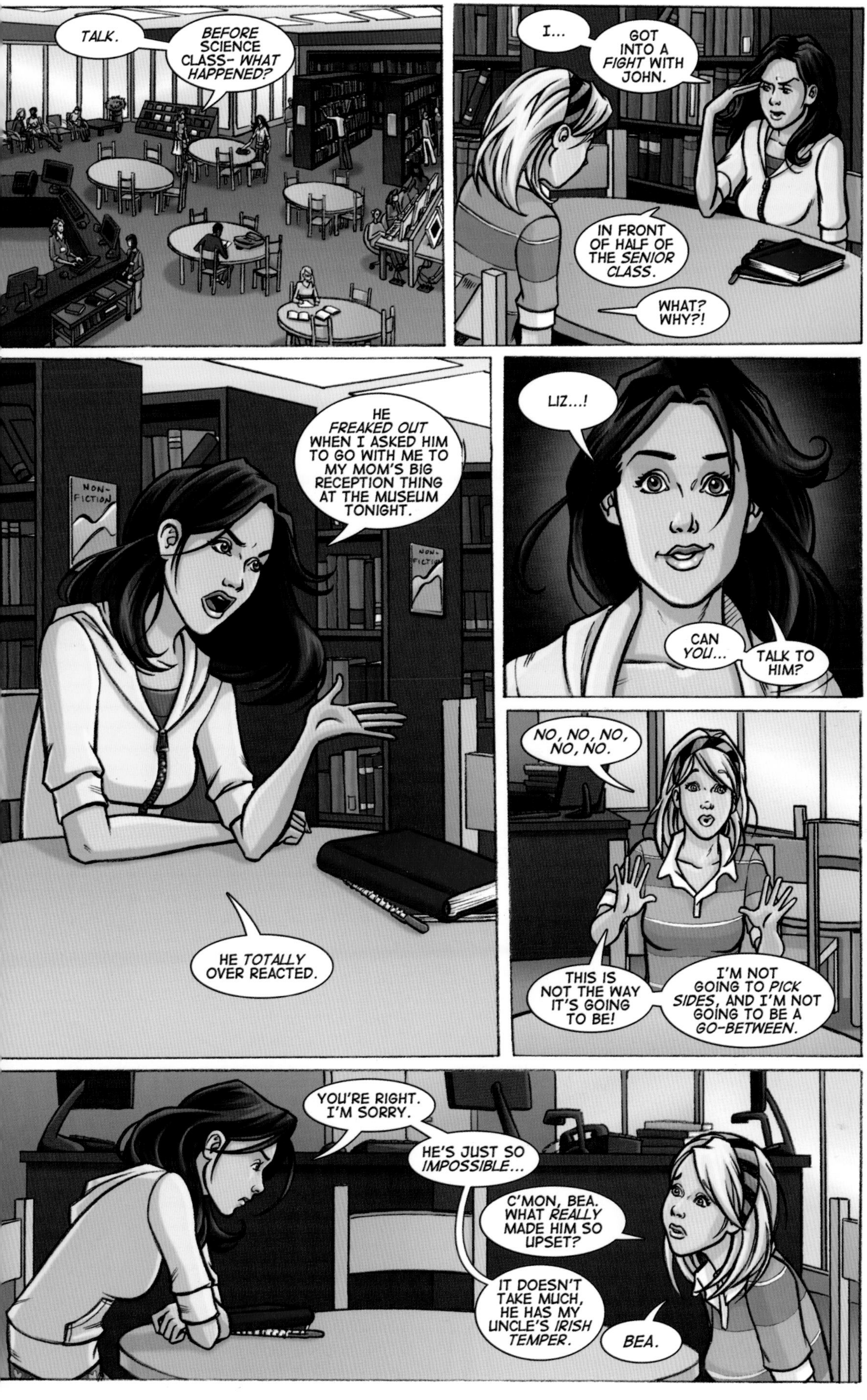

TALK.
BEFORE SCIENCE CLASS- WHAT HAPPENED?
I...
GOT INTO A FIGHT WITH JOHN.
IN FRONT OF HALF OF THE SENIOR CLASS.
WHAT? WHY?!
HE FREAKED OUT WHEN I ASKED HIM TO GO WITH ME TO MY MOM'S BIG RECEPTION THING AT THE MUSEUM TONIGHT.
NON-FICTION
NON-FICTION
HE TOTALLY OVER REACTED.
LIZ...!
CAN YOU...
TALK TO HIM?
NO, NO, NO, NO, NO.
THIS IS NOT THE WAY IT'S GOING TO BE!
I'M NOT GOING TO PICK SIDES, AND I'M NOT GOING TO BE A GO-BETWEEN.
YOU'RE RIGHT. I'M SORRY.
HE'S JUST SO IMPOSSIBLE...
C'MON, BEA. WHAT REALLY MADE HIM SO UPSET?
IT DOESN'T TAKE MUCH, HE HAS MY UNCLE'S IRISH TEMPER.
BEA.

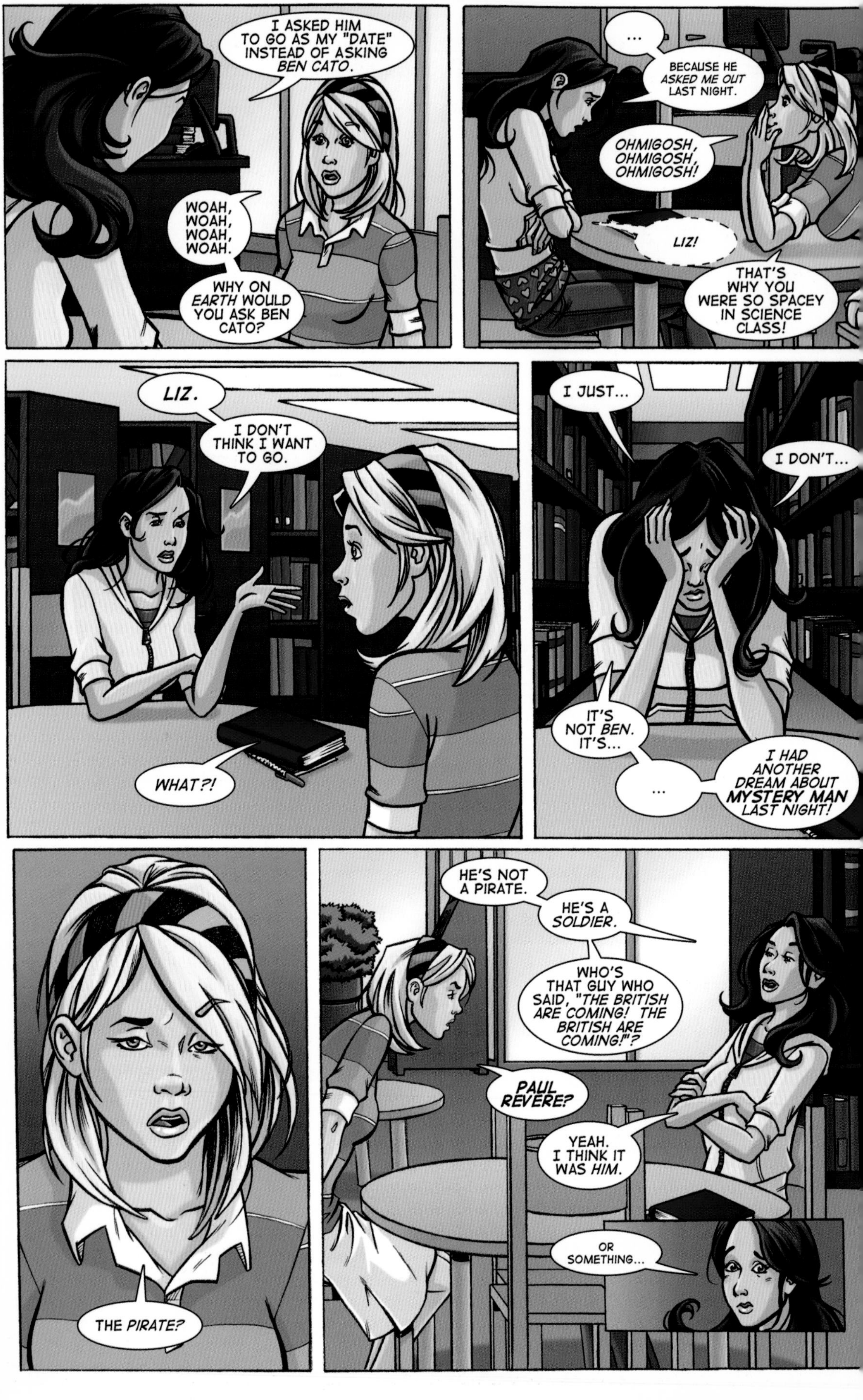

I ASKED HIM TO GO AS MY "DATE" INSTEAD OF ASKING *BEN CATO*.
WOAH, WOAH, WOAH, WOAH.
WHY ON *EARTH* WOULD YOU ASK BEN CATO?
...
BECAUSE HE *ASKED ME OUT* LAST NIGHT.
OHMIGOSH, OHMIGOSH, OHMIGOSH!
LIZ!
THAT'S WHY YOU WERE SO SPACEY IN SCIENCE CLASS!
LIZ.
I DON'T THINK I WANT TO GO.
WHAT?!
I JUST...
I DON'T...
IT'S NOT *BEN*. IT'S...
...
I HAD ANOTHER DREAM ABOUT ***MYSTERY MAN*** *LAST NIGHT!*
THE *PIRATE?*
HE'S NOT A PIRATE.
HE'S A *SOLDIER*.
WHO'S THAT GUY WHO SAID, *"THE BRITISH ARE COMING! THE BRITISH ARE COMING!"*?
PAUL REVERE?
YEAH. I THINK IT WAS *HIM*.
OR SOMETHING...

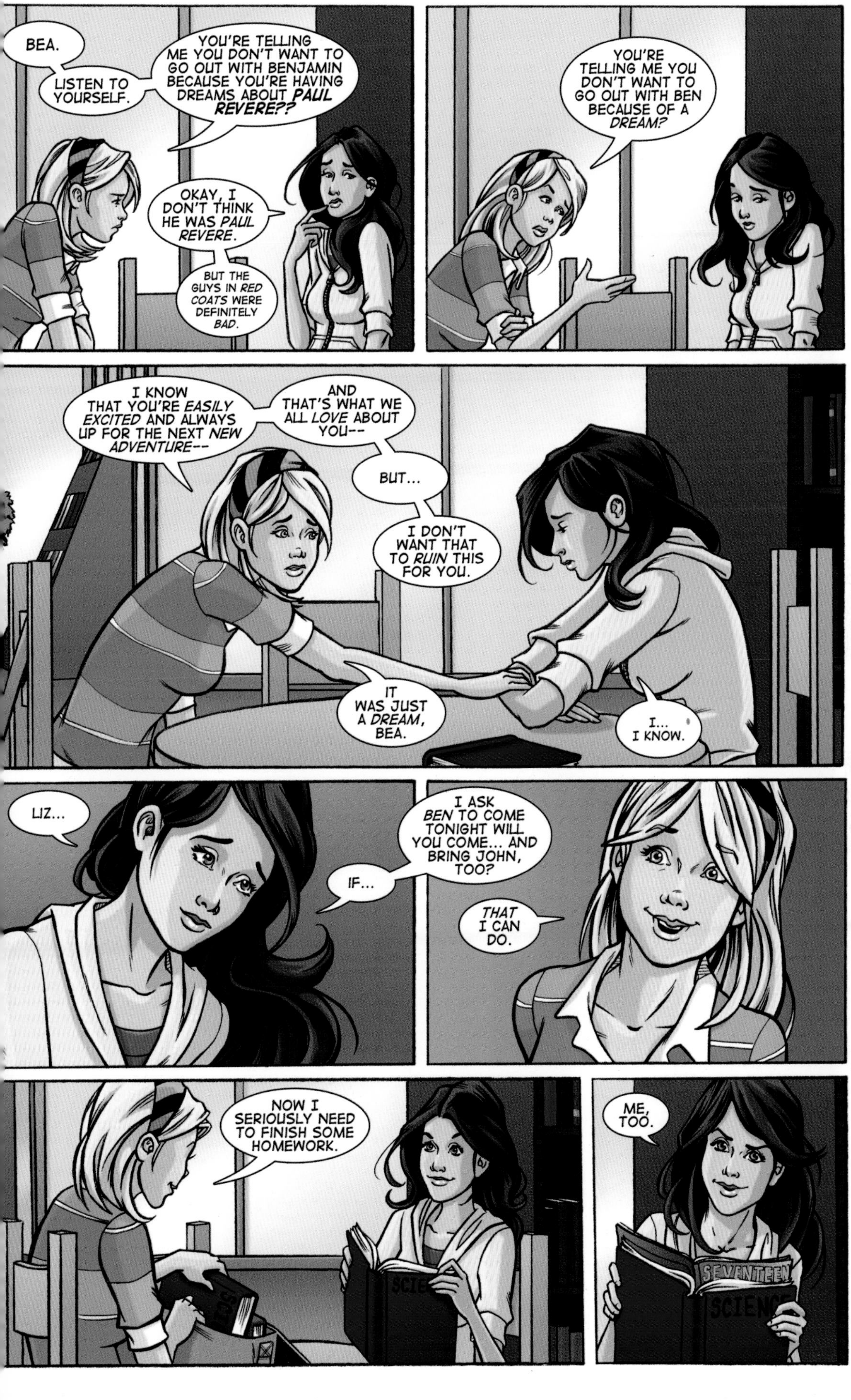
BEA.
LISTEN TO YOURSELF.
YOU'RE TELLING ME YOU DON'T WANT TO GO OUT WITH BENJAMIN BECAUSE YOU'RE HAVING DREAMS ABOUT PAUL REVERE??
OKAY, I DON'T THINK HE WAS PAUL REVERE.
BUT THE GUYS IN RED COATS WERE DEFINITELY BAD.
YOU'RE TELLING ME YOU DON'T WANT TO GO OUT WITH BEN BECAUSE OF A DREAM?
I KNOW THAT YOU'RE EASILY EXCITED AND ALWAYS UP FOR THE NEXT NEW ADVENTURE--
AND THAT'S WHAT WE ALL LOVE ABOUT YOU--
BUT...
I DON'T WANT THAT TO RUIN THIS FOR YOU.
IT WAS JUST A DREAM, BEA.
I... I KNOW.
LIZ...
IF...
I ASK BEN TO COME TONIGHT WILL YOU COME... AND BRING JOHN, TOO?
THAT I CAN DO.
NOW I SERIOUSLY NEED TO FINISH SOME HOMEWORK.
ME, TOO.
SEVENTEEN
SCIENCE

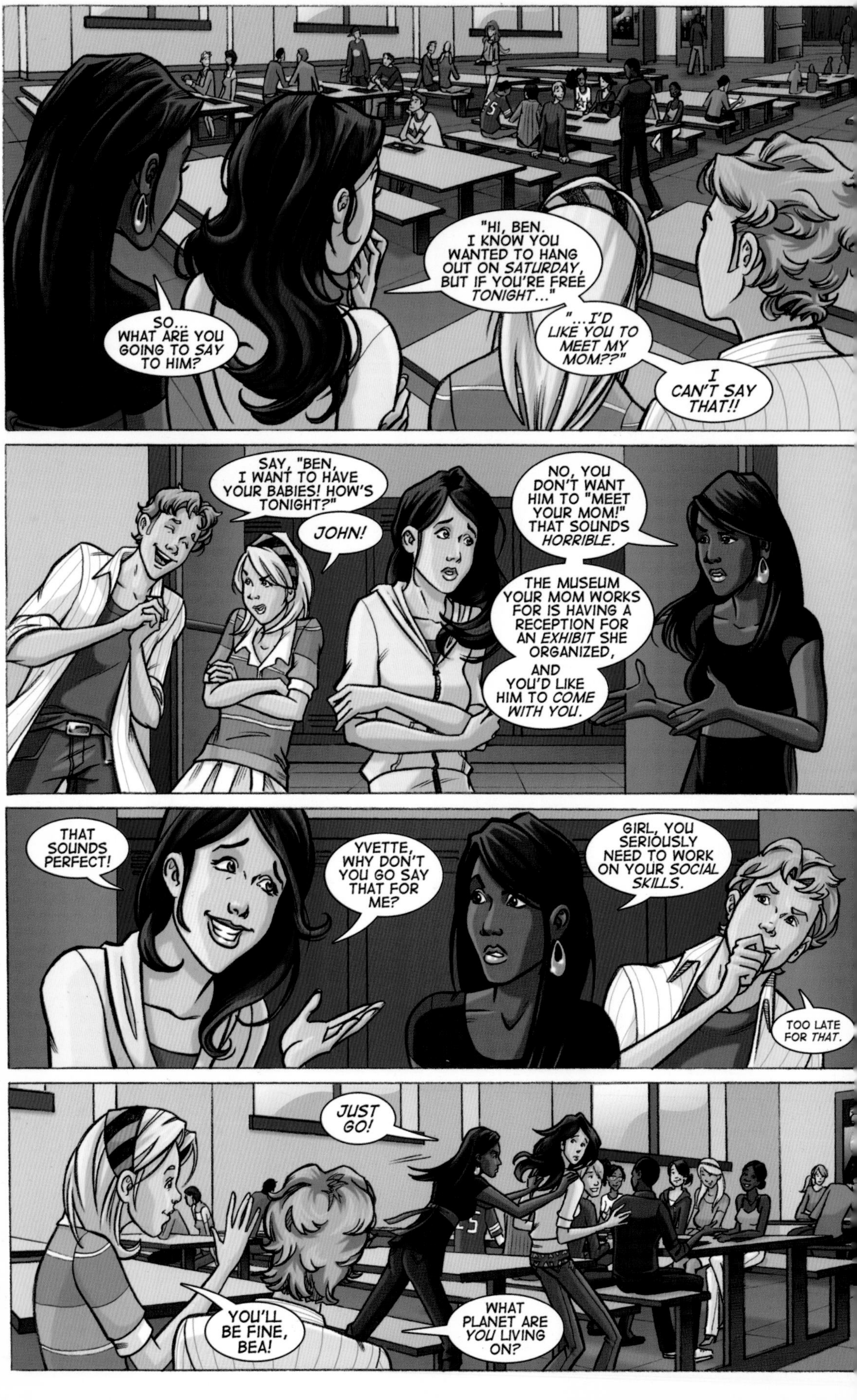
SO... WHAT ARE YOU GOING TO SAY TO HIM?
"HI, BEN. I KNOW YOU WANTED TO HANG OUT ON SATURDAY, BUT IF YOU'RE FREE TONIGHT..."
"...I'D LIKE YOU TO MEET MY MOM??"
I CAN'T SAY THAT!!
SAY, "BEN, I WANT TO HAVE YOUR BABIES! HOW'S TONIGHT?"
JOHN!
NO, YOU DON'T WANT HIM TO "MEET YOUR MOM!" THAT SOUNDS HORRIBLE.
THE MUSEUM YOUR MOM WORKS FOR IS HAVING A RECEPTION FOR AN EXHIBIT SHE ORGANIZED,
AND YOU'D LIKE HIM TO COME WITH YOU.
THAT SOUNDS PERFECT!
YVETTE, WHY DON'T YOU GO SAY THAT FOR ME?
GIRL, YOU SERIOUSLY NEED TO WORK ON YOUR SOCIAL SKILLS.
TOO LATE FOR THAT.
JUST GO!
YOU'LL BE FINE, BEA!
WHAT PLANET ARE YOU LIVING ON?

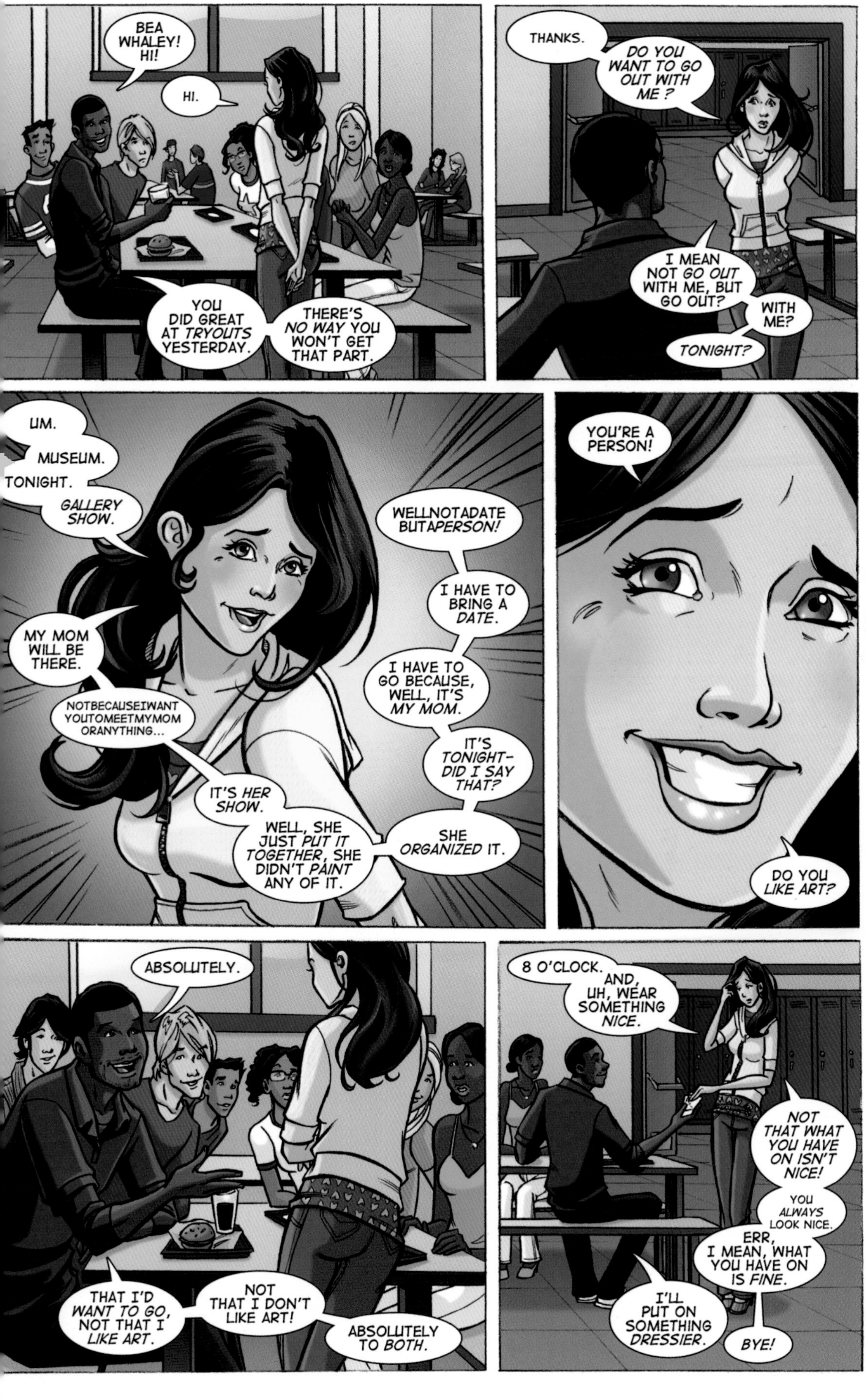
BEA WHALEY! HI!
HI.
YOU DID GREAT AT TRYOUTS YESTERDAY.
THERE'S NO WAY YOU WON'T GET THAT PART.
THANKS.
DO YOU WANT TO GO OUT WITH ME ?
I MEAN NOT GO OUT WITH ME, BUT GO OUT?
WITH ME?
TONIGHT?
UM.
MUSEUM.
TONIGHT.
GALLERY SHOW.
MY MOM WILL BE THERE.
NOTBECAUSEIWANT YOUTOMEETMYMOM ORANYTHING...
WELLNOTADATE BUTAPERSON!
I HAVE TO BRING A DATE.
I HAVE TO GO BECAUSE, WELL, IT'S MY MOM.
IT'S TONIGHT- DID I SAY THAT?
IT'S HER SHOW.
WELL, SHE JUST PUT IT TOGETHER, SHE DIDN'T PAINT ANY OF IT.
SHE ORGANIZED IT.
YOU'RE A PERSON!
DO YOU LIKE ART?
ABSOLUTELY.
THAT I'D WANT TO GO, NOT THAT I LIKE ART.
NOT THAT I DON'T LIKE ART!
ABSOLUTELY TO BOTH.
8 O'CLOCK.
AND, UH, WEAR SOMETHING NICE.
NOT THAT WHAT YOU HAVE ON ISN'T NICE!
YOU ALWAYS LOOK NICE.
ERR, I MEAN, WHAT YOU HAVE ON IS FINE.
I'LL PUT ON SOMETHING DRESSIER.
BYE!

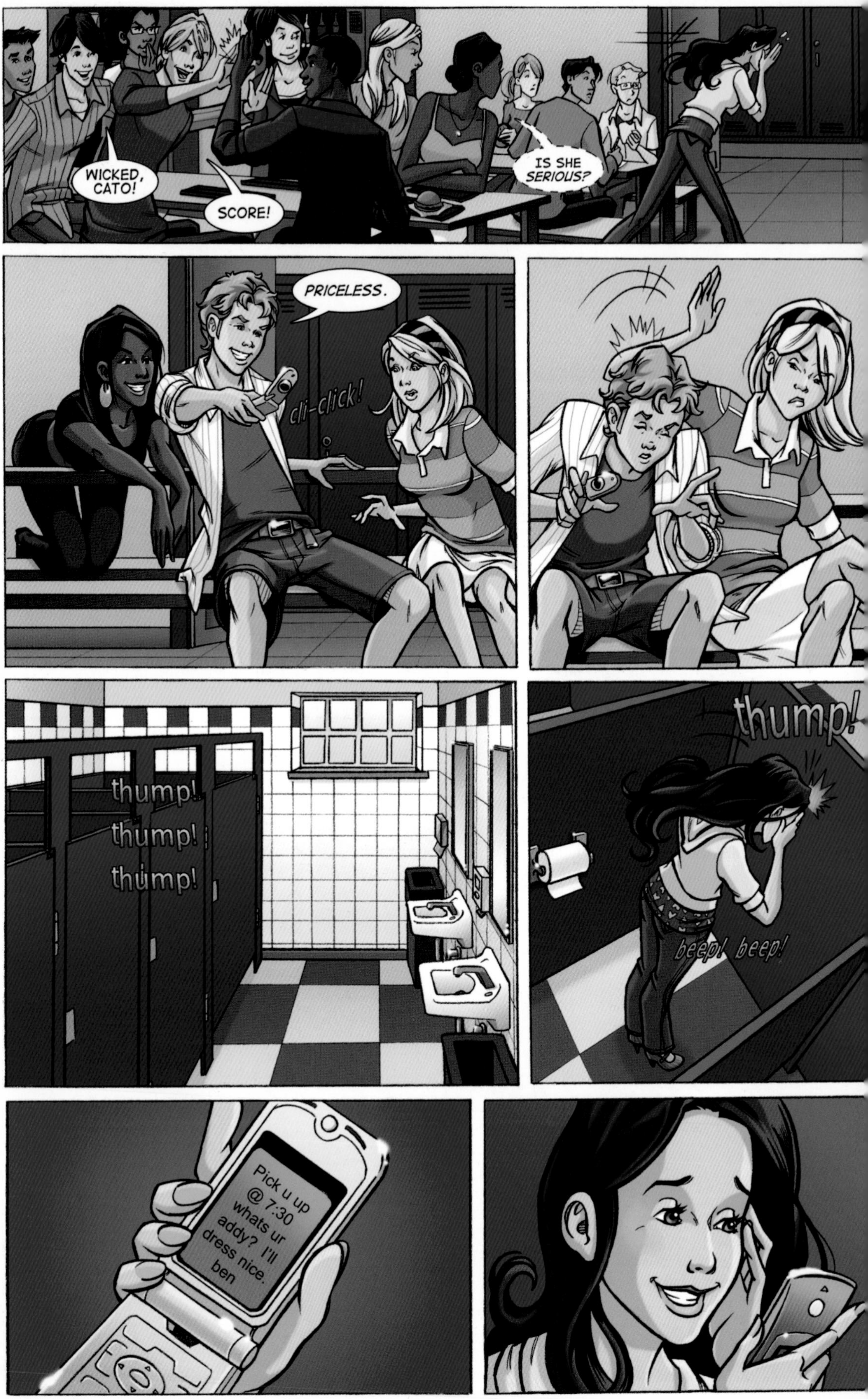
WICKED, CATO!
SCORE!
IS SHE SERIOUS?
PRICELESS.
cli-click!
thump!
thump!
thump!
thump!
beep! beep!
Pick u up @ 7:30 whats ur addy? I'll dress nice. ben

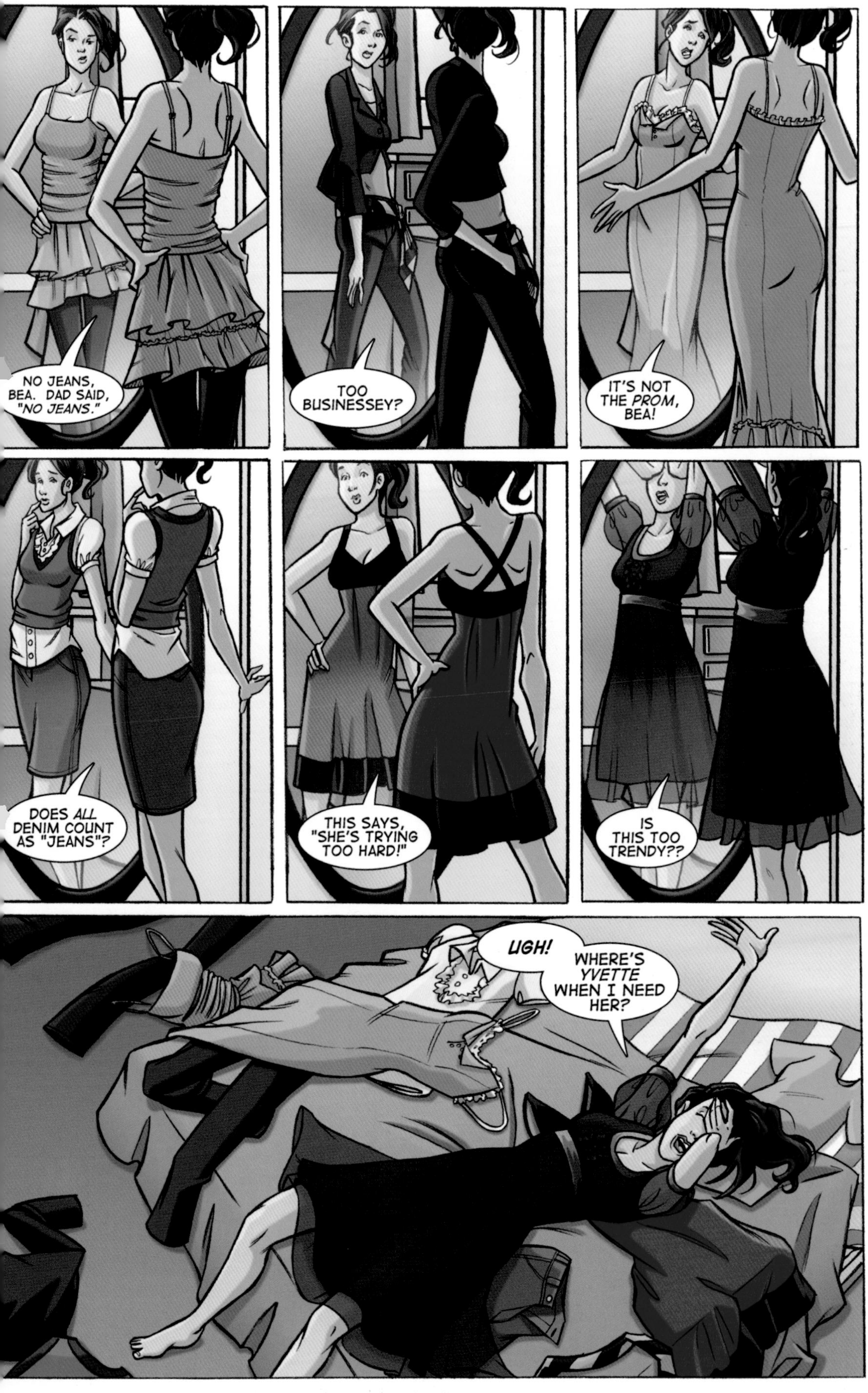
NO JEANS, BEA. DAD SAID, "*NO JEANS.*"
TOO BUSINESSEY?
IT'S NOT THE *PROM*, BEA!
DOES *ALL* DENIM COUNT AS "JEANS"?
THIS SAYS, "SHE'S TRYING TOO HARD!"
IS THIS TOO TRENDY??
UGH!
WHERE'S *YVETTE* WHEN I NEED HER?

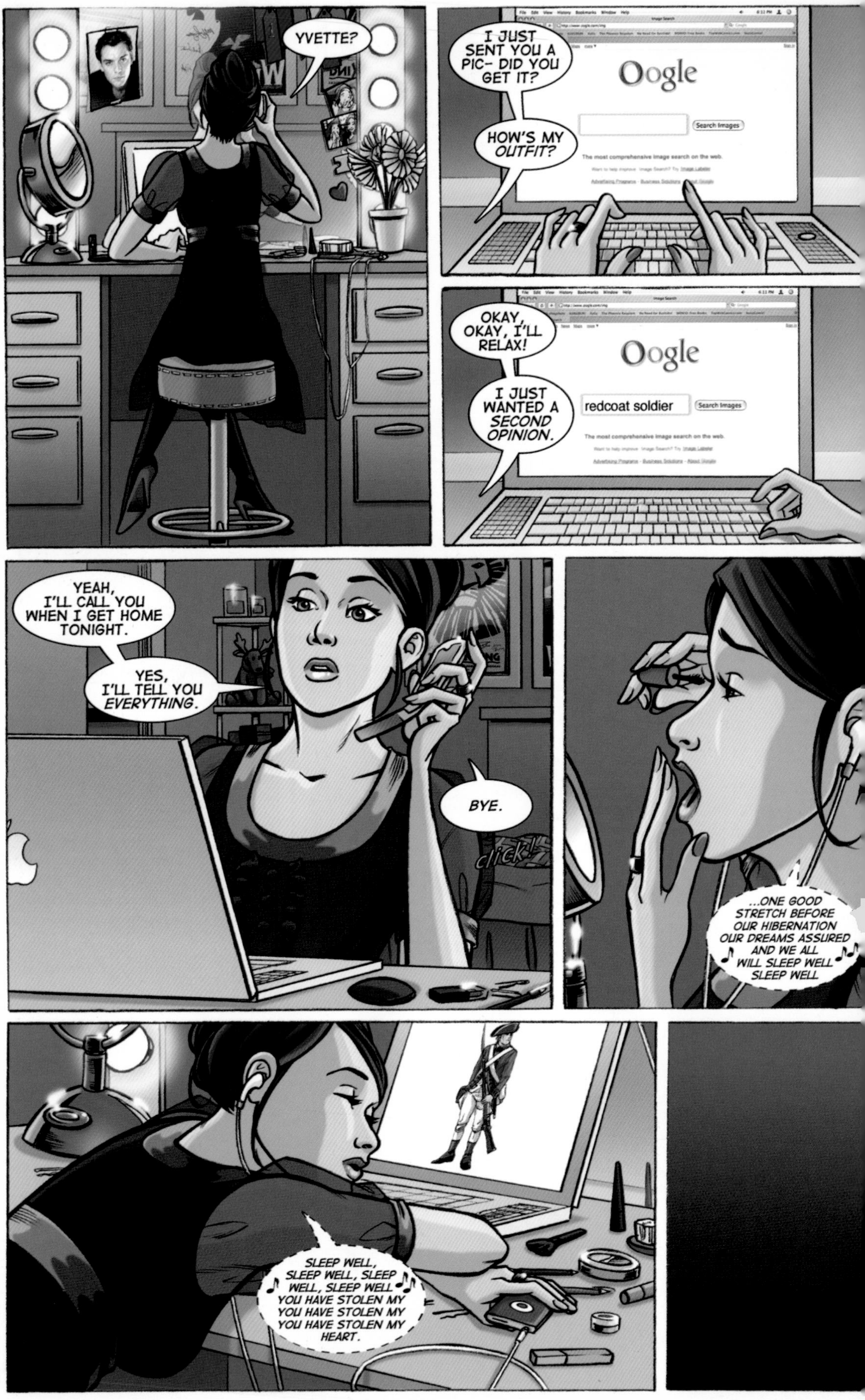
YVETTE?
I JUST SENT YOU A PIC– DID YOU GET IT?
HOW'S MY *OUTFIT?*
Oogle
Search Images
OKAY, OKAY, I'LL RELAX!
I JUST WANTED A *SECOND OPINION.*
Oogle
redcoat soldier
Search Images
YEAH, I'LL CALL YOU WHEN I GET HOME TONIGHT.
YES, I'LL TELL YOU *EVERYTHING.*
BYE.
CLICK!
...ONE GOOD STRETCH BEFORE OUR HIBERNATION OUR DREAMS ASSURED AND WE ALL WILL SLEEP WELL SLEEP WELL
SLEEP WELL, SLEEP WELL, SLEEP WELL, SLEEP WELL YOU HAVE STOLEN MY YOU HAVE STOLEN MY YOU HAVE STOLEN MY HEART.

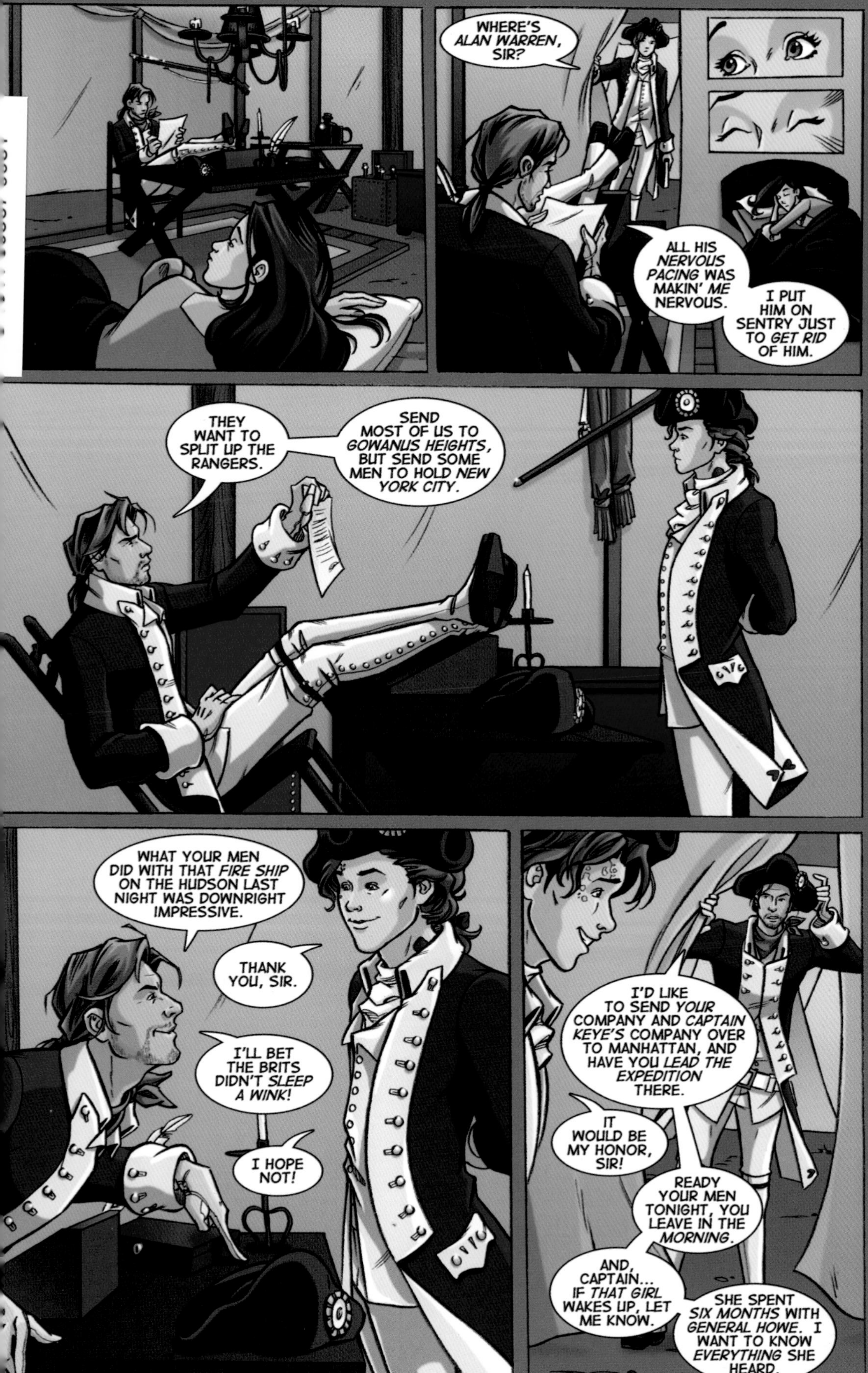
WHERE'S ALAN WARREN, SIR?
ALL HIS NERVOUS PACING WAS MAKIN' ME NERVOUS.
I PUT HIM ON SENTRY JUST TO GET RID OF HIM.
THEY WANT TO SPLIT UP THE RANGERS.
SEND MOST OF US TO GOWANUS HEIGHTS, BUT SEND SOME MEN TO HOLD NEW YORK CITY.
WHAT YOUR MEN DID WITH THAT FIRE SHIP ON THE HUDSON LAST NIGHT WAS DOWNRIGHT IMPRESSIVE.
THANK YOU, SIR.
I'LL BET THE BRITS DIDN'T SLEEP A WINK!
I HOPE NOT!
I'D LIKE TO SEND YOUR COMPANY AND CAPTAIN KEYE'S COMPANY OVER TO MANHATTAN, AND HAVE YOU LEAD THE EXPEDITION THERE.
IT WOULD BE MY HONOR, SIR!
READY YOUR MEN TONIGHT, YOU LEAVE IN THE MORNING.
AND, CAPTAIN... IF THAT GIRL WAKES UP, LET ME KNOW.
SHE SPENT SIX MONTHS WITH GENERAL HOWE. I WANT TO KNOW EVERYTHING SHE HEARD.

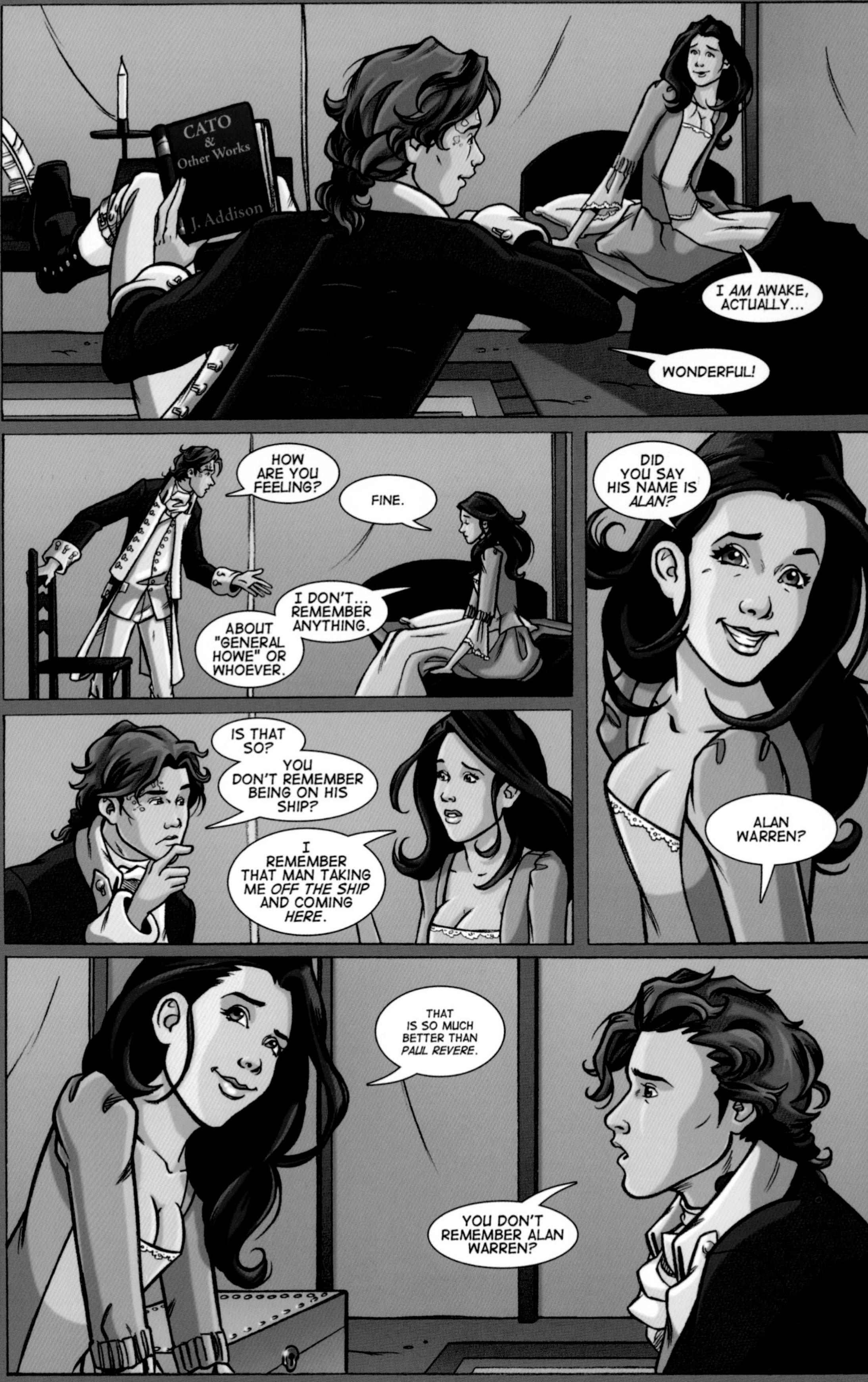
CATO & Other Works
J. Addison
I *AM* AWAKE, ACTUALLY...
WONDERFUL!
HOW ARE YOU FEELING?
FINE.
I DON'T... REMEMBER ANYTHING.
ABOUT "GENERAL HOWE" OR WHOEVER.
IS THAT SO?
YOU DON'T REMEMBER BEING ON HIS SHIP?
I REMEMBER THAT MAN TAKING ME *OFF THE SHIP* AND COMING *HERE*.
DID YOU SAY HIS NAME IS *ALAN?*
ALAN WARREN?
THAT IS SO MUCH BETTER THAN *PAUL REVERE*.
YOU DON'T REMEMBER ALAN WARREN?

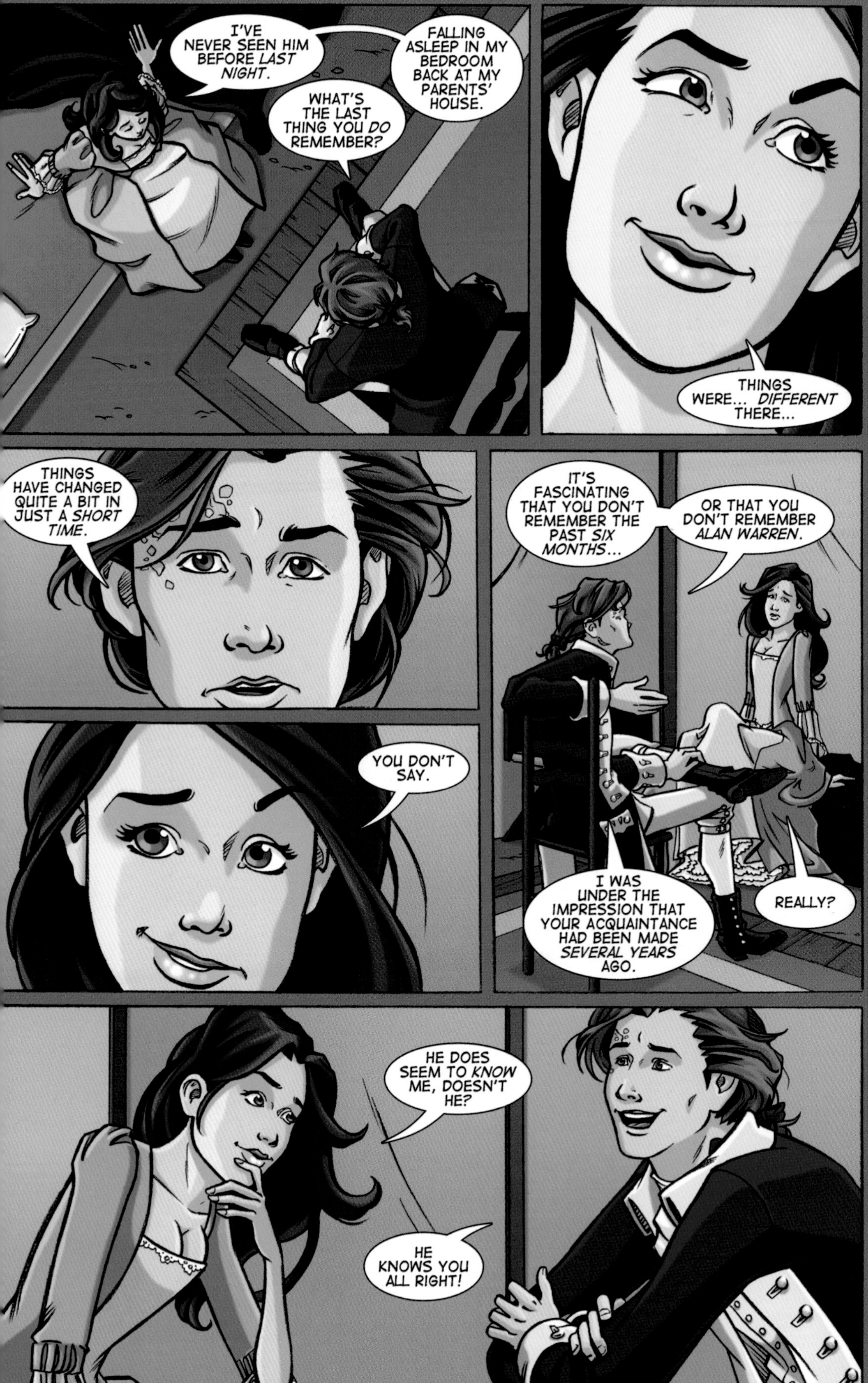
I'VE NEVER SEEN HIM BEFORE *LAST NIGHT*.
WHAT'S THE LAST THING YOU *DO* REMEMBER?
FALLING ASLEEP IN MY BEDROOM BACK AT MY PARENTS' HOUSE.
THINGS WERE... *DIFFERENT* THERE...
THINGS HAVE CHANGED QUITE A BIT IN JUST A *SHORT TIME*.
YOU DON'T SAY.
IT'S FASCINATING THAT YOU DON'T REMEMBER THE PAST *SIX MONTHS*...
OR THAT YOU DON'T REMEMBER *ALAN WARREN*.
I WAS UNDER THE IMPRESSION THAT YOUR ACQUAINTANCE HAD BEEN MADE *SEVERAL YEARS* AGO.
REALLY?
HE DOES SEEM TO *KNOW* ME, DOESN'T HE?
HE KNOWS YOU ALL RIGHT!

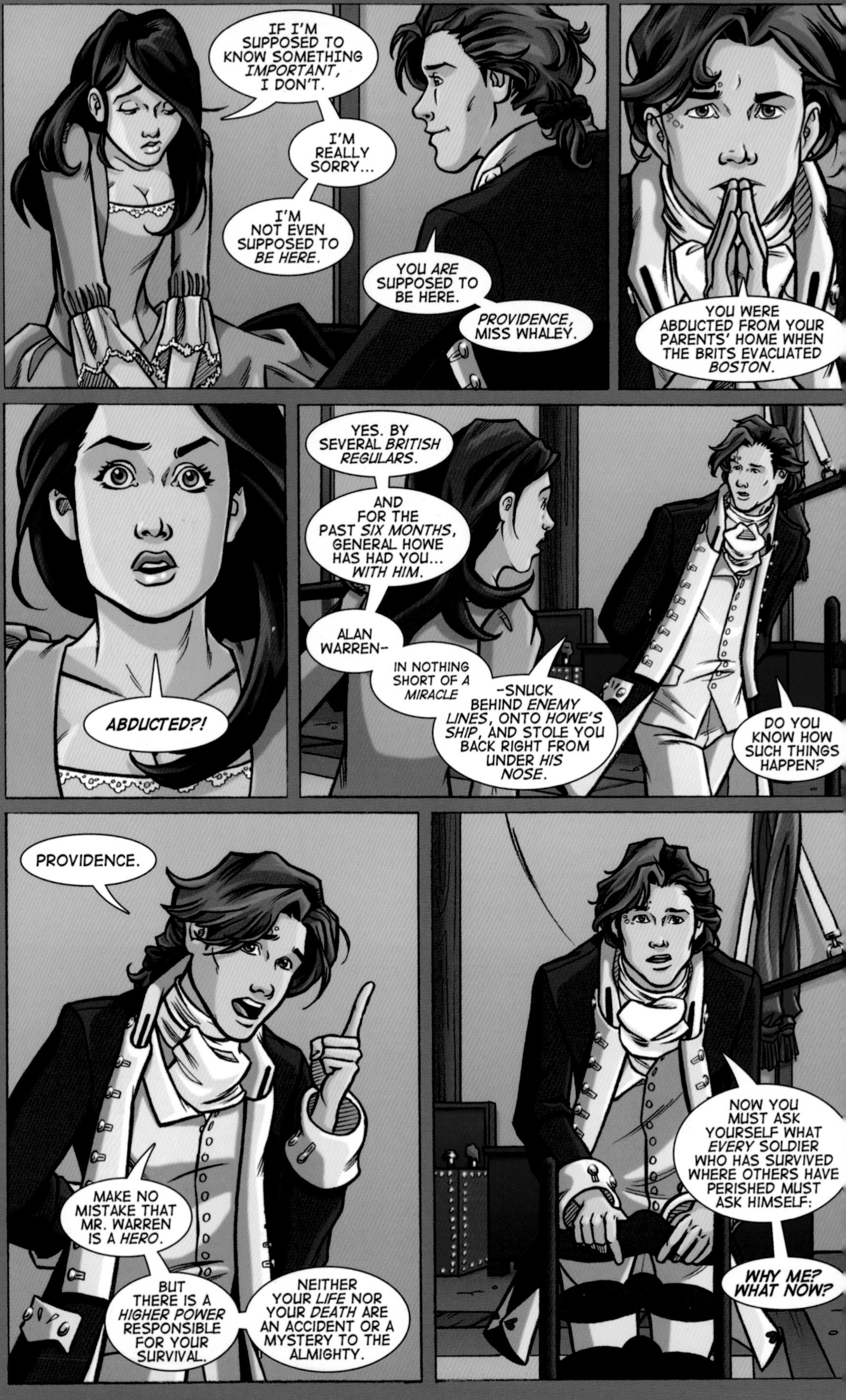
IF I'M SUPPOSED TO KNOW SOMETHING *IMPORTANT,* I DON'T.
I'M REALLY SORRY...
I'M NOT EVEN SUPPOSED TO *BE HERE.*
YOU *ARE* SUPPOSED TO BE HERE.
PROVIDENCE, MISS WHALEY.
YOU WERE ABDUCTED FROM YOUR PARENTS' HOME WHEN THE BRITS EVACUATED *BOSTON.*
ABDUCTED?!
YES. BY SEVERAL *BRITISH REGULARS.*
AND FOR THE PAST *SIX MONTHS,* GENERAL HOWE HAS HAD YOU... *WITH HIM.*
ALAN WARREN-
IN NOTHING SHORT OF A *MIRACLE*
-SNUCK BEHIND *ENEMY LINES,* ONTO *HOWE'S SHIP,* AND STOLE YOU BACK RIGHT FROM UNDER *HIS* NOSE.
DO YOU KNOW HOW SUCH THINGS HAPPEN?
PROVIDENCE.
MAKE NO MISTAKE THAT MR. WARREN IS A *HERO.*
BUT THERE IS A *HIGHER POWER* RESPONSIBLE FOR YOUR SURVIVAL.
NEITHER YOUR *LIFE* NOR YOUR *DEATH* ARE AN ACCIDENT OR A MYSTERY TO THE ALMIGHTY.
NOW YOU MUST ASK YOURSELF WHAT *EVERY* SOLDIER WHO HAS SURVIVED WHERE OTHERS HAVE PERISHED MUST ASK HIMSELF:
WHY ME? WHAT NOW?

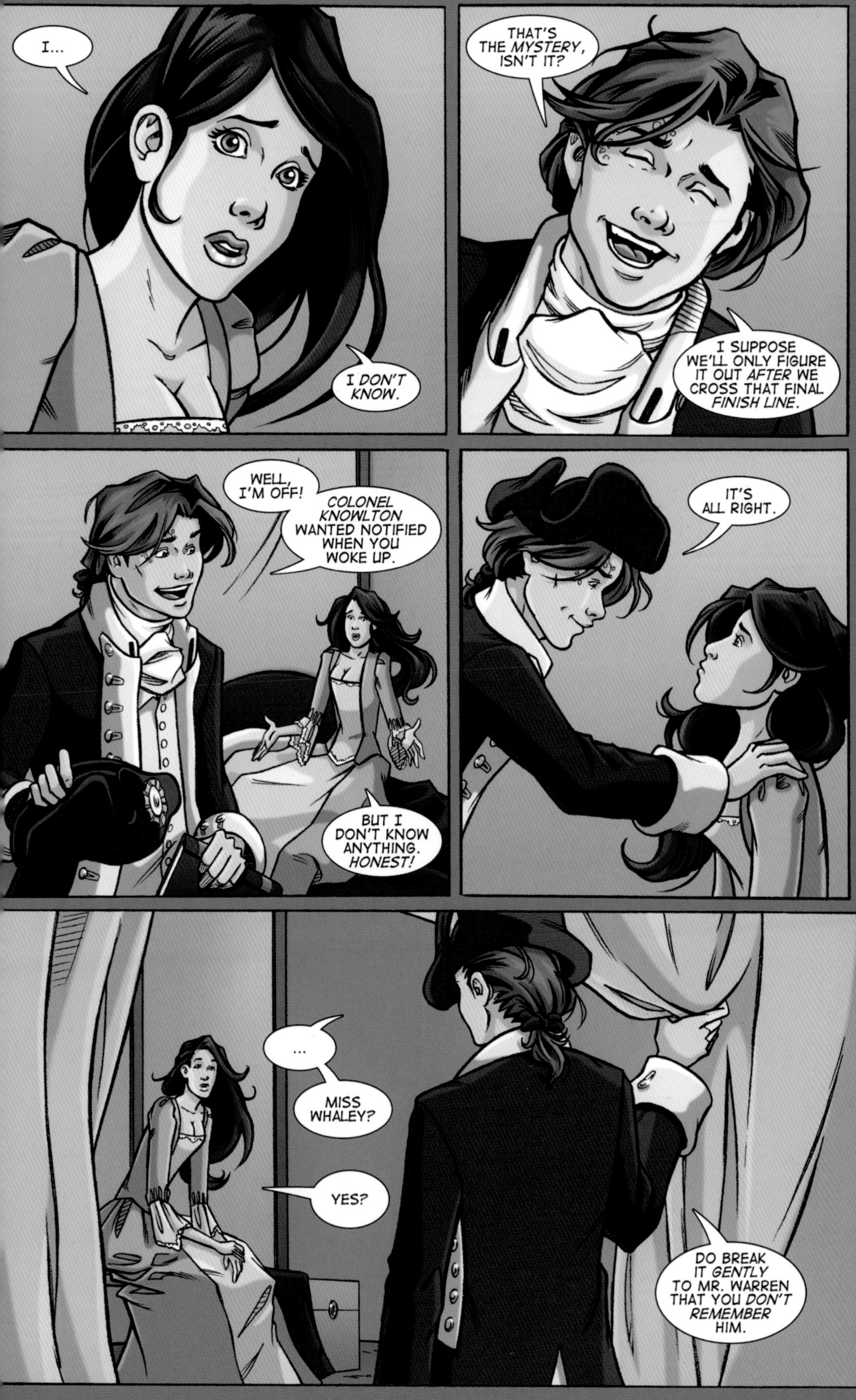
I...
I DON'T KNOW.
THAT'S THE MYSTERY, ISN'T IT?
I SUPPOSE WE'LL ONLY FIGURE IT OUT AFTER WE CROSS THAT FINAL FINISH LINE.
WELL, I'M OFF!
COLONEL KNOWLTON WANTED NOTIFIED WHEN YOU WOKE UP.
BUT I DON'T KNOW ANYTHING. HONEST!
IT'S ALL RIGHT.
...
MISS WHALEY?
YES?
DO BREAK IT GENTLY TO MR. WARREN THAT YOU DON'T REMEMBER HIM.

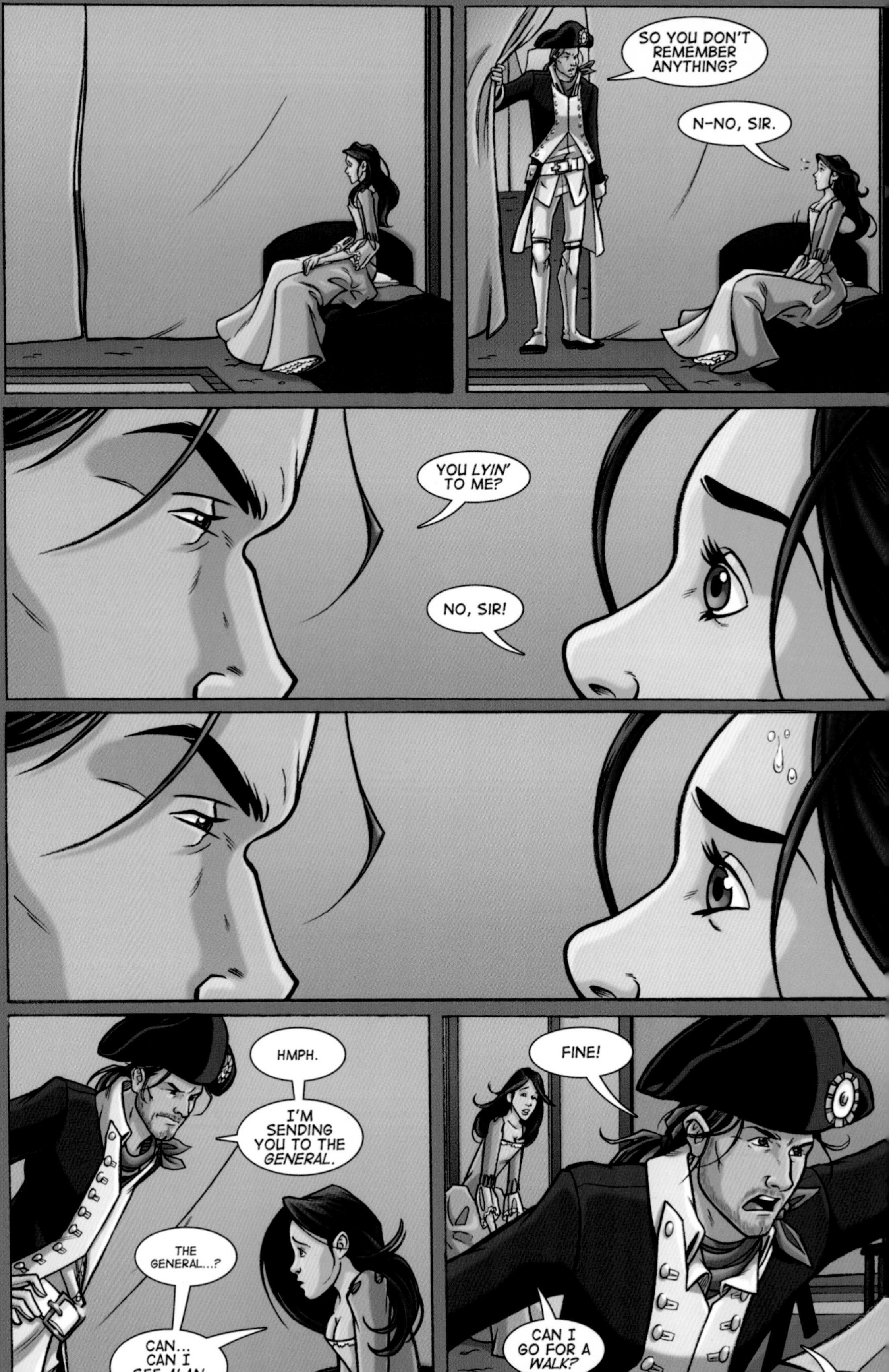
SO YOU DON'T REMEMBER ANYTHING?
N-NO, SIR.
YOU *LYIN'* TO ME?
NO, SIR!
HMPH.
I'M SENDING YOU TO THE *GENERAL*.
THE GENERAL...?
CAN... CAN I SEE *ALAN* FIRST?
FINE!
CAN I GO FOR A *WALK?*
FINE!

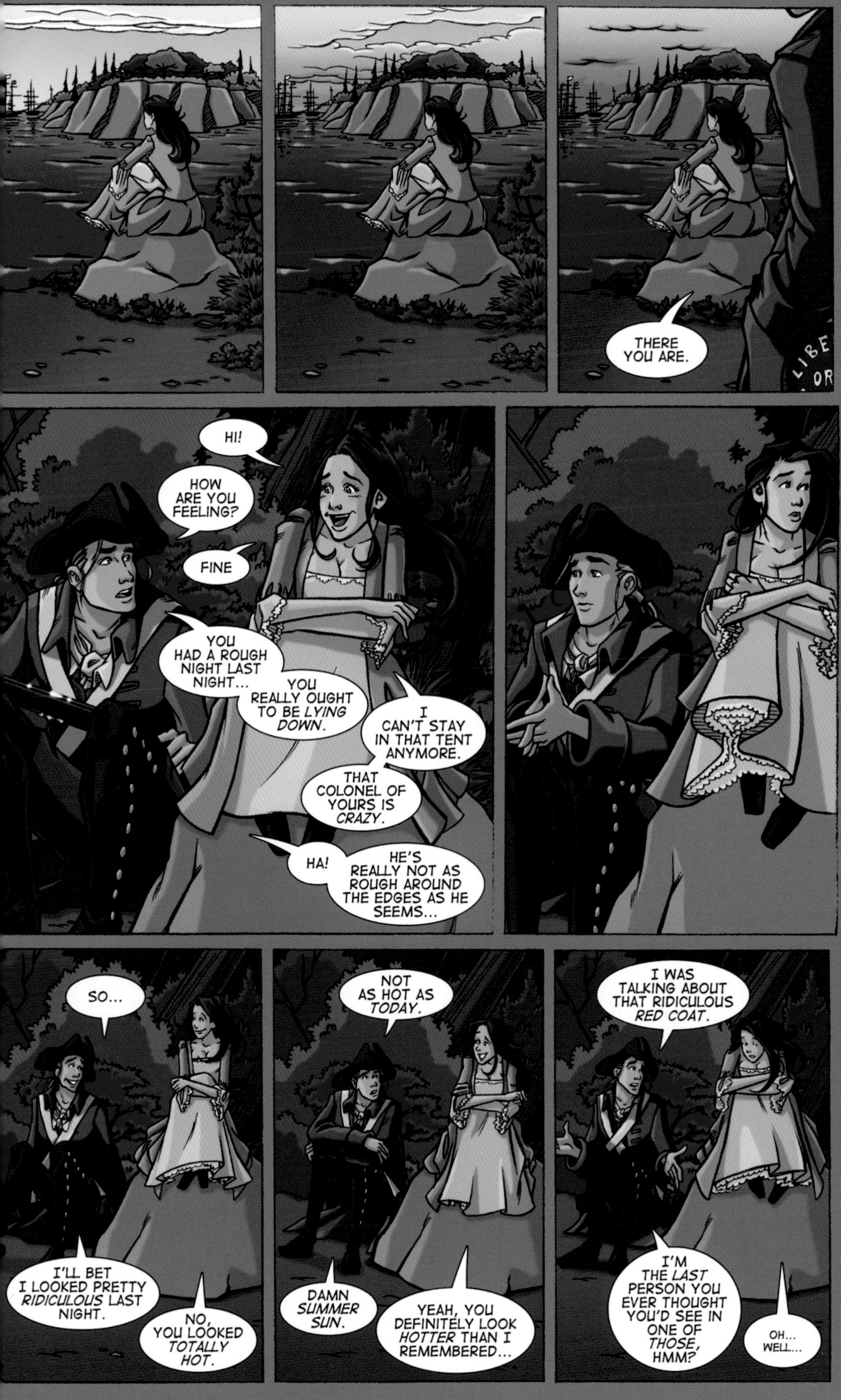
THERE YOU ARE.
LIBE
OR
HI!
HOW ARE YOU FEELING?
FINE
YOU HAD A ROUGH NIGHT LAST NIGHT...
YOU REALLY OUGHT TO BE *LYING DOWN*.
I CAN'T STAY IN THAT TENT ANYMORE.
THAT COLONEL OF YOURS IS *CRAZY*.
HA!
HE'S REALLY NOT AS ROUGH AROUND THE EDGES AS HE SEEMS...
SO...
I'LL BET I LOOKED PRETTY *RIDICULOUS* LAST NIGHT.
NO, YOU LOOKED *TOTALLY HOT*.
NOT AS HOT AS *TODAY*.
DAMN *SUMMER SUN*.
YEAH, YOU DEFINITELY LOOK *HOTTER* THAN I REMEMBERED...
I WAS TALKING ABOUT THAT RIDICULOUS *RED COAT*.
I'M THE *LAST* PERSON YOU EVER THOUGHT YOU'D SEE IN ONE OF *THOSE*, HMM?
OH... WELL...

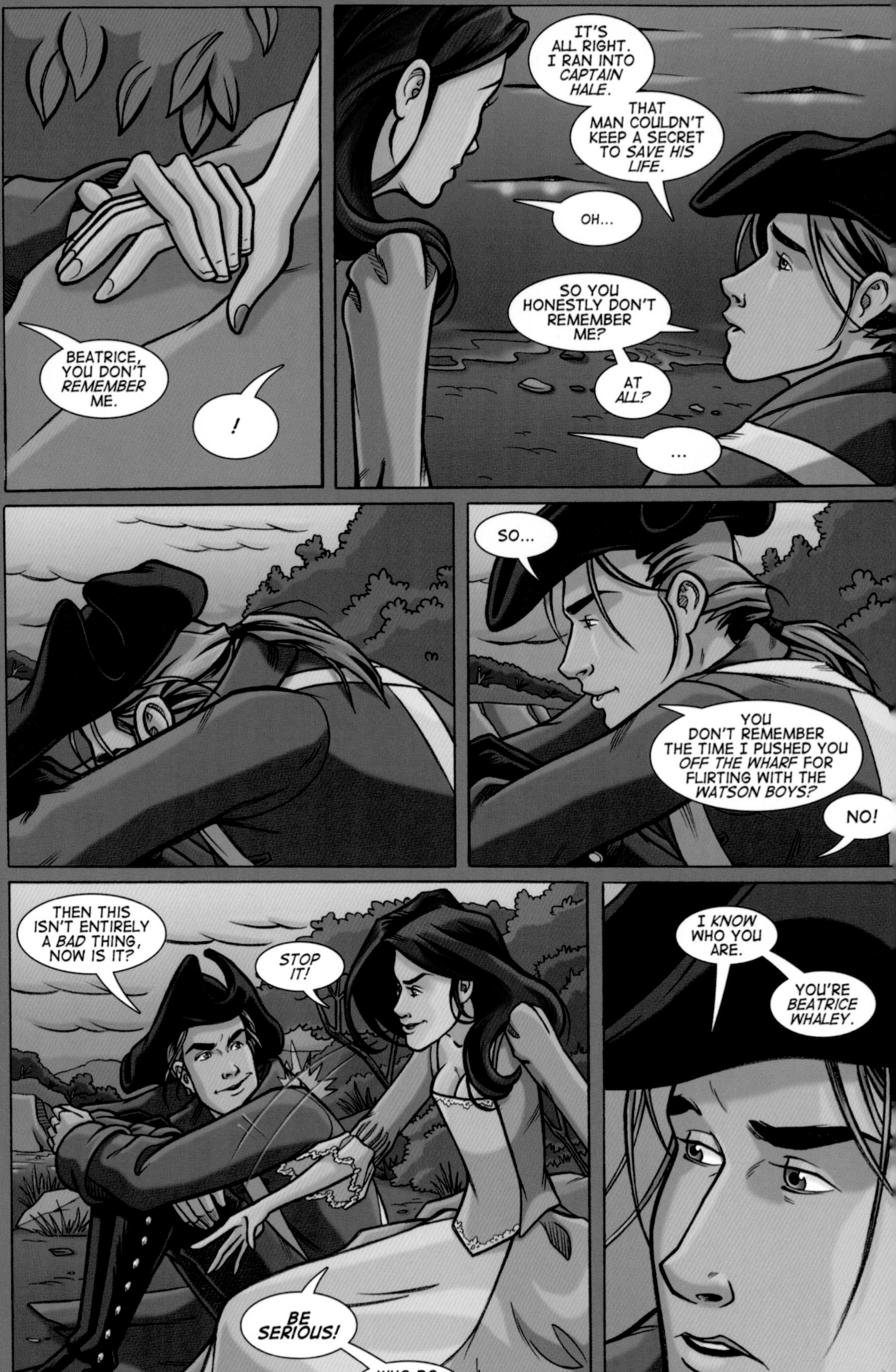
BEATRICE, YOU DON'T *REMEMBER* ME.
!
IT'S ALL RIGHT. I RAN INTO *CAPTAIN HALE*.
THAT MAN COULDN'T KEEP A SECRET TO *SAVE HIS LIFE*.
OH...
SO YOU HONESTLY DON'T REMEMBER ME?
AT *ALL?*
...
SO...
YOU DON'T REMEMBER THE TIME I PUSHED YOU *OFF THE WHARF* FOR FLIRTING WITH THE *WATSON BOYS?*
NO!
THEN THIS ISN'T ENTIRELY A *BAD* THING, NOW IS IT?
STOP IT!
BE SERIOUS!
WHO DO YOU THINK I AM?
I *KNOW* WHO YOU ARE.
YOU'RE *BEATRICE WHALEY*.
YOU'RE...

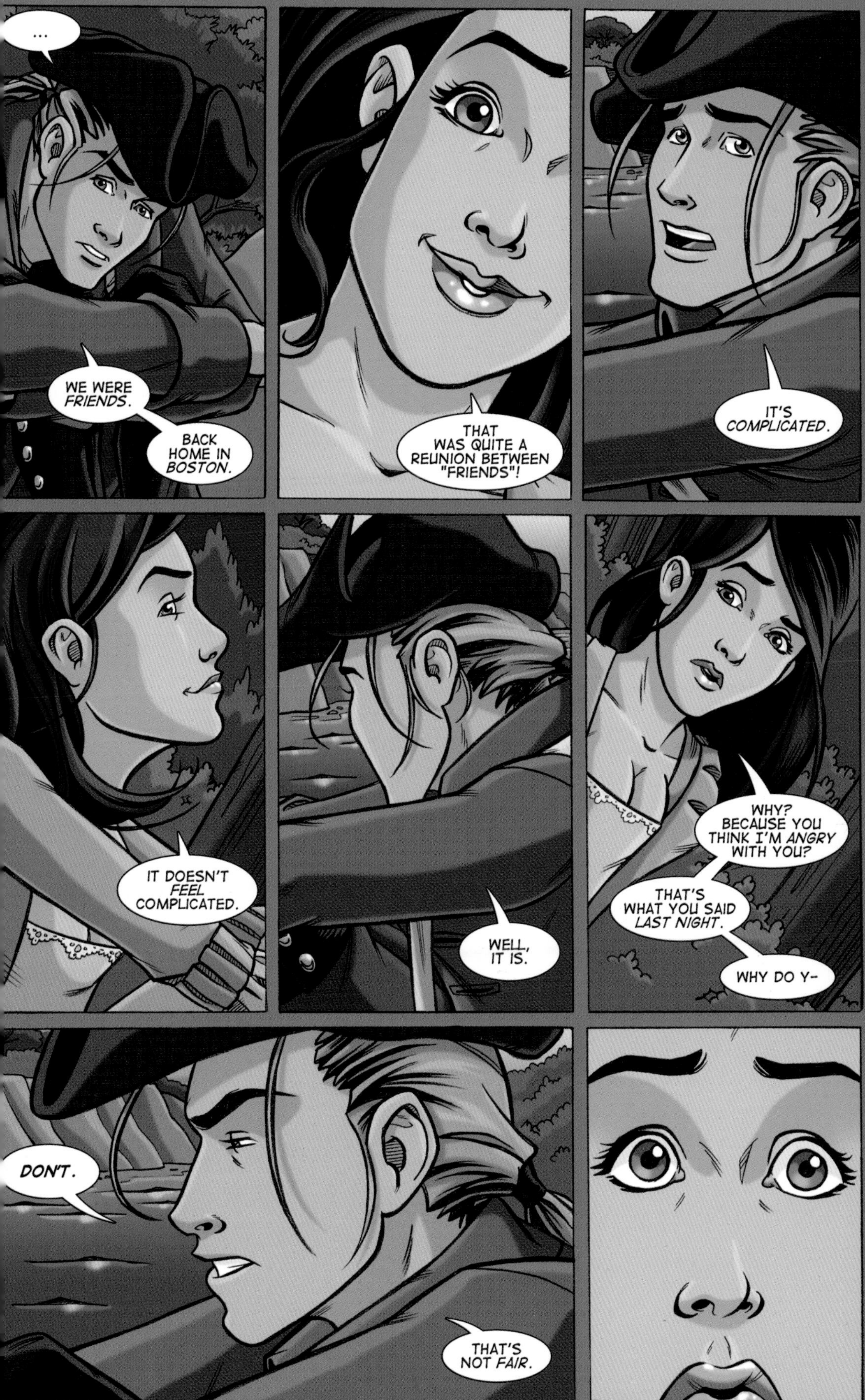
...
WE WERE FRIENDS.
BACK HOME IN BOSTON.
THAT WAS QUITE A REUNION BETWEEN "FRIENDS"!
IT'S COMPLICATED.
IT DOESN'T FEEL COMPLICATED.
WELL, IT IS.
WHY? BECAUSE YOU THINK I'M ANGRY WITH YOU?
THAT'S WHAT YOU SAID LAST NIGHT.
WHY DO Y-
DON'T.
THAT'S NOT FAIR.

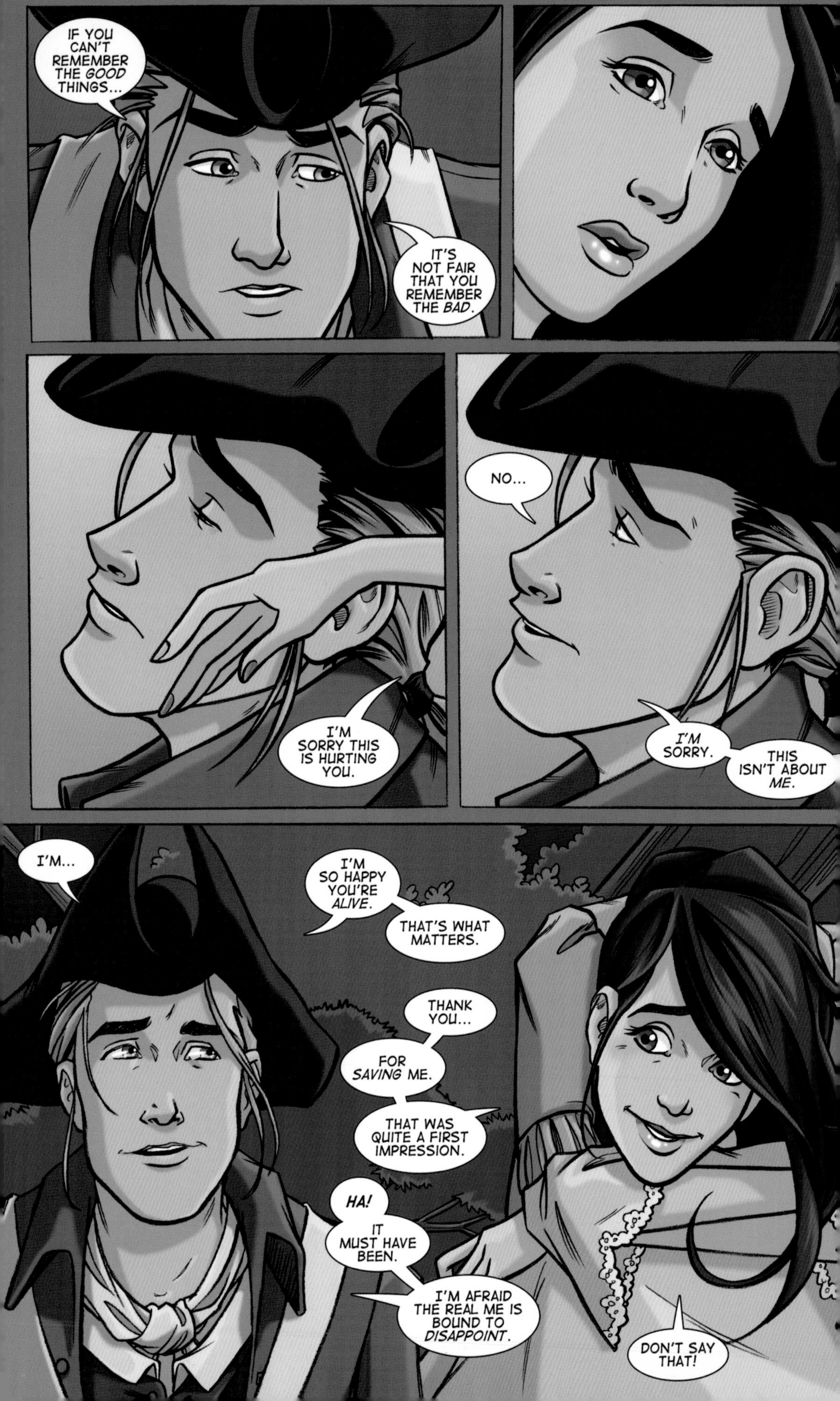
IF YOU CAN'T REMEMBER THE *GOOD* THINGS...
IT'S NOT FAIR THAT YOU REMEMBER THE *BAD*.
I'M SORRY THIS IS HURTING YOU.
NO...
I'M SORRY.
THIS ISN'T ABOUT *ME*.
I'M...
I'M SO HAPPY YOU'RE *ALIVE*.
THAT'S WHAT MATTERS.
THANK YOU...
FOR *SAVING* ME.
THAT WAS QUITE A FIRST IMPRESSION.
HA!
IT MUST HAVE BEEN.
I'M AFRAID THE REAL ME IS BOUND TO *DISAPPOINT*.
DON'T SAY THAT!

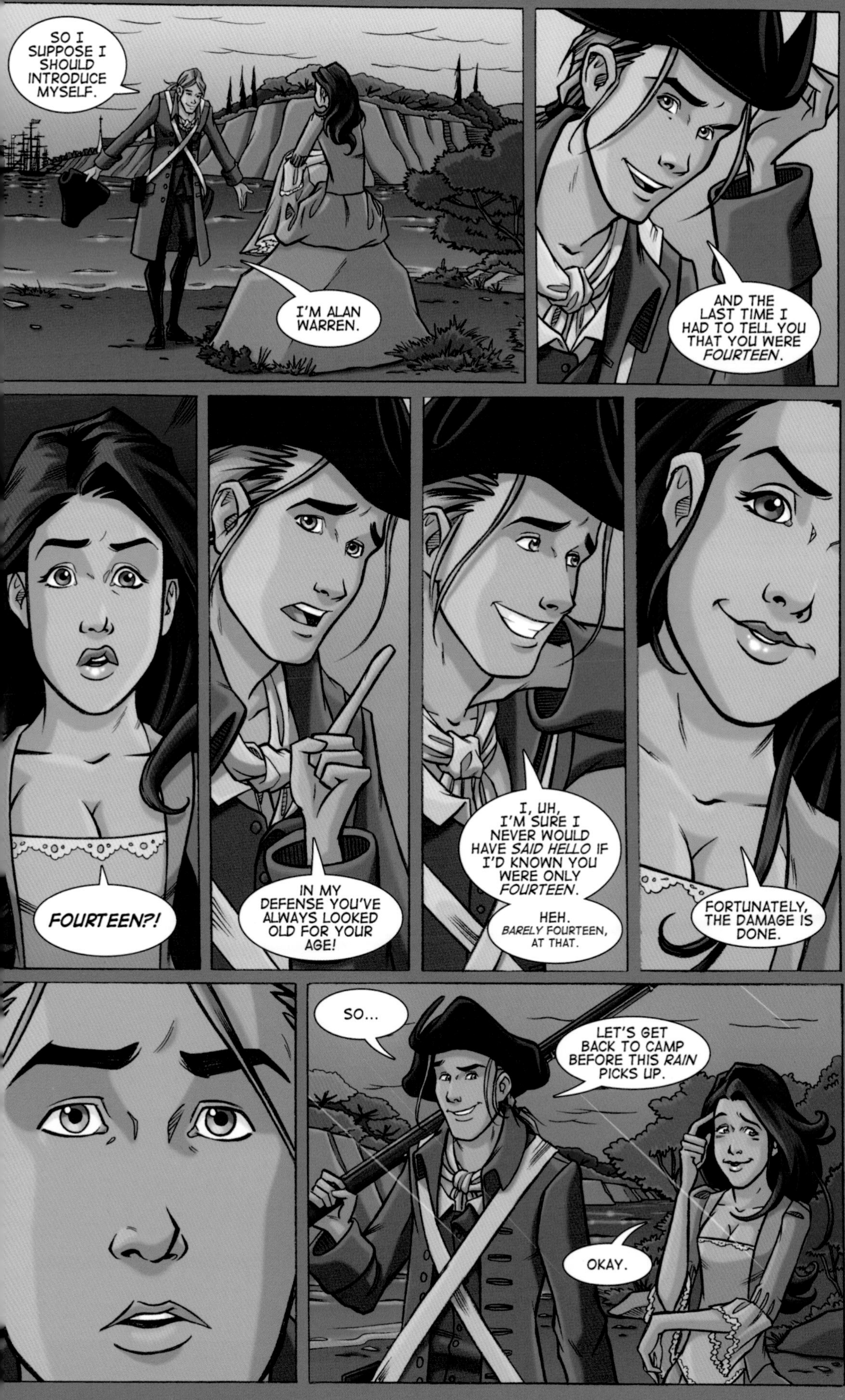

SO I SUPPOSE I SHOULD INTRODUCE MYSELF.
I'M ALAN WARREN.
AND THE LAST TIME I HAD TO TELL YOU THAT YOU WERE *FOURTEEN*.
FOURTEEN?!
IN MY DEFENSE YOU'VE ALWAYS LOOKED OLD FOR YOUR AGE!
I, UH, I'M SURE I NEVER WOULD HAVE *SAID HELLO* IF I'D KNOWN YOU WERE ONLY *FOURTEEN*.
HEH. *BARELY* FOURTEEN, AT THAT.
FORTUNATELY, THE DAMAGE IS DONE.
SO...
LET'S GET BACK TO CAMP BEFORE THIS *RAIN* PICKS UP.
OKAY.

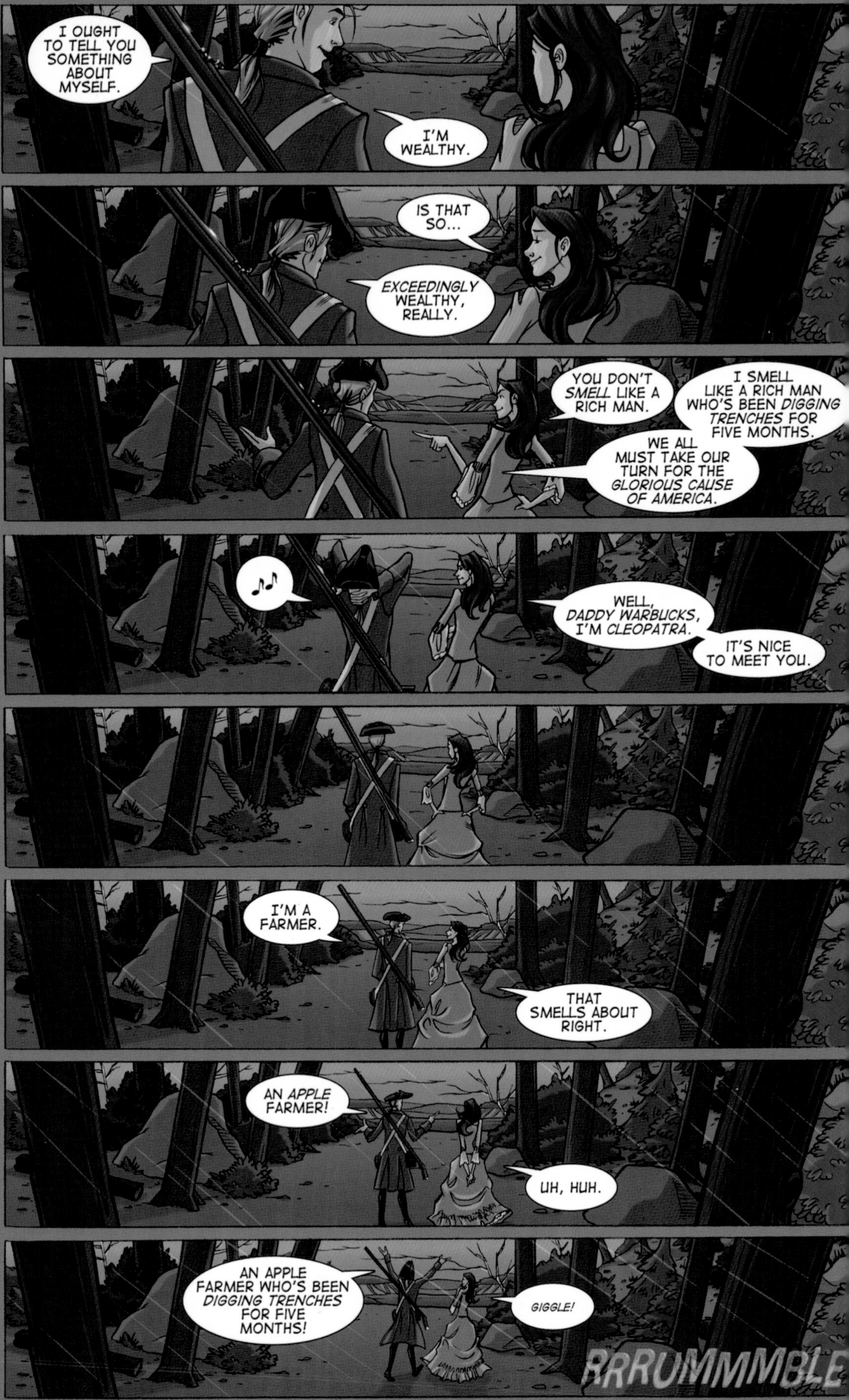
I OUGHT TO TELL YOU SOMETHING ABOUT MYSELF.
I'M WEALTHY.
IS THAT SO...
EXCEEDINGLY WEALTHY, REALLY.
YOU DON'T *SMELL* LIKE A RICH MAN.
I SMELL LIKE A RICH MAN WHO'S BEEN *DIGGING TRENCHES* FOR FIVE MONTHS.
WE ALL MUST TAKE OUR TURN FOR THE *GLORIOUS CAUSE OF AMERICA*.
♪♪
WELL, *DADDY WARBUCKS*, I'M *CLEOPATRA*.
IT'S NICE TO MEET YOU.
I'M A FARMER.
THAT SMELLS ABOUT RIGHT.
AN *APPLE* FARMER!
UH, HUH.
AN APPLE FARMER WHO'S BEEN *DIGGING TRENCHES* FOR FIVE MONTHS!
GIGGLE!
RRRUMMMBLE

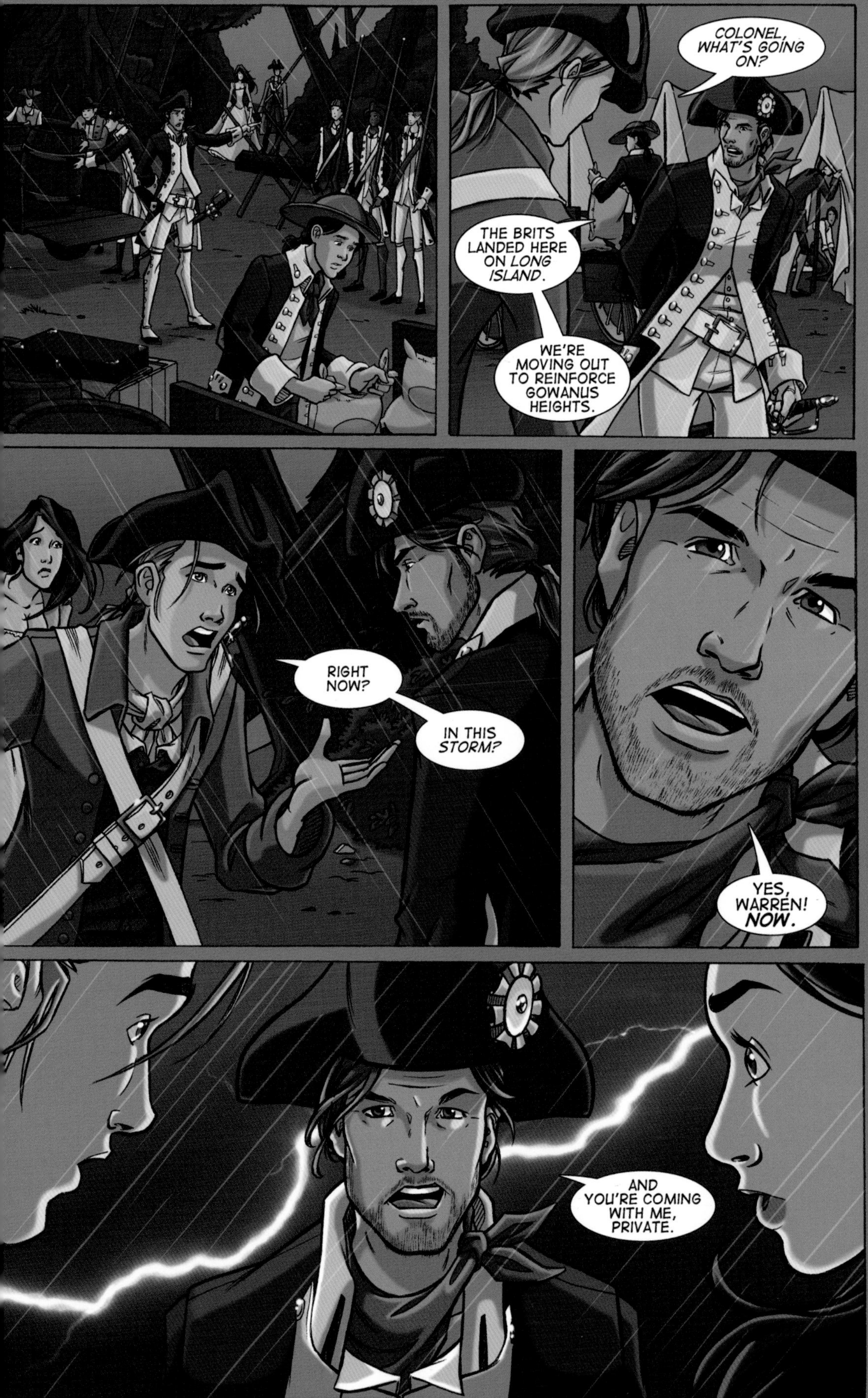
COLONEL, WHAT'S GOING ON?
THE BRITS LANDED HERE ON LONG ISLAND.
WE'RE MOVING OUT TO REINFORCE GOWANUS HEIGHTS.
RIGHT NOW?
IN THIS STORM?
YES, WARREN! NOW.
AND YOU'RE COMING WITH ME, PRIVATE.

Chapter Three

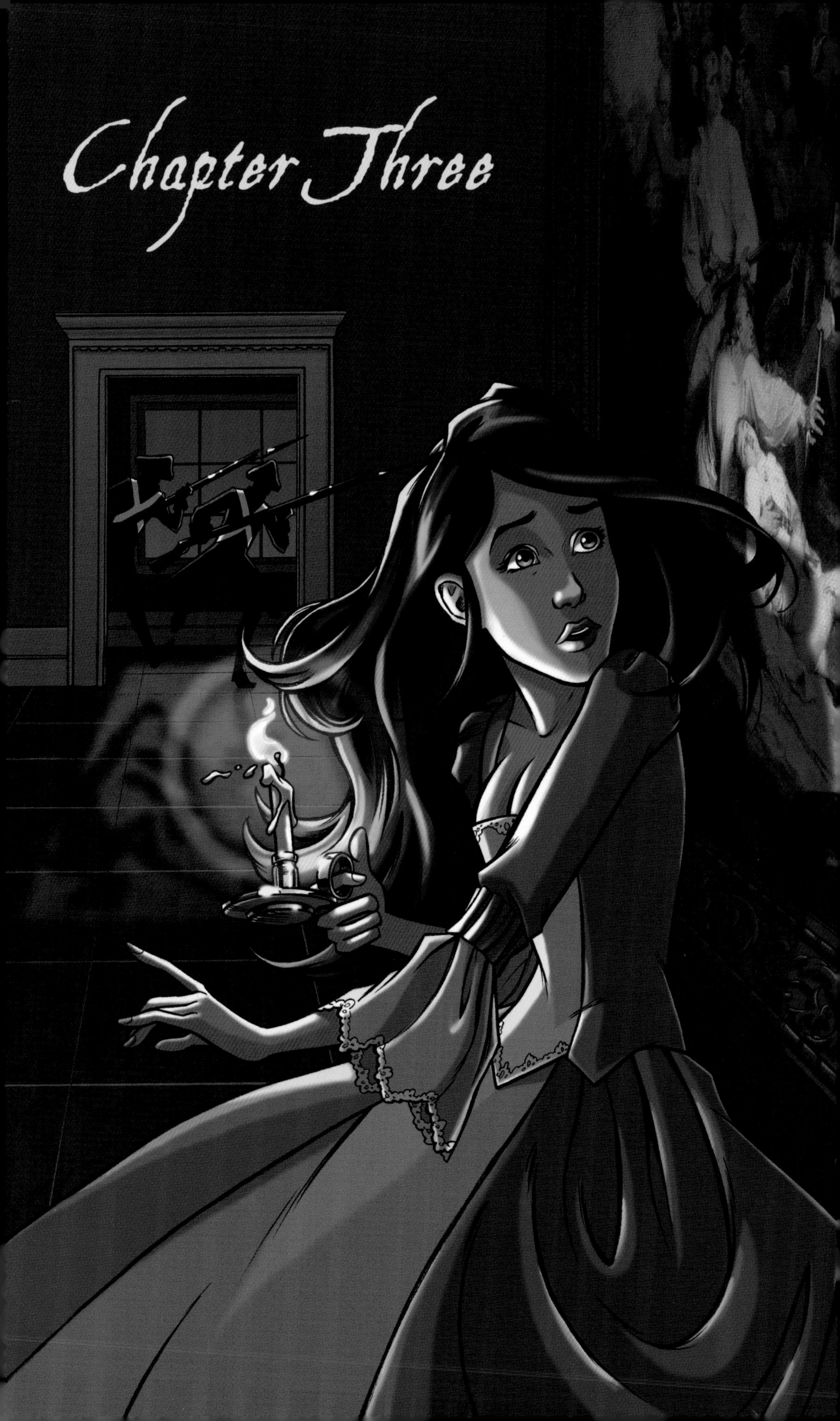

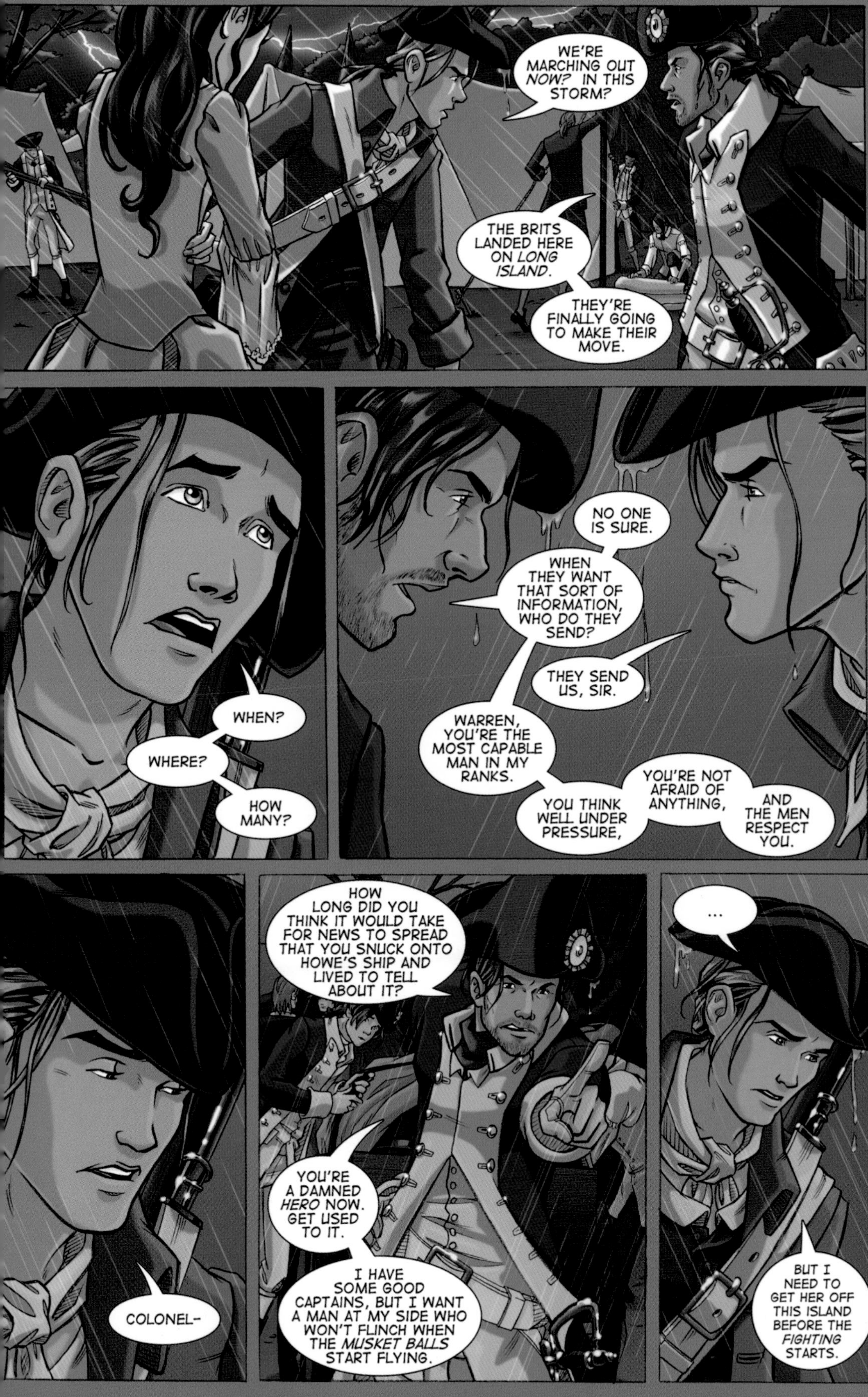

WE'RE MARCHING OUT *NOW?* IN THIS STORM?
THE BRITS LANDED HERE ON *LONG ISLAND*.
THEY'RE FINALLY GOING TO MAKE THEIR MOVE.
WHEN?
WHERE?
HOW MANY?
NO ONE IS SURE.
WHEN THEY WANT THAT SORT OF INFORMATION, WHO DO THEY SEND?
THEY SEND US, SIR.
WARREN, YOU'RE THE MOST CAPABLE MAN IN MY RANKS.
YOU THINK WELL UNDER PRESSURE,
YOU'RE NOT AFRAID OF ANYTHING,
AND THE MEN RESPECT YOU.
COLONEL-
HOW LONG DID YOU THINK IT WOULD TAKE FOR NEWS TO SPREAD THAT YOU SNUCK ONTO HOWE'S SHIP AND LIVED TO TELL ABOUT IT?
YOU'RE A DAMNED *HERO* NOW. GET USED TO IT.
I HAVE SOME GOOD CAPTAINS, BUT I WANT A MAN AT MY SIDE WHO WON'T FLINCH WHEN THE *MUSKET BALLS* START FLYING.
...
BUT I NEED TO GET HER OFF THIS ISLAND BEFORE THE *FIGHTING* STARTS.

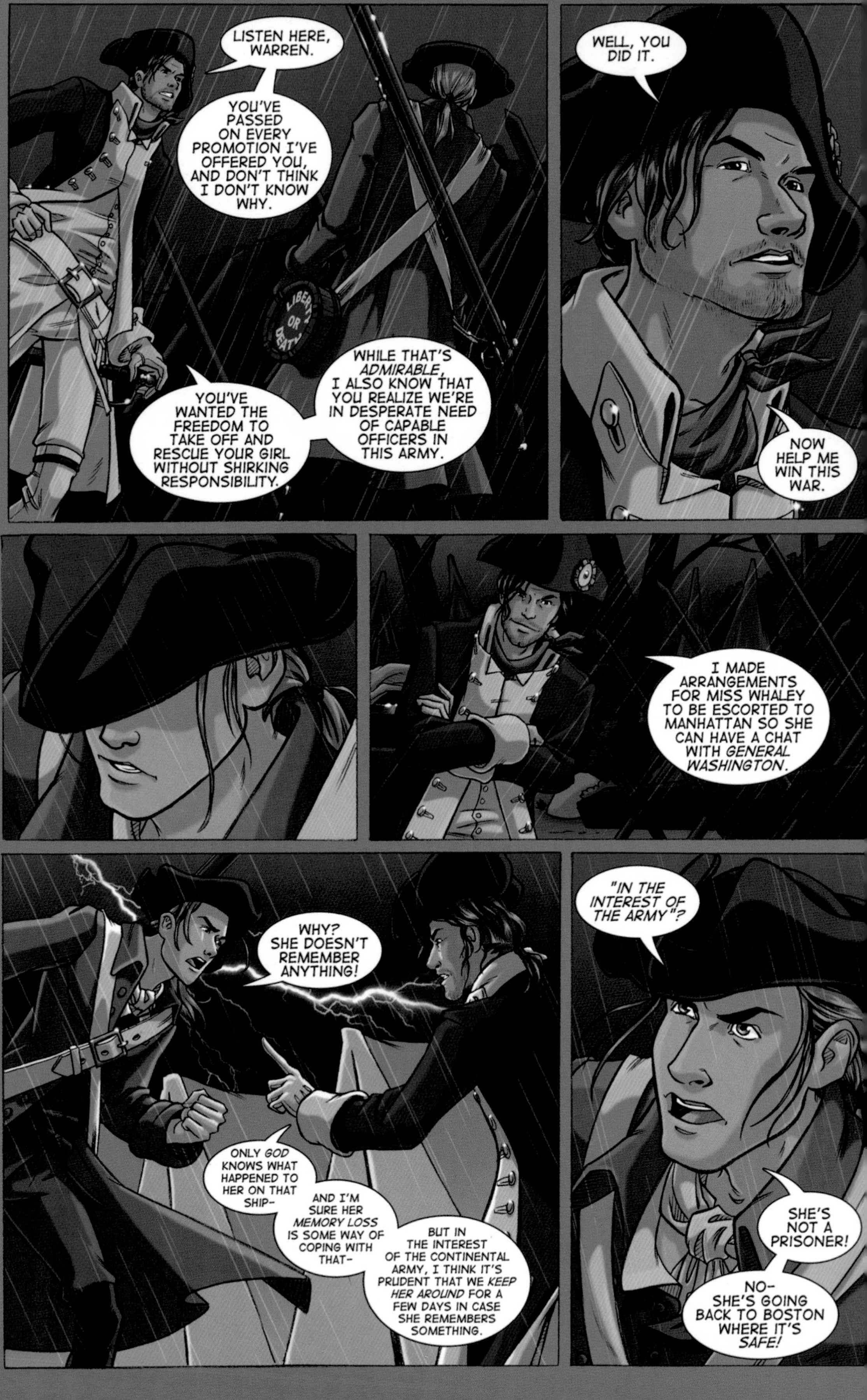
LISTEN HERE, WARREN.
YOU'VE PASSED ON EVERY PROMOTION I'VE OFFERED YOU, AND DON'T THINK I DON'T KNOW WHY.
LIBERTY OR DEATH
YOU'VE WANTED THE FREEDOM TO TAKE OFF AND RESCUE YOUR GIRL WITHOUT SHIRKING RESPONSIBILITY.
WHILE THAT'S *ADMIRABLE*, I ALSO KNOW THAT YOU REALIZE WE'RE IN DESPERATE NEED OF CAPABLE OFFICERS IN THIS ARMY.
WELL, YOU DID IT.
NOW HELP ME WIN THIS WAR.
I MADE ARRANGEMENTS FOR MISS WHALEY TO BE ESCORTED TO MANHATTAN SO SHE CAN HAVE A CHAT WITH *GENERAL WASHINGTON*.
WHY? SHE DOESN'T REMEMBER ANYTHING!
ONLY *GOD* KNOWS WHAT HAPPENED TO HER ON THAT SHIP-
AND I'M SURE HER *MEMORY LOSS* IS SOME WAY OF COPING WITH THAT-
BUT IN THE INTEREST OF THE CONTINENTAL ARMY, I THINK IT'S PRUDENT THAT WE *KEEP HER AROUND* FOR A FEW DAYS IN CASE SHE REMEMBERS SOMETHING.
"IN THE INTEREST OF THE ARMY"?
SHE'S NOT A PRISONER!
NO- SHE'S GOING BACK TO BOSTON WHERE IT'S *SAFE!*

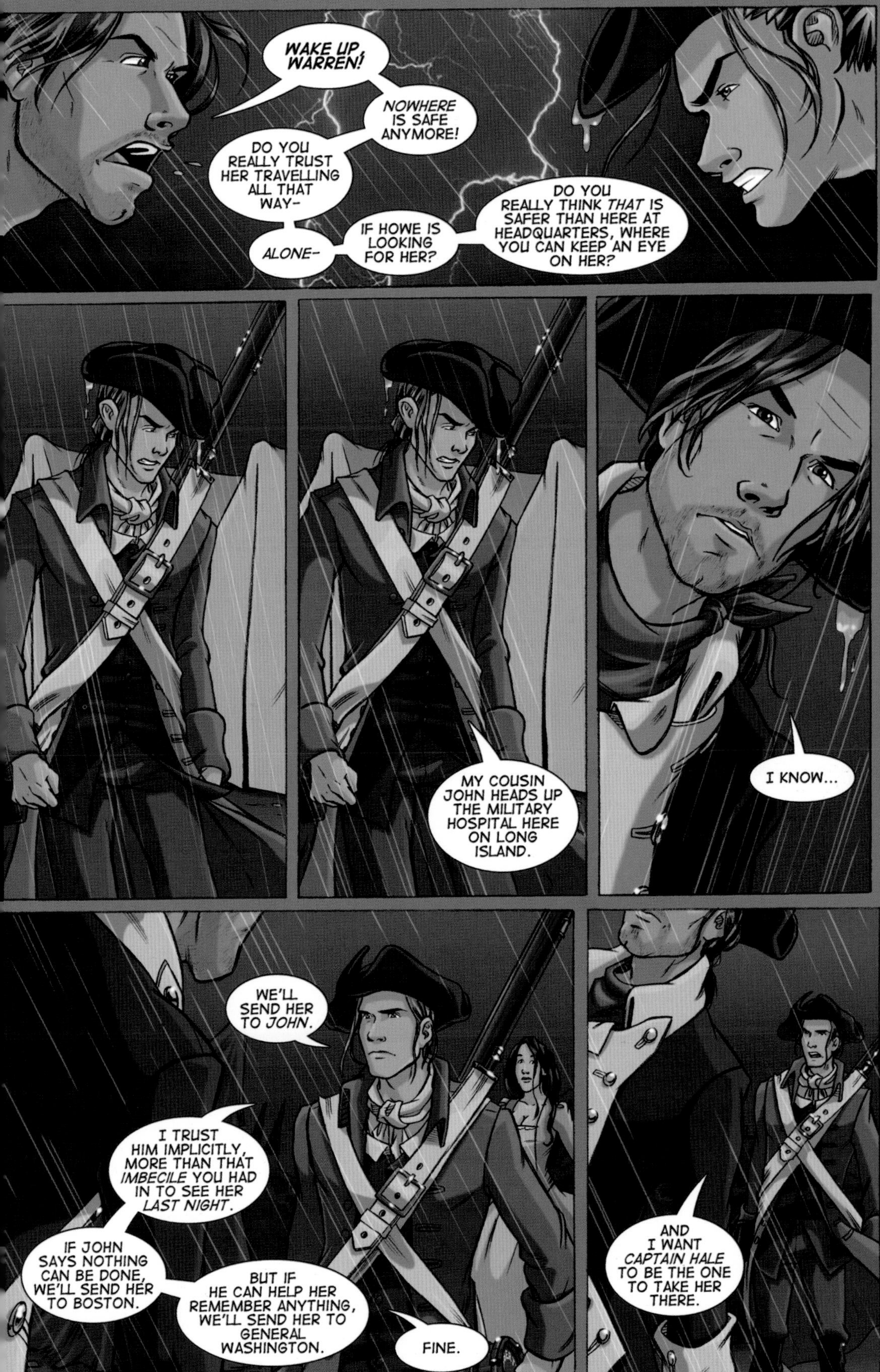
WAKE UP, WARREN!
NOWHERE IS SAFE ANYMORE!
DO YOU REALLY TRUST HER TRAVELLING ALL THAT WAY-
ALONE-
IF HOWE IS LOOKING FOR HER?
DO YOU REALLY THINK THAT IS SAFER THAN HERE AT HEADQUARTERS, WHERE YOU CAN KEEP AN EYE ON HER?
MY COUSIN JOHN HEADS UP THE MILITARY HOSPITAL HERE ON LONG ISLAND.
I KNOW...
WE'LL SEND HER TO JOHN.
I TRUST HIM IMPLICITLY, MORE THAN THAT IMBECILE YOU HAD IN TO SEE HER LAST NIGHT.
IF JOHN SAYS NOTHING CAN BE DONE, WE'LL SEND HER TO BOSTON.
BUT IF HE CAN HELP HER REMEMBER ANYTHING, WE'LL SEND HER TO GENERAL WASHINGTON.
FINE.
AND I WANT CAPTAIN HALE TO BE THE ONE TO TAKE HER THERE.

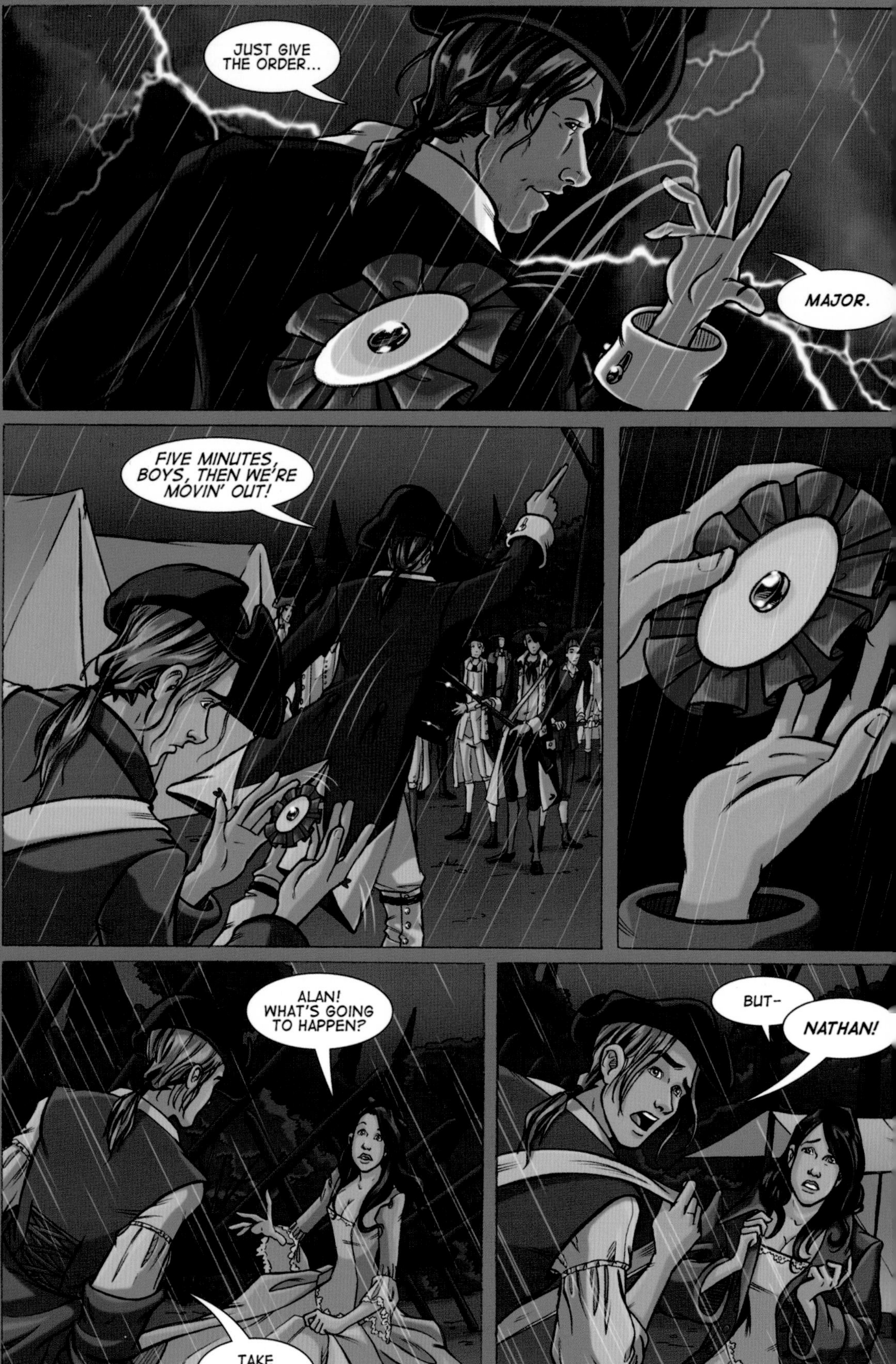
JUST GIVE THE ORDER...
MAJOR.
FIVE MINUTES, BOYS, THEN WE'RE MOVIN' OUT!
ALAN! WHAT'S GOING TO HAPPEN?
TAKE MY JACKET. STAY DRY.
BUT-
NATHAN!

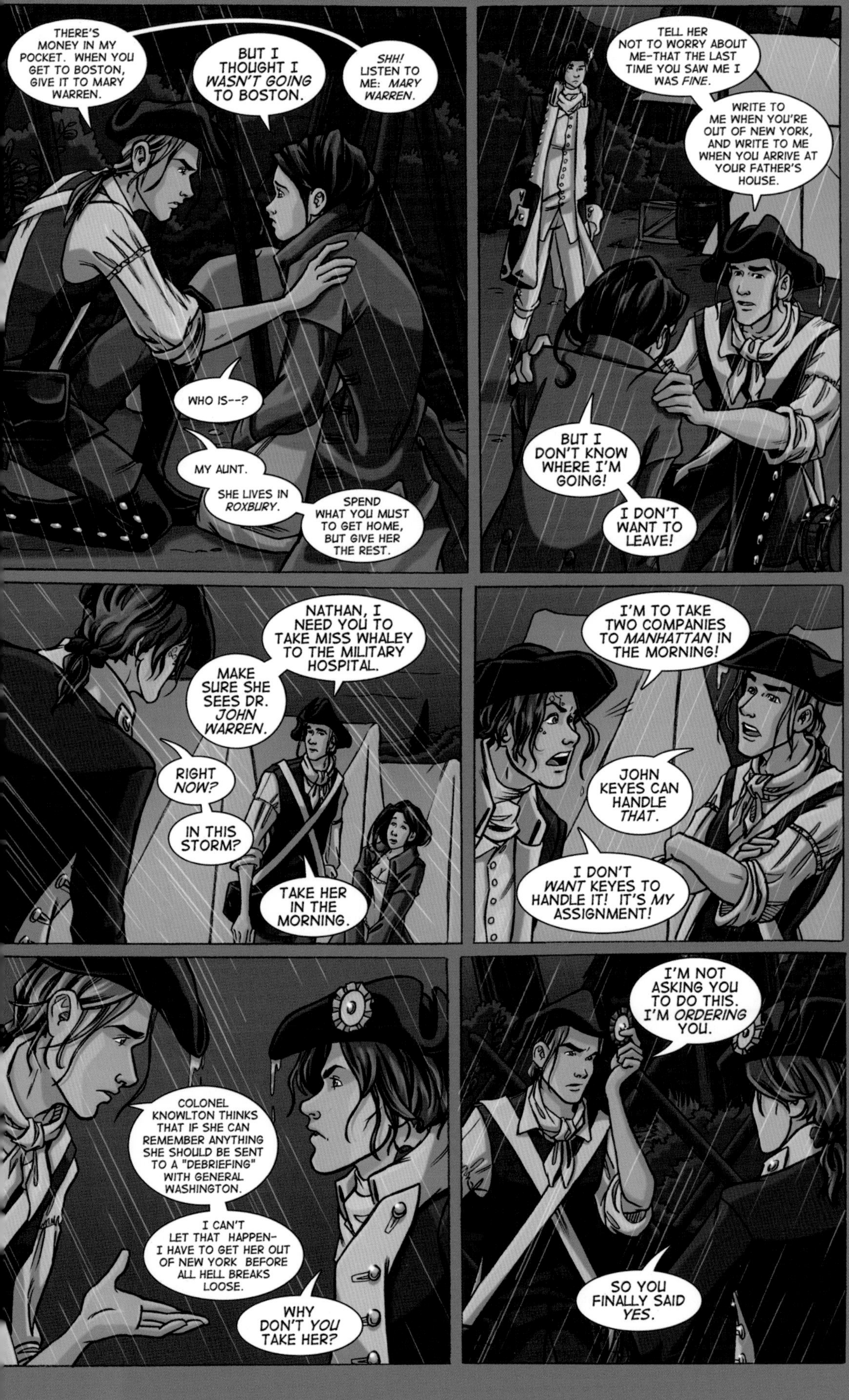
THERE'S MONEY IN MY POCKET. WHEN YOU GET TO BOSTON, GIVE IT TO MARY WARREN.
BUT I THOUGHT I *WASN'T GOING* TO BOSTON.
SHH! LISTEN TO ME: *MARY WARREN*.
WHO IS--?
MY AUNT.
SHE LIVES IN *ROXBURY*.
SPEND WHAT YOU MUST TO GET HOME, BUT GIVE HER THE REST.
TELL HER NOT TO WORRY ABOUT ME—THAT THE LAST TIME YOU SAW ME I WAS *FINE*.
WRITE TO ME WHEN YOU'RE OUT OF NEW YORK, AND WRITE TO ME WHEN YOU ARRIVE AT YOUR FATHER'S HOUSE.
BUT I DON'T KNOW WHERE I'M GOING!
I DON'T WANT TO LEAVE!
NATHAN, I NEED YOU TO TAKE MISS WHALEY TO THE MILITARY HOSPITAL.
MAKE SURE SHE SEES DR. *JOHN WARREN*.
RIGHT *NOW?*
IN THIS STORM?
TAKE HER IN THE MORNING.
I'M TO TAKE TWO COMPANIES TO *MANHATTAN* IN THE MORNING!
JOHN KEYES CAN HANDLE *THAT*.
I DON'T *WANT* KEYES TO HANDLE IT! IT'S *MY* ASSIGNMENT!
COLONEL KNOWLTON THINKS THAT IF SHE CAN REMEMBER ANYTHING SHE SHOULD BE SENT TO A "DEBRIEFING" WITH GENERAL WASHINGTON.
I CAN'T LET THAT HAPPEN—I HAVE TO GET HER OUT OF NEW YORK BEFORE ALL HELL BREAKS LOOSE.
WHY DON'T *YOU* TAKE HER?
I'M NOT ASKING YOU TO DO THIS. I'M *ORDERING* YOU.
SO YOU FINALLY SAID *YES*.

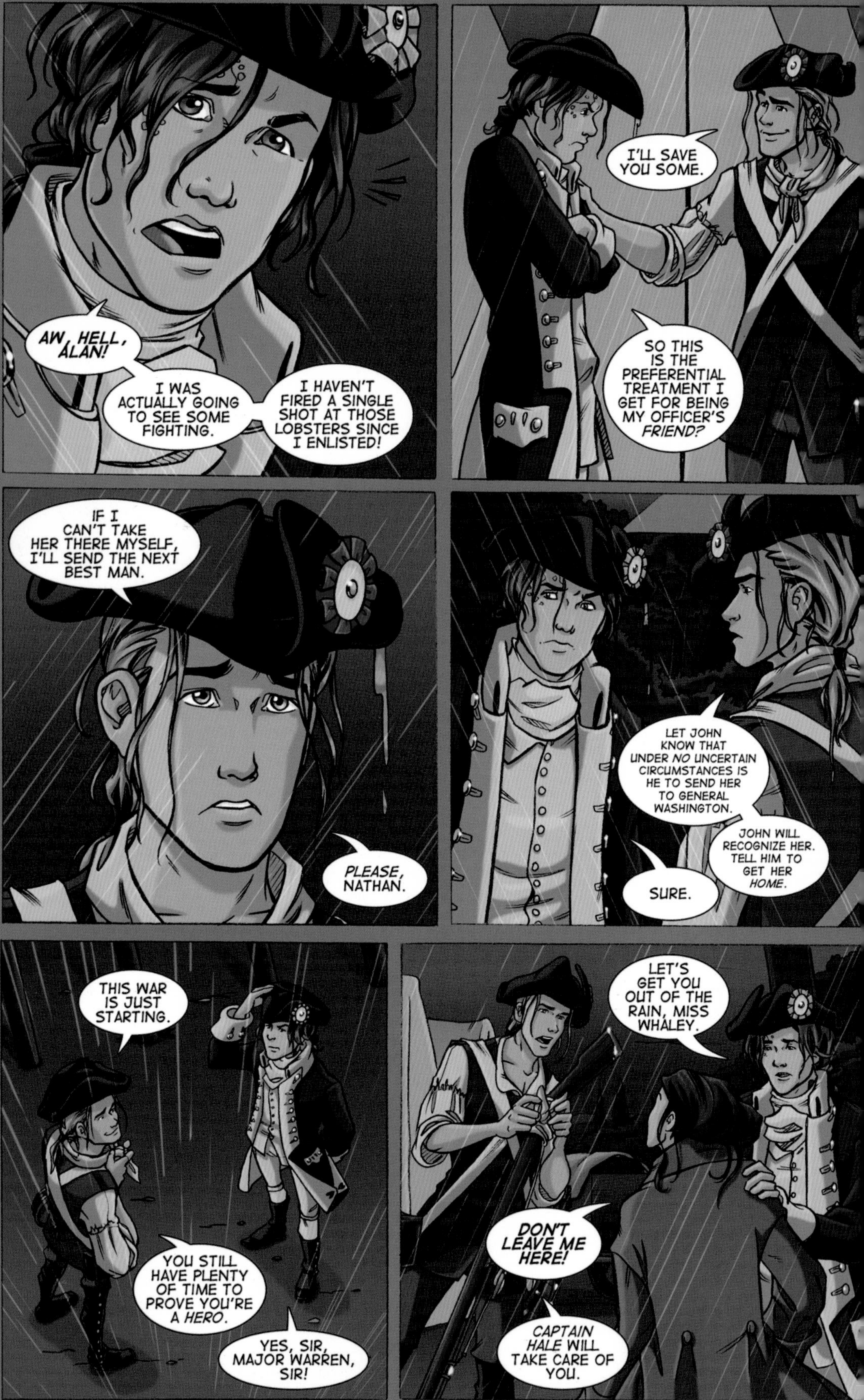
AW, HELL, ALAN!
I WAS ACTUALLY GOING TO SEE SOME FIGHTING.
I HAVEN'T FIRED A SINGLE SHOT AT THOSE LOBSTERS SINCE I ENLISTED!
I'LL SAVE YOU SOME.
SO THIS IS THE PREFERENTIAL TREATMENT I GET FOR BEING MY OFFICER'S *FRIEND?*
IF I CAN'T TAKE HER THERE MYSELF, I'LL SEND THE NEXT BEST MAN.
PLEASE, NATHAN.
LET JOHN KNOW THAT UNDER *NO* UNCERTAIN CIRCUMSTANCES IS HE TO SEND HER TO GENERAL WASHINGTON.
JOHN WILL RECOGNIZE HER. TELL HIM TO GET HER *HOME*.
SURE.
THIS WAR IS JUST STARTING.
YOU STILL HAVE PLENTY OF TIME TO PROVE YOU'RE A *HERO*.
YES, SIR, MAJOR WARREN, SIR!
LET'S GET YOU OUT OF THE RAIN, MISS WHALEY.
DON'T LEAVE ME HERE!
CAPTAIN HALE WILL TAKE CARE OF YOU.

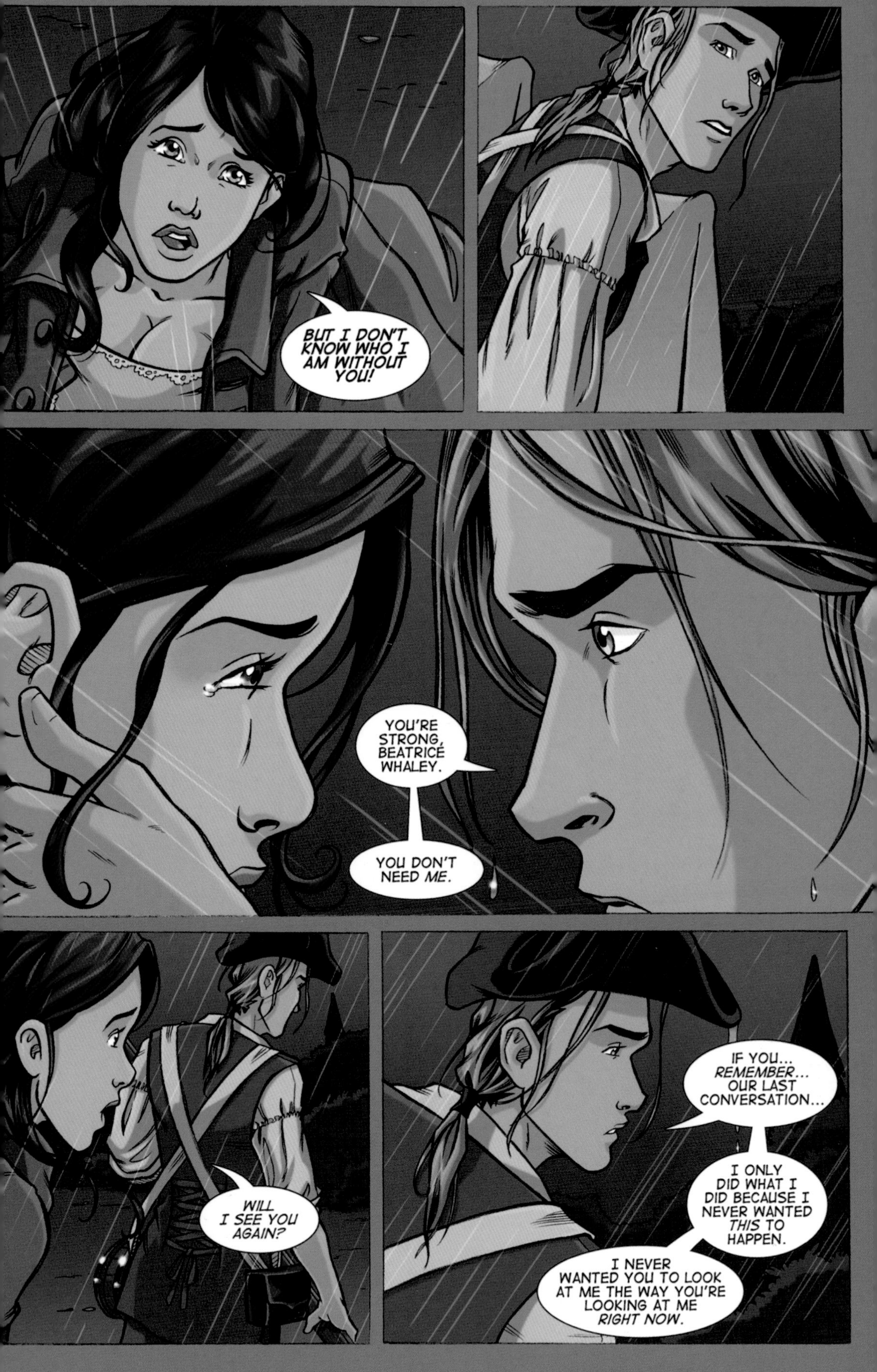

BUT I DON'T KNOW WHO I AM WITHOUT YOU!
YOU'RE STRONG, BEATRICÉ WHALEY.
YOU DON'T NEED *ME*.
WILL I SEE YOU AGAIN?
IF YOU... *REMEMBER*... OUR LAST CONVERSATION...
I ONLY DID WHAT I DID BECAUSE I NEVER WANTED *THIS* TO HAPPEN.
I NEVER WANTED YOU TO LOOK AT ME THE WAY YOU'RE LOOKING AT ME *RIGHT NOW*.

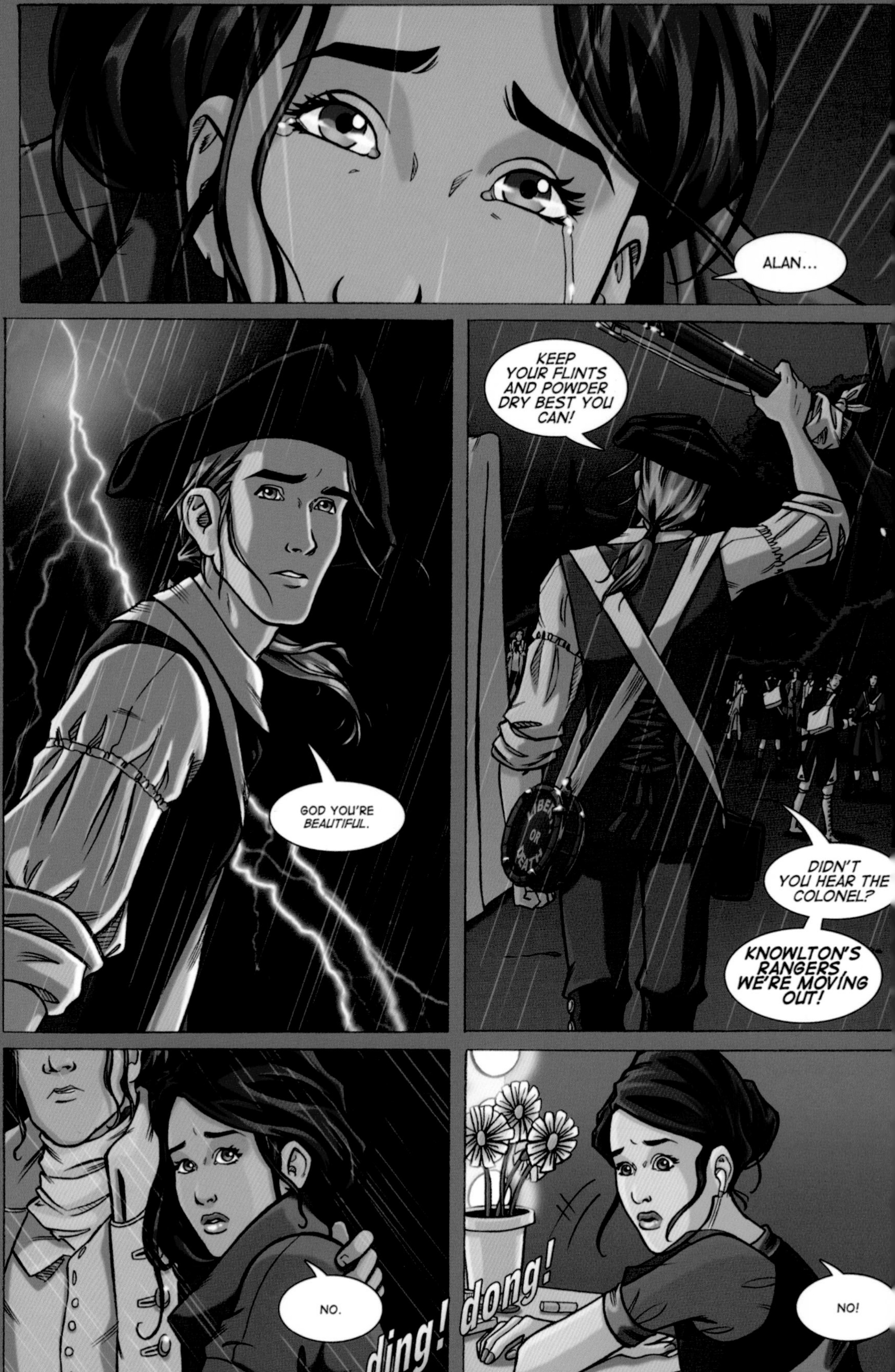
ALAN...
GOD YOU'RE BEAUTIFUL.
KEEP YOUR FLINTS AND POWDER DRY BEST YOU CAN!
DIDN'T YOU HEAR THE COLONEL?
KNOWLTON'S RANGERS, WE'RE MOVING OUT!
NO.
ding! dong!
NO!

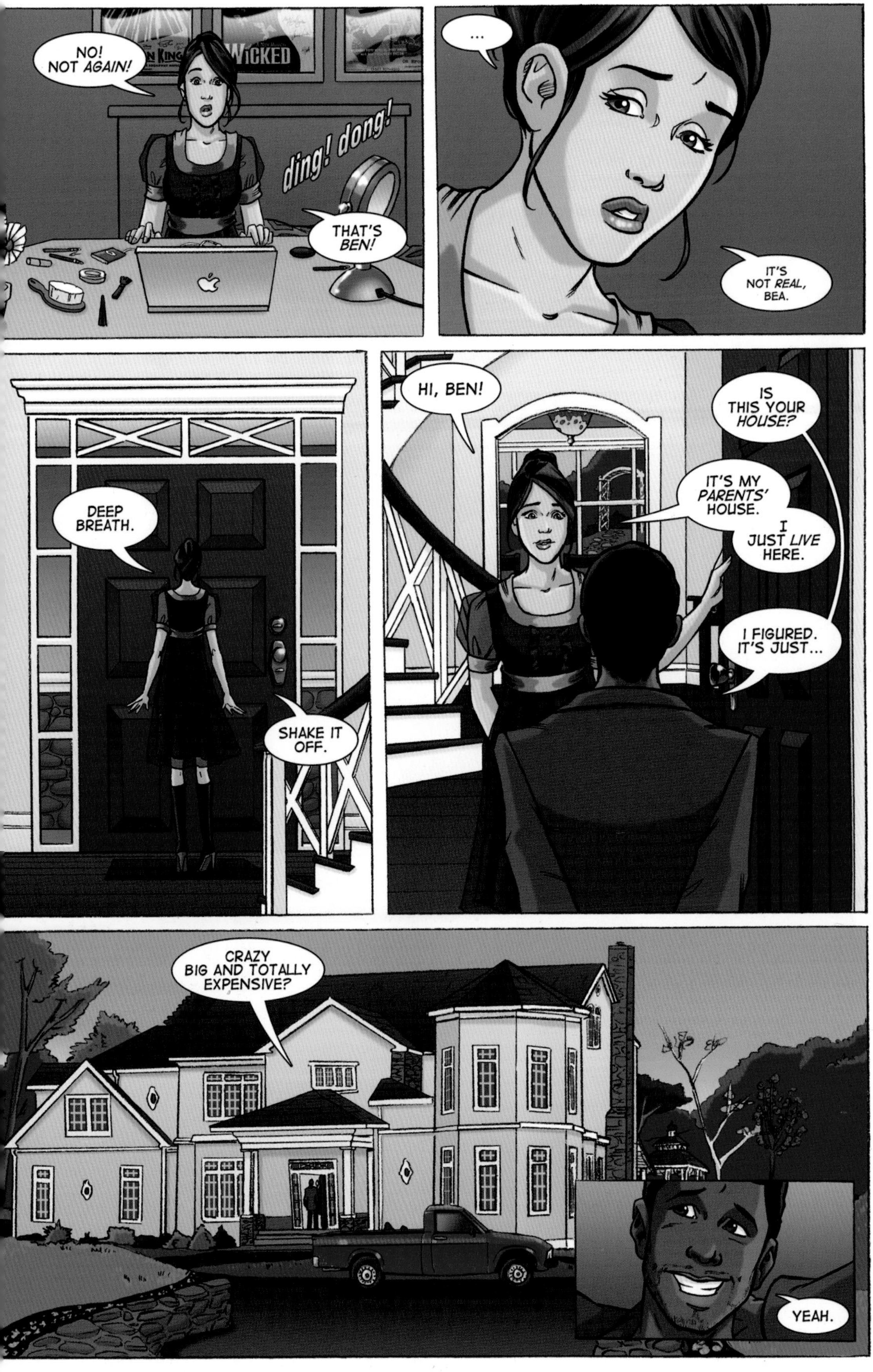

NO! NOT AGAIN!
ding! dong!
THAT'S BEN!
...
IT'S NOT REAL, BEA.
DEEP BREATH.
SHAKE IT OFF.
HI, BEN!
IS THIS YOUR HOUSE?
IT'S MY PARENTS' HOUSE.
I JUST LIVE HERE.
I FIGURED. IT'S JUST...
CRAZY BIG AND TOTALLY EXPENSIVE?
YEAH.

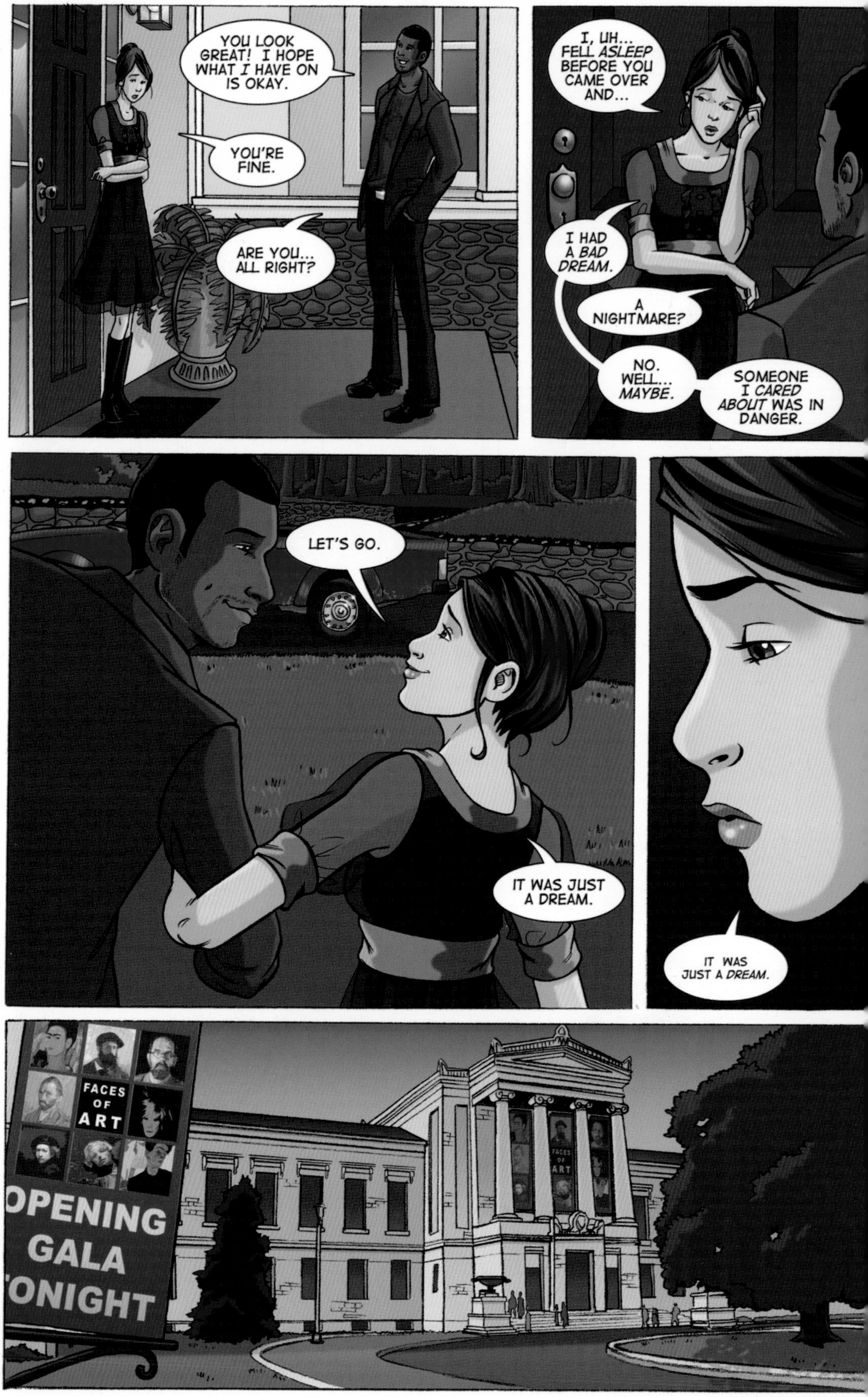
YOU LOOK GREAT! I HOPE WHAT *I* HAVE ON IS OKAY.
YOU'RE FINE.
ARE YOU... ALL RIGHT?
I, UH... FELL *ASLEEP* BEFORE YOU CAME OVER AND...
I HAD A *BAD DREAM*.
A NIGHTMARE?
NO. WELL... *MAYBE*.
SOMEONE I *CARED ABOUT* WAS IN DANGER.
LET'S GO.
IT WAS JUST A DREAM.
IT WAS JUST A *DREAM*.
FACES OF ART
OPENING GALA TONIGHT
FACES OF ART

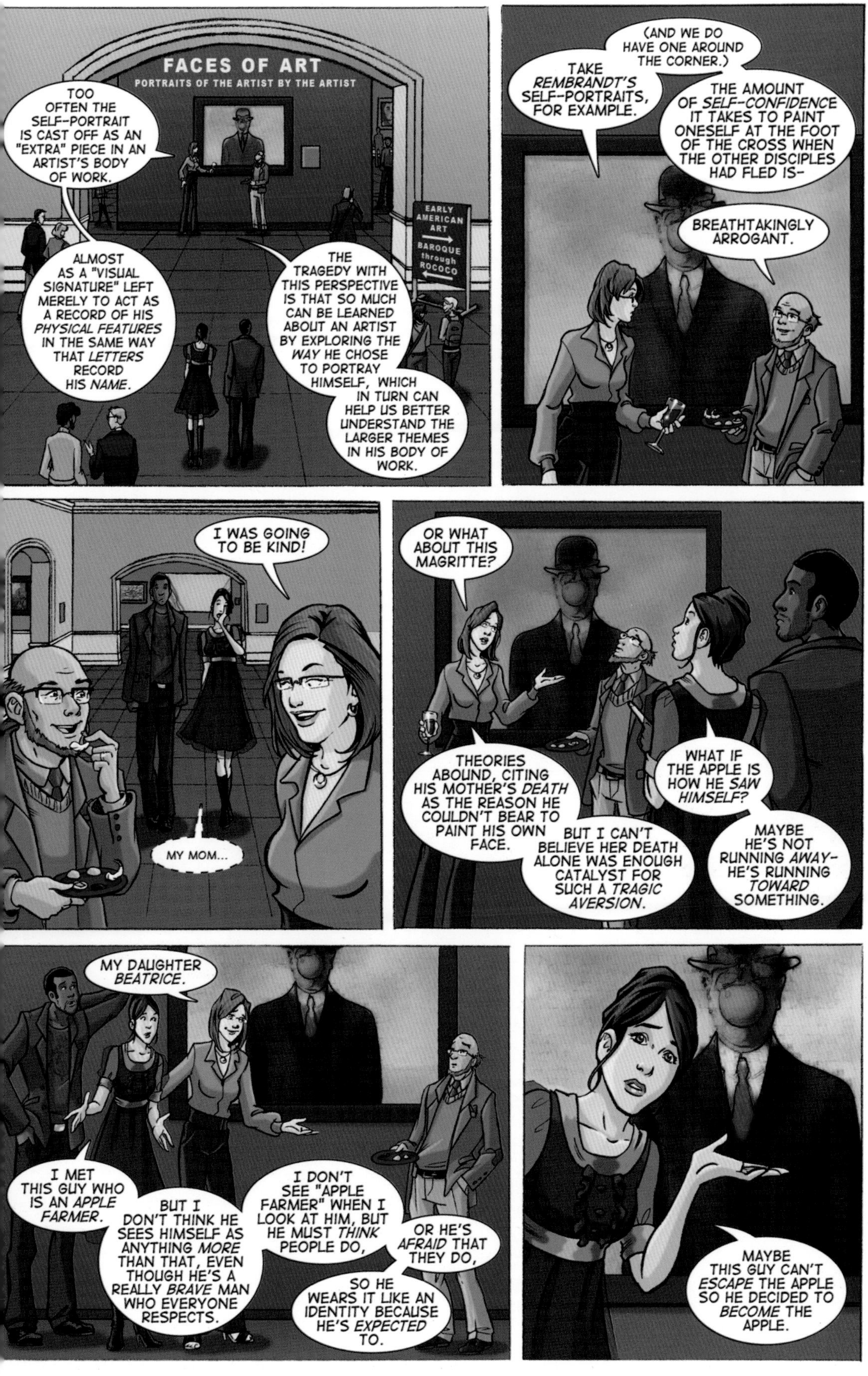
FACES OF ART
PORTRAITS OF THE ARTIST BY THE ARTIST
TOO OFTEN THE SELF-PORTRAIT IS CAST OFF AS AN "EXTRA" PIECE IN AN ARTIST'S BODY OF WORK.
ALMOST AS A "VISUAL SIGNATURE" LEFT MERELY TO ACT AS A RECORD OF HIS *PHYSICAL FEATURES* IN THE SAME WAY THAT *LETTERS* RECORD HIS *NAME*.
EARLY AMERICAN ART
BAROQUE through ROCOCO
THE TRAGEDY WITH THIS PERSPECTIVE IS THAT SO MUCH CAN BE LEARNED ABOUT AN ARTIST BY EXPLORING THE *WAY* HE CHOSE TO PORTRAY HIMSELF, WHICH IN TURN CAN HELP US BETTER UNDERSTAND THE LARGER THEMES IN HIS BODY OF WORK.
TAKE *REMBRANDT'S* SELF-PORTRAITS, FOR EXAMPLE.
(AND WE DO HAVE ONE AROUND THE CORNER.)
THE AMOUNT OF *SELF-CONFIDENCE* IT TAKES TO PAINT ONESELF AT THE FOOT OF THE CROSS WHEN THE OTHER DISCIPLES HAD FLED IS-
BREATHTAKINGLY ARROGANT.
I WAS GOING TO BE KIND!
MY MOM...
OR WHAT ABOUT THIS MAGRITTE?
THEORIES ABOUND, CITING HIS MOTHER'S *DEATH* AS THE REASON HE COULDN'T BEAR TO PAINT HIS OWN FACE.
BUT I CAN'T BELIEVE HER DEATH ALONE WAS ENOUGH CATALYST FOR SUCH A *TRAGIC AVERSION*.
WHAT IF THE APPLE IS HOW HE *SAW HIMSELF?*
MAYBE HE'S NOT RUNNING *AWAY*- HE'S RUNNING *TOWARD* SOMETHING.
MY DAUGHTER *BEATRICE*.
I MET THIS GUY WHO IS AN *APPLE FARMER*.
BUT I DON'T THINK HE SEES HIMSELF AS ANYTHING *MORE* THAN THAT, EVEN THOUGH HE'S A REALLY *BRAVE* MAN WHO EVERYONE RESPECTS.
I DON'T SEE "APPLE FARMER" WHEN I LOOK AT HIM, BUT HE MUST *THINK* PEOPLE DO,
OR HE'S *AFRAID* THAT THEY DO,
SO HE WEARS IT LIKE AN IDENTITY BECAUSE HE'S *EXPECTED* TO.
MAYBE THIS GUY CAN'T *ESCAPE* THE APPLE SO HE DECIDED TO *BECOME* THE APPLE.

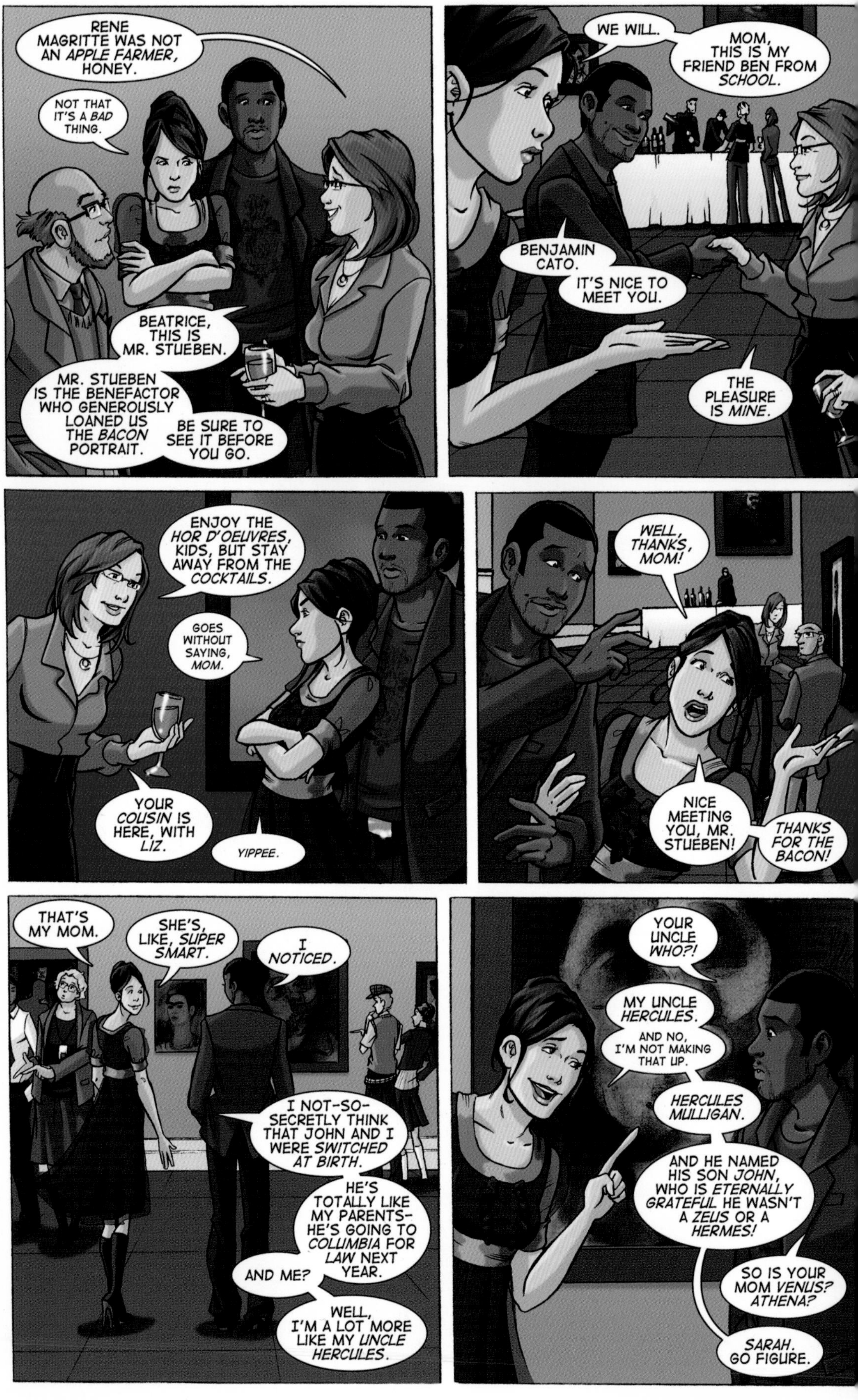
RENE MAGRITTE WAS NOT AN *APPLE FARMER*, HONEY.
NOT THAT IT'S A *BAD* THING.
BEATRICE, THIS IS MR. STUEBEN.
MR. STUEBEN IS THE BENEFACTOR WHO GENEROUSLY LOANED US THE *BACON* PORTRAIT.
BE SURE TO SEE IT BEFORE YOU GO.
WE WILL.
MOM, THIS IS MY FRIEND BEN FROM *SCHOOL*.
BENJAMIN CATO.
IT'S NICE TO MEET YOU.
THE PLEASURE IS *MINE*.
ENJOY THE *HOR D'OEUVRES*, KIDS, BUT STAY AWAY FROM THE *COCKTAILS*.
GOES WITHOUT SAYING, *MOM*.
YOUR *COUSIN* IS HERE, WITH *LIZ*.
YIPPEE.
WELL, THANKS, MOM!
NICE MEETING YOU, MR. STUEBEN!
THANKS FOR THE BACON!
THAT'S MY MOM.
SHE'S, LIKE, *SUPER SMART*.
I *NOTICED*.
I NOT-SO-SECRETLY THINK THAT JOHN AND I WERE *SWITCHED AT BIRTH*.
HE'S TOTALLY LIKE MY PARENTS-HE'S GOING TO *COLUMBIA* FOR *LAW* NEXT YEAR.
AND ME?
WELL, I'M A LOT MORE LIKE MY *UNCLE HERCULES*.
YOUR UNCLE *WHO?!*
MY UNCLE *HERCULES*.
AND NO, I'M NOT MAKING THAT UP.
HERCULES MULLIGAN.
AND HE NAMED HIS SON *JOHN*, WHO IS *ETERNALLY GRATEFUL* HE WASN'T A *ZEUS* OR A *HERMES!*
SO IS YOUR MOM *VENUS? ATHENA?*
SARAH. GO FIGURE.

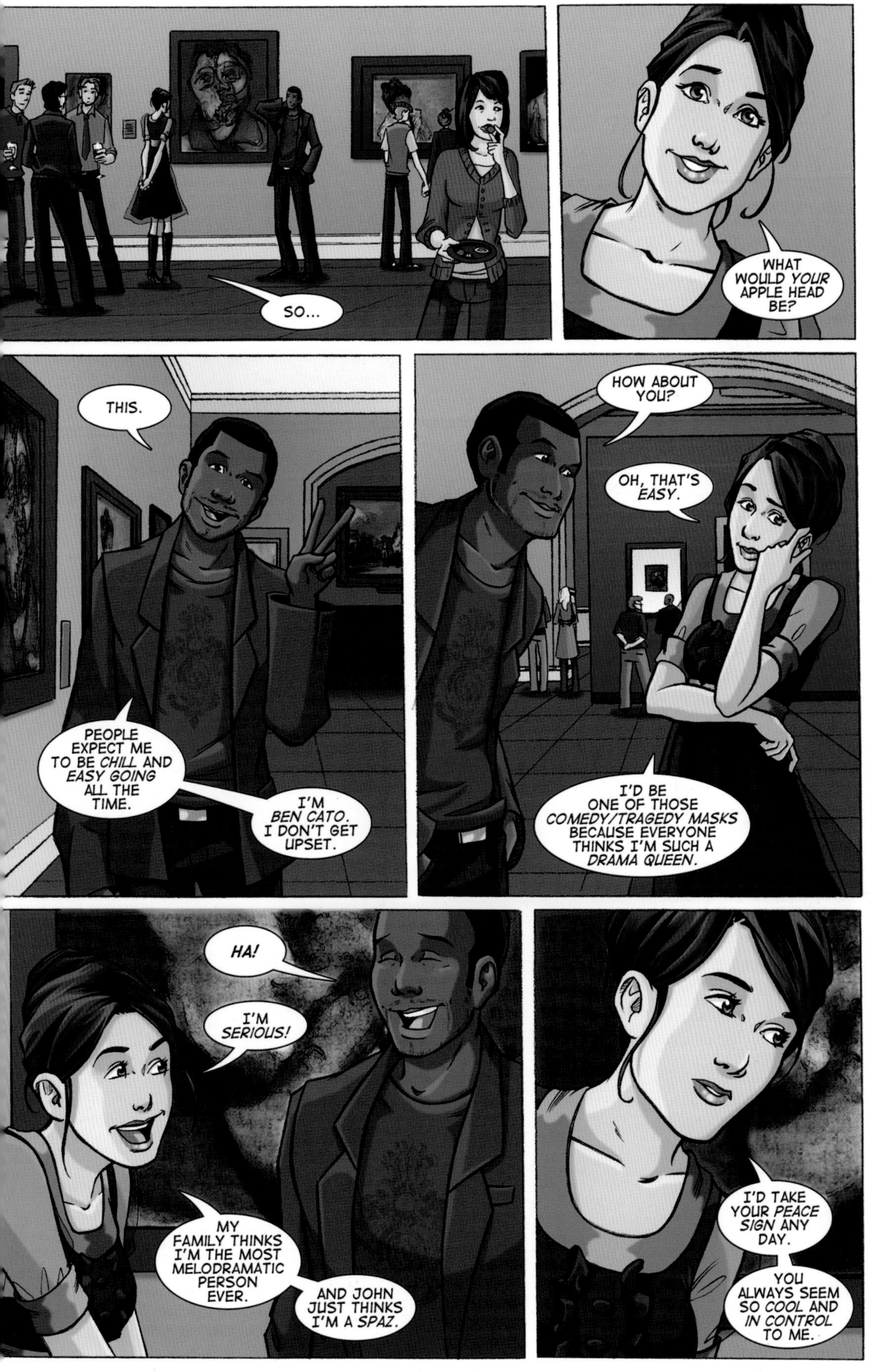

SO...
WHAT WOULD YOUR APPLE HEAD BE?
THIS.
PEOPLE EXPECT ME TO BE CHILL AND EASY GOING ALL THE TIME.
I'M BEN CATO. I DON'T GET UPSET.
HOW ABOUT YOU?
OH, THAT'S EASY.
I'D BE ONE OF THOSE COMEDY/TRAGEDY MASKS BECAUSE EVERYONE THINKS I'M SUCH A DRAMA QUEEN.
HA!
I'M SERIOUS!
MY FAMILY THINKS I'M THE MOST MELODRAMATIC PERSON EVER.
AND JOHN JUST THINKS I'M A SPAZ.
I'D TAKE YOUR PEACE SIGN ANY DAY.
YOU ALWAYS SEEM SO COOL AND IN CONTROL TO ME.

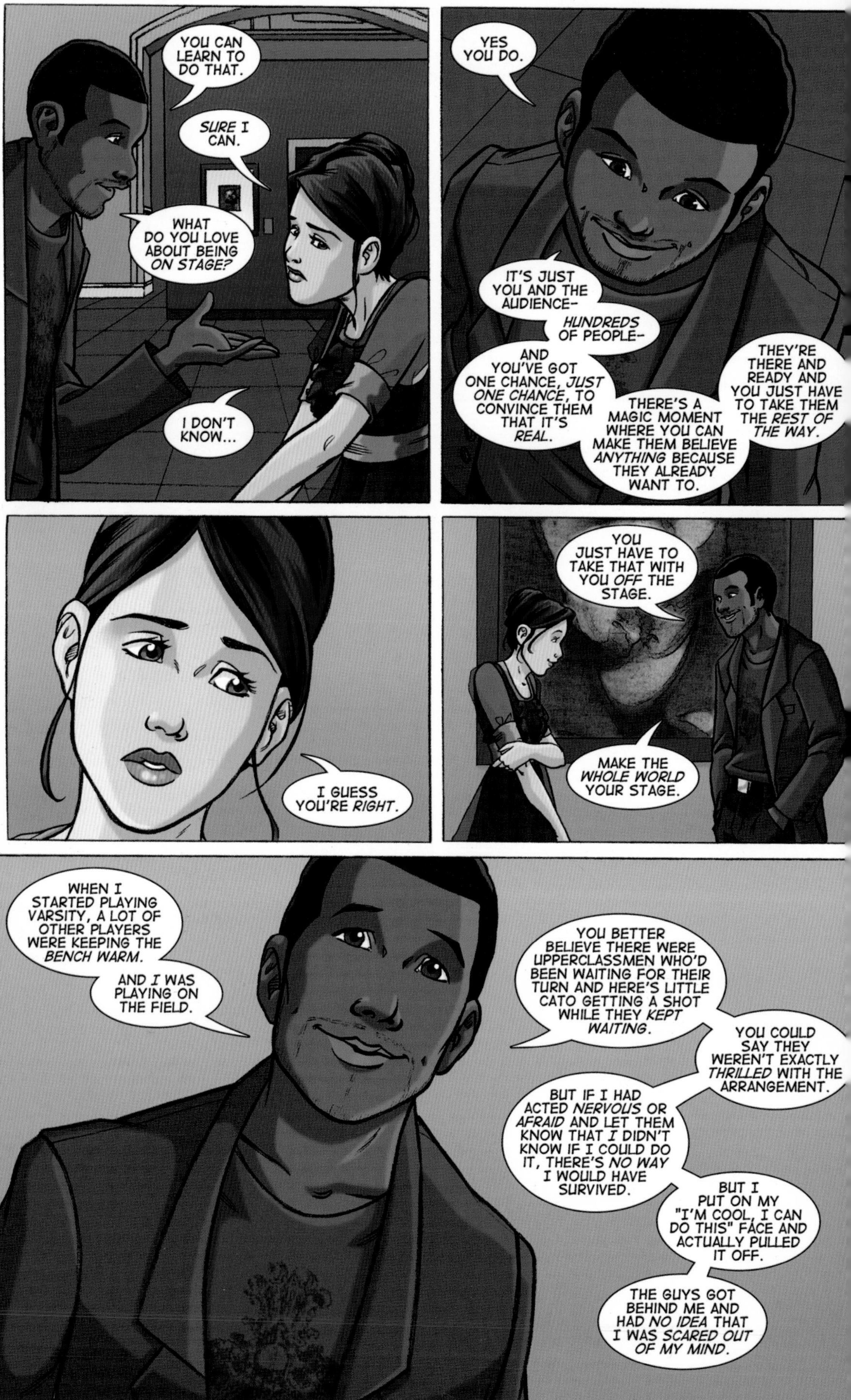
YOU CAN LEARN TO DO THAT.
SURE I CAN.
WHAT DO YOU LOVE ABOUT BEING ON STAGE?
I DON'T KNOW...
YES YOU DO.
IT'S JUST YOU AND THE AUDIENCE-
HUNDREDS OF PEOPLE-
AND YOU'VE GOT ONE CHANCE, JUST ONE CHANCE, TO CONVINCE THEM THAT IT'S REAL.
THERE'S A MAGIC MOMENT WHERE YOU CAN MAKE THEM BELIEVE ANYTHING BECAUSE THEY ALREADY WANT TO.
THEY'RE THERE AND READY AND YOU JUST HAVE TO TAKE THEM THE REST OF THE WAY.
I GUESS YOU'RE RIGHT.
YOU JUST HAVE TO TAKE THAT WITH YOU OFF THE STAGE.
MAKE THE WHOLE WORLD YOUR STAGE.
WHEN I STARTED PLAYING VARSITY, A LOT OF OTHER PLAYERS WERE KEEPING THE BENCH WARM.
AND I WAS PLAYING ON THE FIELD.
YOU BETTER BELIEVE THERE WERE UPPERCLASSMEN WHO'D BEEN WAITING FOR THEIR TURN AND HERE'S LITTLE CATO GETTING A SHOT WHILE THEY KEPT WAITING.
YOU COULD SAY THEY WEREN'T EXACTLY THRILLED WITH THE ARRANGEMENT.
BUT IF I HAD ACTED NERVOUS OR AFRAID AND LET THEM KNOW THAT I DIDN'T KNOW IF I COULD DO IT, THERE'S NO WAY I WOULD HAVE SURVIVED.
BUT I PUT ON MY "I'M COOL, I CAN DO THIS" FACE AND ACTUALLY PULLED IT OFF.
THE GUYS GOT BEHIND ME AND HAD NO IDEA THAT I WAS SCARED OUT OF MY MIND.

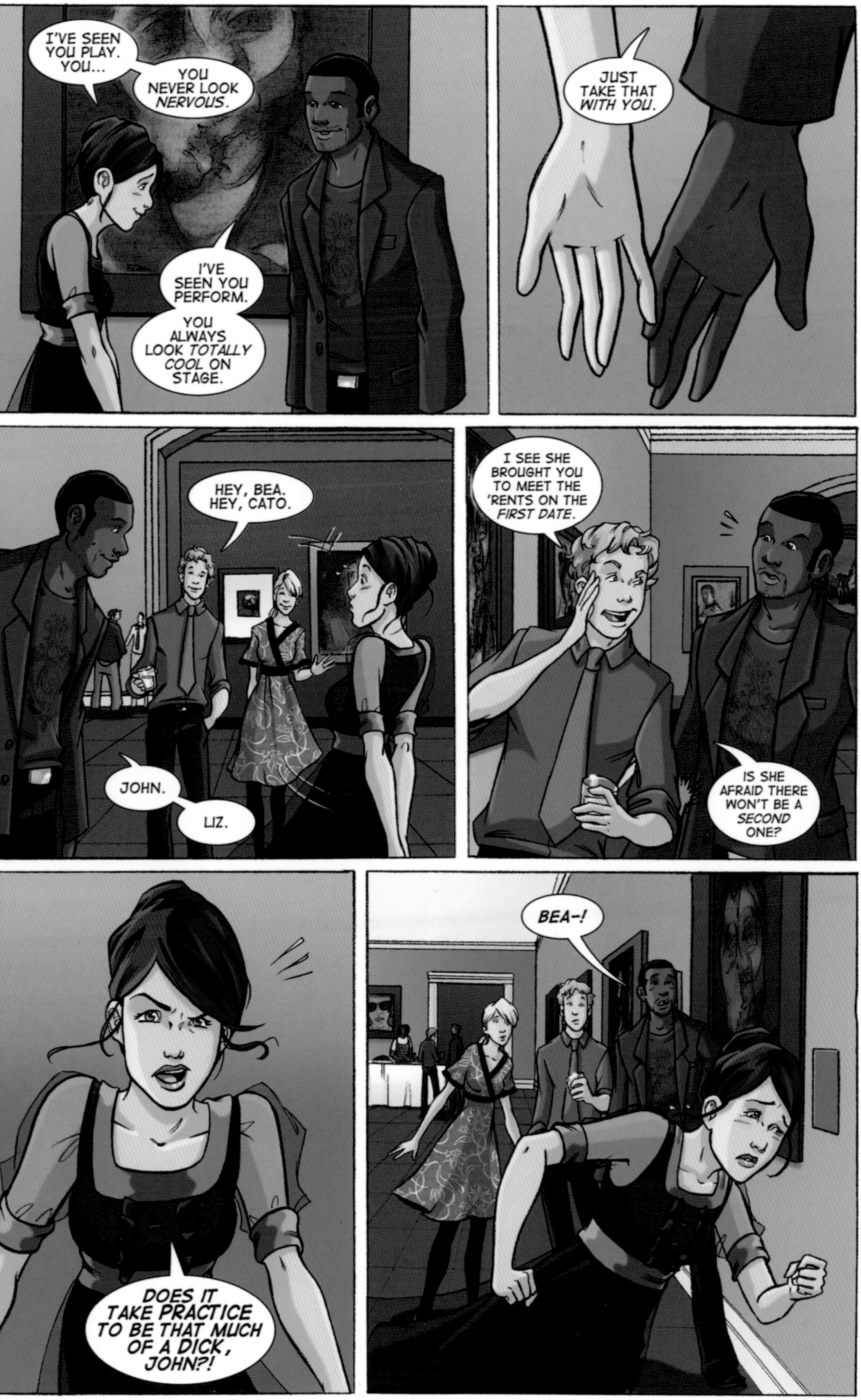
I'VE SEEN YOU PLAY. YOU...
YOU NEVER LOOK NERVOUS.
I'VE SEEN YOU PERFORM.
YOU ALWAYS LOOK TOTALLY COOL ON STAGE.
JUST TAKE THAT WITH YOU.
HEY, BEA. HEY, CATO.
JOHN.
LIZ.
I SEE SHE BROUGHT YOU TO MEET THE 'RENTS ON THE FIRST DATE.
IS SHE AFRAID THERE WON'T BE A SECOND ONE?
DOES IT TAKE PRACTICE TO BE THAT MUCH OF A DICK, JOHN?!
BEA-!

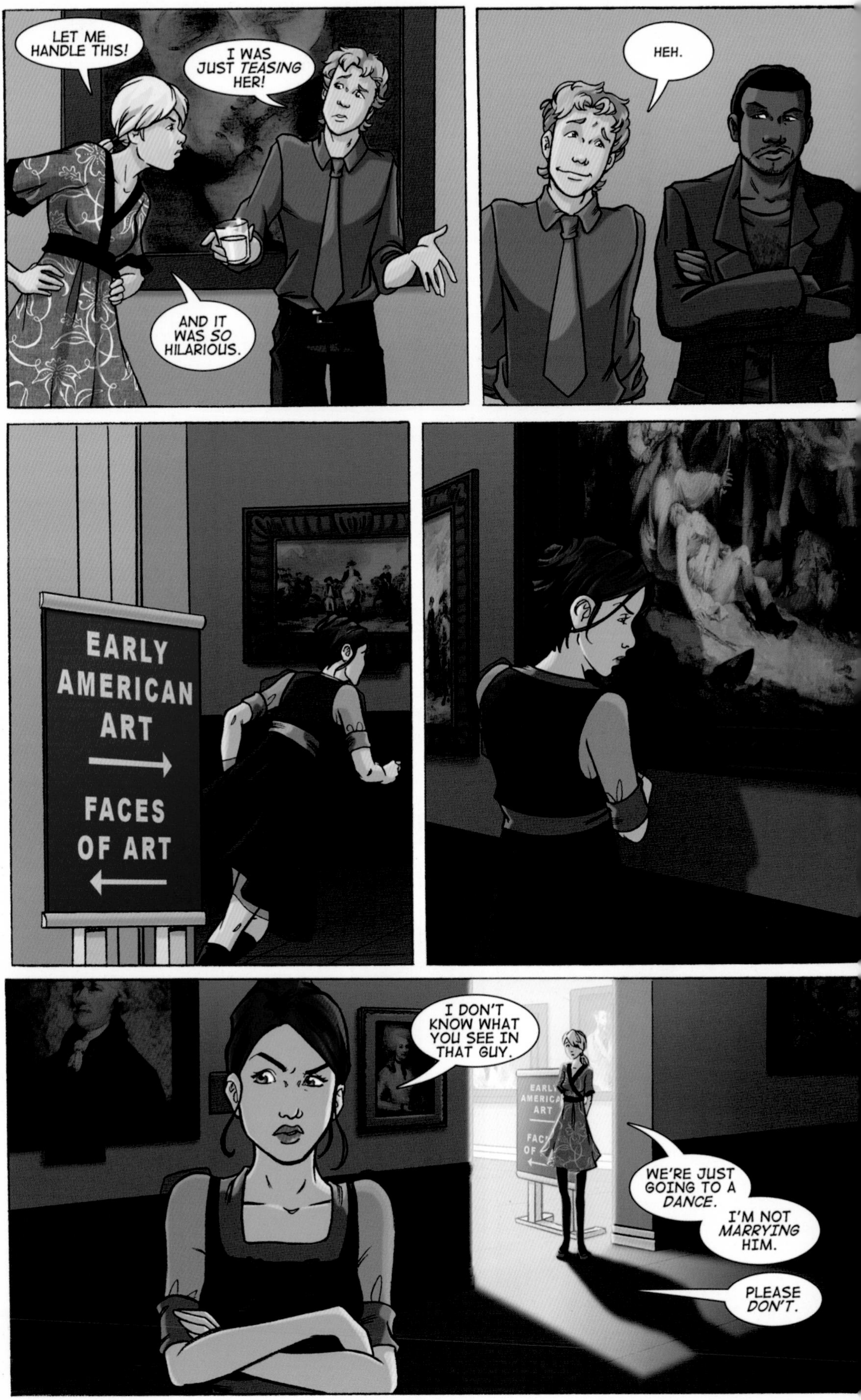
LET ME HANDLE THIS!
I WAS JUST *TEASING* HER!
AND IT WAS *SO* HILARIOUS.
HEH.
EARLY AMERICAN ART
FACES OF ART
I DON'T KNOW WHAT YOU SEE IN THAT GUY.
WE'RE JUST GOING TO A *DANCE*.
I'M NOT *MARRYING* HIM.
PLEASE *DON'T*.

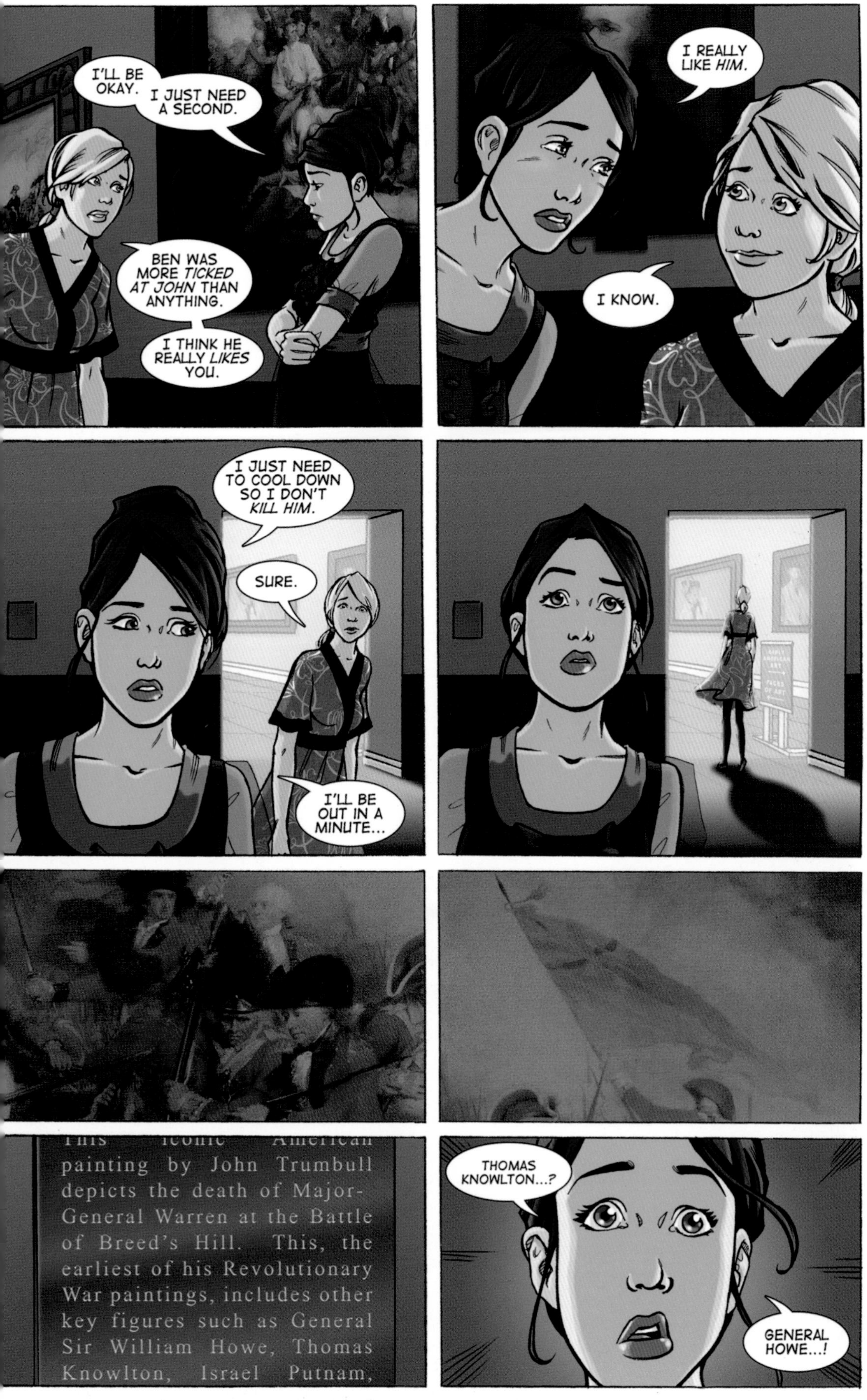
I'LL BE OKAY.
I JUST NEED A SECOND.
BEN WAS MORE *TICKED AT JOHN* THAN ANYTHING.
I THINK HE REALLY *LIKES* YOU.
I REALLY LIKE *HIM*.
I KNOW.
I JUST NEED TO COOL DOWN SO I DON'T *KILL HIM*.
SURE.
I'LL BE OUT IN A MINUTE...
This iconic American painting by John Trumbull depicts the death of Major-General Warren at the Battle of Breed's Hill. This, the earliest of his Revolutionary War paintings, includes other key figures such as General Sir William Howe, Thomas Knowlton, Israel Putnam,
THOMAS KNOWLTON...?
GENERAL HOWE...!

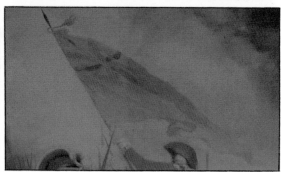

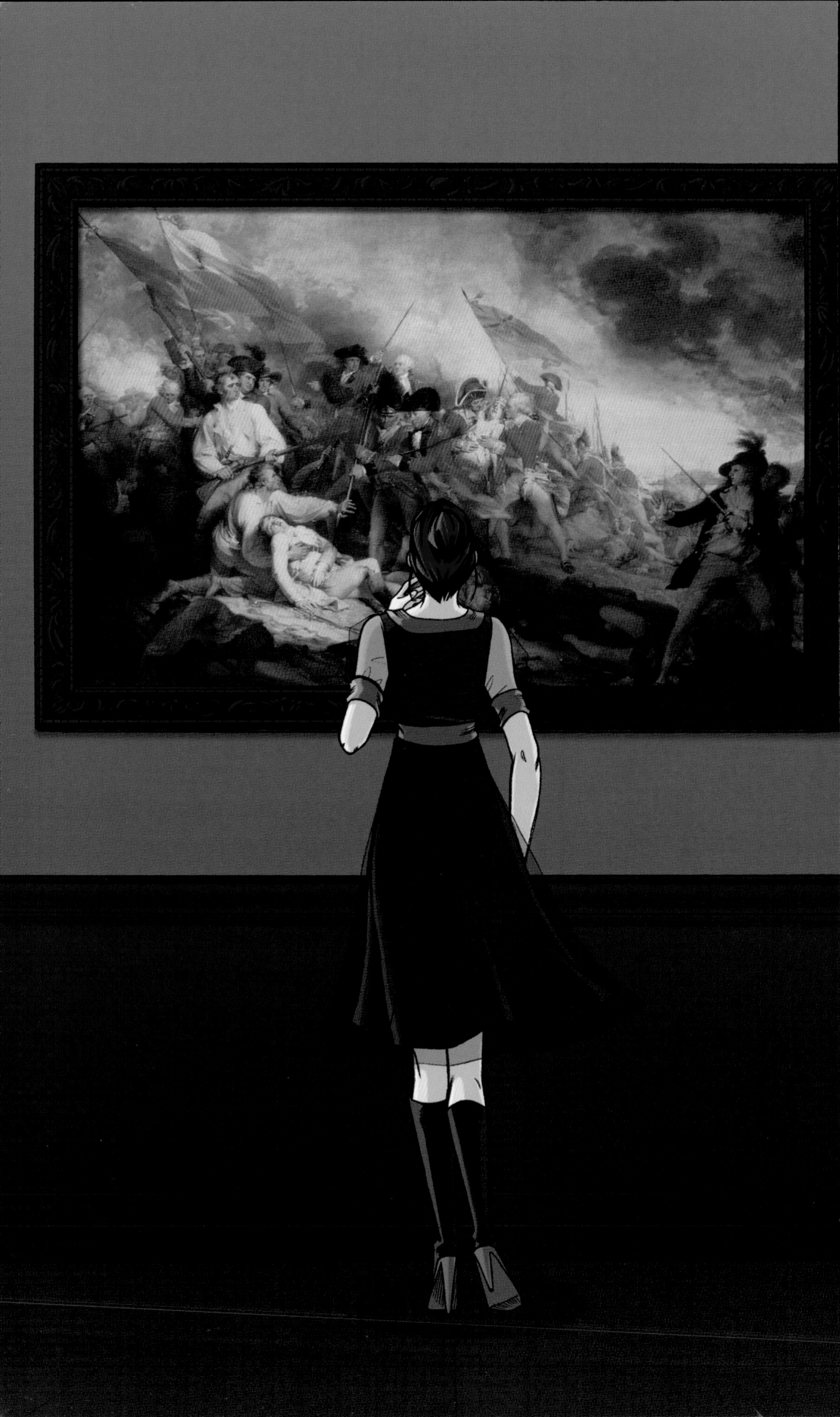

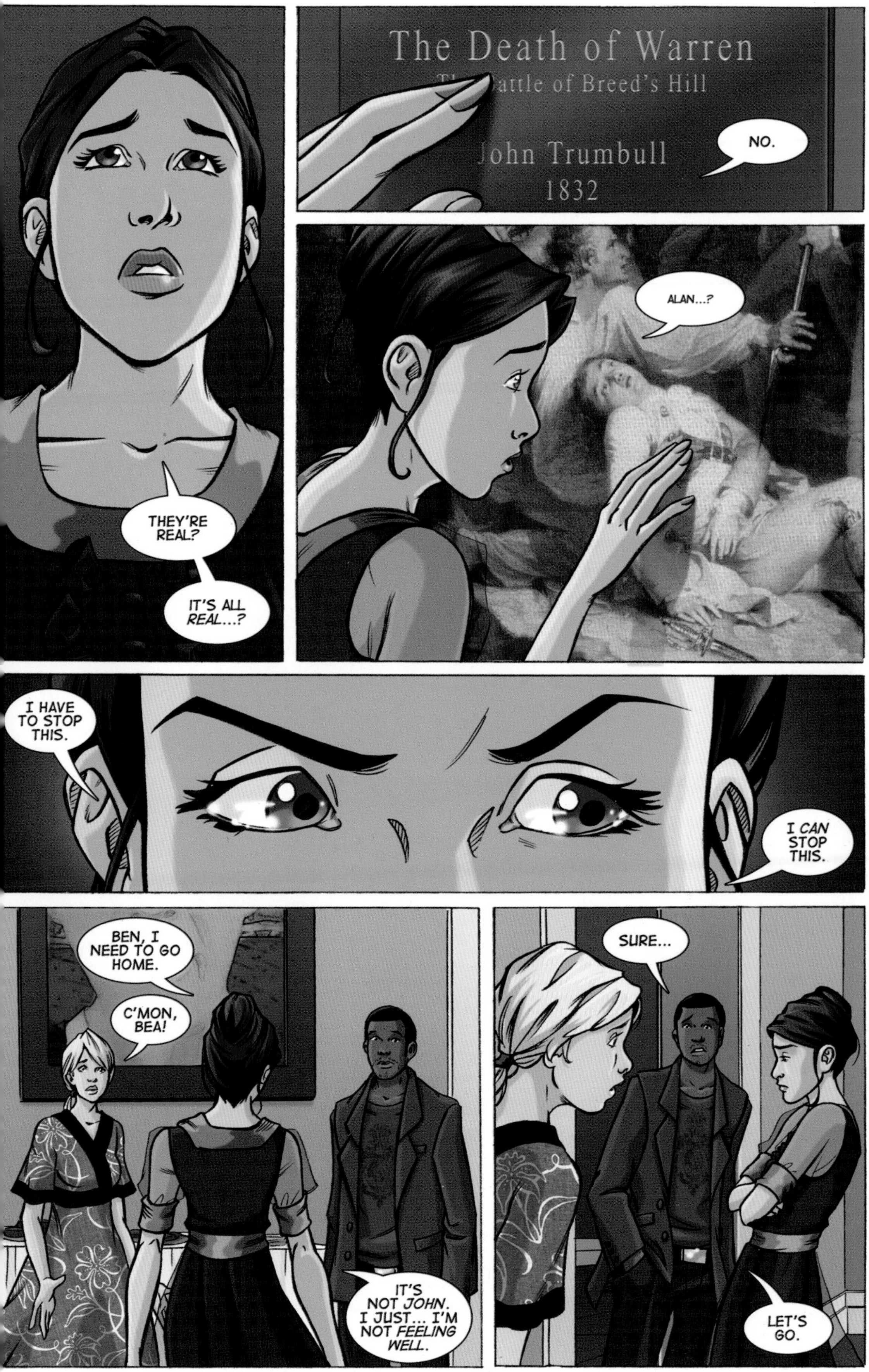
THEY'RE REAL?
IT'S ALL *REAL*...?
The Death of Warren
The Battle of Breed's Hill
John Trumbull
1832
NO.
ALAN...?
I HAVE TO STOP THIS.
I *CAN* STOP THIS.
BEN, I NEED TO GO HOME.
C'MON, BEA!
IT'S NOT *JOHN*. I JUST... I'M NOT *FEELING* *WELL*.
SURE...
LET'S GO.

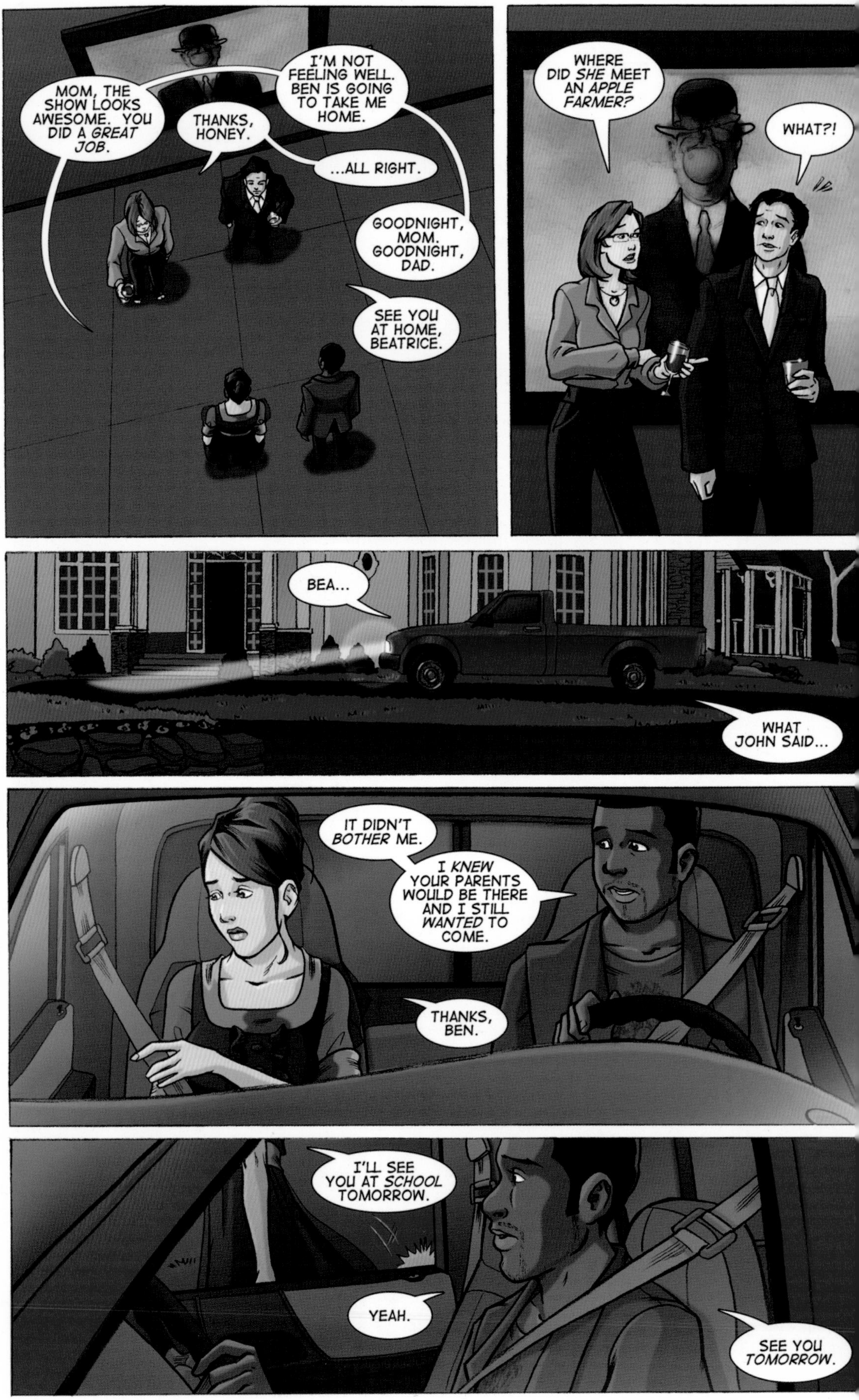
MOM, THE SHOW LOOKS AWESOME. YOU DID A *GREAT* *JOB*.
THANKS, HONEY.
I'M NOT FEELING WELL. BEN IS GOING TO TAKE ME HOME.
...ALL RIGHT.
GOODNIGHT, MOM. GOODNIGHT, DAD.
SEE YOU AT HOME, BEATRICE.
WHERE DID *SHE* MEET AN *APPLE FARMER?*
WHAT?!
BEA...
WHAT JOHN SAID...
IT DIDN'T *BOTHER* ME.
I *KNEW* YOUR PARENTS WOULD BE THERE AND I STILL *WANTED* TO COME.
THANKS, BEN.
I'LL SEE YOU AT *SCHOOL* TOMORROW.
YEAH.
SEE YOU *TOMORROW*.

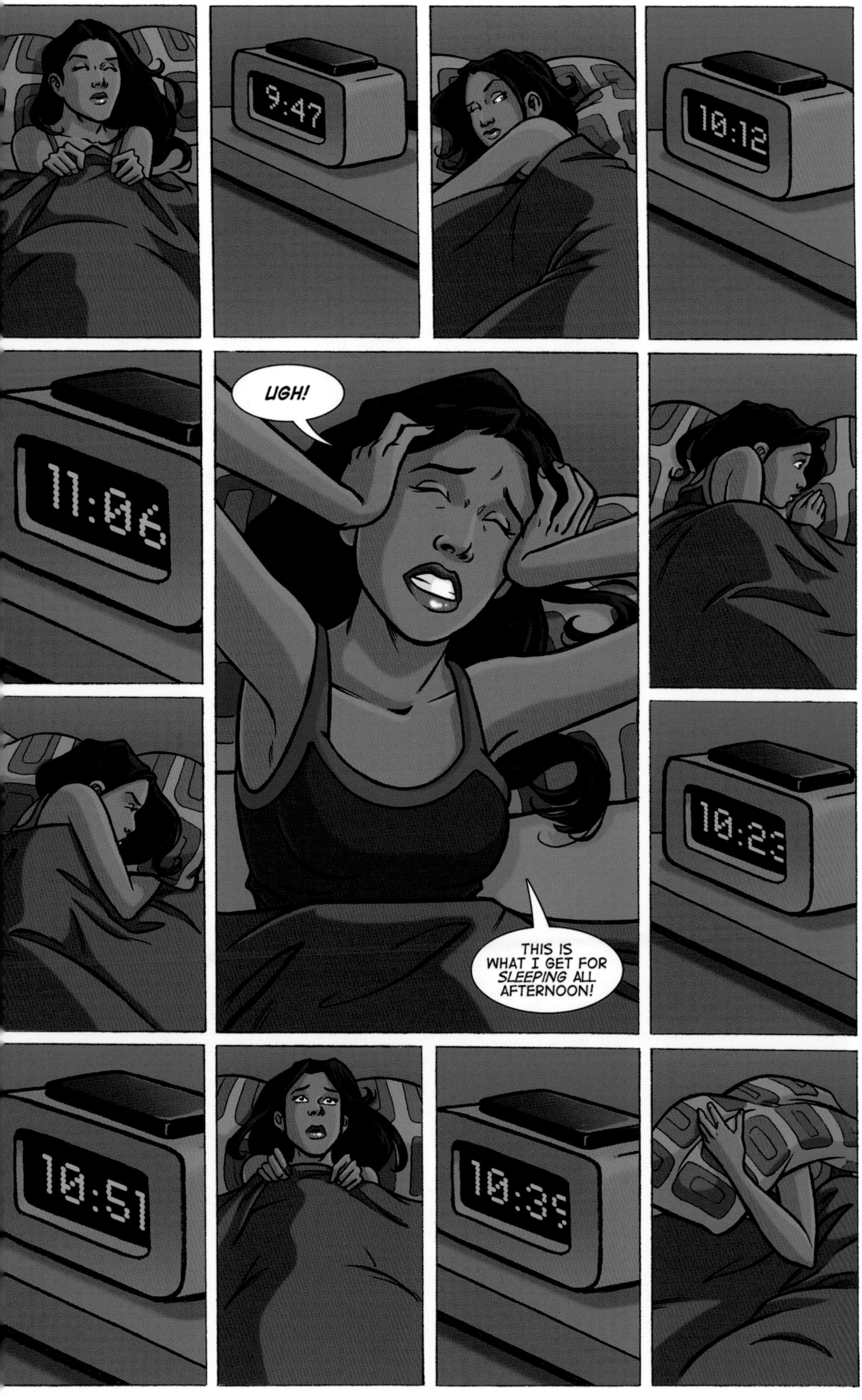
9:47
10:12
11:06
UGH!
THIS IS WHAT I GET FOR SLEEPING ALL AFTERNOON!
10:51

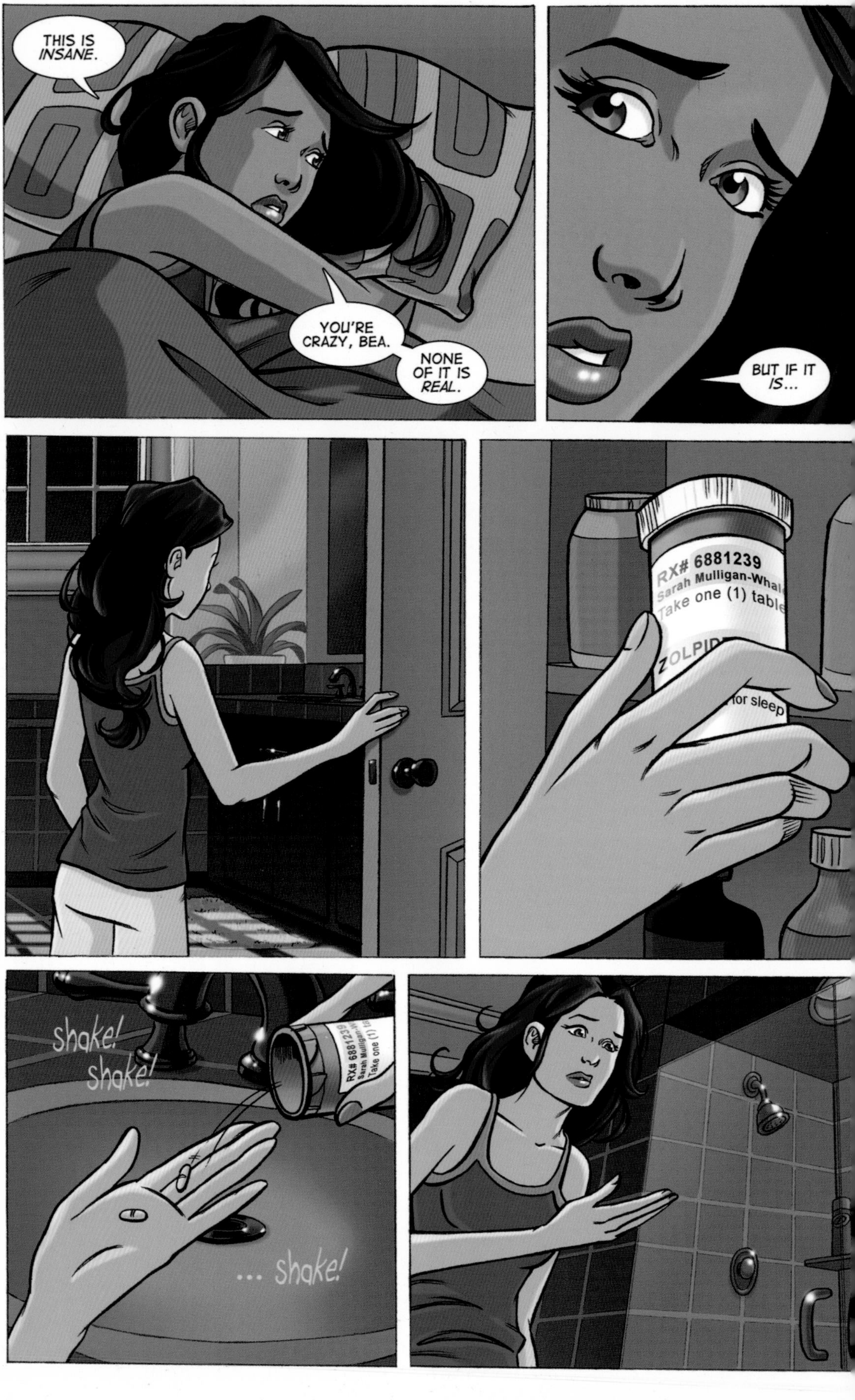
THIS IS INSANE.
YOU'RE CRAZY, BEA.
NONE OF IT IS REAL.
BUT IF IT IS...
RX# 6881239
Sarah Mulligan-Whal
Take one (1) table
ZOLPID
for sleep
shake! shake!
RX# 6881239
Sarah Mulligan-W
Take one (1) ta
... shake!

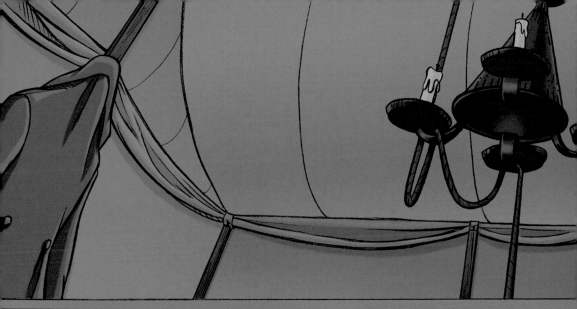

IT WORKED.

I CAN'T BELIEVE THAT WORKED!

THIS IS SO WEIRD.

NATHAN?

OOPS!

SORRY!

NATHAN...?

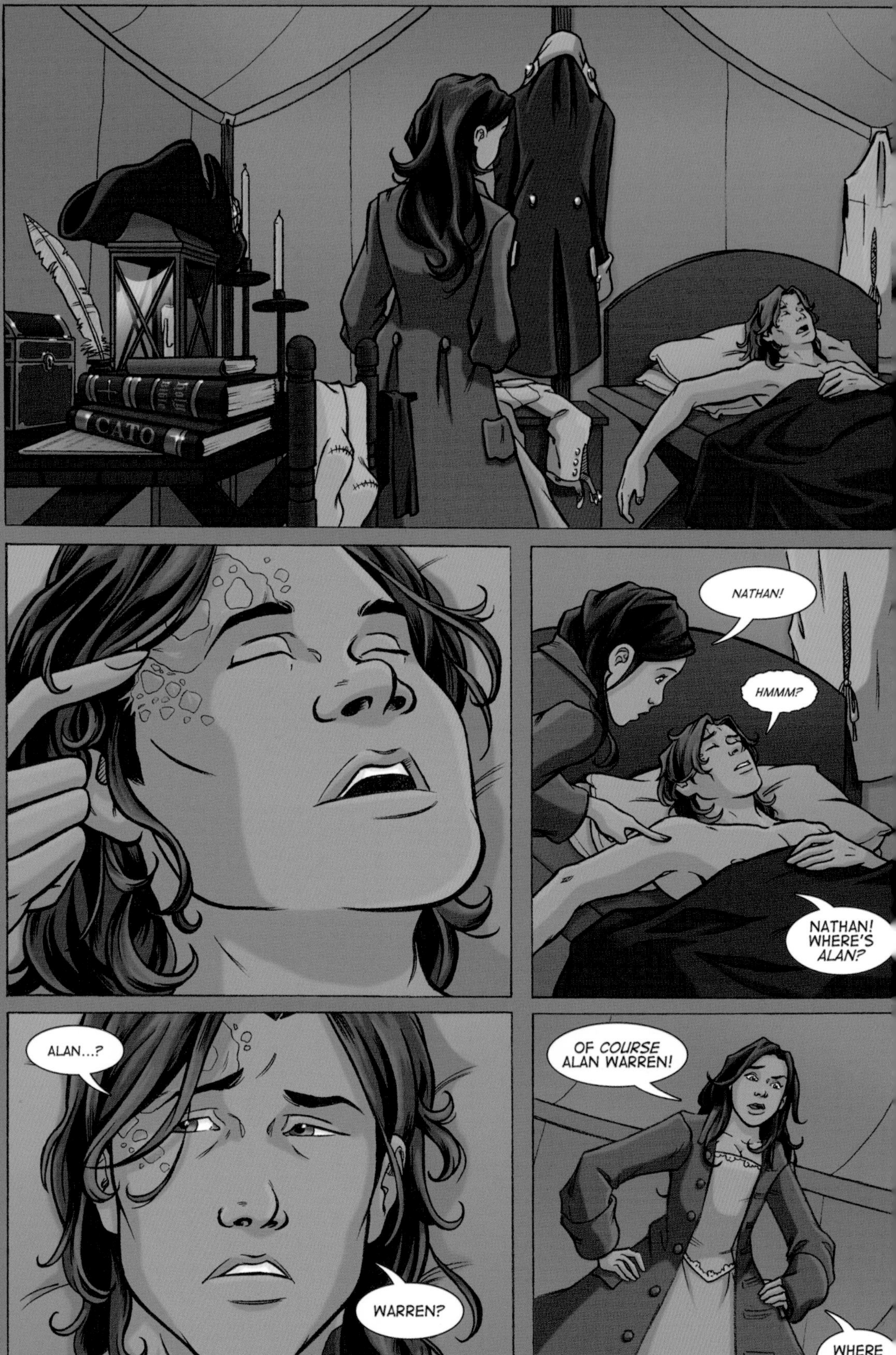
CATO
NATHAN!
HMMM?
NATHAN! WHERE'S *ALAN?*
ALAN...?
WARREN?
OF *COURSE* ALAN WARREN!
WHERE IS HE?

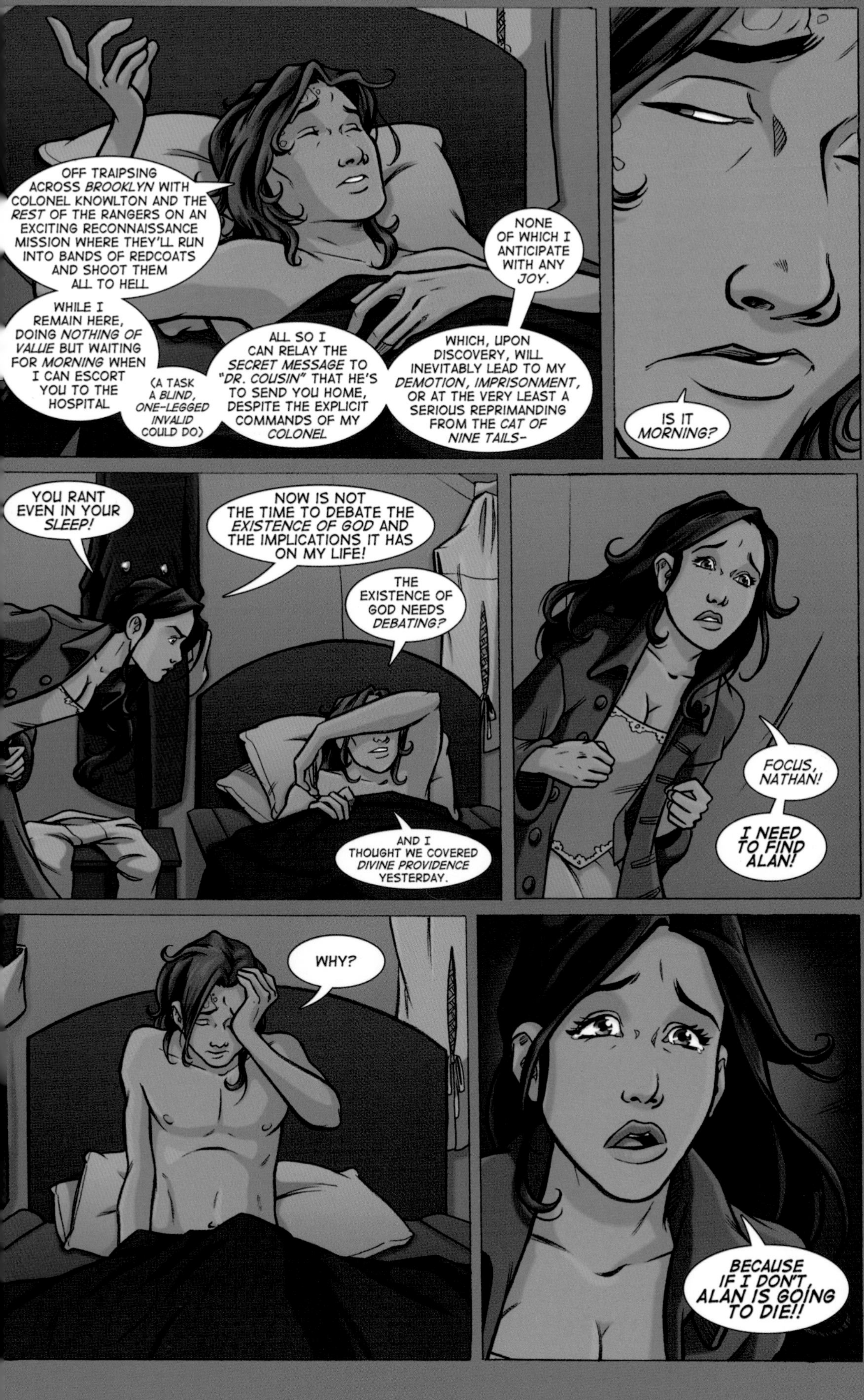

OFF TRAIPSING ACROSS BROOKLYN WITH COLONEL KNOWLTON AND THE REST OF THE RANGERS ON AN EXCITING RECONNAISSANCE MISSION WHERE THEY'LL RUN INTO BANDS OF REDCOATS AND SHOOT THEM ALL TO HELL
WHILE I REMAIN HERE, DOING NOTHING OF VALUE BUT WAITING FOR MORNING WHEN I CAN ESCORT YOU TO THE HOSPITAL
(A TASK A BLIND, ONE-LEGGED INVALID COULD DO)
ALL SO I CAN RELAY THE SECRET MESSAGE TO "DR. COUSIN" THAT HE'S TO SEND YOU HOME, DESPITE THE EXPLICIT COMMANDS OF MY COLONEL
WHICH, UPON DISCOVERY, WILL INEVITABLY LEAD TO MY DEMOTION, IMPRISONMENT, OR AT THE VERY LEAST A SERIOUS REPRIMANDING FROM THE CAT OF NINE TAILS-
NONE OF WHICH I ANTICIPATE WITH ANY JOY.
IS IT MORNING?
YOU RANT EVEN IN YOUR SLEEP!
NOW IS NOT THE TIME TO DEBATE THE EXISTENCE OF GOD AND THE IMPLICATIONS IT HAS ON MY LIFE!
THE EXISTENCE OF GOD NEEDS DEBATING?
AND I THOUGHT WE COVERED DIVINE PROVIDENCE YESTERDAY.
FOCUS, NATHAN!
I NEED TO FIND ALAN!
WHY?
BECAUSE IF I DON'T, ALAN IS GOING TO DIE!!

Chapter Four

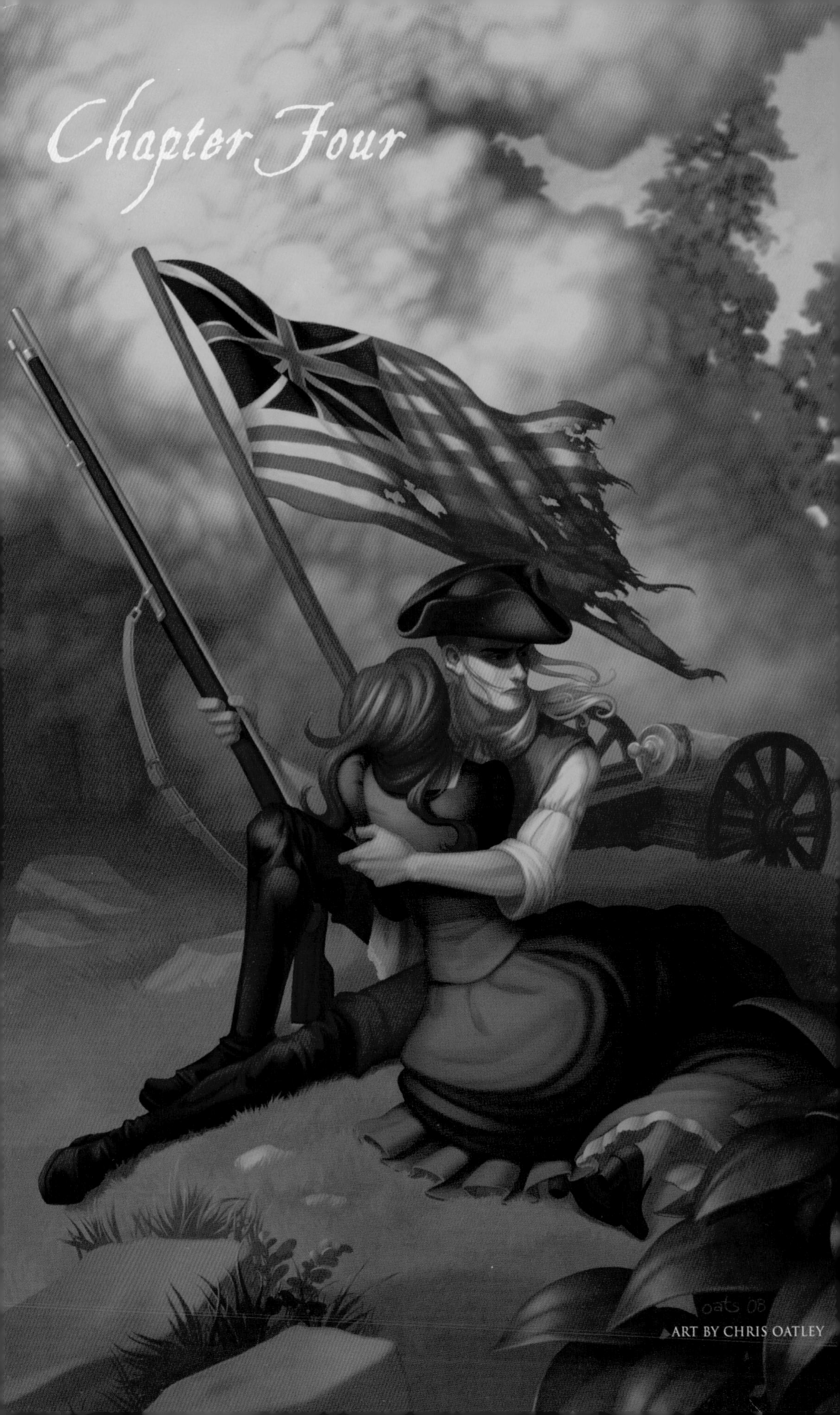
oats 08

ART BY CHRIS OATLEY

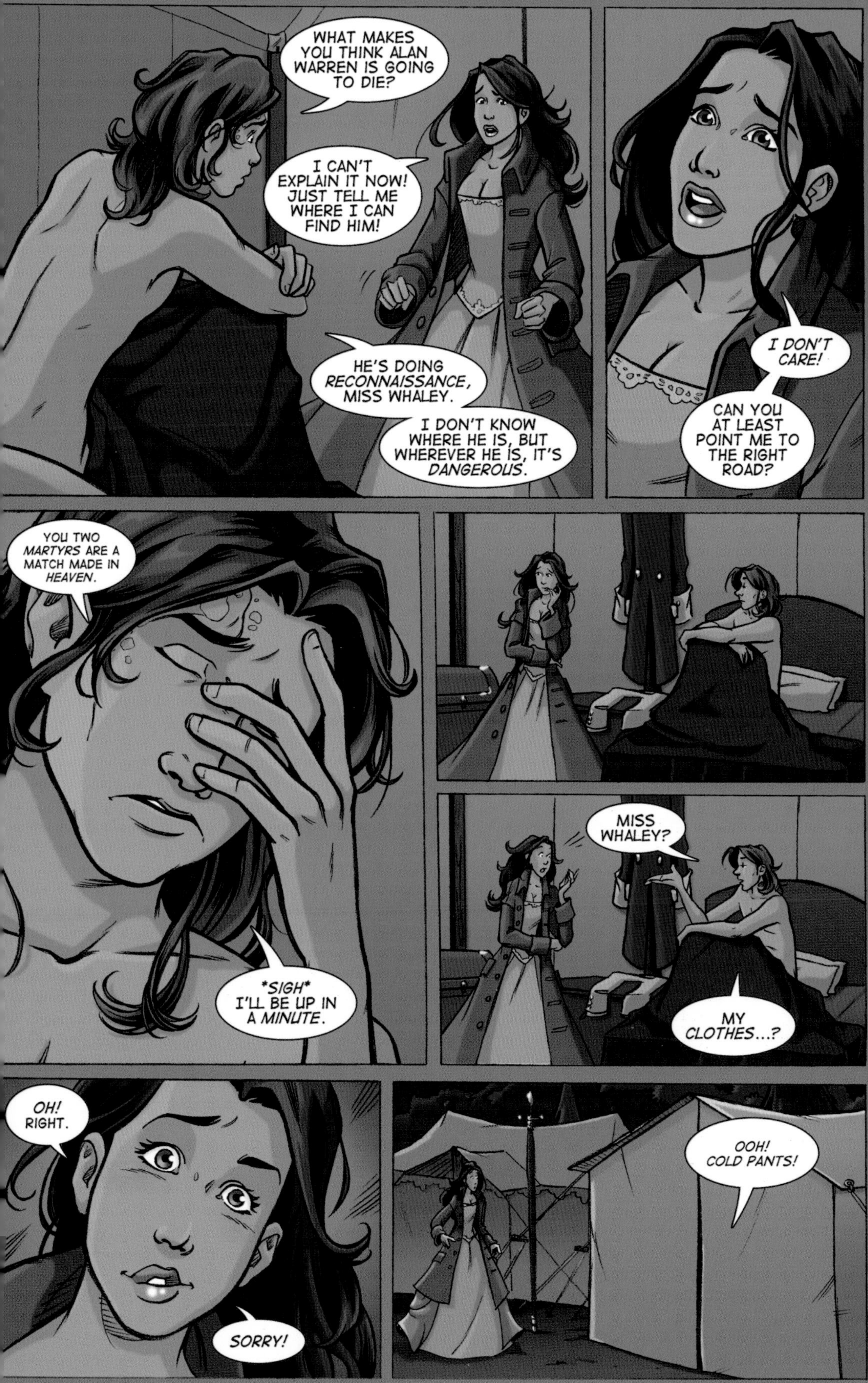
WHAT MAKES YOU THINK ALAN WARREN IS GOING TO DIE?
I CAN'T EXPLAIN IT NOW! JUST TELL ME WHERE I CAN FIND HIM!
HE'S DOING *RECONNAISSANCE*, MISS WHALEY.
I DON'T KNOW WHERE HE IS, BUT WHEREVER HE IS, IT'S *DANGEROUS*.
I DON'T CARE!
CAN YOU AT LEAST POINT ME TO THE RIGHT ROAD?
YOU TWO *MARTYRS* ARE A MATCH MADE IN *HEAVEN*.
SIGH I'LL BE UP IN A *MINUTE*.
MISS WHALEY?
MY *CLOTHES...?*
OH! RIGHT.
SORRY!
OOH! COLD PANTS!

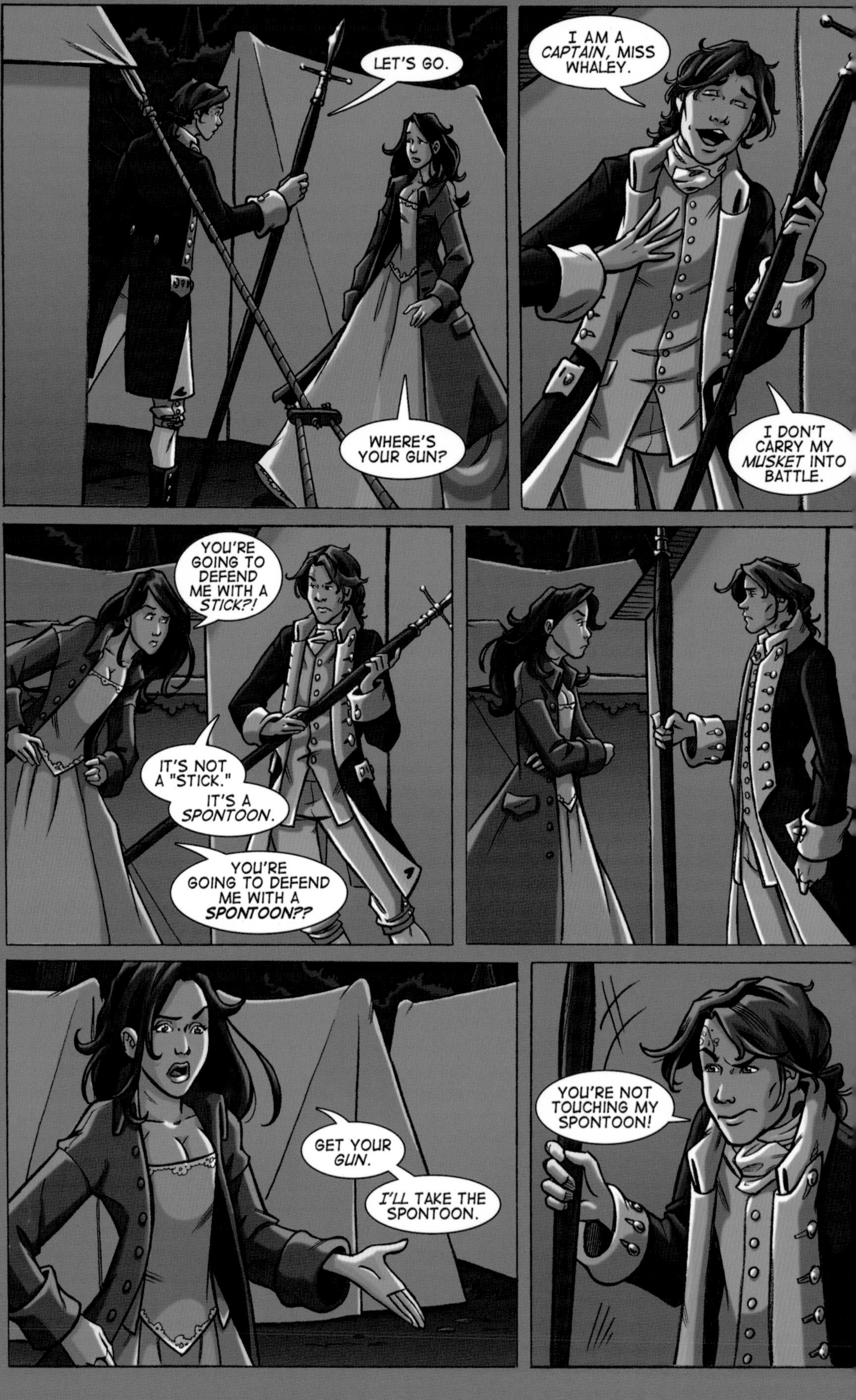
LET'S GO.
WHERE'S YOUR GUN?
I AM A CAPTAIN, MISS WHALEY.
I DON'T CARRY MY MUSKET INTO BATTLE.
YOU'RE GOING TO DEFEND ME WITH A STICK?!
IT'S NOT A "STICK."
IT'S A SPONTOON.
YOU'RE GOING TO DEFEND ME WITH A SPONTOON??
GET YOUR GUN.
I'LL TAKE THE SPONTOON.
YOU'RE NOT TOUCHING MY SPONTOON!

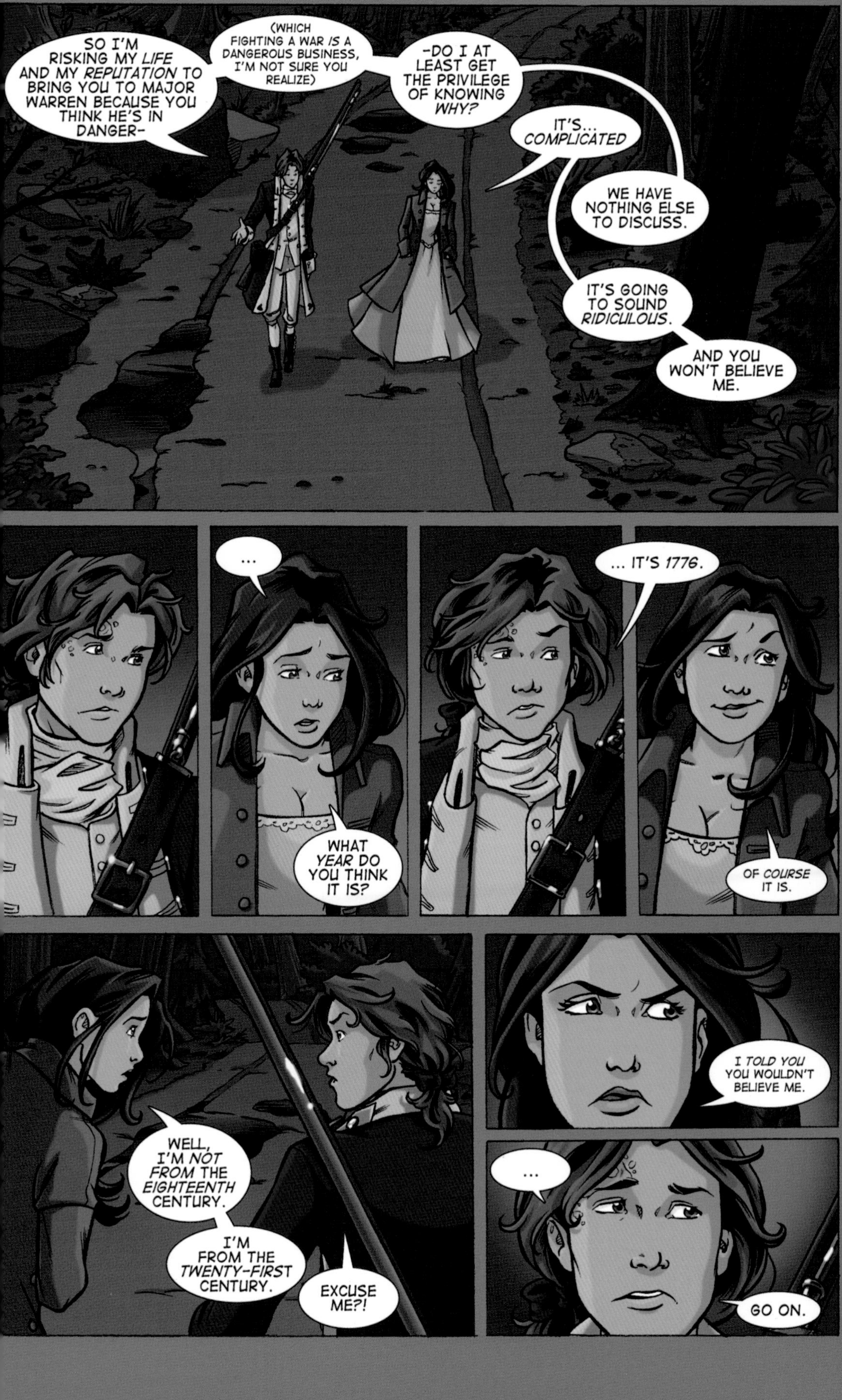
SO I'M RISKING MY LIFE AND MY REPUTATION TO BRING YOU TO MAJOR WARREN BECAUSE YOU THINK HE'S IN DANGER-
(WHICH FIGHTING A WAR IS A DANGEROUS BUSINESS, I'M NOT SURE YOU REALIZE)
-DO I AT LEAST GET THE PRIVILEGE OF KNOWING WHY?
IT'S... COMPLICATED
WE HAVE NOTHING ELSE TO DISCUSS.
IT'S GOING TO SOUND RIDICULOUS.
AND YOU WON'T BELIEVE ME.
...
WHAT YEAR DO YOU THINK IT IS?
... IT'S 1776.
OF COURSE IT IS.
WELL, I'M NOT FROM THE EIGHTEENTH CENTURY.
I'M FROM THE TWENTY-FIRST CENTURY.
EXCUSE ME?!
I TOLD YOU YOU WOULDN'T BELIEVE ME.
...
GO ON.

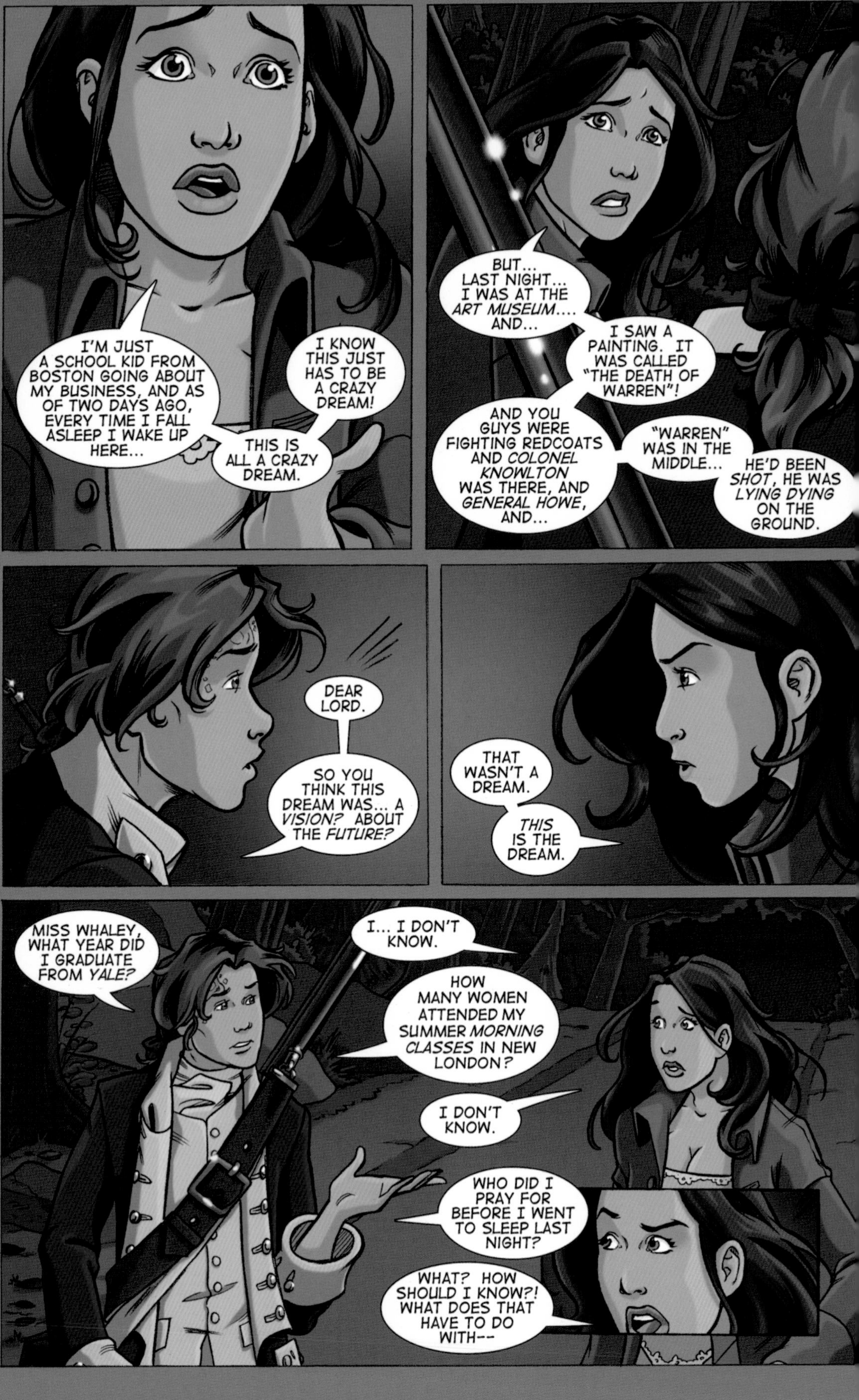

I'M JUST A SCHOOL KID FROM BOSTON GOING ABOUT MY BUSINESS, AND AS OF TWO DAYS AGO, EVERY TIME I FALL ASLEEP I WAKE UP HERE...
THIS IS ALL A CRAZY DREAM.
I KNOW THIS JUST HAS TO BE A CRAZY DREAM!
BUT... LAST NIGHT... I WAS AT THE *ART MUSEUM*.... AND...
I SAW A PAINTING. IT WAS CALLED "THE DEATH OF WARREN"!
AND YOU GUYS WERE FIGHTING REDCOATS AND *COLONEL KNOWLTON* WAS THERE, AND *GENERAL HOWE*, AND...
"WARREN" WAS IN THE MIDDLE...
HE'D BEEN *SHOT*, HE WAS *LYING DYING* ON THE GROUND.
DEAR LORD.
SO YOU THINK THIS DREAM WAS... A *VISION?* ABOUT THE *FUTURE?*
THAT WASN'T A DREAM.
THIS IS THE DREAM.
MISS WHALEY, WHAT YEAR DID I GRADUATE FROM *YALE?*
I... I DON'T KNOW.
HOW MANY WOMEN ATTENDED MY SUMMER *MORNING CLASSES* IN NEW LONDON?
I DON'T KNOW.
WHO DID I PRAY FOR BEFORE I WENT TO SLEEP LAST NIGHT?
WHAT? HOW SHOULD I KNOW?! WHAT DOES THAT HAVE TO DO WITH--

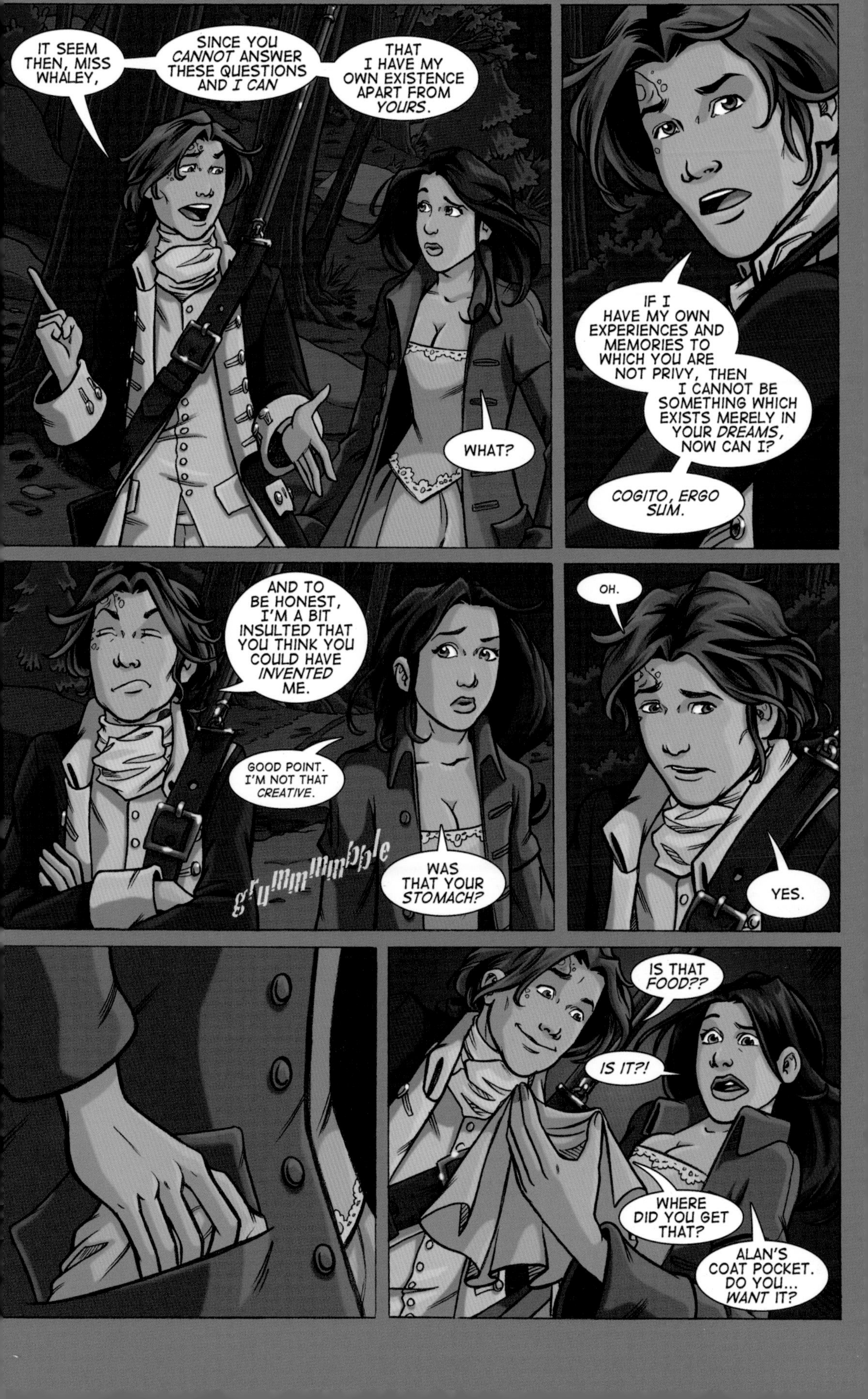
IT SEEM THEN, MISS WHALEY,
SINCE YOU CANNOT ANSWER THESE QUESTIONS AND I CAN
THAT I HAVE MY OWN EXISTENCE APART FROM YOURS.
WHAT?
IF I HAVE MY OWN EXPERIENCES AND MEMORIES TO WHICH YOU ARE NOT PRIVY, THEN I CANNOT BE SOMETHING WHICH EXISTS MERELY IN YOUR DREAMS, NOW CAN I?
COGITO, ERGO SUM.
AND TO BE HONEST, I'M A BIT INSULTED THAT YOU THINK YOU COULD HAVE INVENTED ME.
GOOD POINT. I'M NOT THAT CREATIVE.
grummmmmble
WAS THAT YOUR STOMACH?
OH.
YES.
IS THAT FOOD??
IS IT?!
WHERE DID YOU GET THAT?
ALAN'S COAT POCKET. DO YOU... WANT IT?

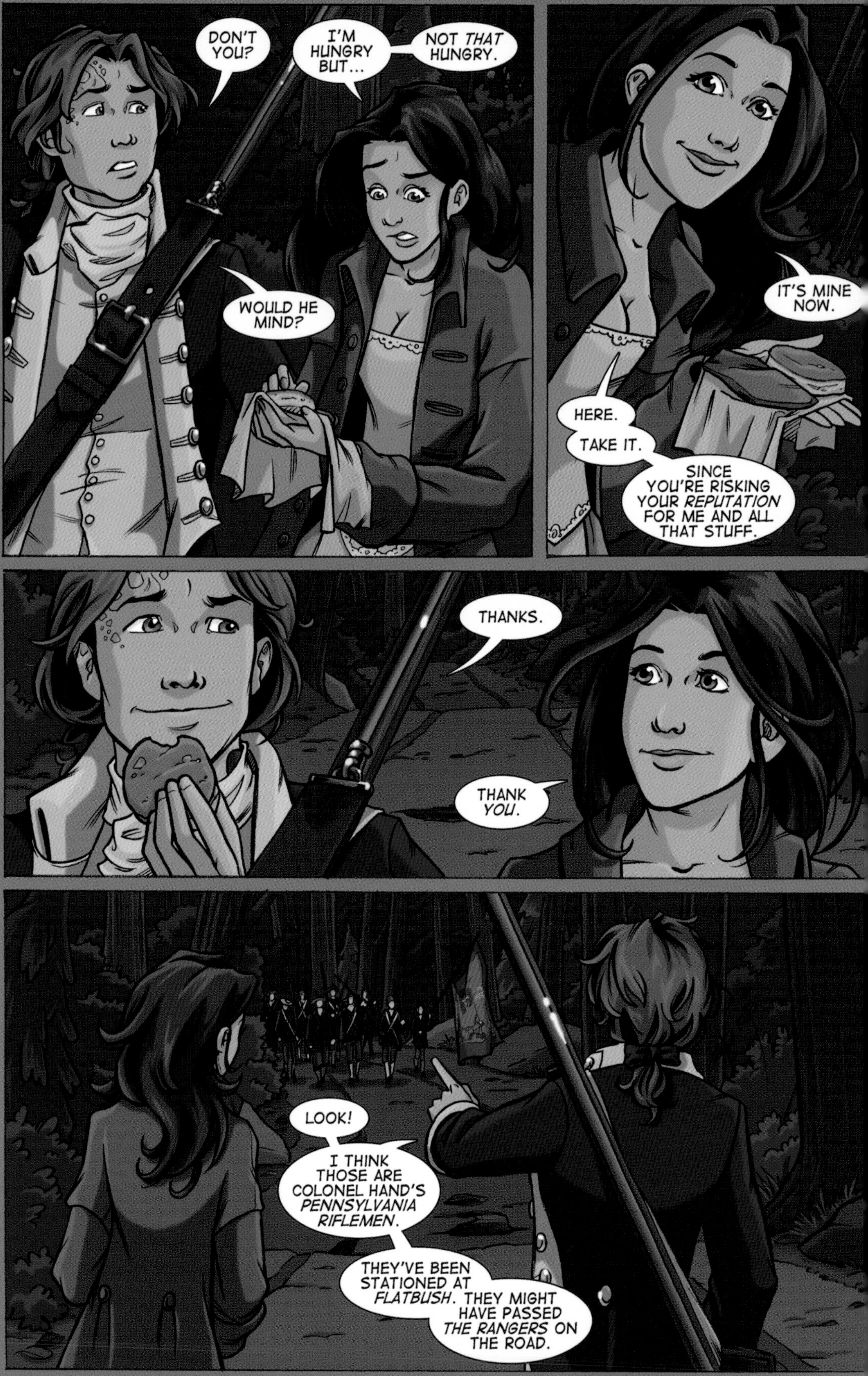
DON'T YOU?
I'M HUNGRY BUT...
NOT *THAT* HUNGRY.
WOULD HE MIND?
IT'S MINE NOW.
HERE.
TAKE IT.
SINCE YOU'RE RISKING YOUR *REPUTATION* FOR ME AND ALL THAT STUFF.
THANKS.
THANK *YOU*.
LOOK!
I THINK THOSE ARE COLONEL HAND'S *PENNSYLVANIA RIFLEMEN*.
THEY'VE BEEN STATIONED AT *FLATBUSH*. THEY MIGHT HAVE PASSED *THE RANGERS* ON THE ROAD.

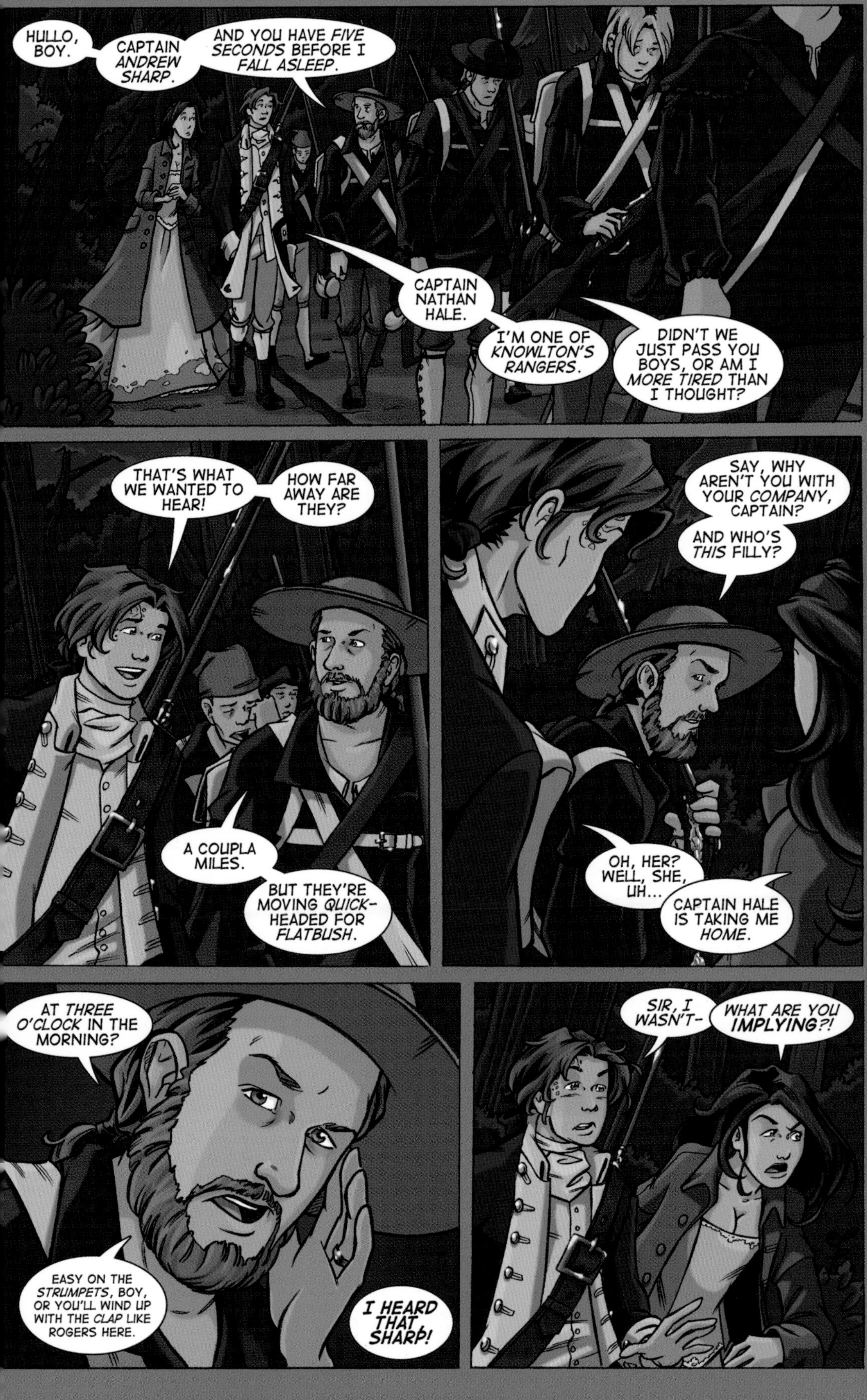
HULLO, BOY.
CAPTAIN ANDREW SHARP.
AND YOU HAVE *FIVE SECONDS* BEFORE I *FALL ASLEEP*.
CAPTAIN NATHAN HALE.
I'M ONE OF *KNOWLTON'S RANGERS*.
DIDN'T WE JUST PASS YOU BOYS, OR AM I *MORE TIRED* THAN I THOUGHT?
THAT'S WHAT WE WANTED TO HEAR!
HOW FAR AWAY ARE THEY?
A COUPLA MILES.
BUT THEY'RE MOVING *QUICK*- HEADED FOR *FLATBUSH*.
SAY, WHY AREN'T YOU WITH YOUR *COMPANY*, CAPTAIN?
AND WHO'S *THIS* FILLY?
OH, HER? WELL, SHE, UH...
CAPTAIN HALE IS TAKING ME *HOME*.
AT *THREE O'CLOCK* IN THE MORNING?
EASY ON THE *STRUMPETS*, BOY, OR YOU'LL WIND UP WITH THE *CLAP* LIKE ROGERS HERE.
I HEARD THAT, SHARP!
SIR, I WASN'T-
WHAT ARE YOU ***IMPLYING***?!

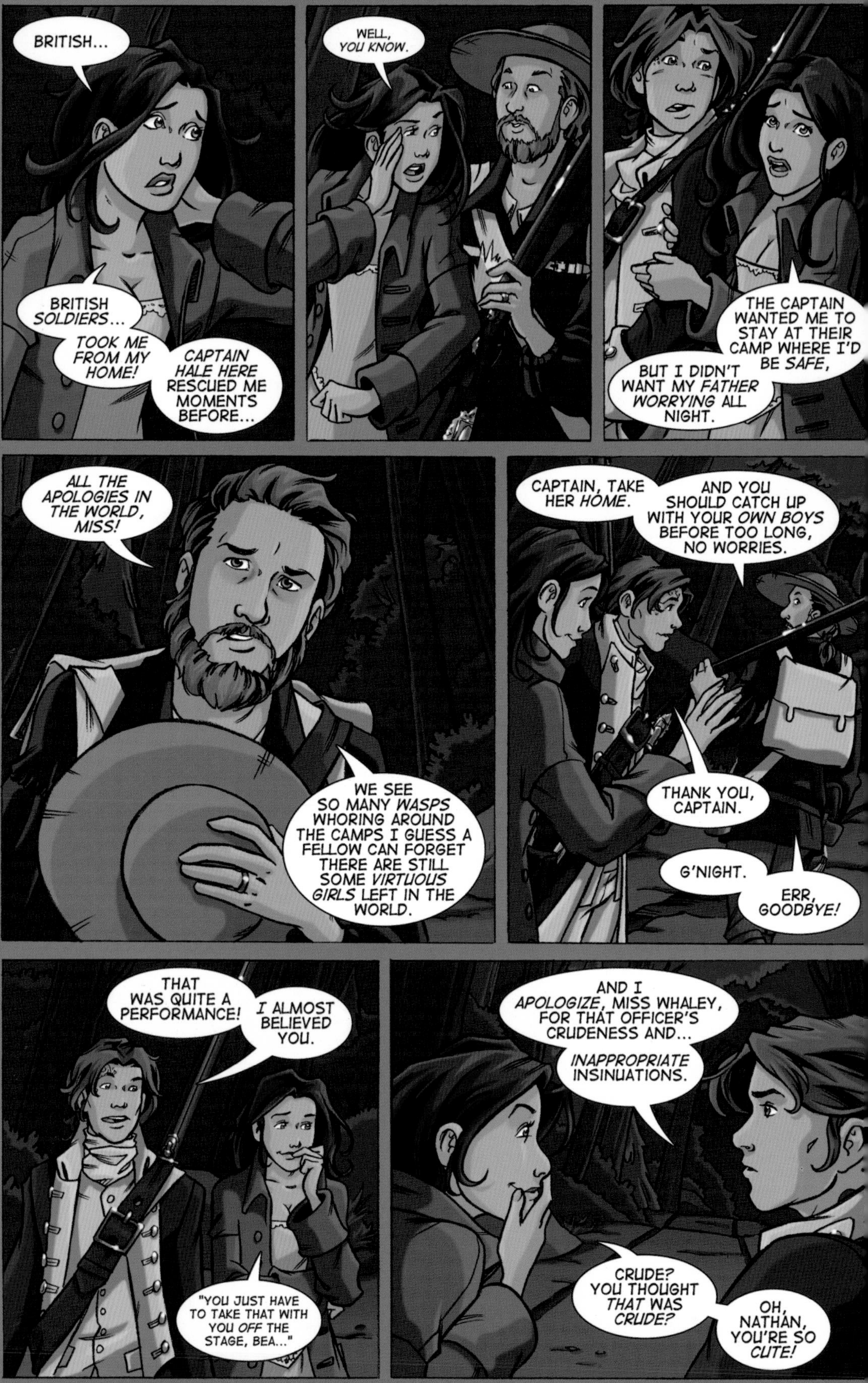
BRITISH...
BRITISH SOLDIERS...
TOOK ME FROM MY HOME!
CAPTAIN HALE HERE RESCUED ME MOMENTS BEFORE...
WELL, YOU KNOW.
THE CAPTAIN WANTED ME TO STAY AT THEIR CAMP WHERE I'D BE SAFE,
BUT I DIDN'T WANT MY FATHER WORRYING ALL NIGHT.
ALL THE APOLOGIES IN THE WORLD, MISS!
WE SEE SO MANY WASPS WHORING AROUND THE CAMPS I GUESS A FELLOW CAN FORGET THERE ARE STILL SOME VIRTUOUS GIRLS LEFT IN THE WORLD.
CAPTAIN, TAKE HER HOME.
AND YOU SHOULD CATCH UP WITH YOUR OWN BOYS BEFORE TOO LONG, NO WORRIES.
THANK YOU, CAPTAIN.
G'NIGHT.
ERR, GOODBYE!
THAT WAS QUITE A PERFORMANCE!
I ALMOST BELIEVED YOU.
"YOU JUST HAVE TO TAKE THAT WITH YOU OFF THE STAGE, BEA..."
AND I APOLOGIZE, MISS WHALEY, FOR THAT OFFICER'S CRUDENESS AND...
INAPPROPRIATE INSINUATIONS.
CRUDE? YOU THOUGHT THAT WAS CRUDE?
OH, NATHAN, YOU'RE SO CUTE!

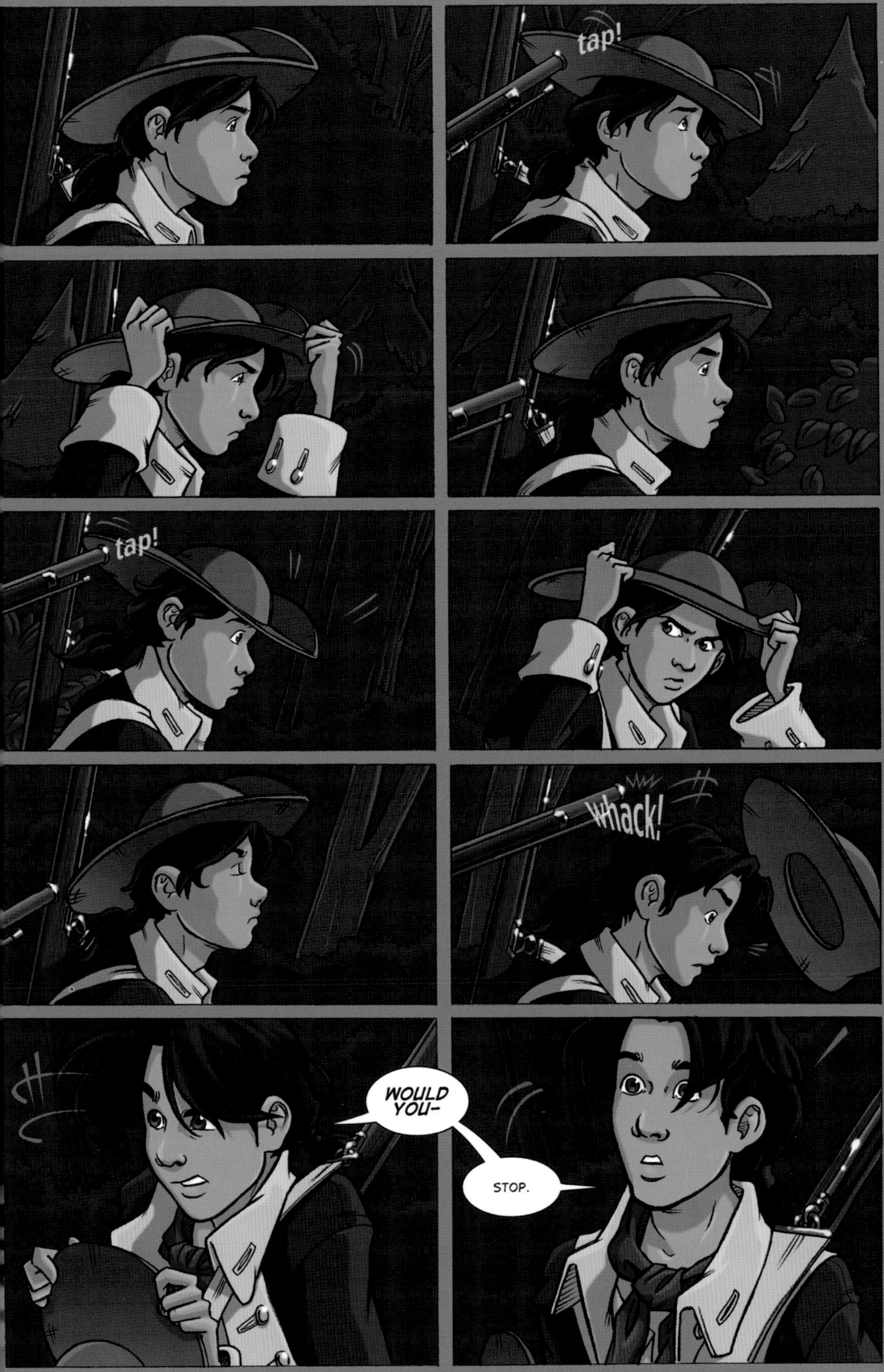
tap!
tap!
whack!
WOULD YOU-
STOP.

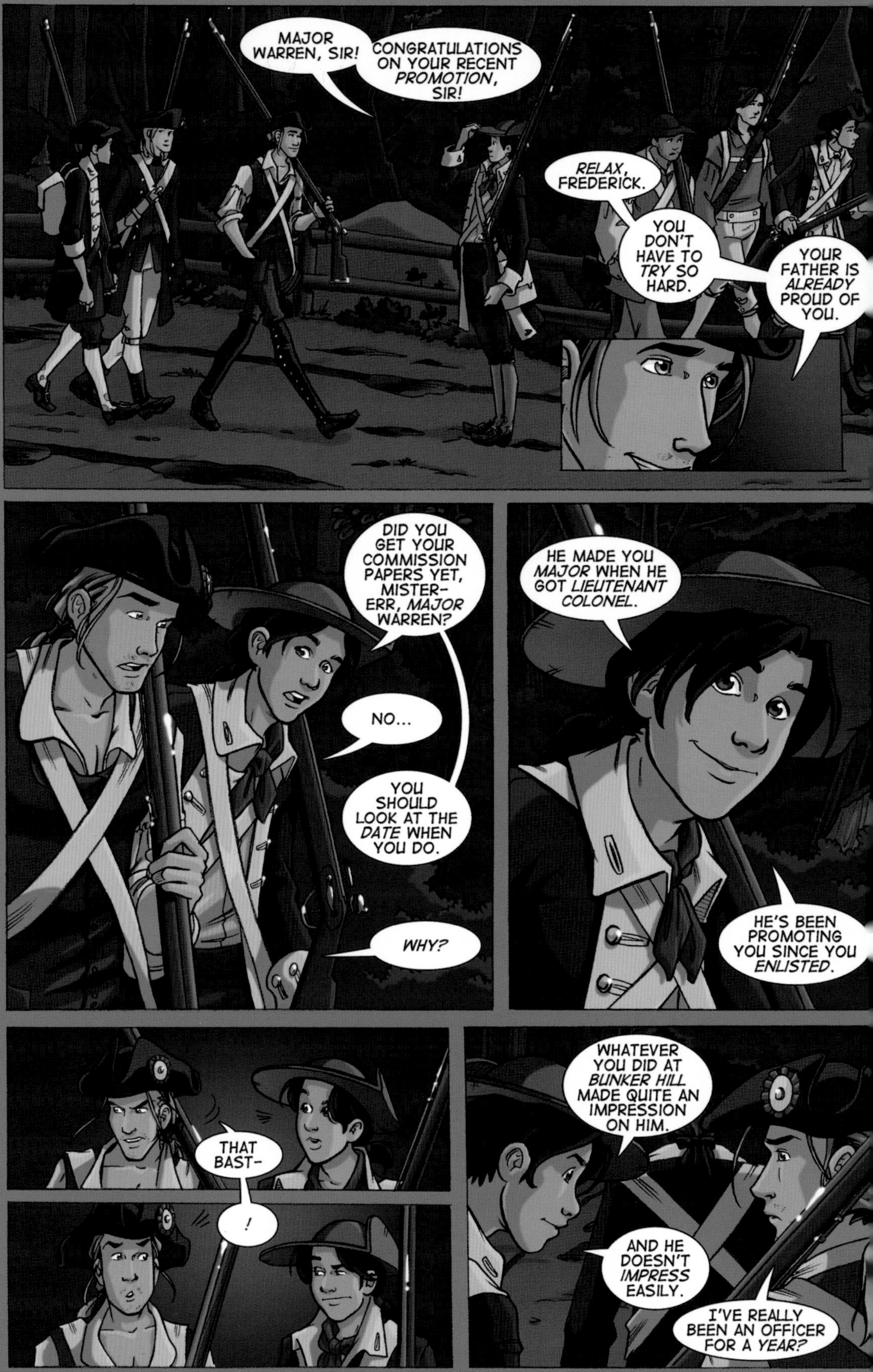
MAJOR WARREN, SIR!
CONGRATULATIONS ON YOUR RECENT *PROMOTION*, SIR!
RELAX, FREDERICK.
YOU DON'T HAVE TO *TRY* SO HARD.
YOUR FATHER IS *ALREADY* PROUD OF YOU.
DID YOU GET YOUR COMMISSION PAPERS YET, MISTER- ERR, *MAJOR* WARREN?
NO...
YOU SHOULD LOOK AT THE *DATE* WHEN YOU DO.
WHY?
HE MADE YOU *MAJOR* WHEN HE GOT *LIEUTENANT COLONEL*.
HE'S BEEN PROMOTING YOU SINCE YOU *ENLISTED*.
THAT BAST-
!
WHATEVER YOU DID AT *BUNKER HILL* MADE QUITE AN IMPRESSION ON HIM.
AND HE DOESN'T *IMPRESS* EASILY.
I'VE REALLY BEEN AN OFFICER FOR A *YEAR?*

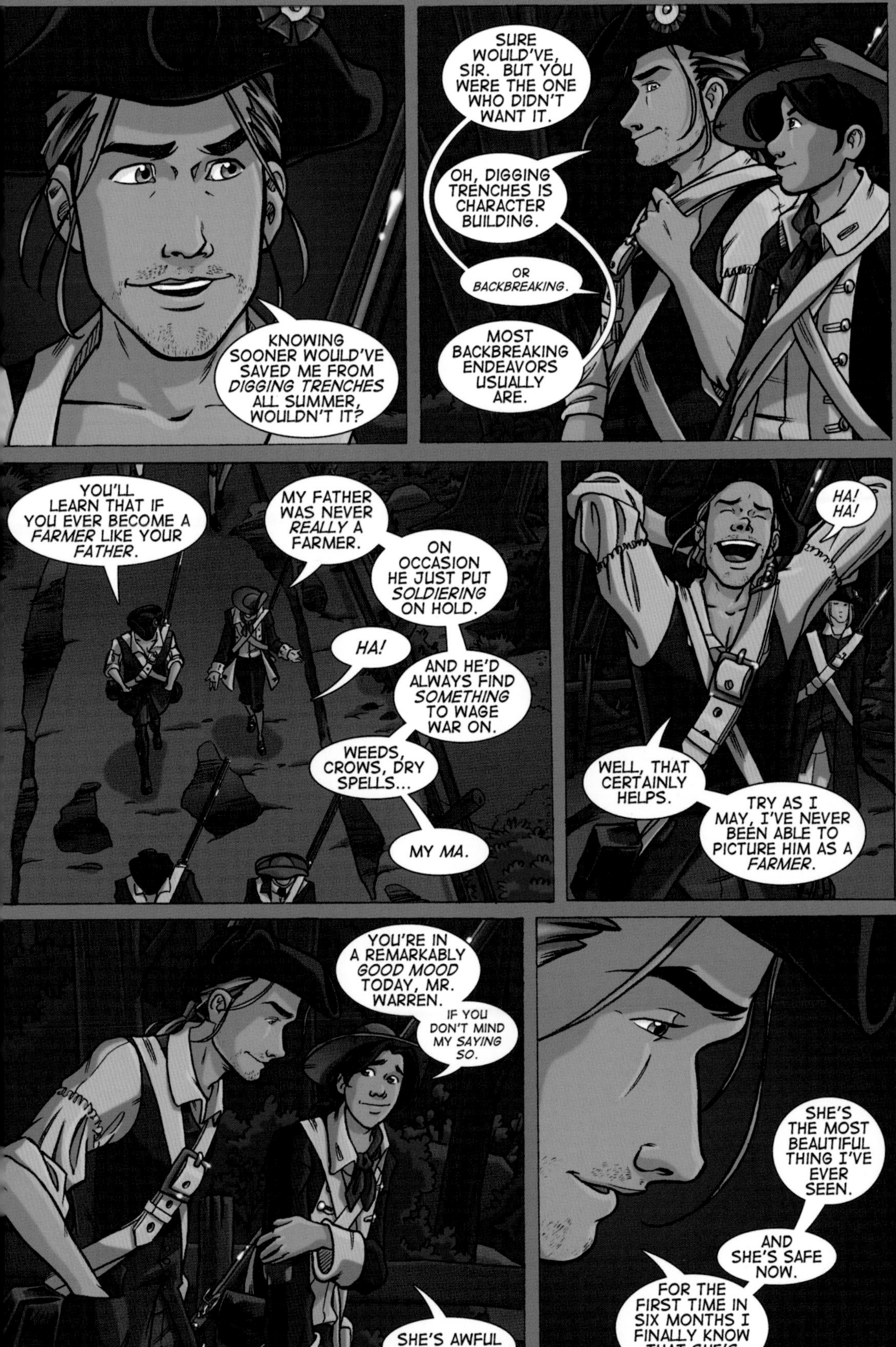
KNOWING SOONER WOULD'VE SAVED ME FROM *DIGGING TRENCHES* ALL SUMMER, WOULDN'T IT?
SURE WOULD'VE, SIR. BUT YOU WERE THE ONE WHO DIDN'T WANT IT.
OH, DIGGING TRENCHES IS CHARACTER BUILDING.
OR *BACKBREAKING*.
MOST BACKBREAKING ENDEAVORS USUALLY ARE.
YOU'LL LEARN THAT IF YOU EVER BECOME A *FARMER* LIKE YOUR *FATHER*.
MY FATHER WAS NEVER *REALLY* A FARMER.
ON OCCASION HE JUST PUT *SOLDIERING* ON HOLD.
HA!
AND HE'D ALWAYS FIND *SOMETHING* TO WAGE WAR ON.
WEEDS, CROWS, DRY SPELLS...
MY *MA*.
HA! HA!
WELL, THAT CERTAINLY HELPS.
TRY AS I MAY, I'VE NEVER BEEN ABLE TO PICTURE HIM AS A *FARMER*.
YOU'RE IN A REMARKABLY *GOOD MOOD* TODAY, MR. WARREN.
IF YOU DON'T MIND MY *SAYING* SO.
SHE'S AWFUL *PRETTY*.
SHE'S THE MOST BEAUTIFUL THING I'VE EVER SEEN.
AND SHE'S SAFE NOW.
FOR THE FIRST TIME IN SIX MONTHS I FINALLY KNOW THAT SHE'S *SAFE*.

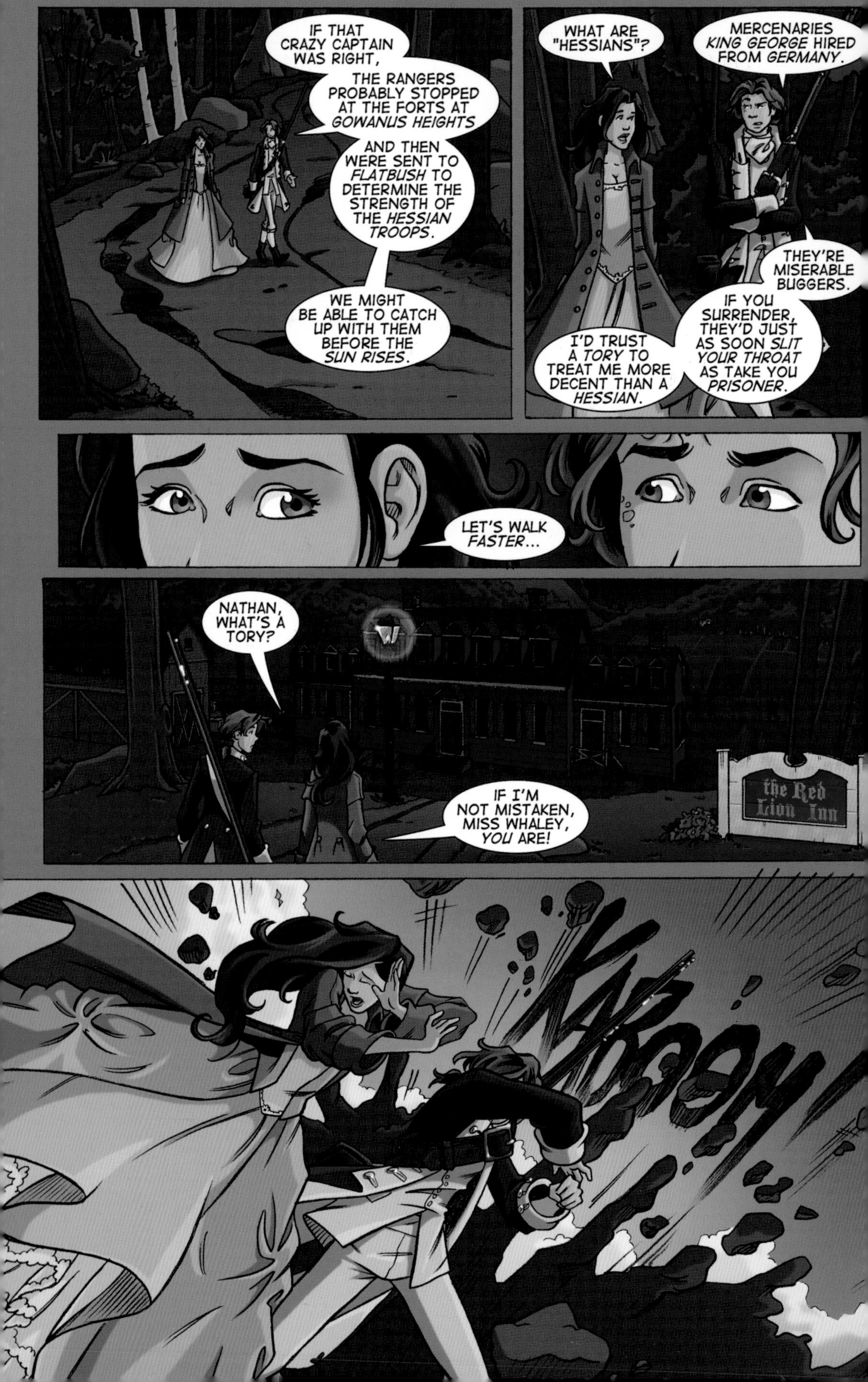
IF THAT CRAZY CAPTAIN WAS RIGHT,
THE RANGERS PROBABLY STOPPED AT THE FORTS AT GOWANUS HEIGHTS
AND THEN WERE SENT TO FLATBUSH TO DETERMINE THE STRENGTH OF THE HESSIAN TROOPS.
WE MIGHT BE ABLE TO CATCH UP WITH THEM BEFORE THE SUN RISES.
WHAT ARE "HESSIANS"?
MERCENARIES KING GEORGE HIRED FROM GERMANY.
THEY'RE MISERABLE BUGGERS.
IF YOU SURRENDER, THEY'D JUST AS SOON SLIT YOUR THROAT AS TAKE YOU PRISONER.
I'D TRUST A TORY TO TREAT ME MORE DECENT THAN A HESSIAN.
LET'S WALK FASTER...
NATHAN, WHAT'S A TORY?
IF I'M NOT MISTAKEN, MISS WHALEY, YOU ARE!
the Red Lion Inn
KABOOM

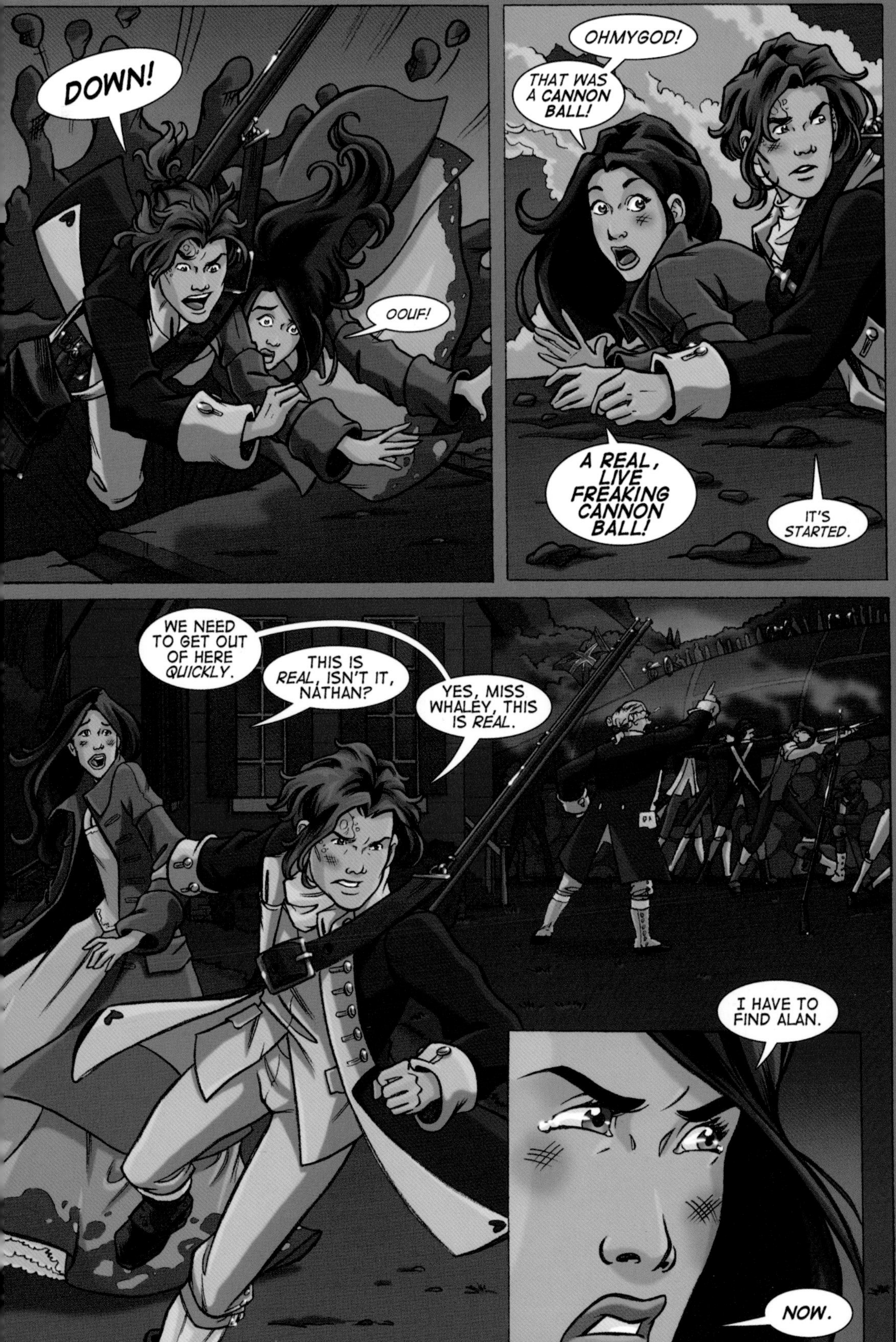
DOWN!
OOUF!
OHMYGOD!
THAT WAS A CANNON BALL!
A REAL, LIVE FREAKING CANNON BALL!
IT'S STARTED.
WE NEED TO GET OUT OF HERE *QUICKLY*.
THIS IS *REAL*, ISN'T IT, NATHAN?
YES, MISS WHALEY, THIS IS *REAL*.
I HAVE TO FIND ALAN.
NOW.

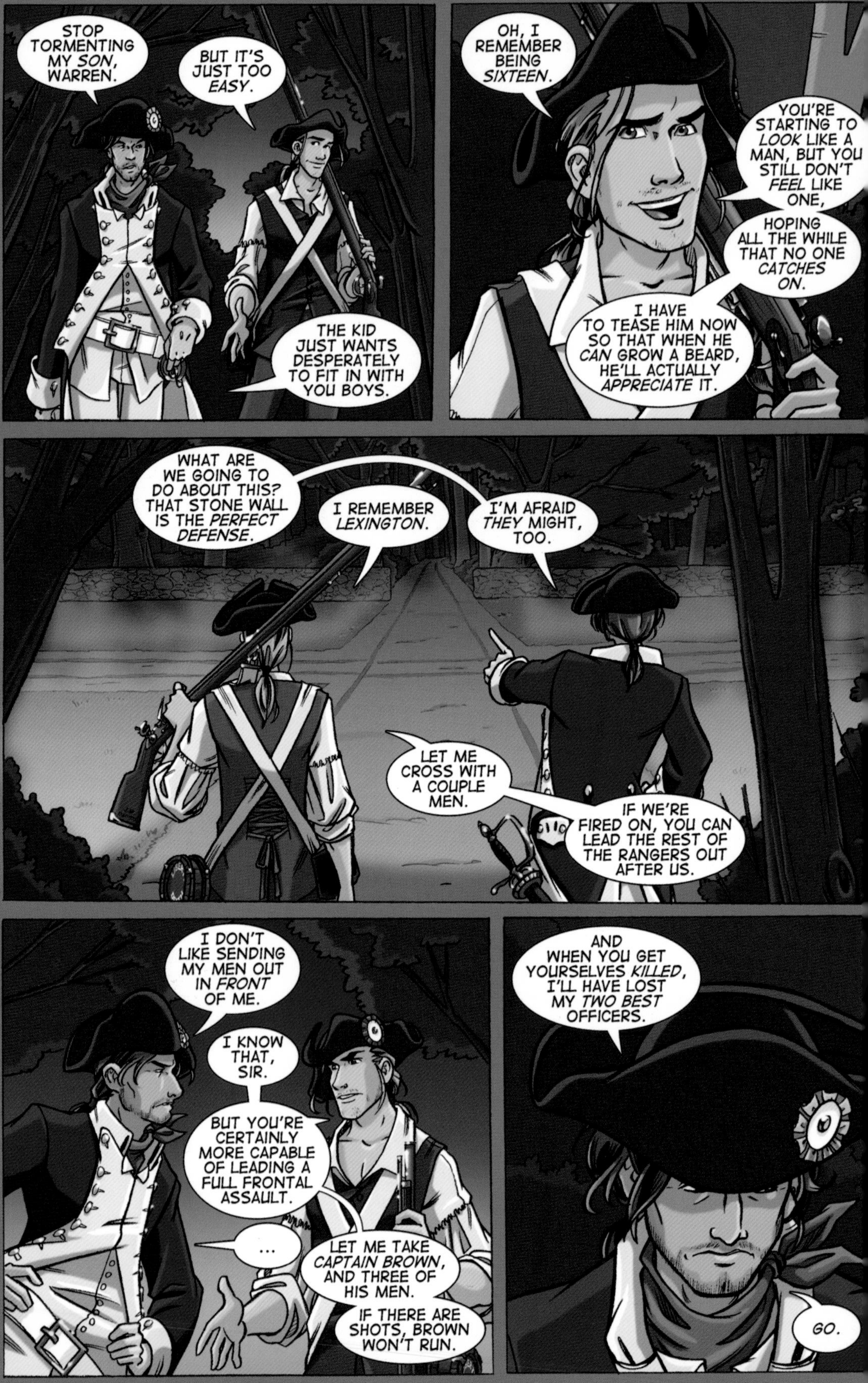
STOP TORMENTING MY SON, WARREN.
BUT IT'S JUST TOO EASY.
THE KID JUST WANTS DESPERATELY TO FIT IN WITH YOU BOYS.
OH, I REMEMBER BEING SIXTEEN.
YOU'RE STARTING TO LOOK LIKE A MAN, BUT YOU STILL DON'T FEEL LIKE ONE,
HOPING ALL THE WHILE THAT NO ONE CATCHES ON.
I HAVE TO TEASE HIM NOW SO THAT WHEN HE CAN GROW A BEARD, HE'LL ACTUALLY APPRECIATE IT.
WHAT ARE WE GOING TO DO ABOUT THIS? THAT STONE WALL IS THE PERFECT DEFENSE.
I REMEMBER LEXINGTON.
I'M AFRAID THEY MIGHT, TOO.
LET ME CROSS WITH A COUPLE MEN.
IF WE'RE FIRED ON, YOU CAN LEAD THE REST OF THE RANGERS OUT AFTER US.
I DON'T LIKE SENDING MY MEN OUT IN FRONT OF ME.
I KNOW THAT, SIR.
BUT YOU'RE CERTAINLY MORE CAPABLE OF LEADING A FULL FRONTAL ASSAULT.
...
LET ME TAKE CAPTAIN BROWN, AND THREE OF HIS MEN.
IF THERE ARE SHOTS, BROWN WON'T RUN.
AND WHEN YOU GET YOURSELVES KILLED, I'LL HAVE LOST MY TWO BEST OFFICERS.
GO.

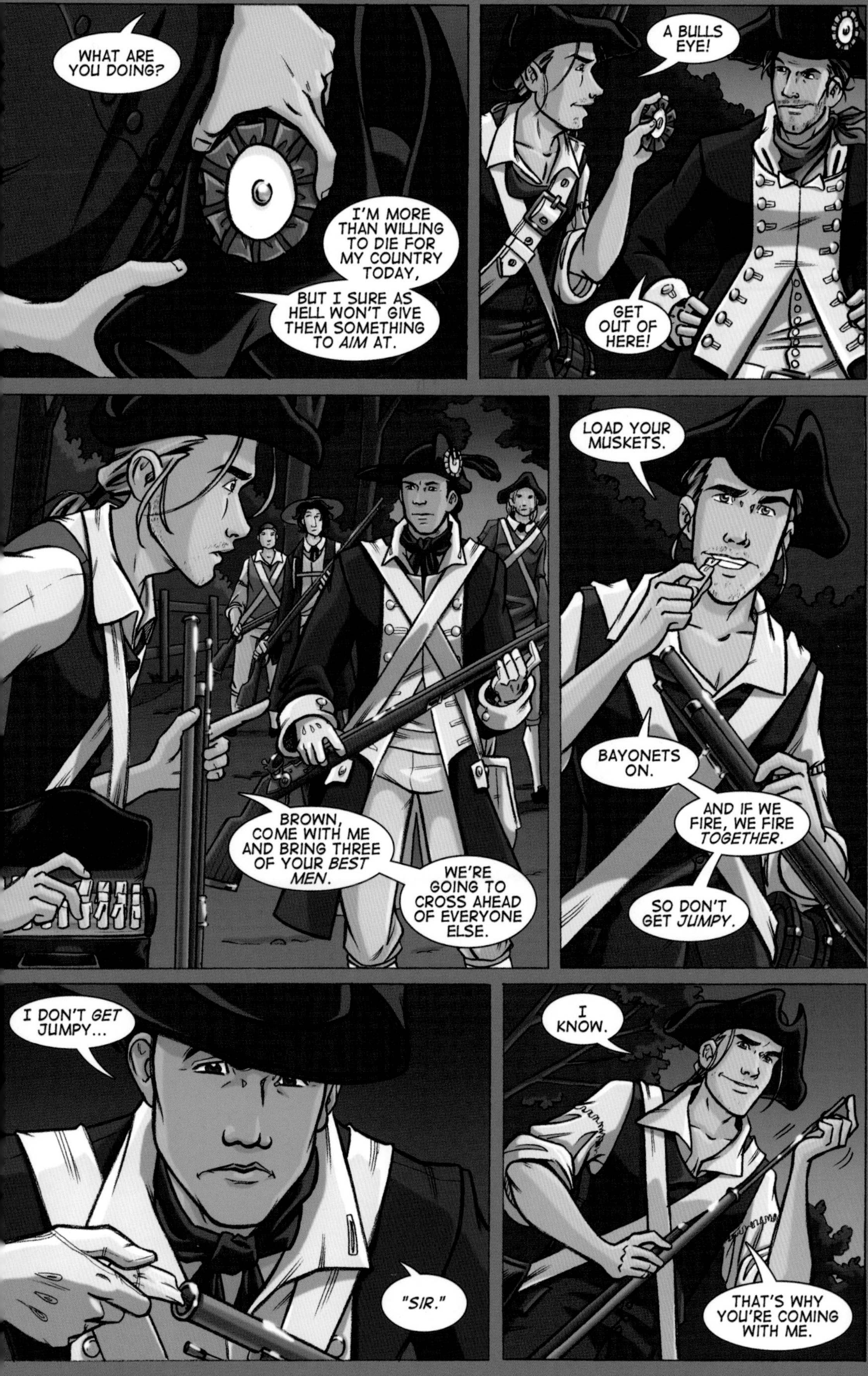
WHAT ARE YOU DOING?
I'M MORE THAN WILLING TO DIE FOR MY COUNTRY TODAY,
BUT I SURE AS HELL WON'T GIVE THEM SOMETHING TO *AIM* AT.
A BULLS EYE!
GET OUT OF HERE!
BROWN, COME WITH ME AND BRING THREE OF YOUR *BEST MEN*.
WE'RE GOING TO CROSS AHEAD OF EVERYONE ELSE.
LOAD YOUR MUSKETS.
BAYONETS ON.
AND IF WE FIRE, WE FIRE *TOGETHER*.
SO DON'T GET *JUMPY*.
I DON'T *GET* JUMPY...
"*SIR*."
I KNOW.
THAT'S WHY YOU'RE COMING WITH ME.

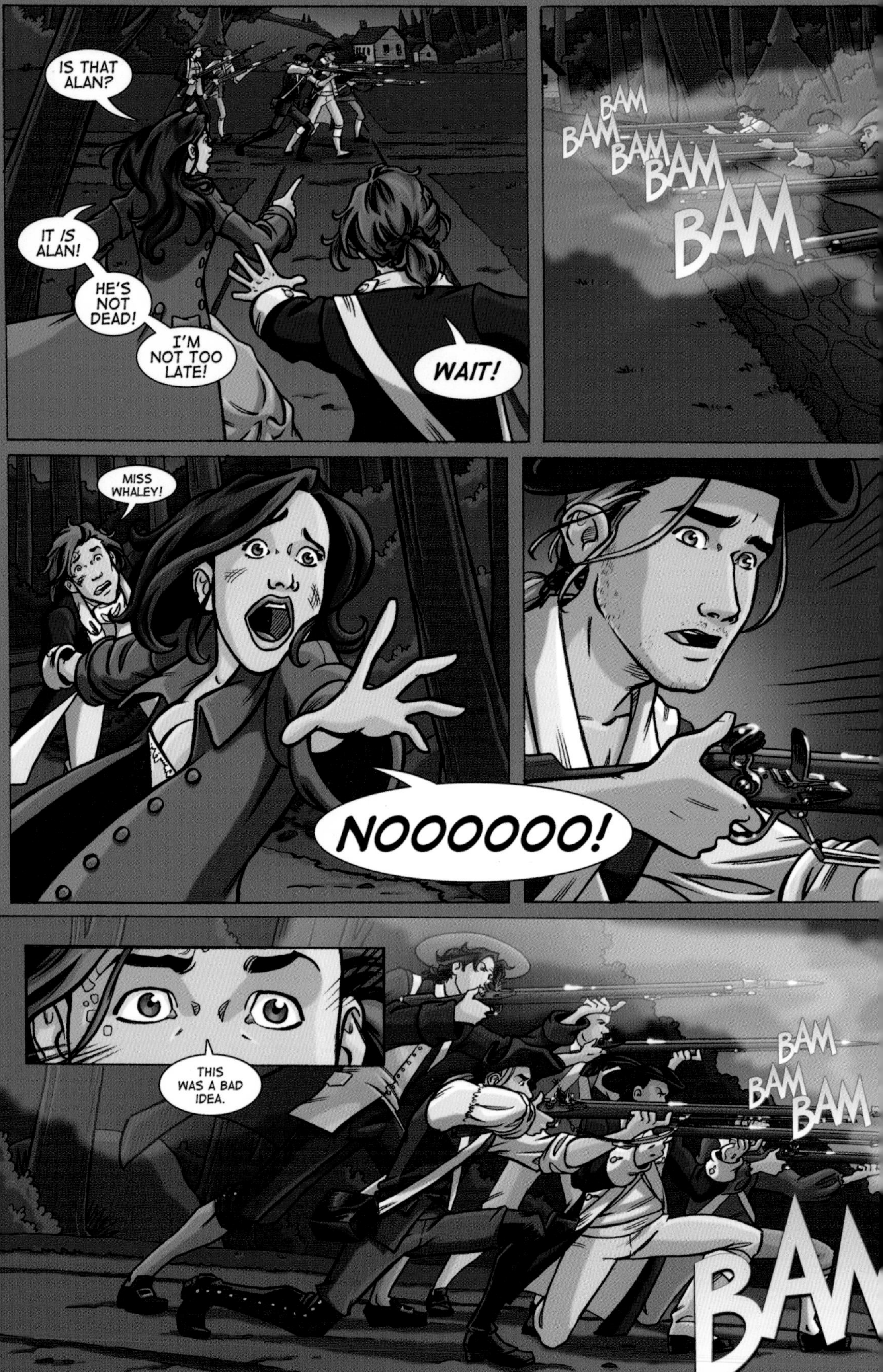
IS THAT ALAN?
IT IS ALAN!
HE'S NOT DEAD!
I'M NOT TOO LATE!
WAIT!
BAM
BAM-BAM
BAM
BAM
BAM
MISS WHALEY!
NOOOOOO!
THIS WAS A BAD IDEA.
BAM
BAM
BAM
BAM

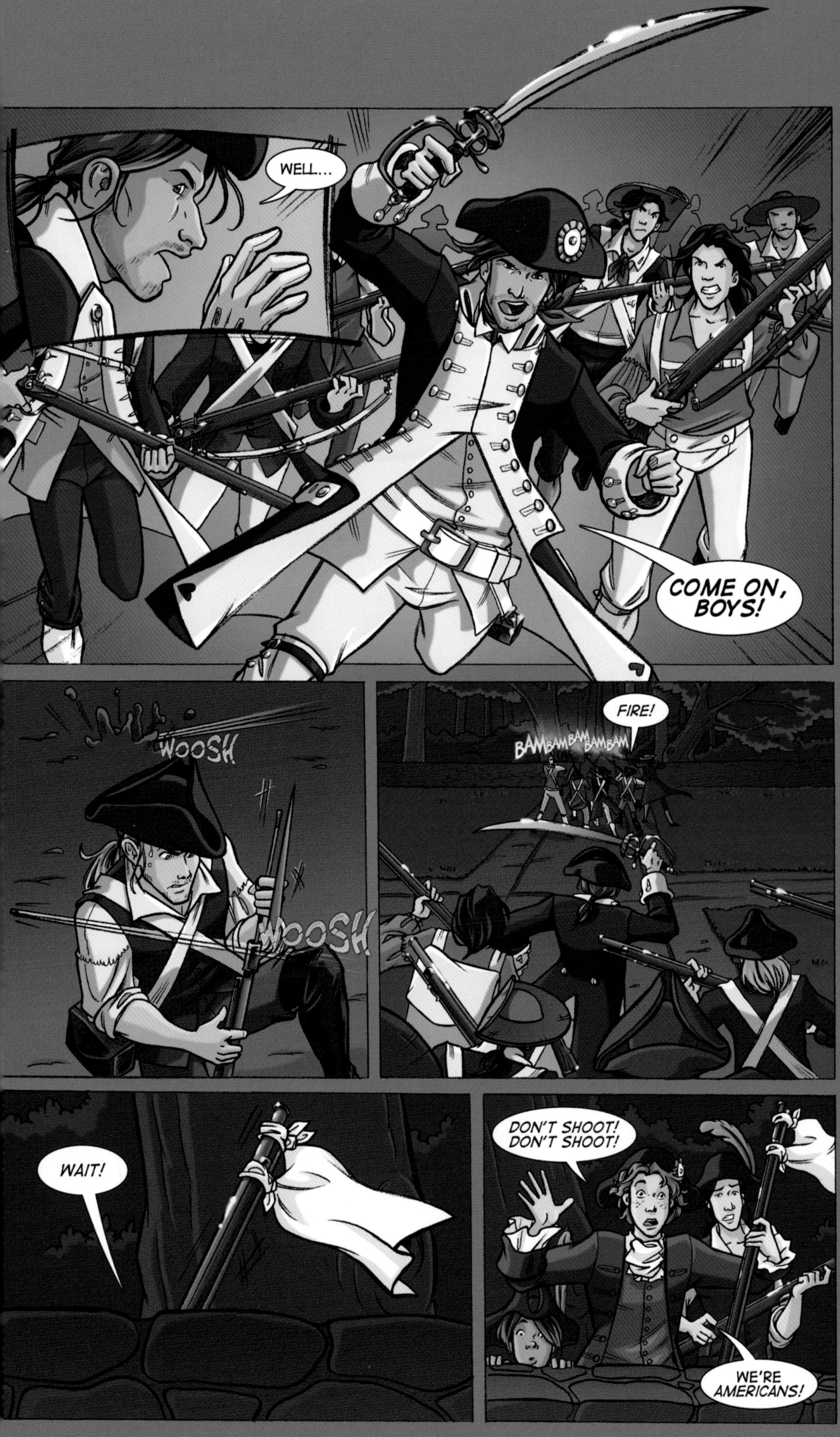
WELL...
COME ON, BOYS!
WOOSH
WOOSH
FIRE!
BAMBAMBAMBAMBAM
WAIT!
DON'T SHOOT! DON'T SHOOT!
WE'RE AMERICANS!

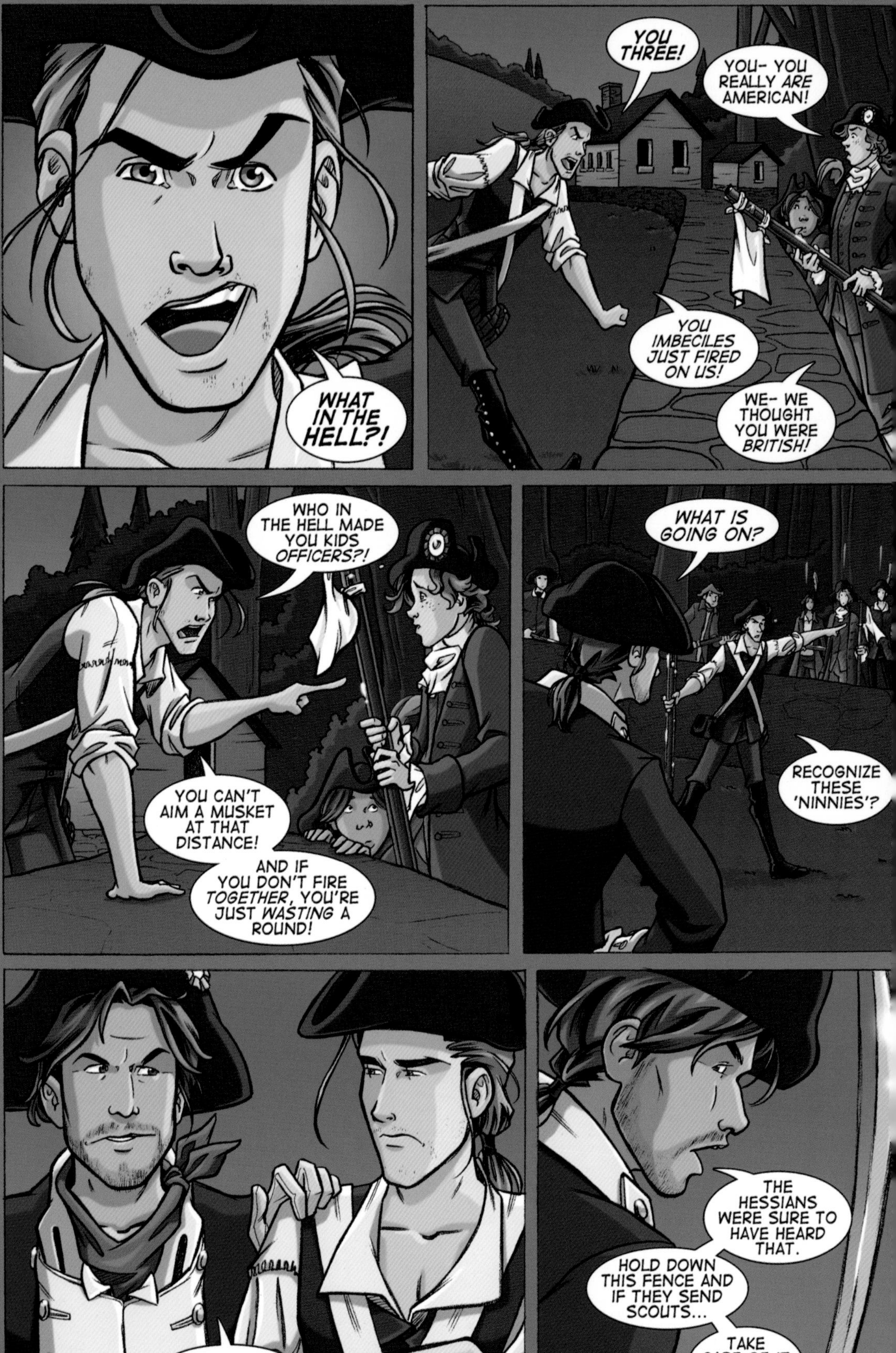
WHAT IN THE HELL?!
YOU THREE!
YOU IMBECILES JUST FIRED ON US!
YOU- YOU REALLY ARE AMERICAN!
WE- WE THOUGHT YOU WERE BRITISH!
WHO IN THE HELL MADE YOU KIDS OFFICERS?!
YOU CAN'T AIM A MUSKET AT THAT DISTANCE!
AND IF YOU DON'T FIRE TOGETHER, YOU'RE JUST WASTING A ROUND!
WHAT IS GOING ON?
RECOGNIZE THESE 'NINNIES'?
YOU CAN DEAL WITH THIS.
THE HESSIANS WERE SURE TO HAVE HEARD THAT.
HOLD DOWN THIS FENCE AND IF THEY SEND SCOUTS...
TAKE CARE OF IT WITHOUT NOISE.

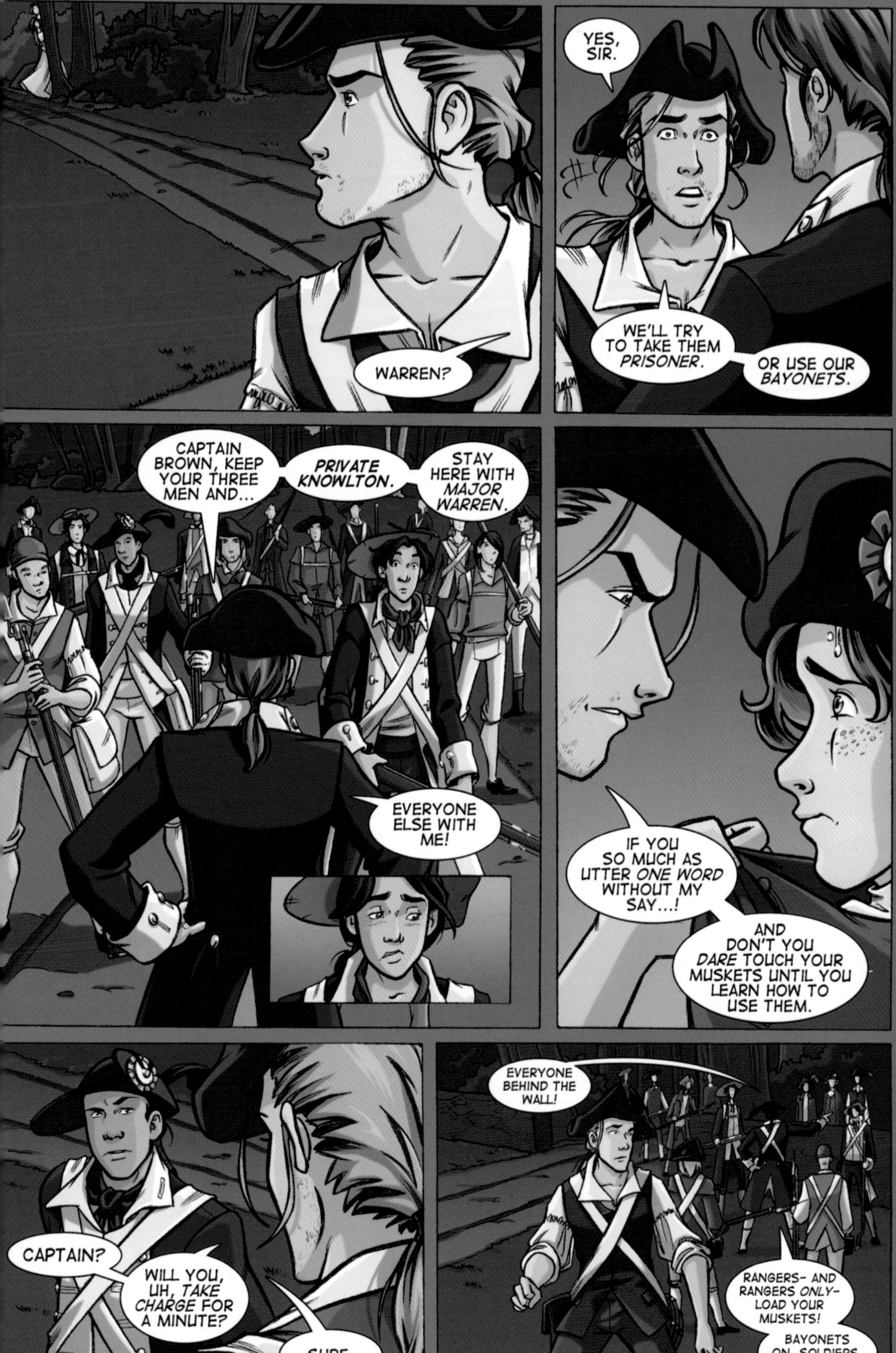
WARREN?
YES, SIR.
WE'LL TRY TO TAKE THEM *PRISONER*.
OR USE OUR *BAYONETS*.
CAPTAIN BROWN, KEEP YOUR THREE MEN AND...
PRIVATE KNOWLTON.
STAY HERE WITH *MAJOR WARREN*.
EVERYONE ELSE WITH ME!
IF YOU SO MUCH AS UTTER *ONE WORD* WITHOUT MY SAY...!
AND DON'T YOU *DARE* TOUCH YOUR MUSKETS UNTIL YOU LEARN HOW TO USE THEM.
CAPTAIN?
WILL YOU, UH, *TAKE CHARGE* FOR A MINUTE?
SURE.
EVERYONE BEHIND THE WALL!
RANGERS- AND RANGERS *ONLY*- LOAD YOUR MUSKETS!
BAYONETS ON, SOLDIERS, HURRY UP!

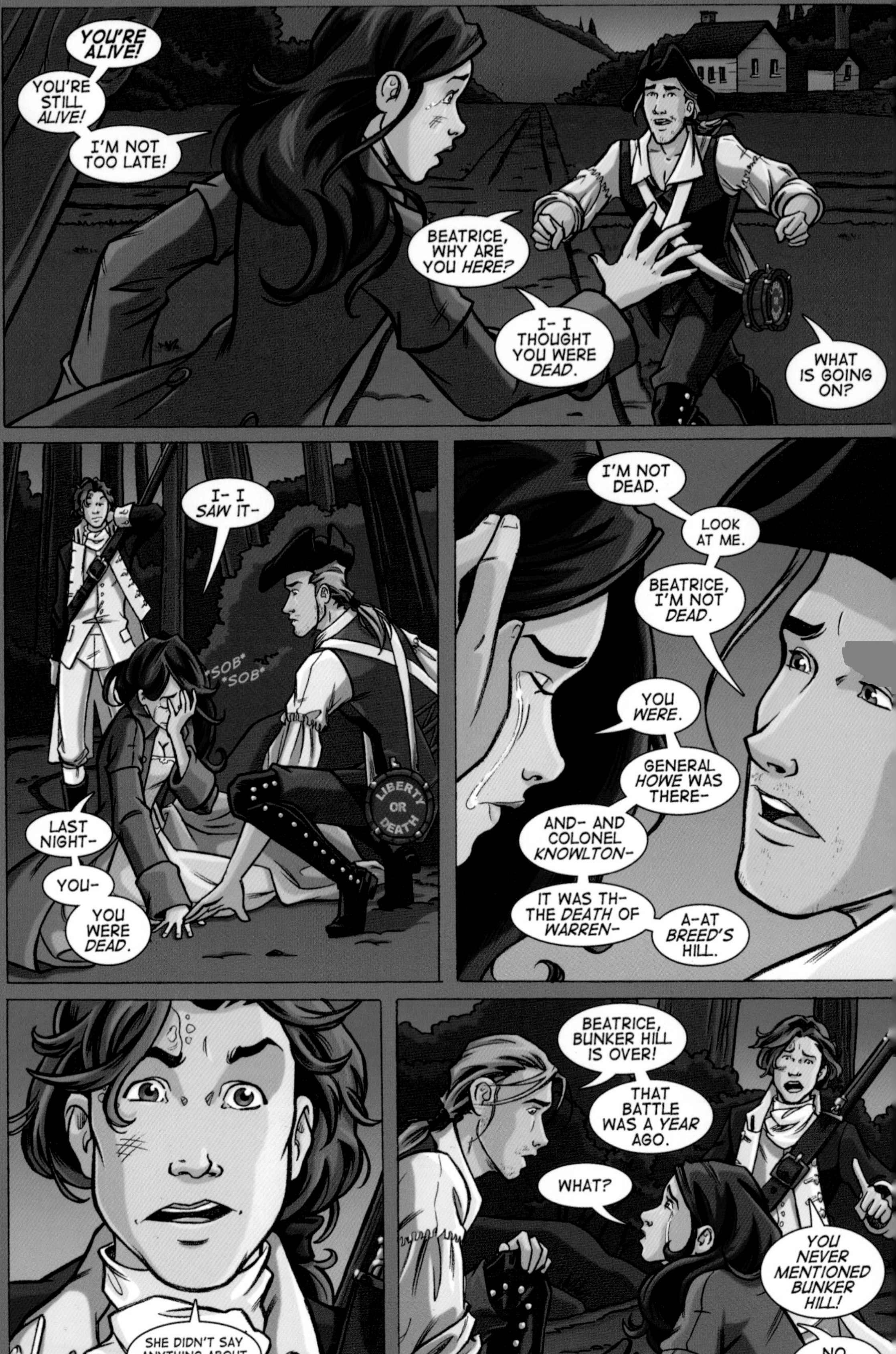
YOU'RE ALIVE!
YOU'RE STILL ALIVE!
I'M NOT TOO LATE!
BEATRICE, WHY ARE YOU HERE?
I- I THOUGHT YOU WERE DEAD.
WHAT IS GOING ON?
I- I SAW IT-
SOB *SOB*
LIBERTY OR DEATH
LAST NIGHT-
YOU-
YOU WERE DEAD.
I'M NOT DEAD.
LOOK AT ME.
BEATRICE, I'M NOT DEAD.
YOU WERE.
GENERAL HOWE WAS THERE-
AND- AND COLONEL KNOWLTON-
IT WAS TH- THE DEATH OF WARREN-
A-AT BREED'S HILL.
SHE DIDN'T SAY ANYTHING ABOUT BUNKER HILL!
BEATRICE, BUNKER HILL IS OVER!
THAT BATTLE WAS A YEAR AGO.
WHAT?
YOU NEVER MENTIONED BUNKER HILL!
NO, BREED'S HILL!

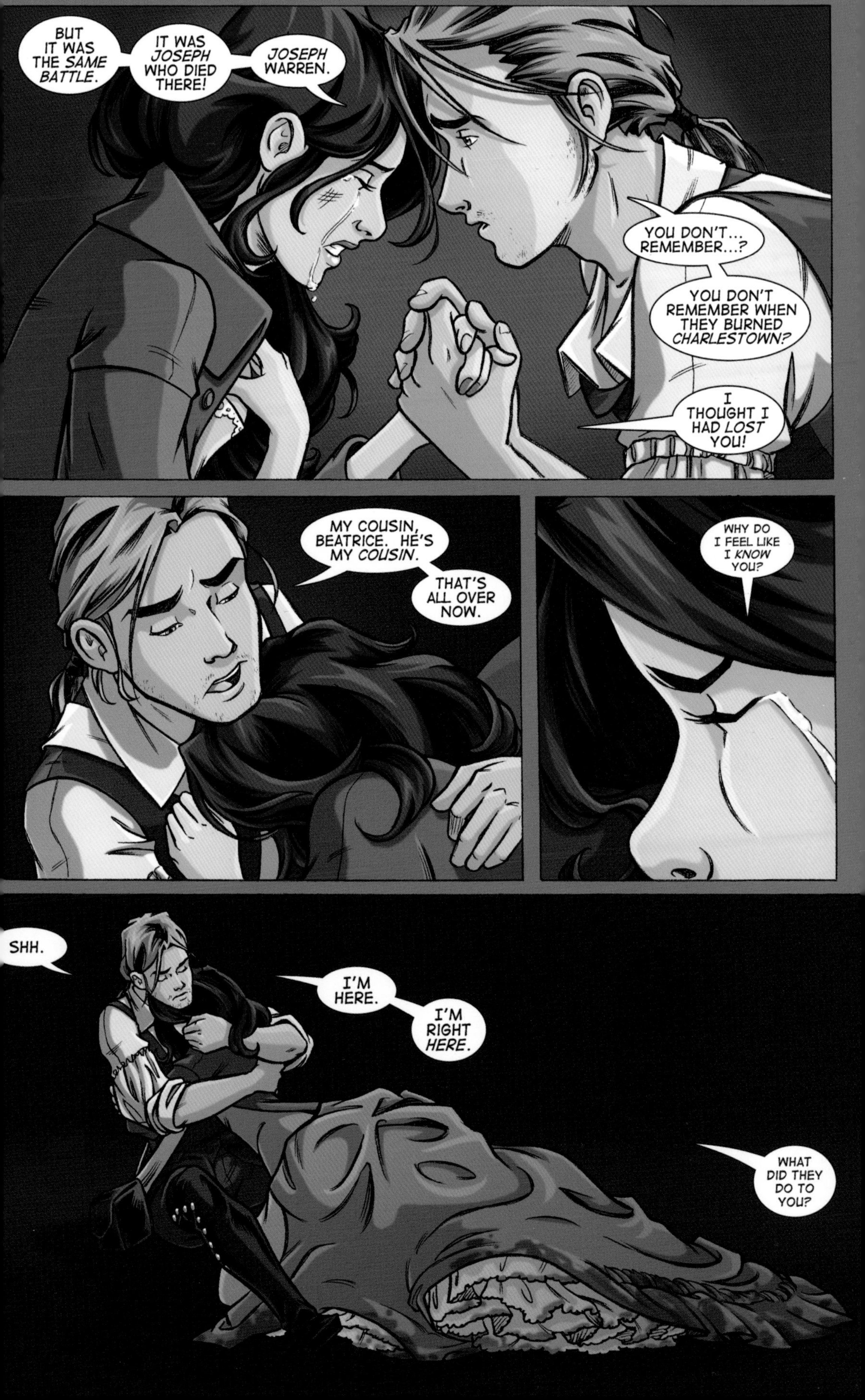
BUT IT WAS THE SAME BATTLE.
IT WAS JOSEPH WHO DIED THERE!
JOSEPH WARREN.
YOU DON'T... REMEMBER...?
YOU DON'T REMEMBER WHEN THEY BURNED CHARLESTOWN?
I THOUGHT I HAD LOST YOU!
MY COUSIN, BEATRICE. HE'S MY COUSIN.
THAT'S ALL OVER NOW.
WHY DO I FEEL LIKE I KNOW YOU?
SHH.
I'M HERE.
I'M RIGHT HERE.
WHAT DID THEY DO TO YOU?

YOU HAVE TO GO NOW.
THE HESSIANS ARE COMING.
OKAY.
I'M NOT DYING TODAY.
I PROMISE.
GO.
GOODBYE.
THAT IS SO HOT.
APPLE FARMER.
HE'S GOOD AT CLIMBING TREES.
I KNOW.
ARE YOU SURE YOU DON'T REMEMBER HIM?
...
I DON'T KNOW.
COME ON. LET'S GO.
HE TOLD US TO LEAVE.

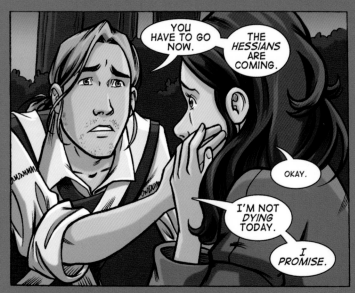

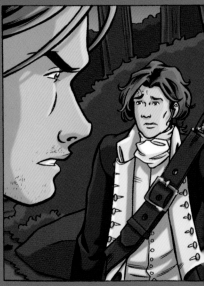

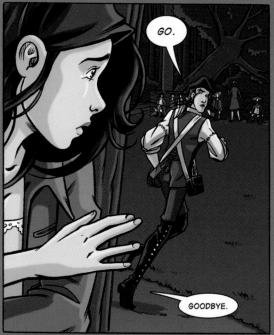

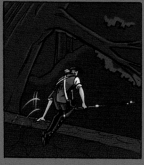

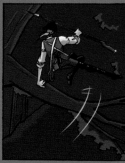

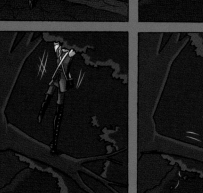

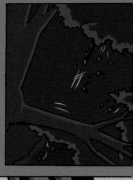

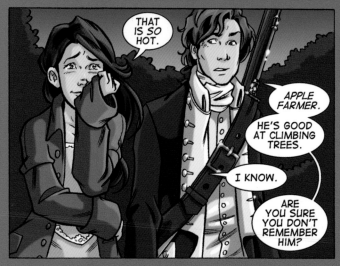

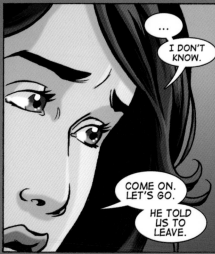

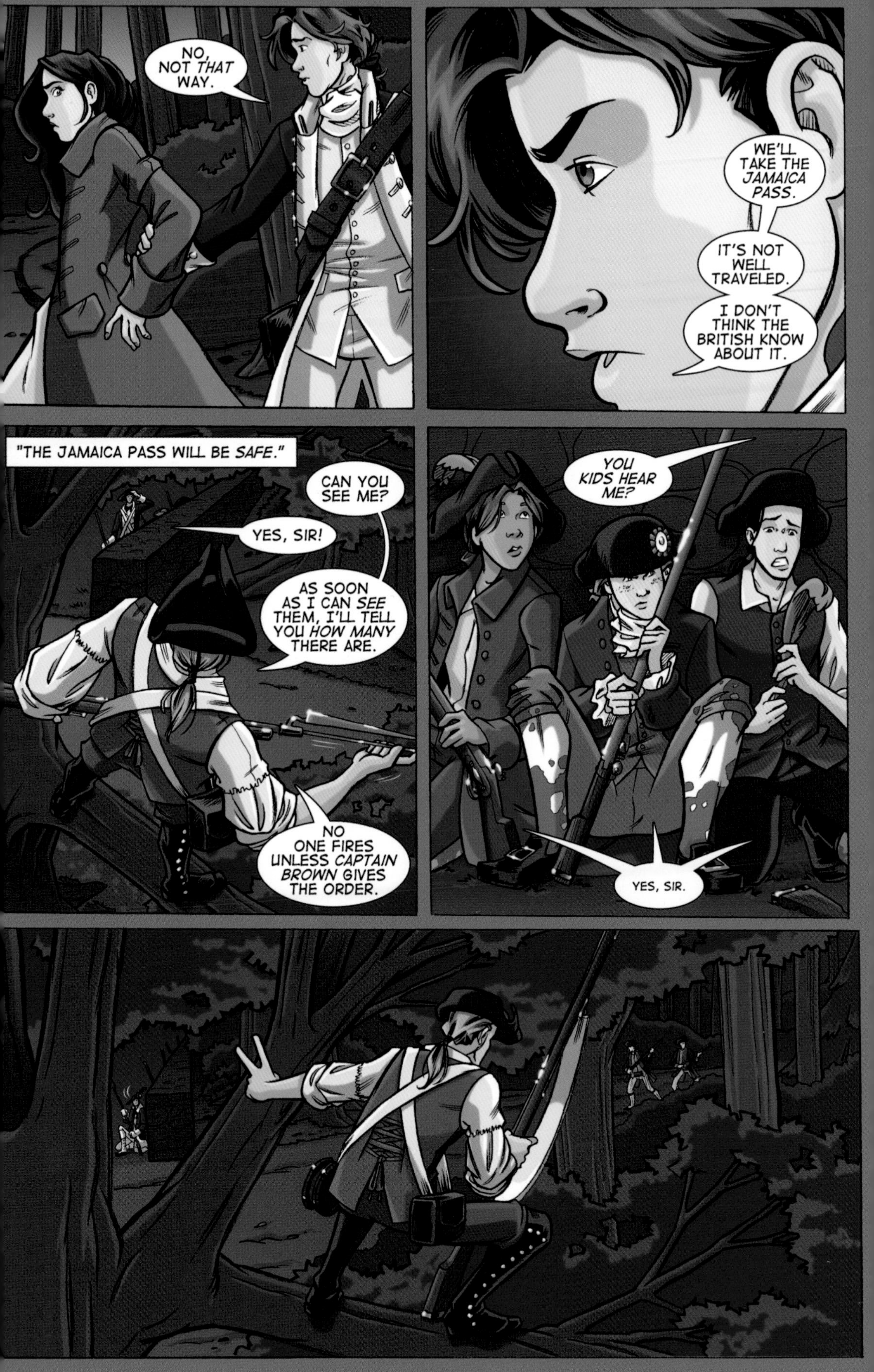
NO, NOT *THAT* WAY.
WE'LL TAKE THE *JAMAICA PASS*.
IT'S NOT WELL TRAVELED.
I DON'T THINK THE BRITISH KNOW ABOUT IT.
"THE JAMAICA PASS WILL BE *SAFE*."
CAN YOU SEE ME?
YES, SIR!
AS SOON AS I CAN *SEE* THEM, I'LL TELL YOU *HOW MANY* THERE ARE.
NO ONE FIRES UNLESS *CAPTAIN BROWN* GIVES THE ORDER.
YOU KIDS HEAR ME?
YES, SIR.

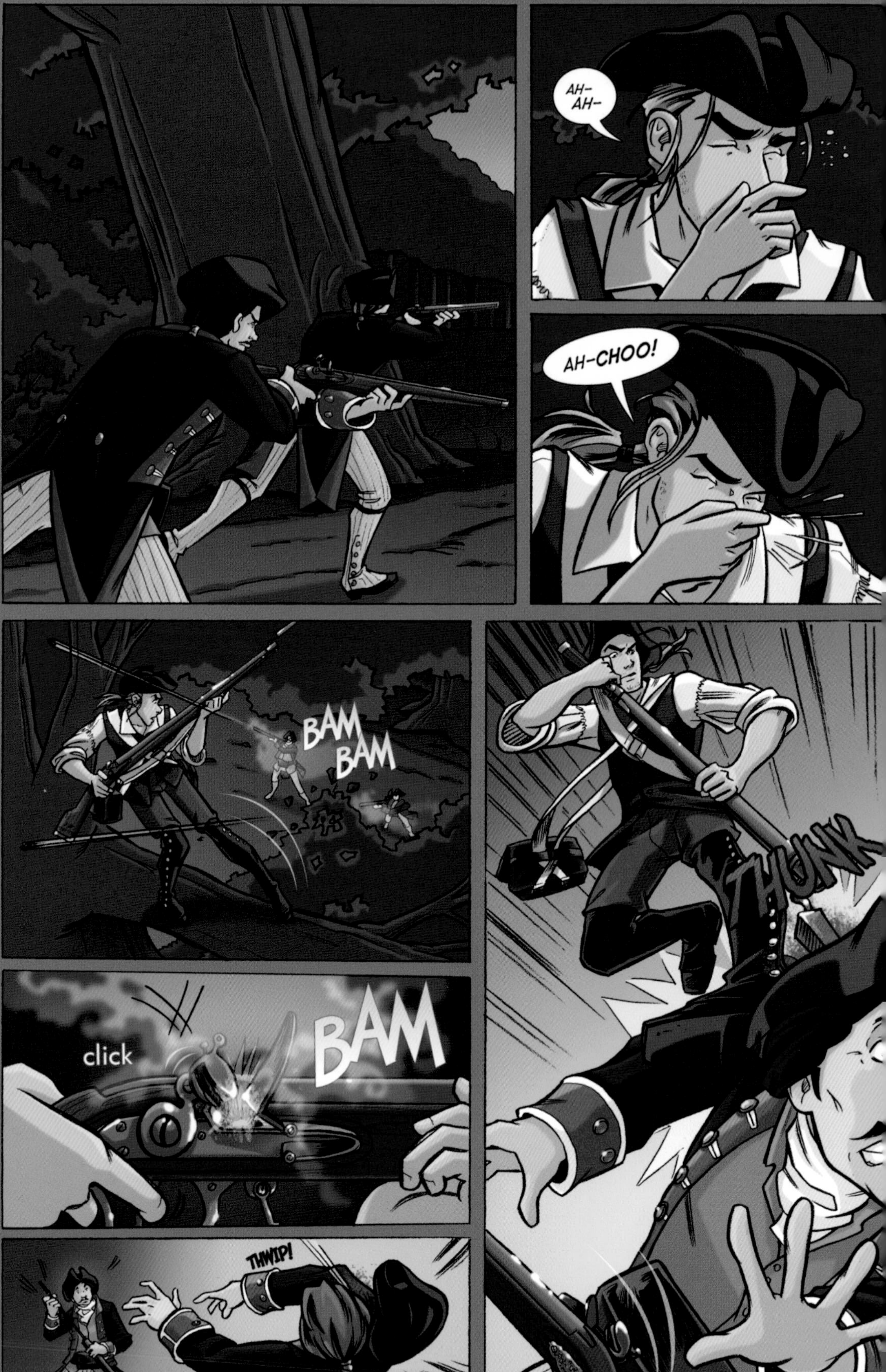
AH-
AH-
AH-CHOO!
BAM
BAM
THUNK
click
BAM
THWIP!

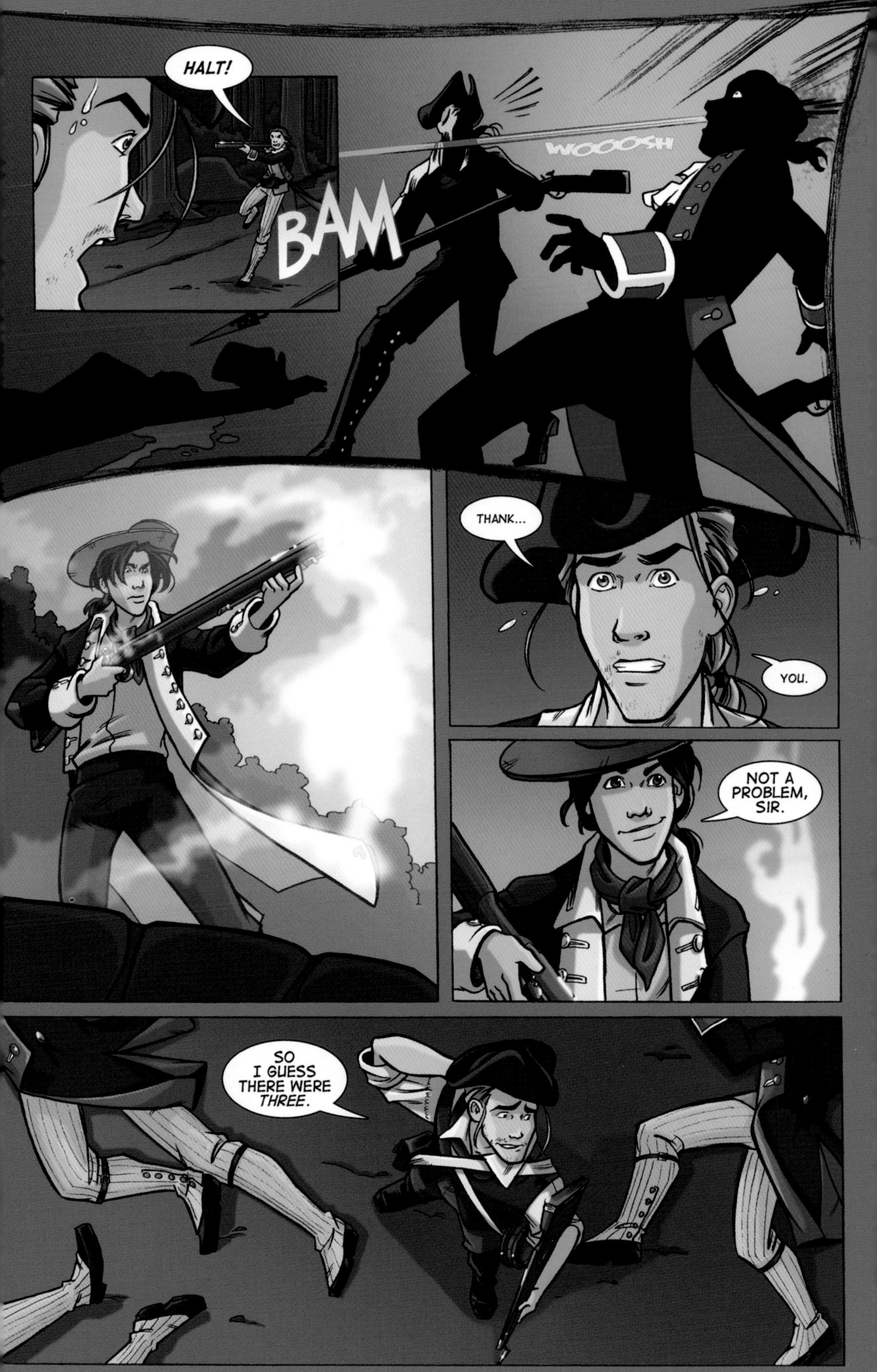
HALT!
WOOOSH
BAM
THANK...
YOU.
NOT A PROBLEM, SIR.
SO I GUESS THERE WERE *THREE*.

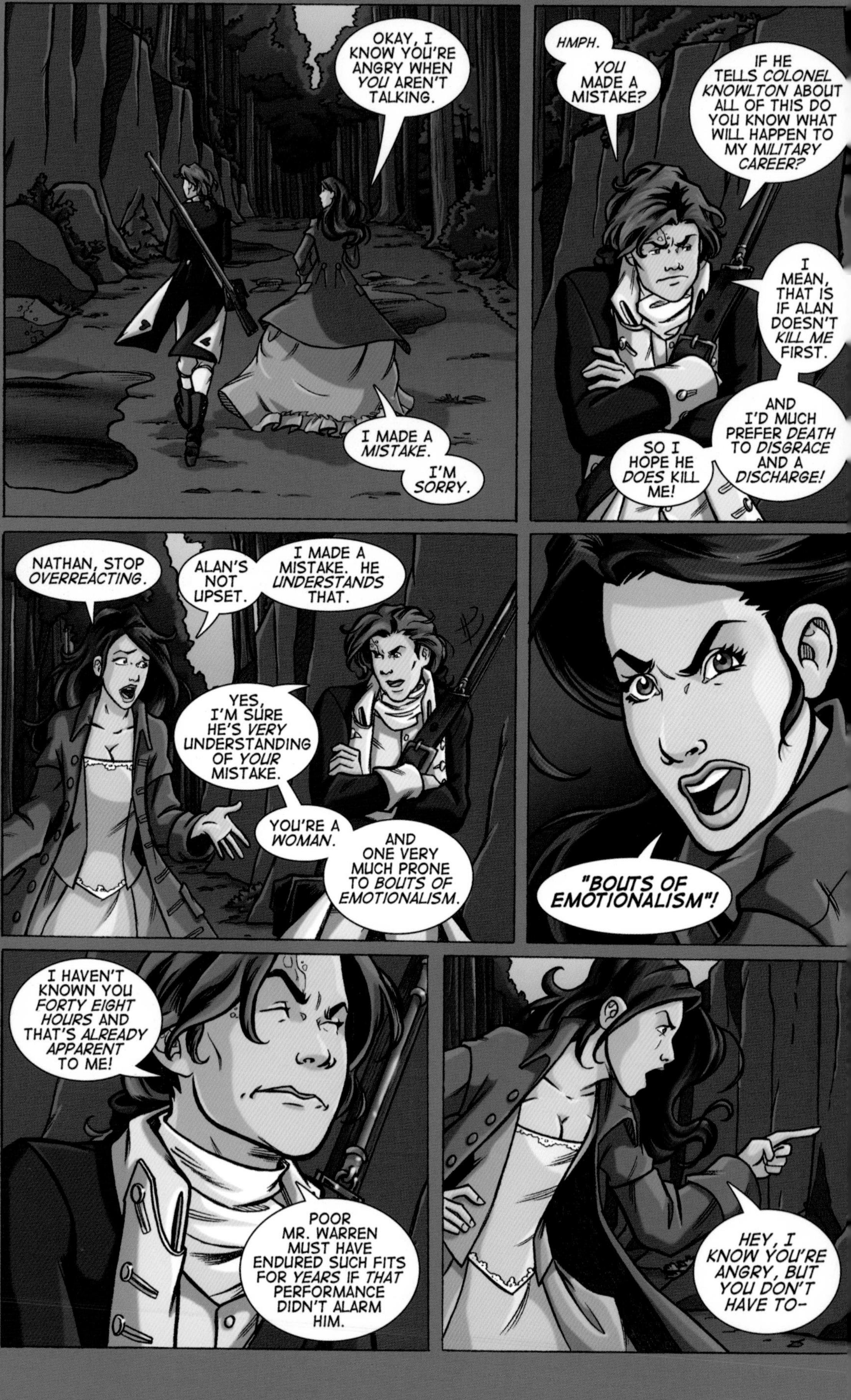
OKAY, I KNOW YOU'RE ANGRY WHEN *YOU* AREN'T TALKING.
I MADE A *MISTAKE*.
I'M *SORRY*.
HMPH.
YOU MADE A MISTAKE?
IF HE TELLS *COLONEL KNOWLTON* ABOUT ALL OF THIS DO YOU KNOW WHAT WILL HAPPEN TO MY *MILITARY CAREER?*
I MEAN, THAT IS IF ALAN DOESN'T *KILL ME* FIRST.
AND I'D MUCH PREFER *DEATH* TO *DISGRACE* AND A *DISCHARGE!*
SO I HOPE HE *DOES* KILL ME!
NATHAN, STOP *OVERREACTING*.
ALAN'S NOT UPSET.
I MADE A MISTAKE. HE *UNDERSTANDS* THAT.
YES, I'M SURE HE'S *VERY* UNDERSTANDING OF *YOUR* MISTAKE.
YOU'RE A *WOMAN*.
AND ONE VERY MUCH PRONE TO *BOUTS OF EMOTIONALISM*.
"BOUTS OF EMOTIONALISM"!
I HAVEN'T KNOWN YOU *FORTY EIGHT HOURS* AND THAT'S *ALREADY APPARENT* TO ME!
POOR MR. WARREN MUST HAVE ENDURED SUCH FITS FOR *YEARS* IF *THAT* PERFORMANCE DIDN'T ALARM HIM.
HEY, I KNOW YOU'RE ANGRY, BUT YOU DON'T HAVE TO–

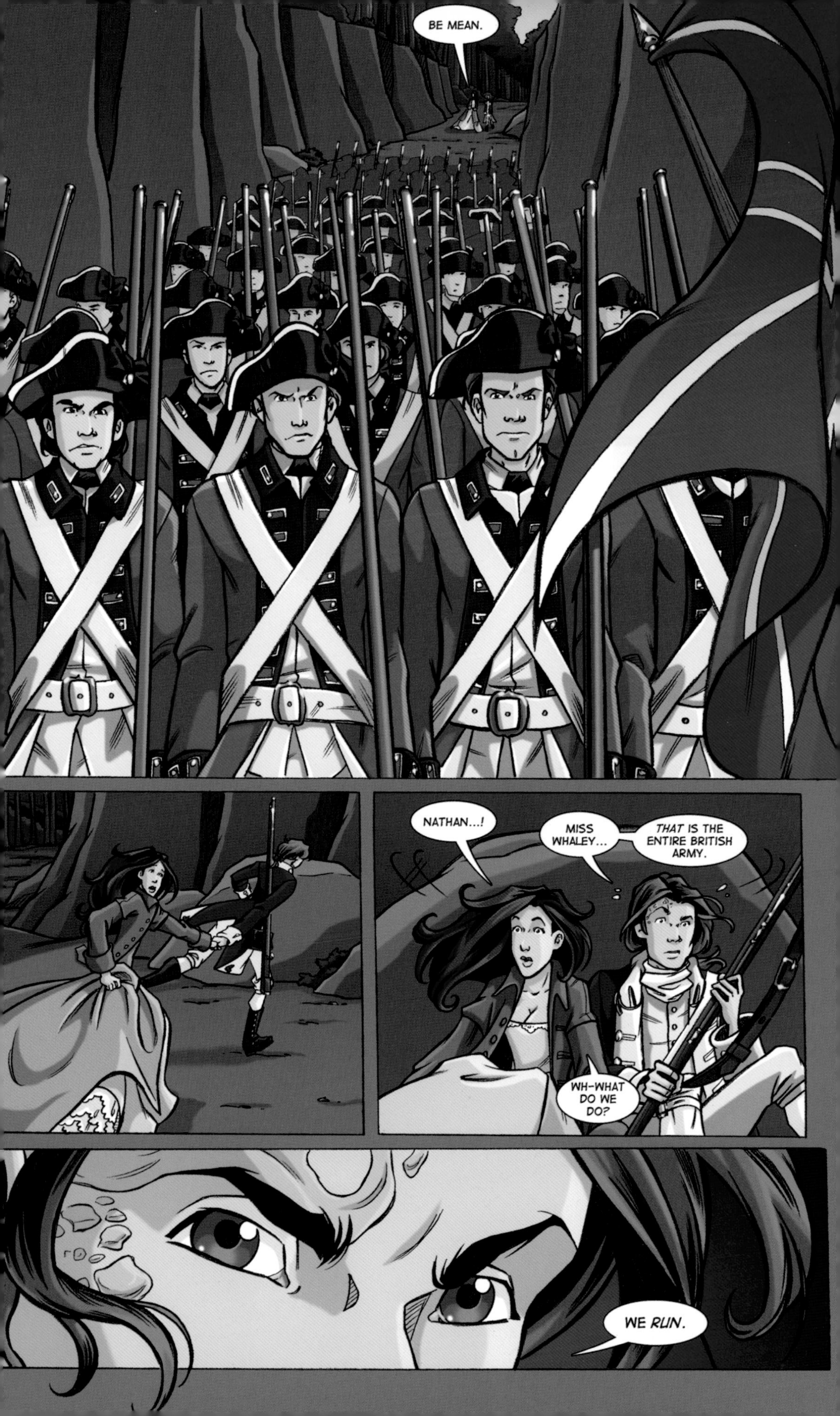
BE MEAN.
NATHAN...!
MISS WHALEY...
THAT IS THE ENTIRE BRITISH ARMY.
WH-WHAT DO WE DO?
WE *RUN*.

Chapter Five

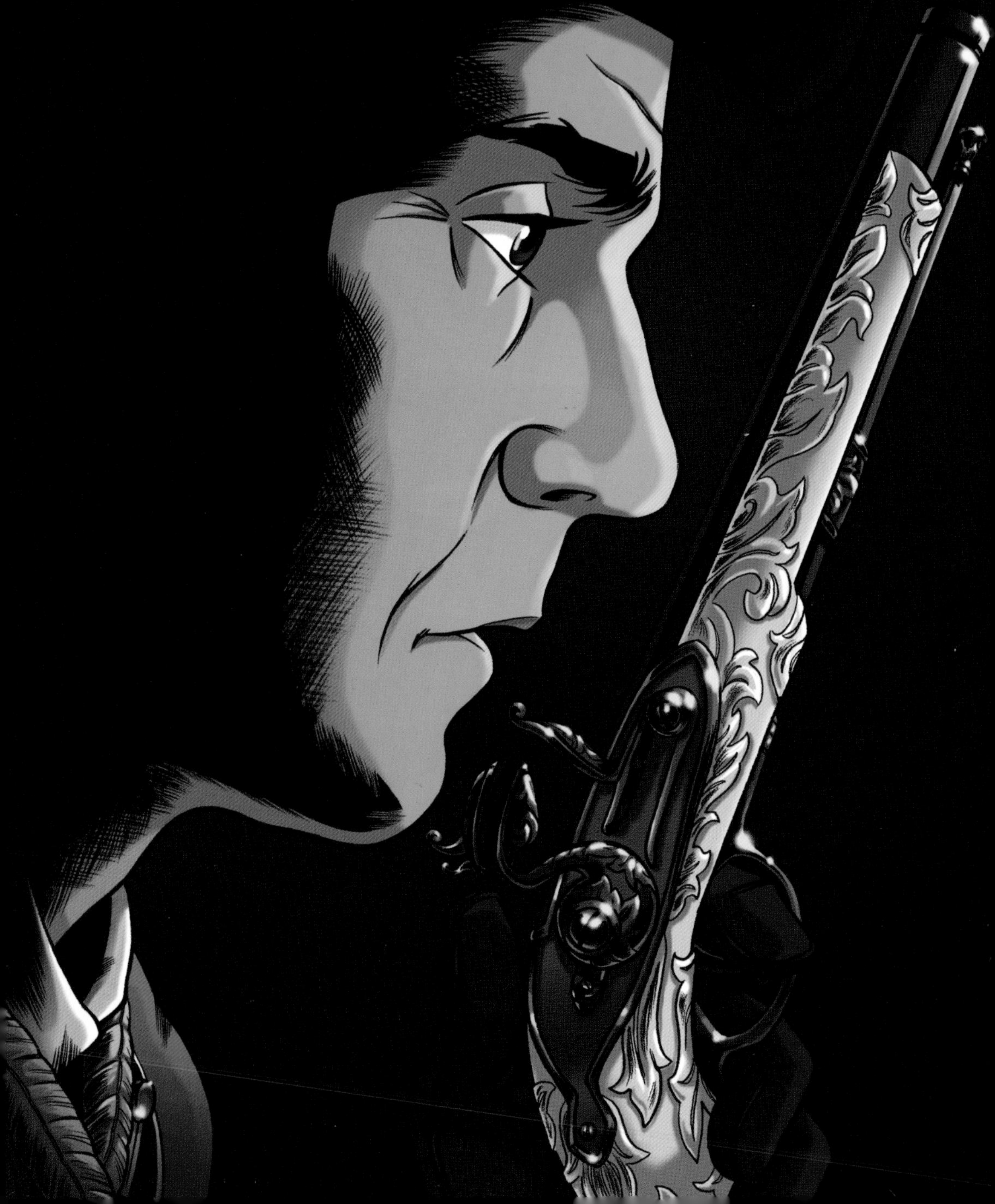

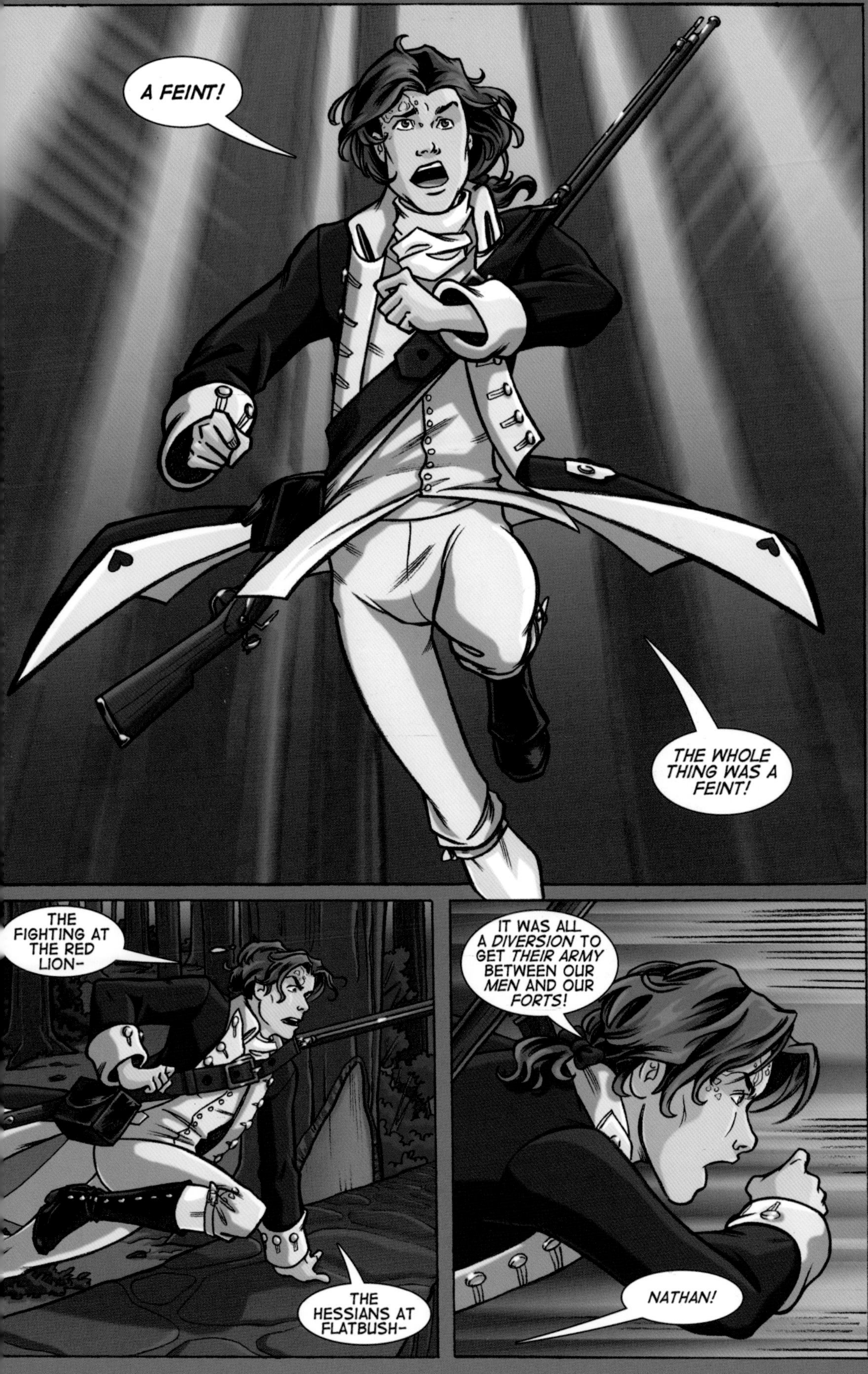
A FEINT!
THE WHOLE THING WAS A FEINT!
THE FIGHTING AT THE RED LION-
THE HESSIANS AT FLATBUSH-
IT WAS ALL A DIVERSION TO GET THEIR ARMY BETWEEN OUR MEN AND OUR FORTS!
NATHAN!

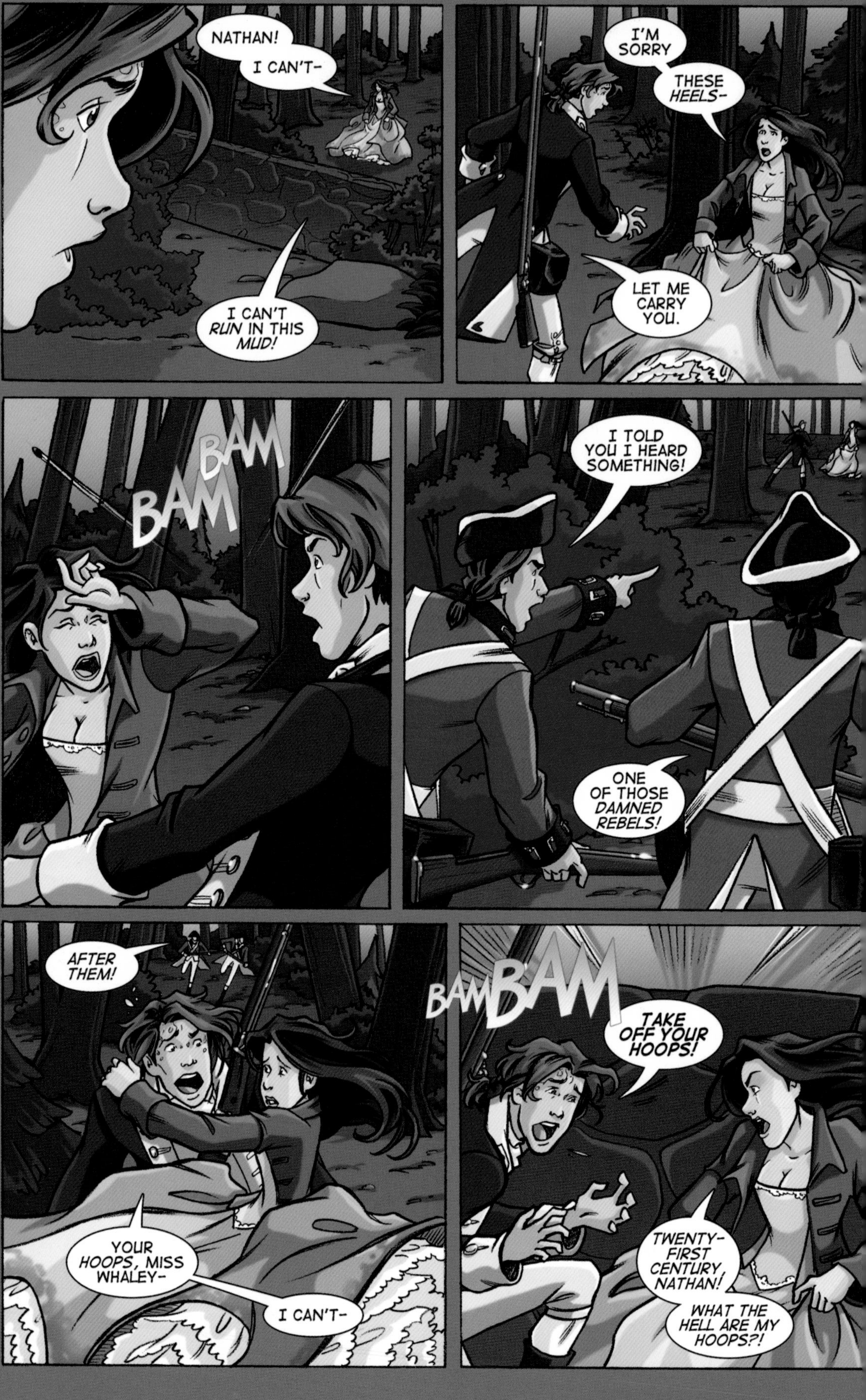

NATHAN!
I CAN'T-
I CAN'T *RUN* IN THIS *MUD!*
I'M SORRY
THESE *HEELS*-
LET ME CARRY YOU.
BAM
BAM
I TOLD YOU I HEARD SOMETHING!
ONE OF THOSE *DAMNED REBELS!*
AFTER THEM!
YOUR HOOPS, MISS WHALEY-
I CAN'T-
BAM
BAM
TAKE OFF YOUR HOOPS!
TWENTY-FIRST CENTURY, NATHAN!
WHAT THE HELL ARE MY HOOPS?!

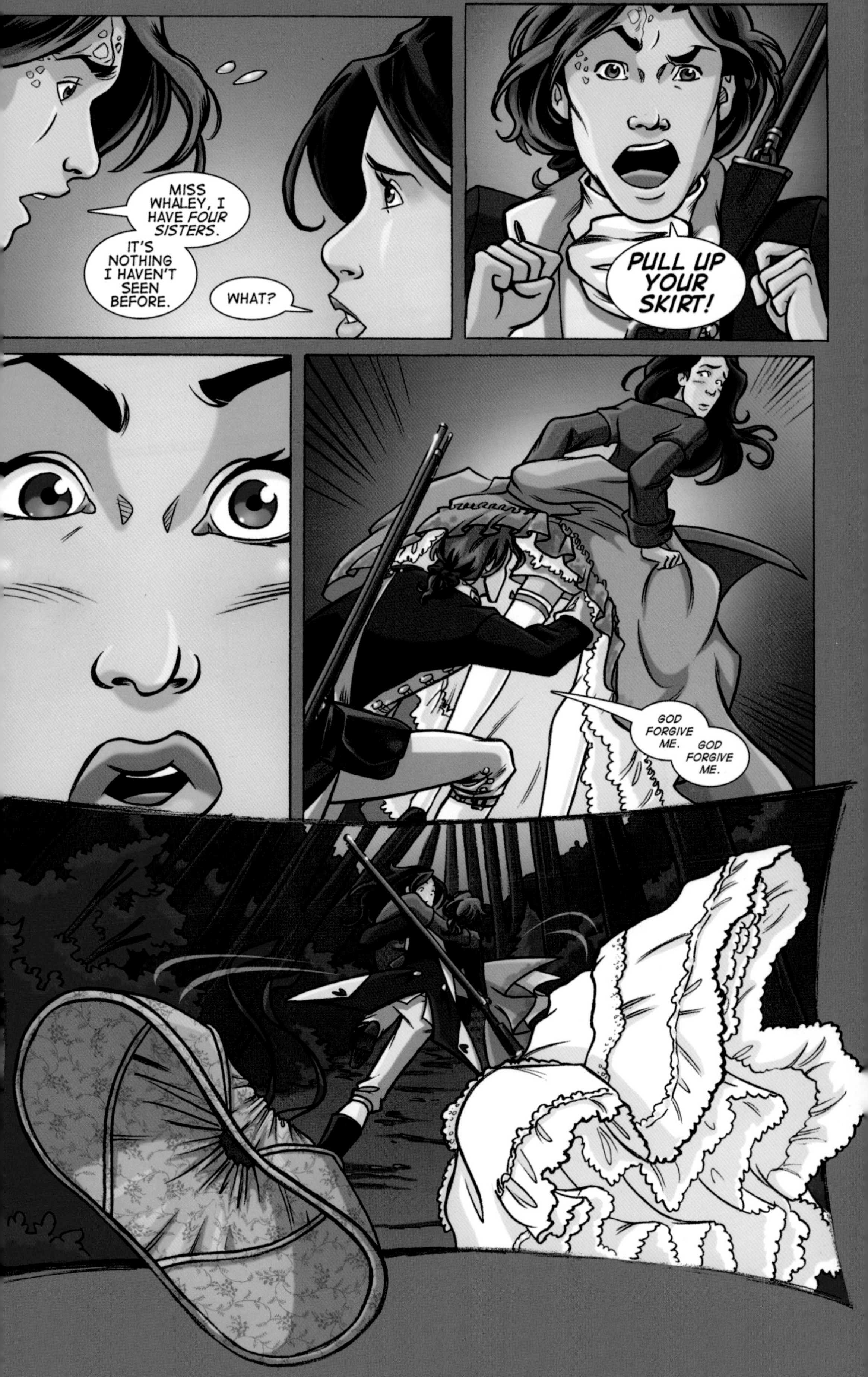

MISS WHALEY, I HAVE FOUR SISTERS.
IT'S NOTHING I HAVEN'T SEEN BEFORE.
WHAT?
PULL UP YOUR SKIRT!
GOD FORGIVE ME.
GOD FORGIVE ME.

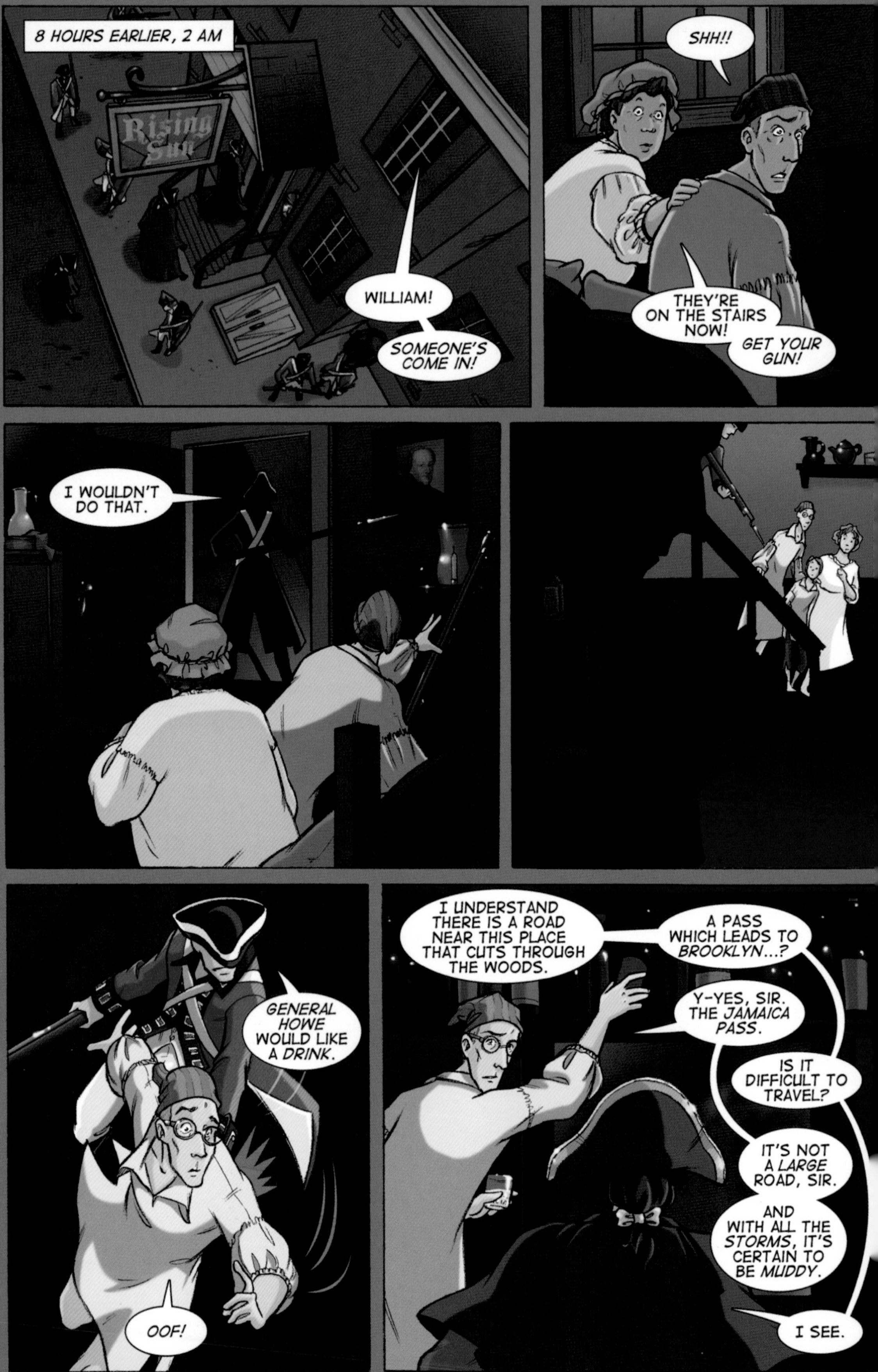
8 HOURS EARLIER, 2 AM
Rising Sun
WILLIAM!
SOMEONE'S COME IN!
SHH!!
THEY'RE ON THE STAIRS NOW!
GET YOUR GUN!
I WOULDN'T DO THAT.
GENERAL HOWE WOULD LIKE A DRINK.
OOF!
I UNDERSTAND THERE IS A ROAD NEAR THIS PLACE THAT CUTS THROUGH THE WOODS.
A PASS WHICH LEADS TO BROOKLYN...?
Y-YES, SIR. THE JAMAICA PASS.
IS IT DIFFICULT TO TRAVEL?
IT'S NOT A LARGE ROAD, SIR.
AND WITH ALL THE STORMS, IT'S CERTAIN TO BE MUDDY.
I SEE.

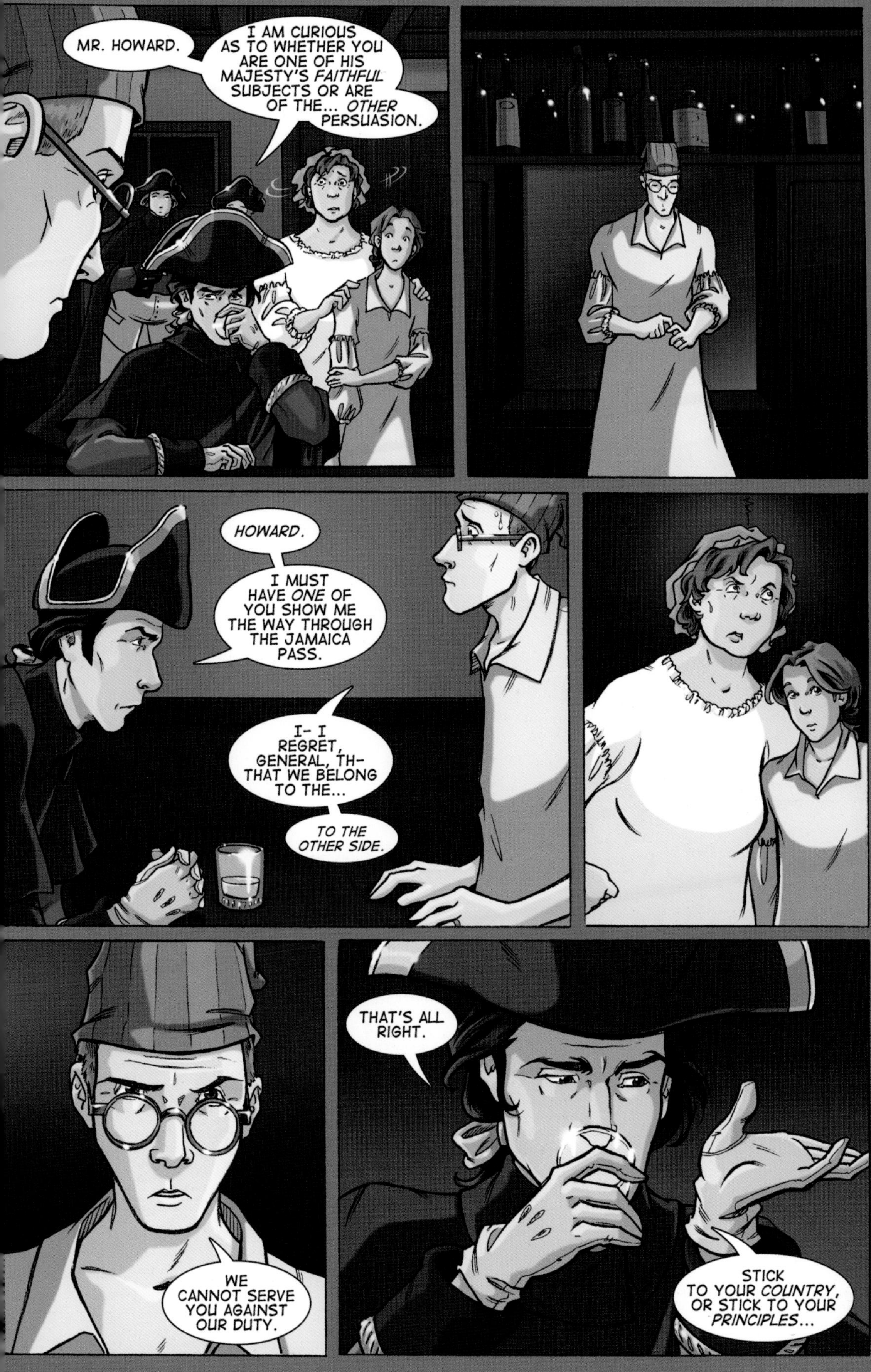
MR. HOWARD.
I AM CURIOUS AS TO WHETHER YOU ARE ONE OF HIS MAJESTY'S *FAITHFUL* SUBJECTS OR ARE OF THE... *OTHER* PERSUASION.
HOWARD.
I MUST HAVE *ONE* OF YOU SHOW ME THE WAY THROUGH THE JAMAICA PASS.
I- I REGRET, GENERAL, TH- THAT WE BELONG TO THE...
TO THE OTHER SIDE.
WE CANNOT SERVE YOU AGAINST OUR DUTY.
THAT'S ALL RIGHT.
STICK TO YOUR *COUNTRY*, OR STICK TO YOUR *PRINCIPLES*...

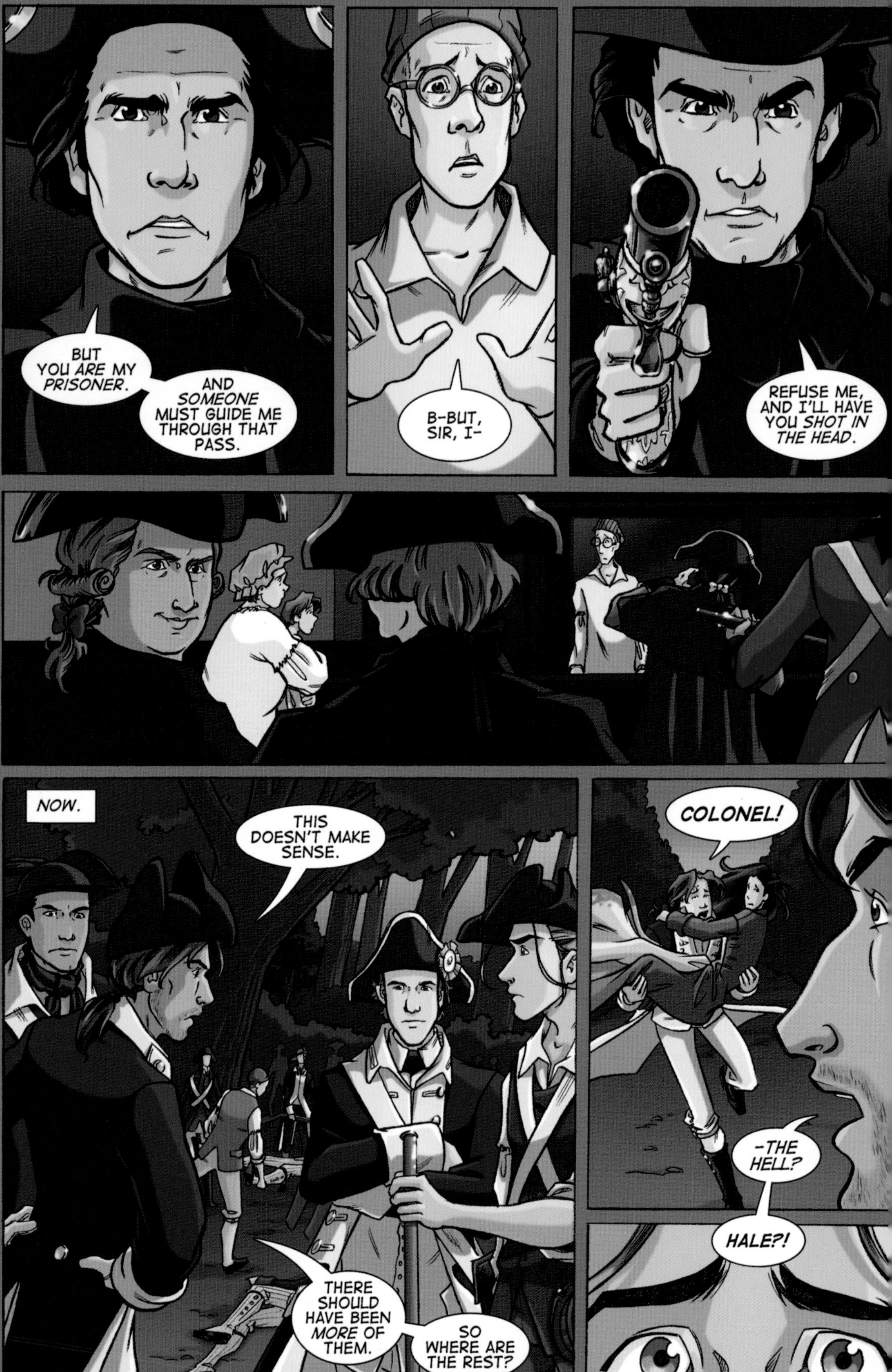
BUT YOU ARE MY PRISONER.
AND SOMEONE MUST GUIDE ME THROUGH THAT PASS.
B-BUT, SIR, I-
REFUSE ME, AND I'LL HAVE YOU SHOT IN THE HEAD.
NOW.
THIS DOESN'T MAKE SENSE.
THERE SHOULD HAVE BEEN MORE OF THEM.
SO WHERE ARE THE REST?
COLONEL!
-THE HELL?
HALE?!

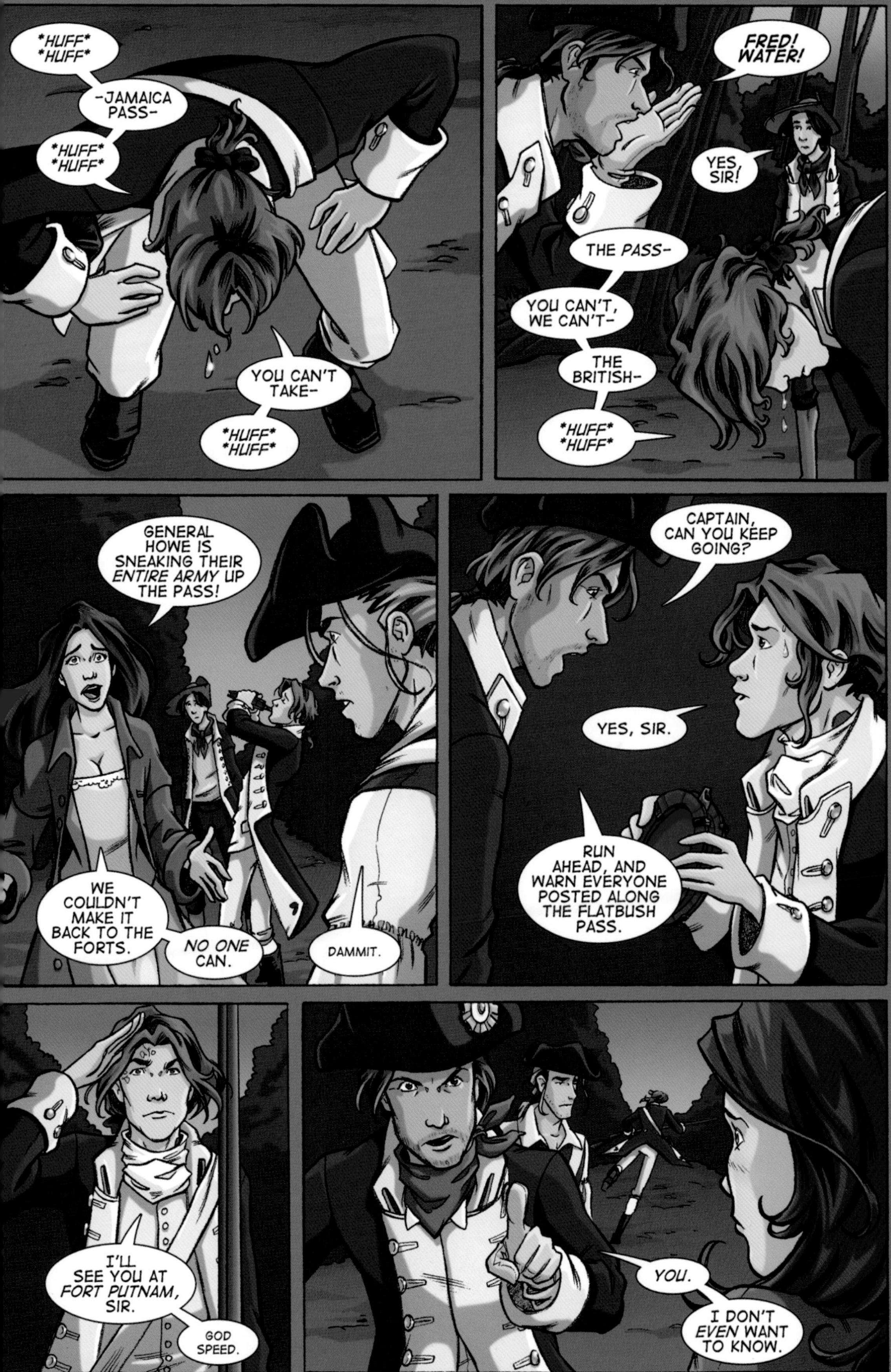
HUFF *HUFF*
-JAMAICA PASS-
HUFF *HUFF*
YOU CAN'T TAKE-
HUFF *HUFF*
FRED! WATER!
YES, SIR!
THE PASS-
YOU CAN'T, WE CAN'T-
THE BRITISH-
HUFF *HUFF*
GENERAL HOWE IS SNEAKING THEIR ENTIRE ARMY UP THE PASS!
WE COULDN'T MAKE IT BACK TO THE FORTS.
NO ONE CAN.
DAMMIT.
CAPTAIN, CAN YOU KEEP GOING?
YES, SIR.
RUN AHEAD, AND WARN EVERYONE POSTED ALONG THE FLATBUSH PASS.
I'LL SEE YOU AT FORT PUTNAM, SIR.
GOD SPEED.
YOU.
I DON'T EVEN WANT TO KNOW.

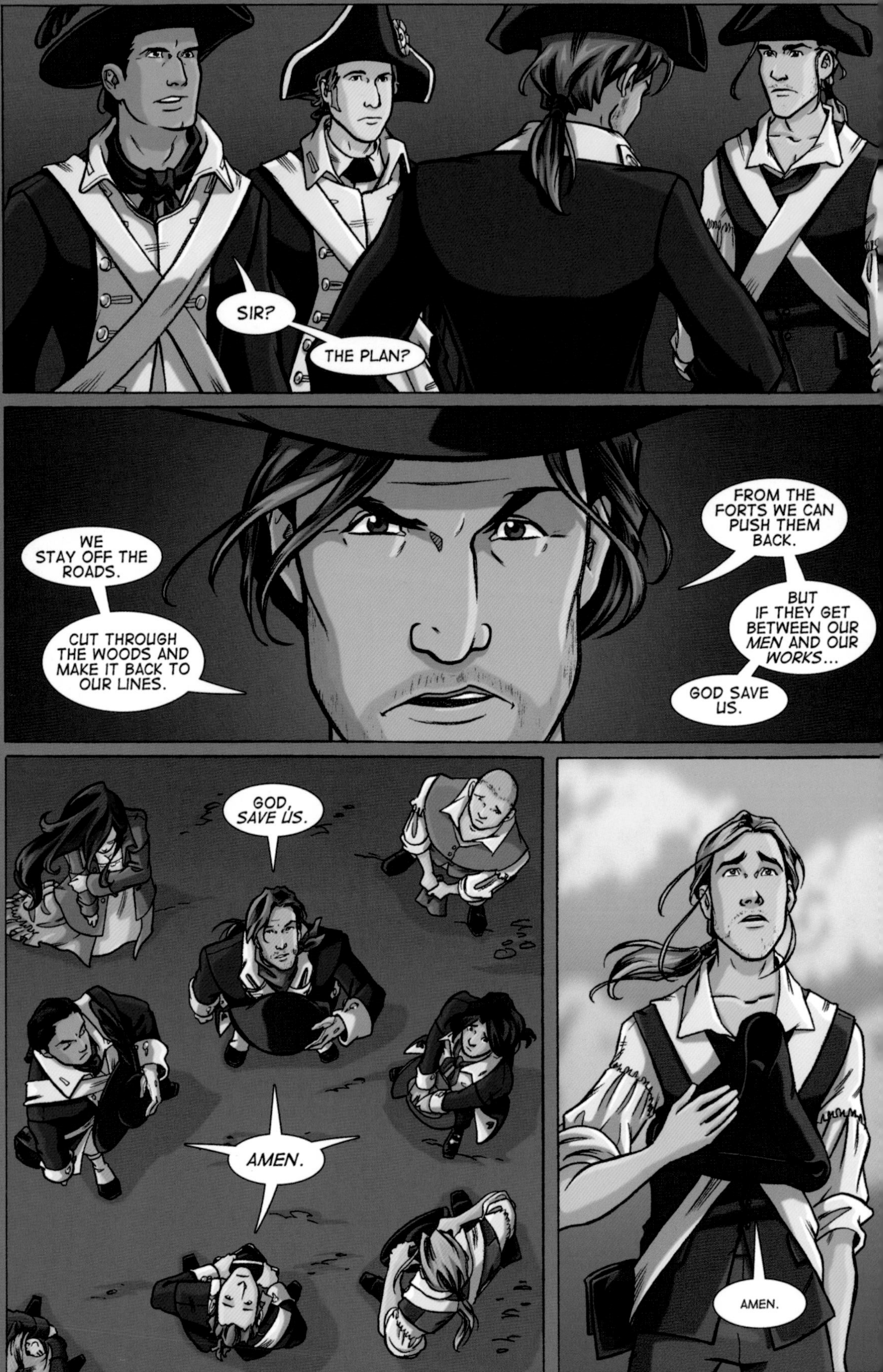
SIR?
THE PLAN?
WE STAY OFF THE ROADS.
CUT THROUGH THE WOODS AND MAKE IT BACK TO OUR LINES.
FROM THE FORTS WE CAN PUSH THEM BACK.
BUT IF THEY GET BETWEEN OUR *MEN* AND OUR *WORKS*...
GOD SAVE US.
GOD, *SAVE US.*
AMEN.
AMEN.

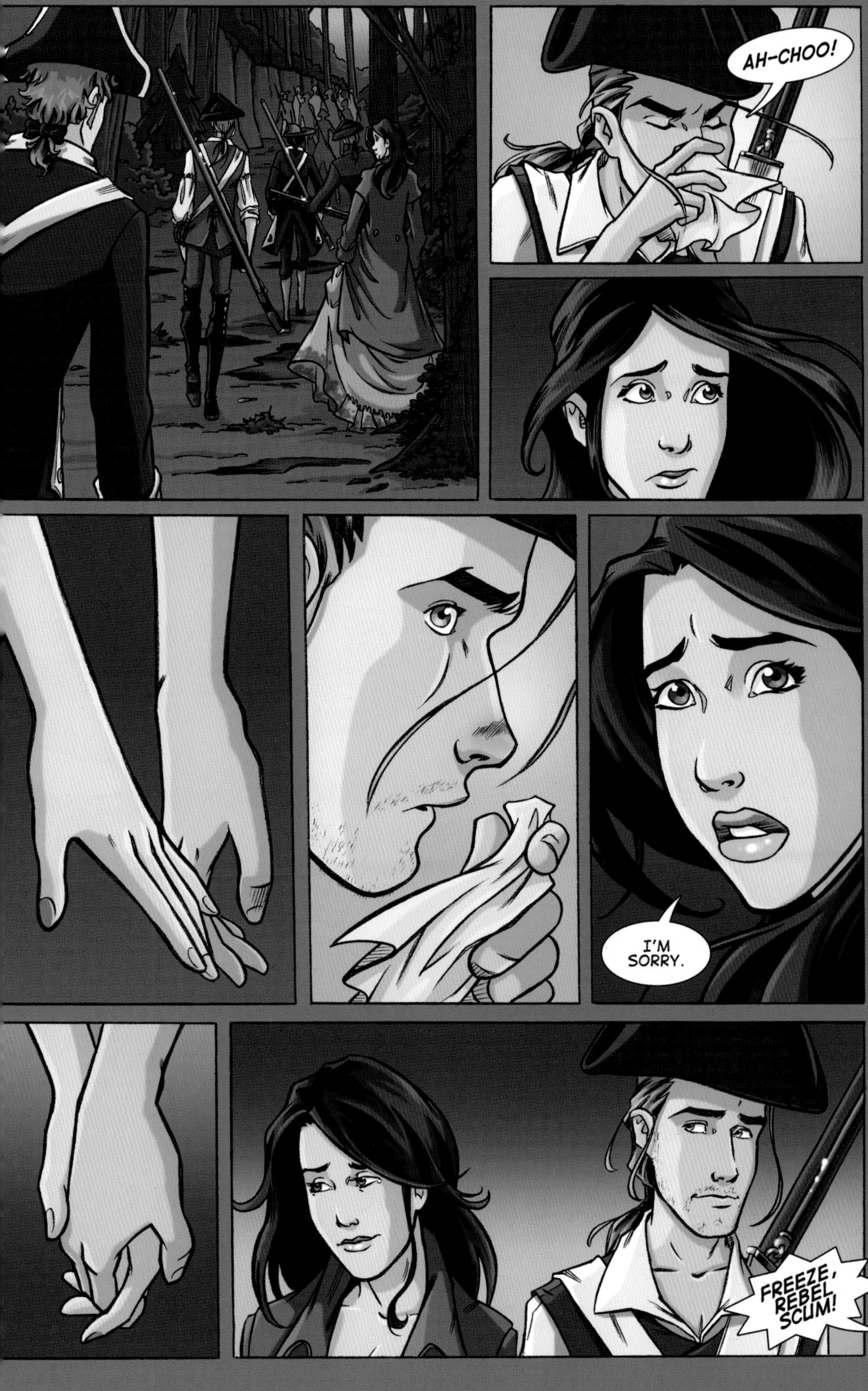
AH-CHOO!
I'M SORRY.
FREEZE, REBEL SCUM!

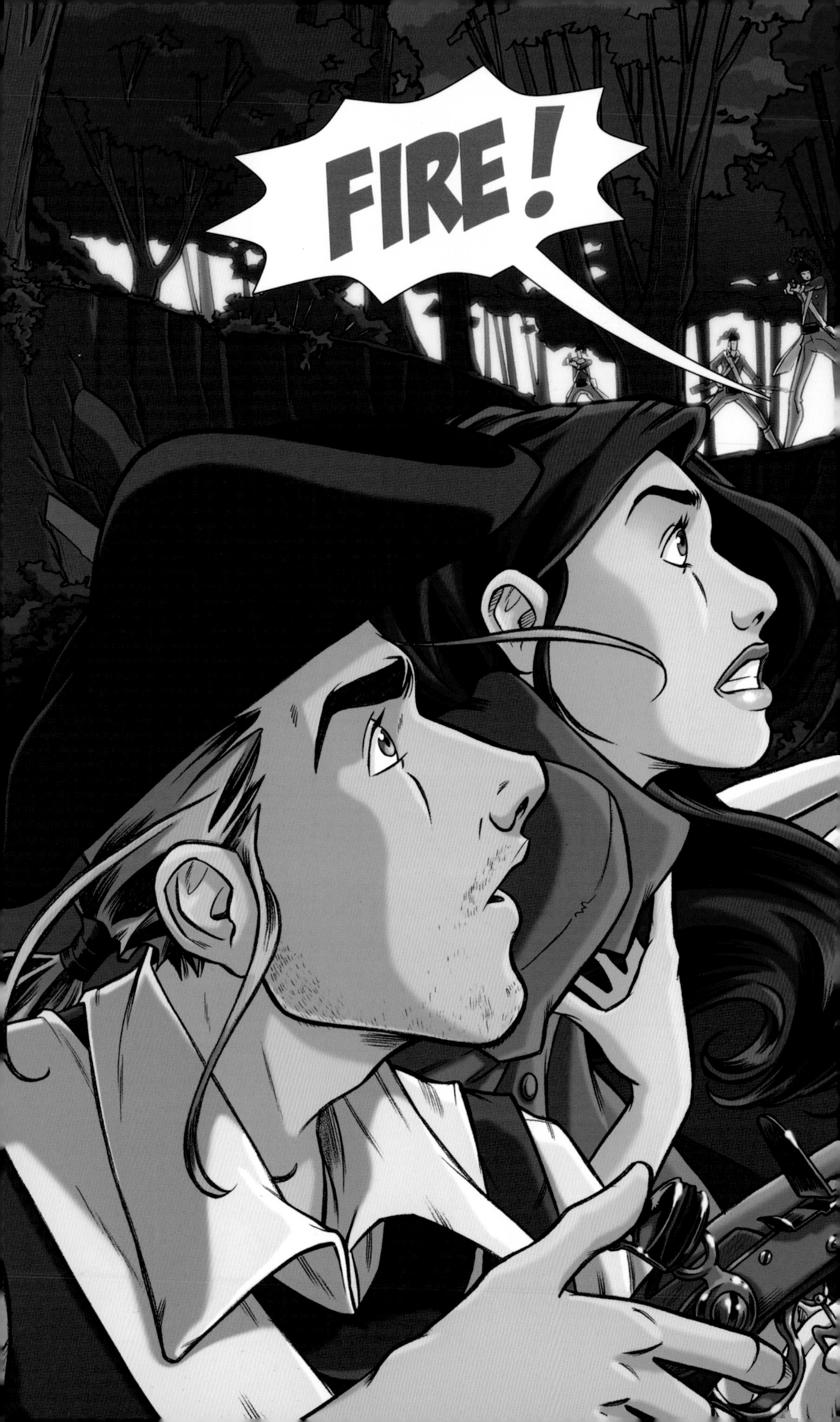
FIRE!

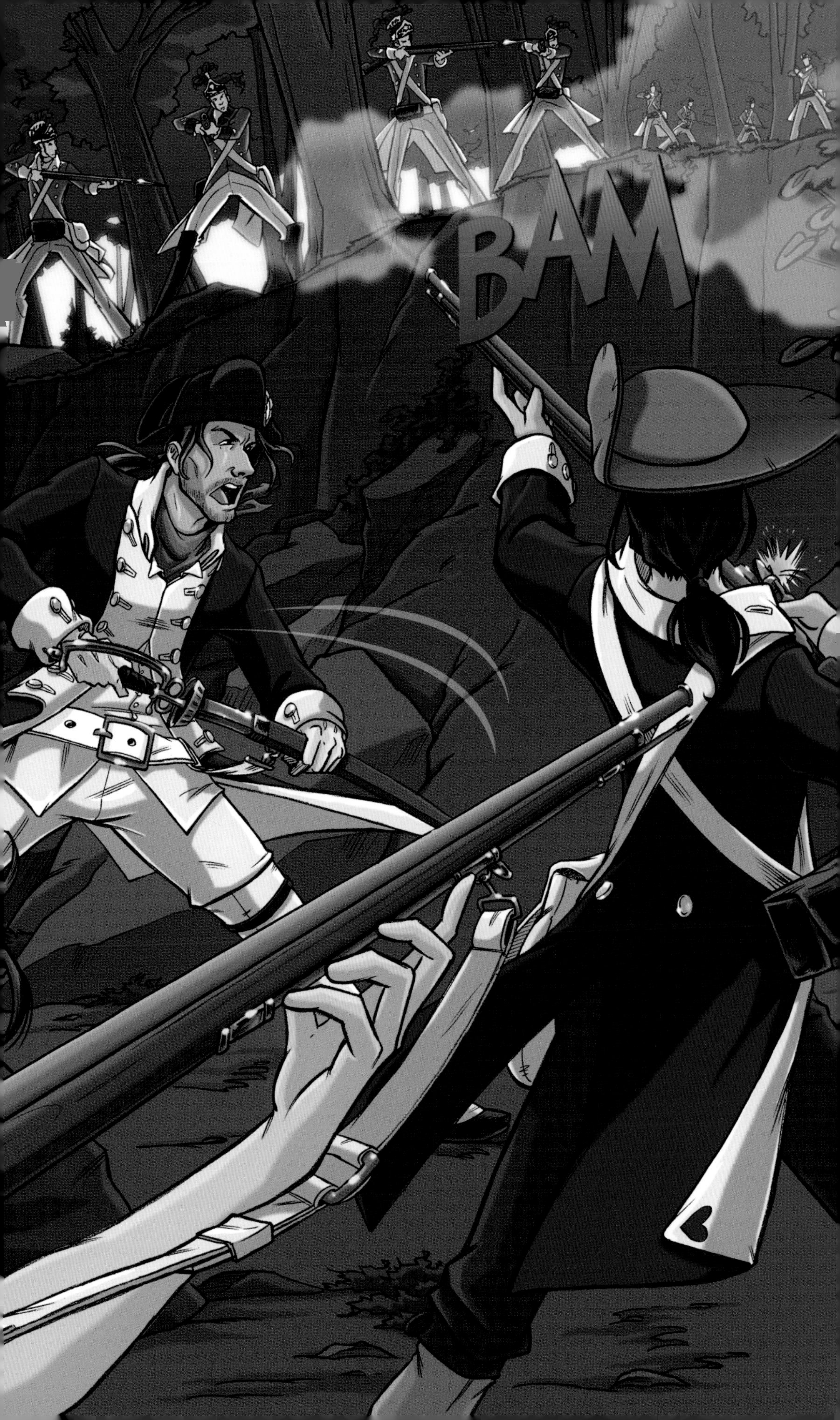
BAM

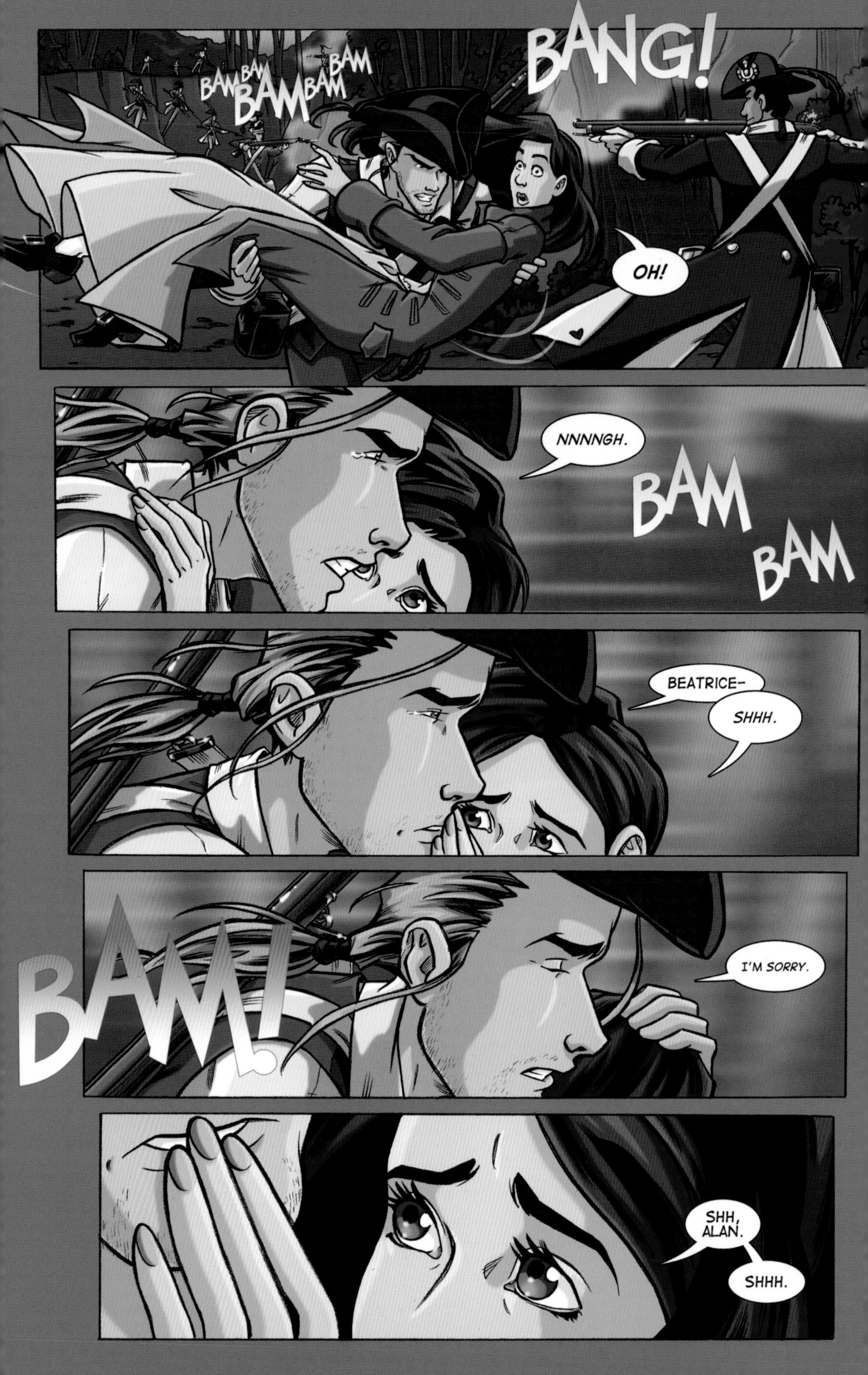
BAM BAM BAM BAM BAM
BANG!
OH!
NNNNGH.
BAM
BAM
BEATRICE-
SHHH.
BAM!
I'M SORRY.
SHH, ALAN.
SHHH.

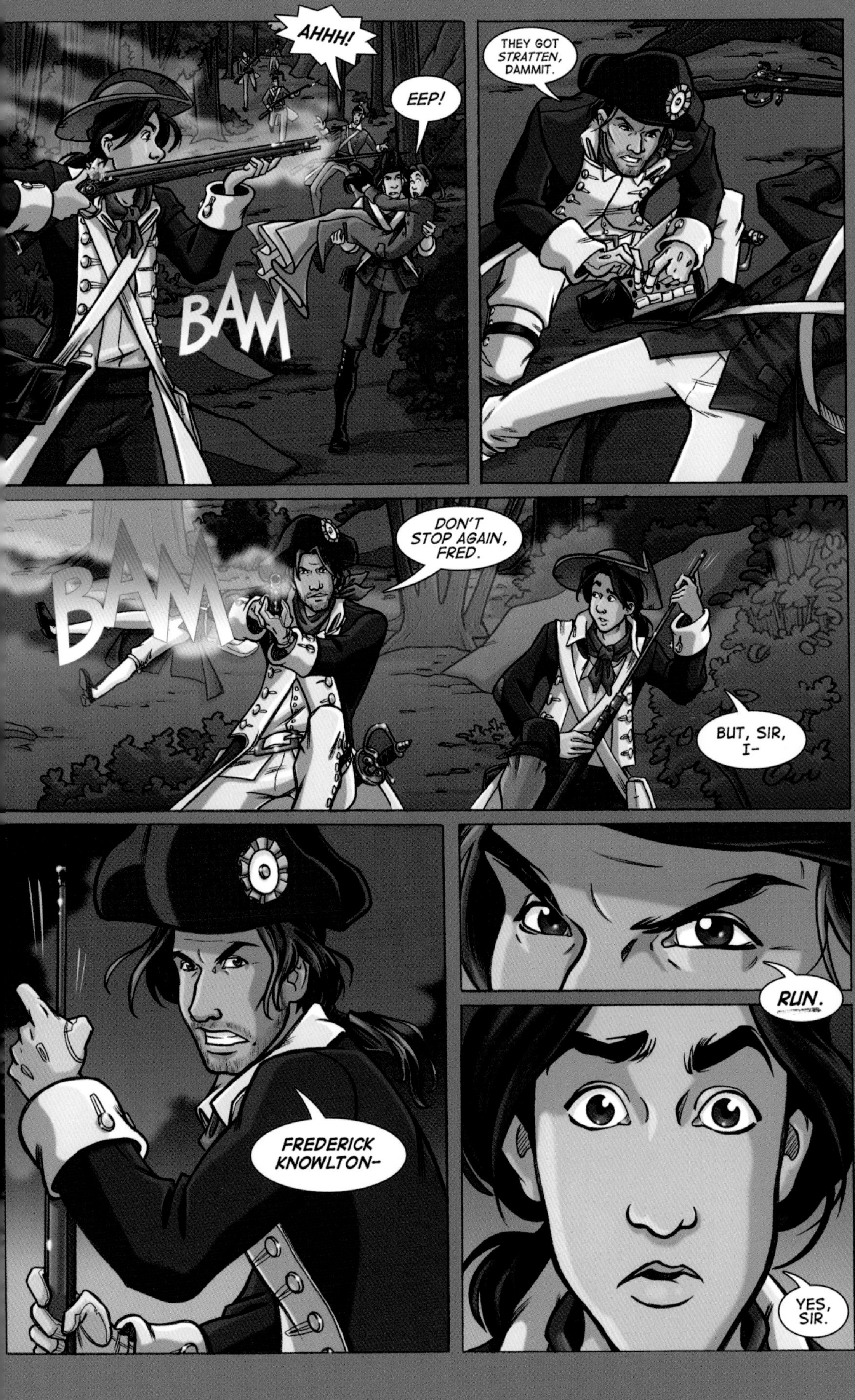
AHHH!
EEP!
BAM
THEY GOT STRATTEN, DAMMIT.
BAM
DON'T STOP AGAIN, FRED.
BUT, SIR, I-
FREDERICK KNOWLTON-
RUN.
YES, SIR.

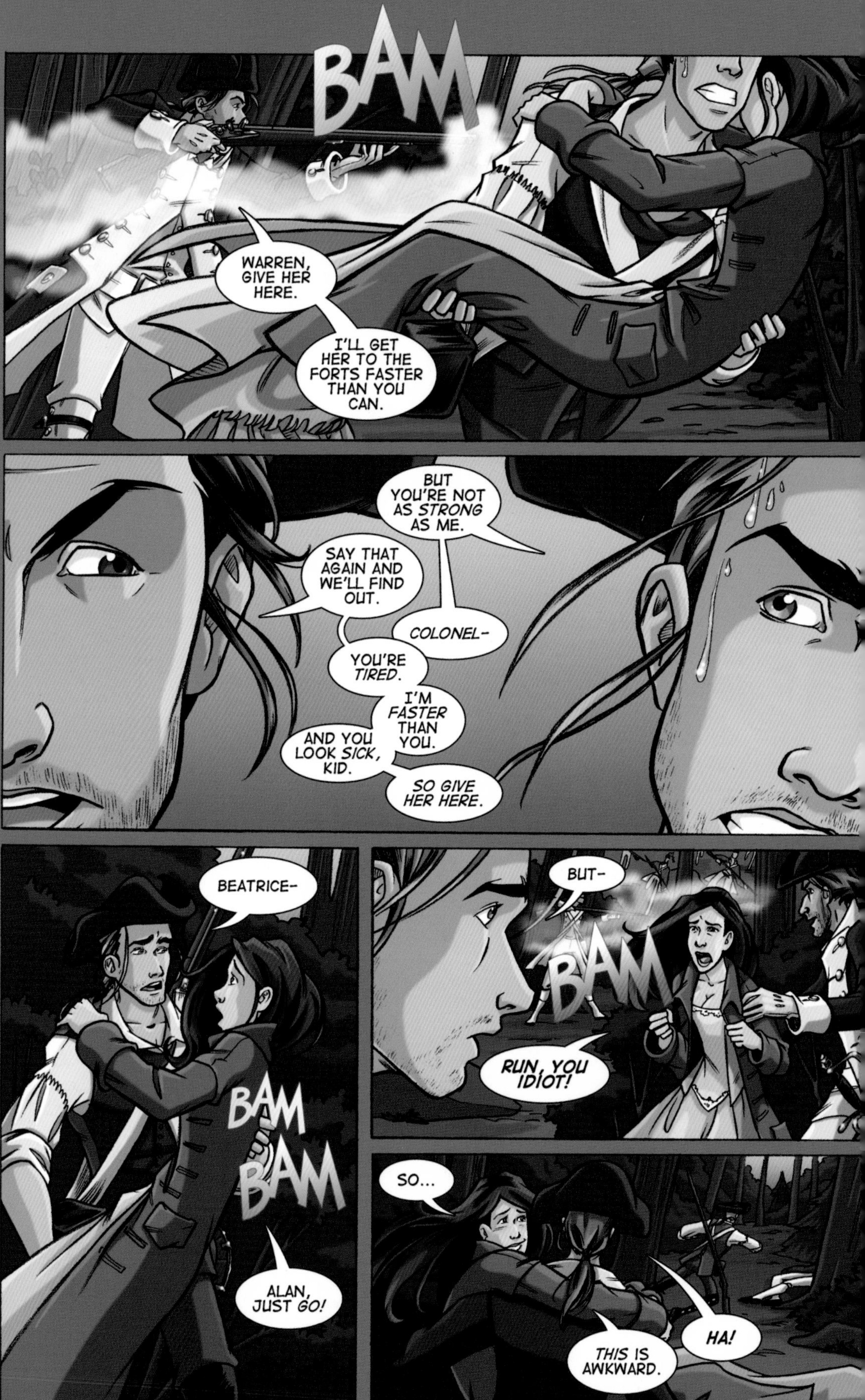
BAM
WARREN, GIVE HER HERE.
I'LL GET HER TO THE FORTS FASTER THAN YOU CAN.
BUT YOU'RE NOT AS STRONG AS ME.
SAY THAT AGAIN AND WE'LL FIND OUT.
COLONEL-
YOU'RE TIRED.
I'M FASTER THAN YOU.
AND YOU LOOK SICK, KID.
SO GIVE HER HERE.
BEATRICE-
BAM
BAM
ALAN, JUST GO!
BUT-
BAM
RUN, YOU IDIOT!
SO...
HA!
THIS IS AWKWARD.

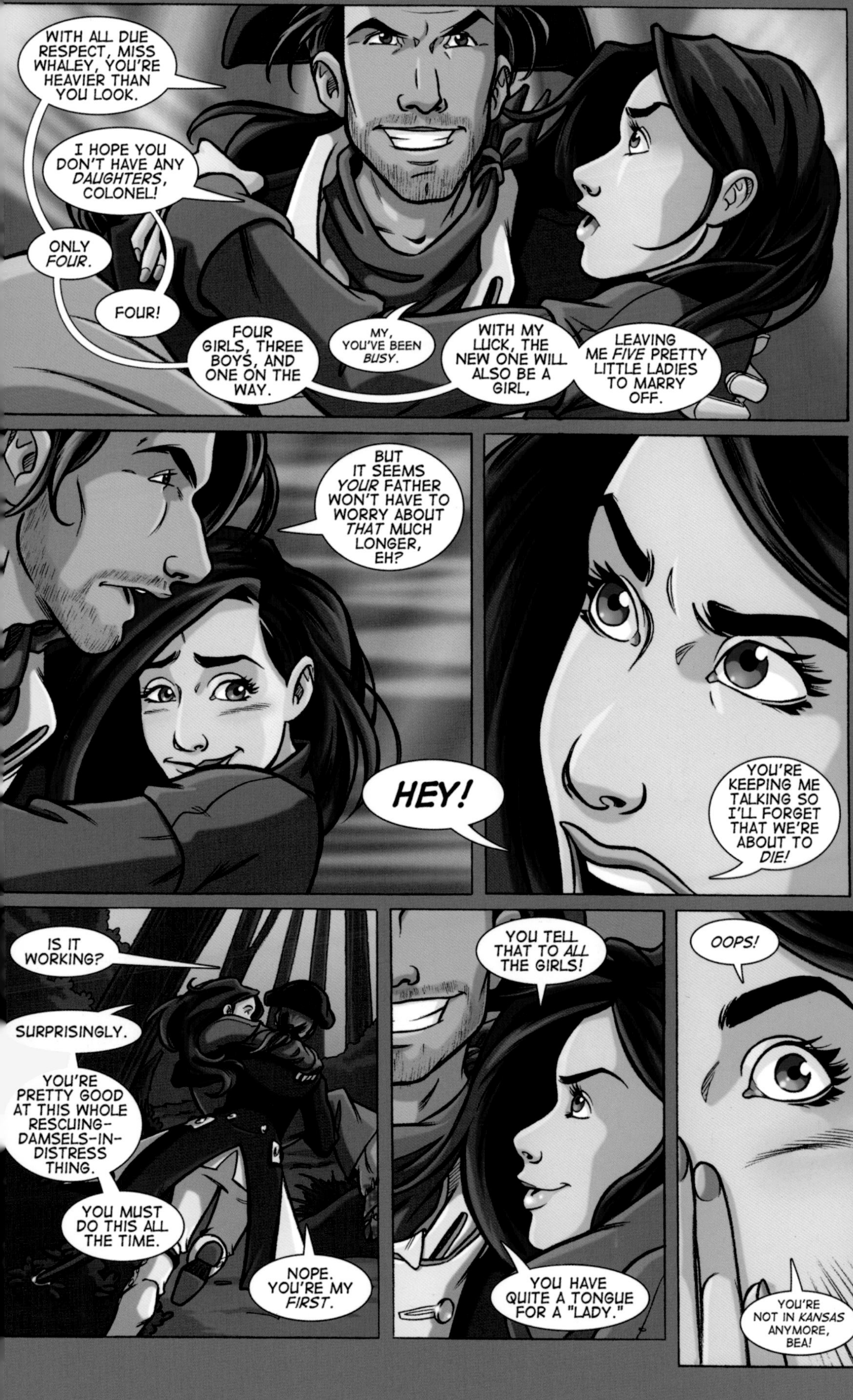
WITH ALL DUE RESPECT, MISS WHALEY, YOU'RE HEAVIER THAN YOU LOOK.
I HOPE YOU DON'T HAVE ANY *DAUGHTERS*, COLONEL!
ONLY *FOUR*.
FOUR!
FOUR GIRLS, THREE BOYS, AND ONE ON THE WAY.
MY, YOU'VE BEEN *BUSY*.
WITH MY LUCK, THE NEW ONE WILL ALSO BE A GIRL,
LEAVING ME *FIVE* PRETTY LITTLE LADIES TO MARRY OFF.
BUT IT SEEMS *YOUR* FATHER WON'T HAVE TO WORRY ABOUT *THAT* MUCH LONGER, EH?
HEY!
YOU'RE KEEPING ME TALKING SO I'LL FORGET THAT WE'RE ABOUT TO *DIE!*
IS IT WORKING?
SURPRISINGLY.
YOU'RE PRETTY GOOD AT THIS WHOLE RESCUING-DAMSELS-IN-DISTRESS THING.
YOU MUST DO THIS ALL THE TIME.
NOPE. YOU'RE MY *FIRST*.
YOU TELL THAT TO *ALL* THE GIRLS!
YOU HAVE QUITE A TONGUE FOR A "LADY."
OOPS!
YOU'RE NOT IN *KANSAS* ANYMORE, BEA!

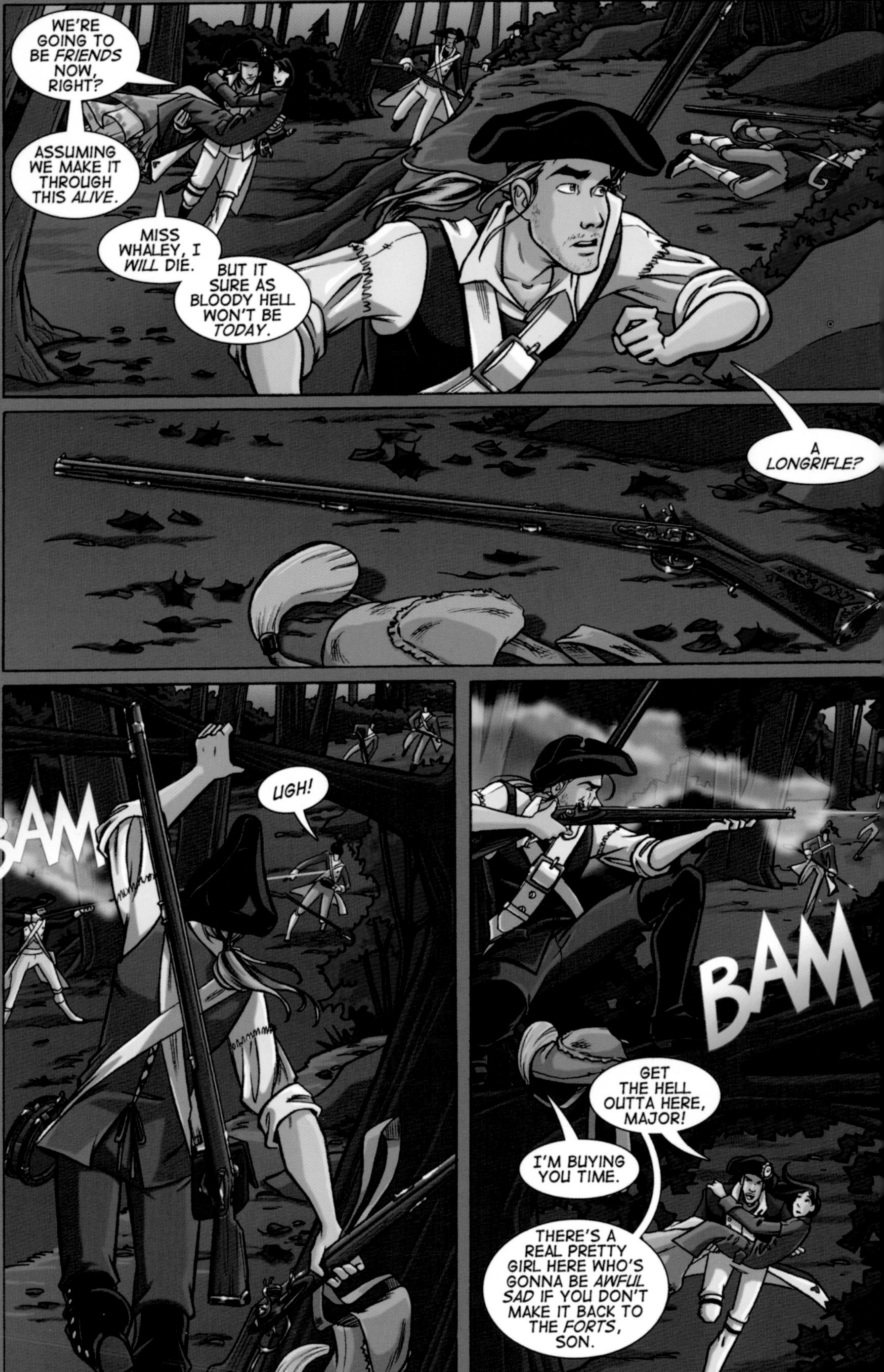
WE'RE GOING TO BE *FRIENDS* NOW, RIGHT?
ASSUMING WE MAKE IT THROUGH THIS *ALIVE*.
MISS WHALEY, I *WILL* DIE.
BUT IT SURE AS BLOODY HELL WON'T BE *TODAY*.
A *LONGRIFLE?*
BAM
UGH!
BAM
GET THE HELL OUTTA HERE, MAJOR!
I'M BUYING YOU TIME.
THERE'S A REAL PRETTY GIRL HERE WHO'S GONNA BE *AWFUL SAD* IF YOU DON'T MAKE IT BACK TO THE *FORTS*, SON.

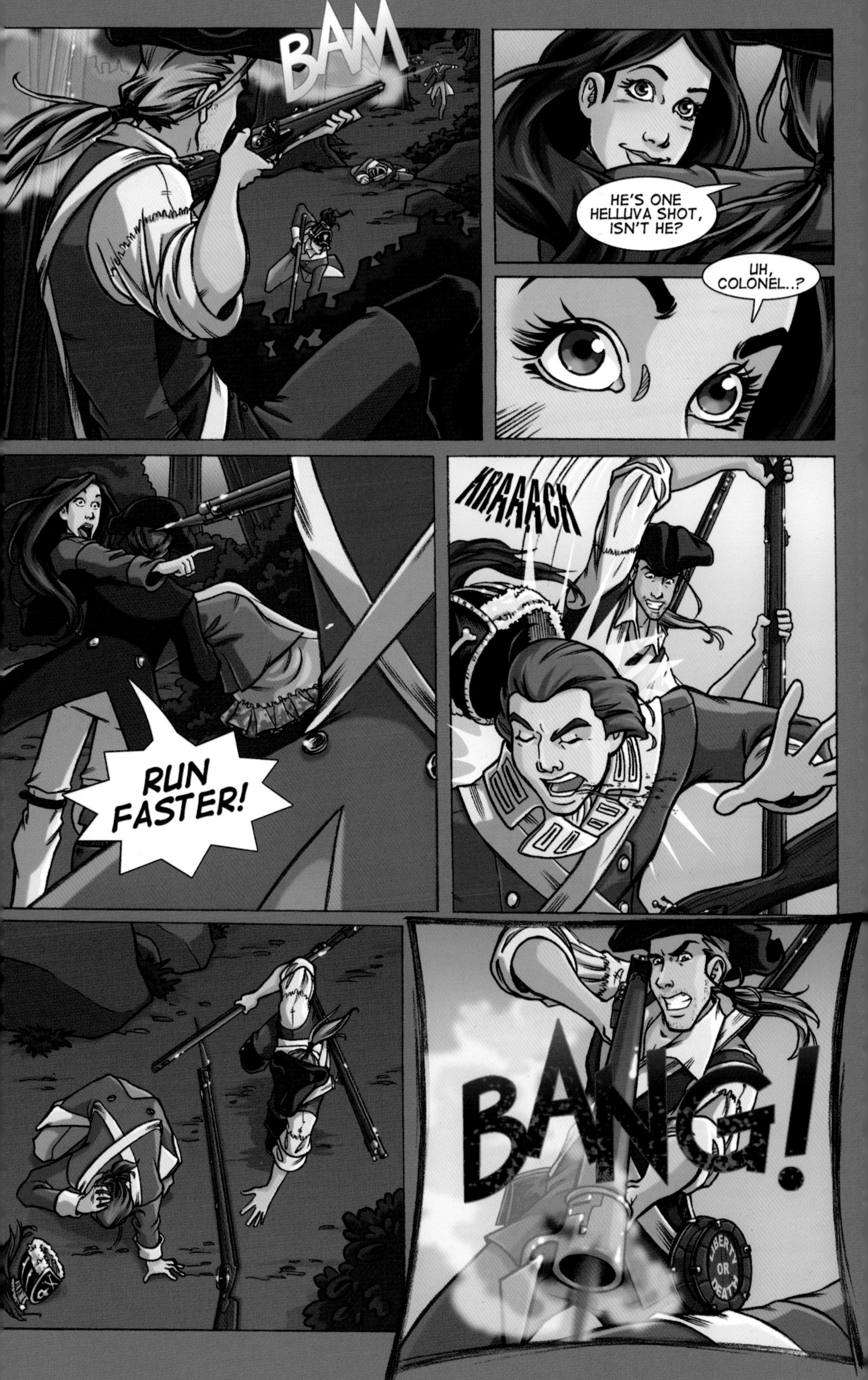
BAM
HE'S ONE HELLUVA SHOT, ISN'T HE?
UH, COLONEL..?
RUN FASTER!
KRRAACH
BANG!
LIBERTY OR DEATH

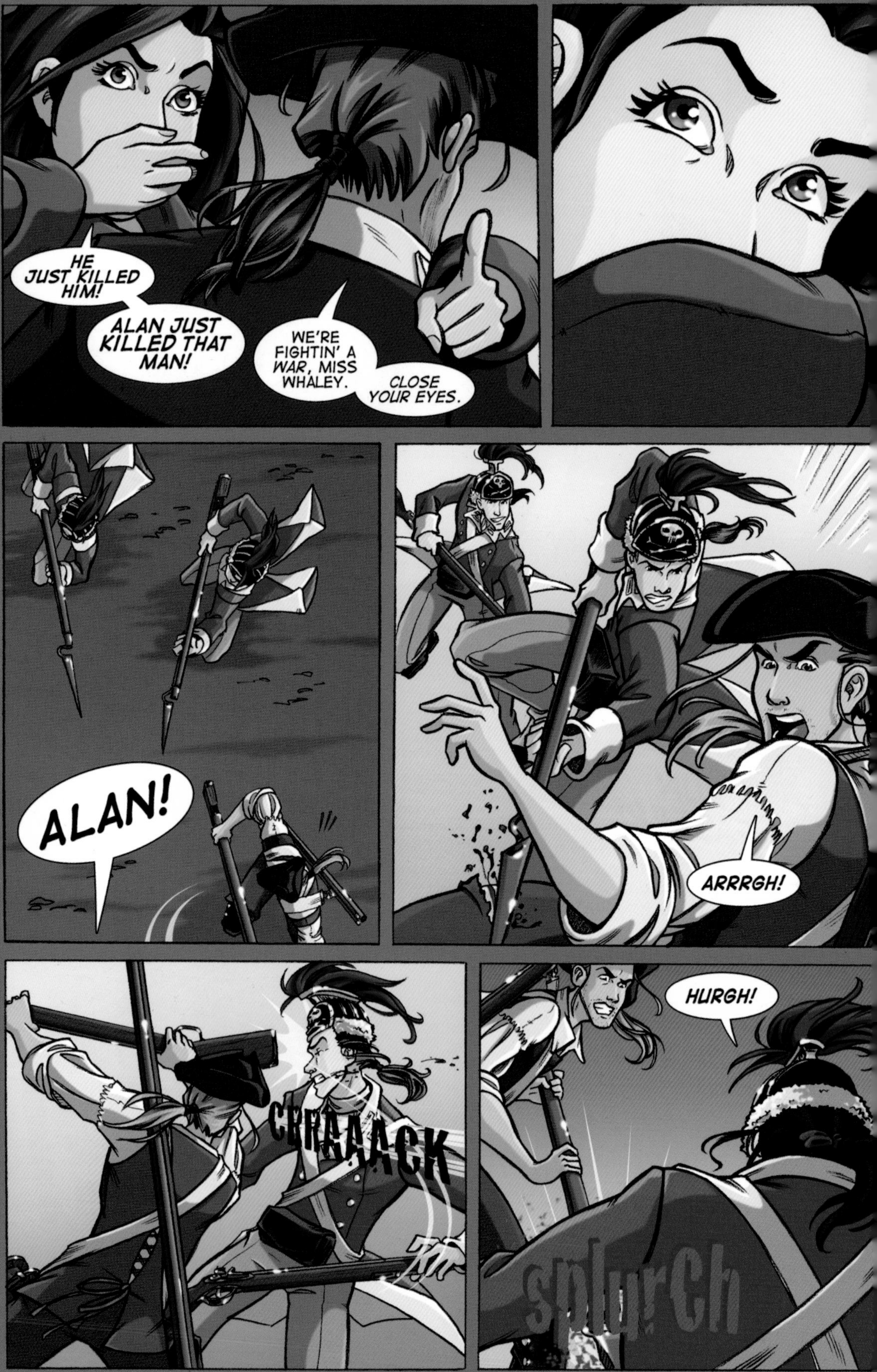
HE JUST KILLED HIM!
ALAN JUST KILLED THAT MAN!
WE'RE FIGHTIN' A WAR, MISS WHALEY.
CLOSE YOUR EYES.
ALAN!
ARRRGH!
CRRAAACK
HURGH!
splurCh

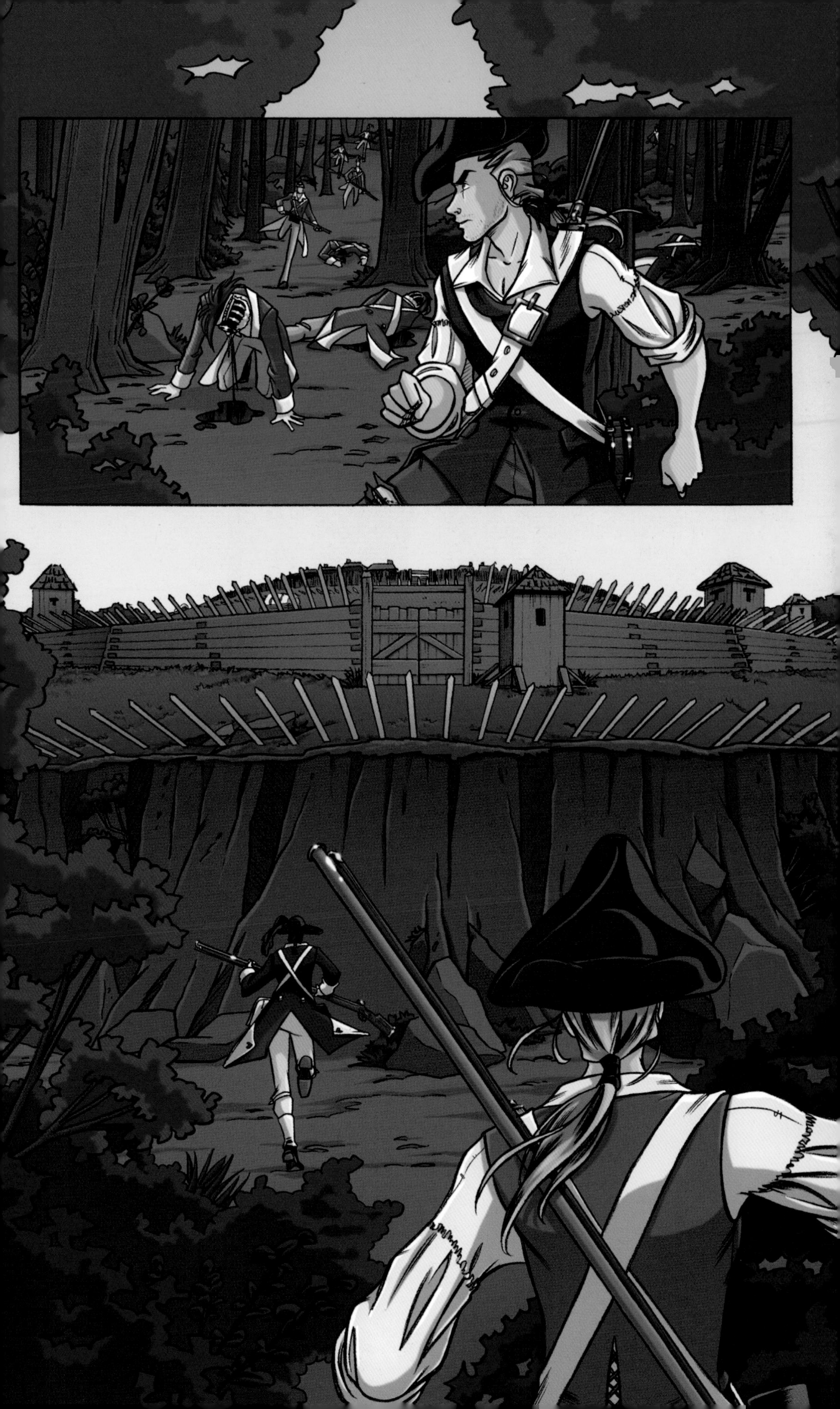

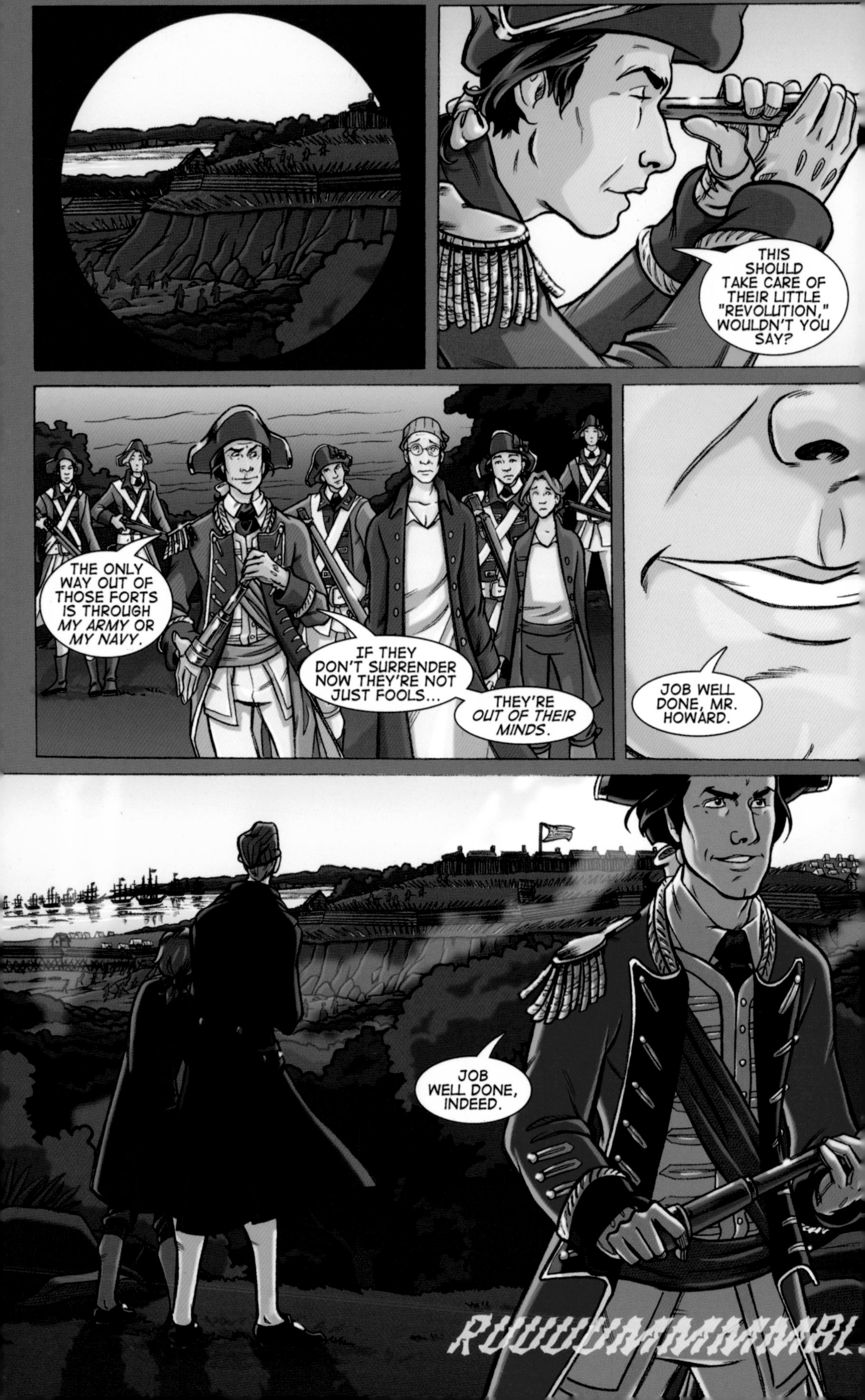

THIS SHOULD TAKE CARE OF THEIR LITTLE "REVOLUTION," WOULDN'T YOU SAY?
THE ONLY WAY OUT OF THOSE FORTS IS THROUGH *MY ARMY* OR *MY NAVY*.
IF THEY DON'T SURRENDER NOW THEY'RE NOT JUST FOOLS...
THEY'RE *OUT OF THEIR MINDS*.
JOB WELL DONE, MR. HOWARD.
JOB WELL DONE, INDEED.
RUUUUMMMMMMMBL

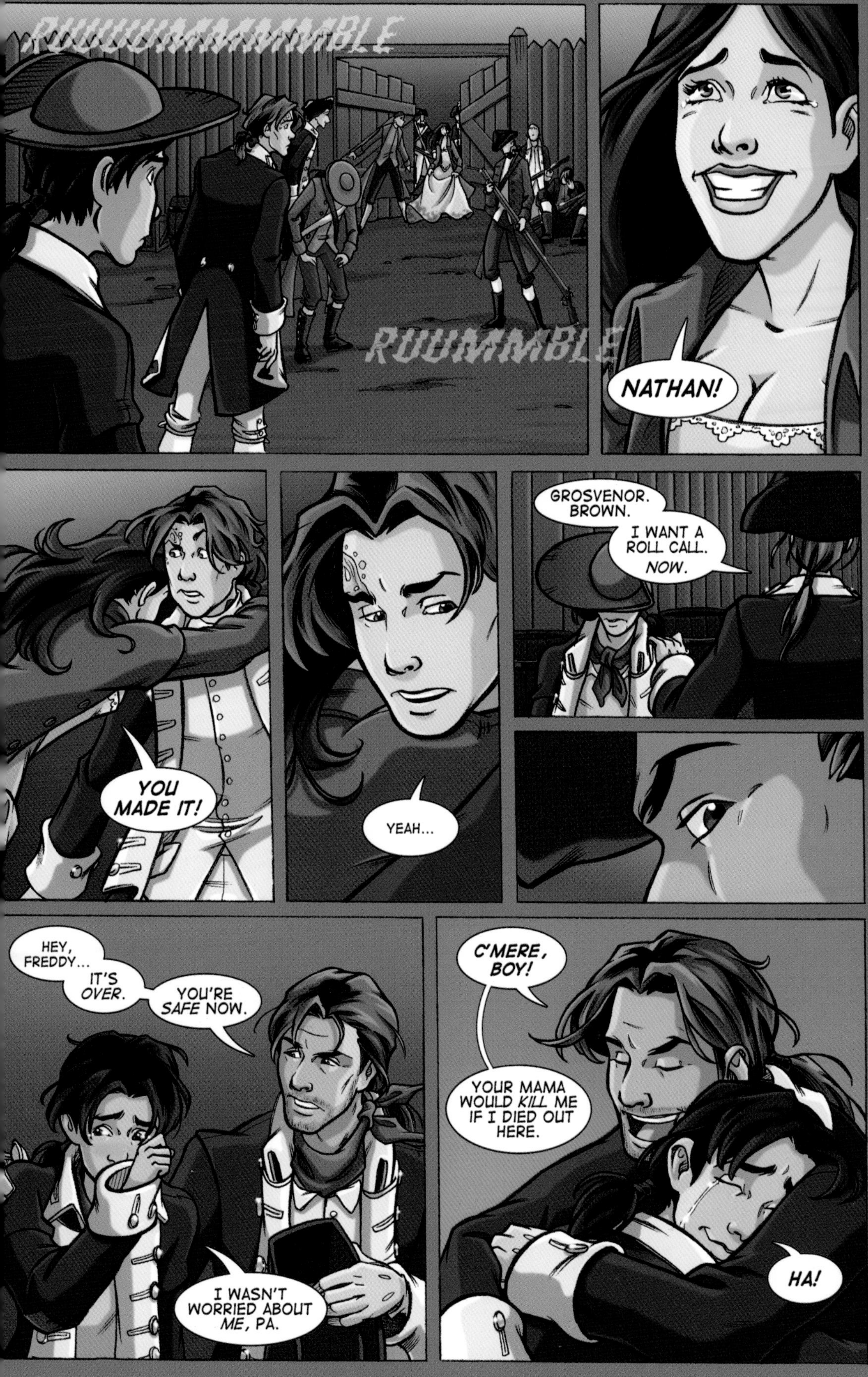
RUUUMMMMMBLE
RUUMMMBLE
NATHAN!
YOU MADE IT!
YEAH...
GROSVENOR. BROWN.
I WANT A ROLL CALL. NOW.
HEY, FREDDY...
IT'S OVER.
YOU'RE SAFE NOW.
I WASN'T WORRIED ABOUT ME, PA.
C'MERE, BOY!
YOUR MAMA WOULD KILL ME IF I DIED OUT HERE.
HA!

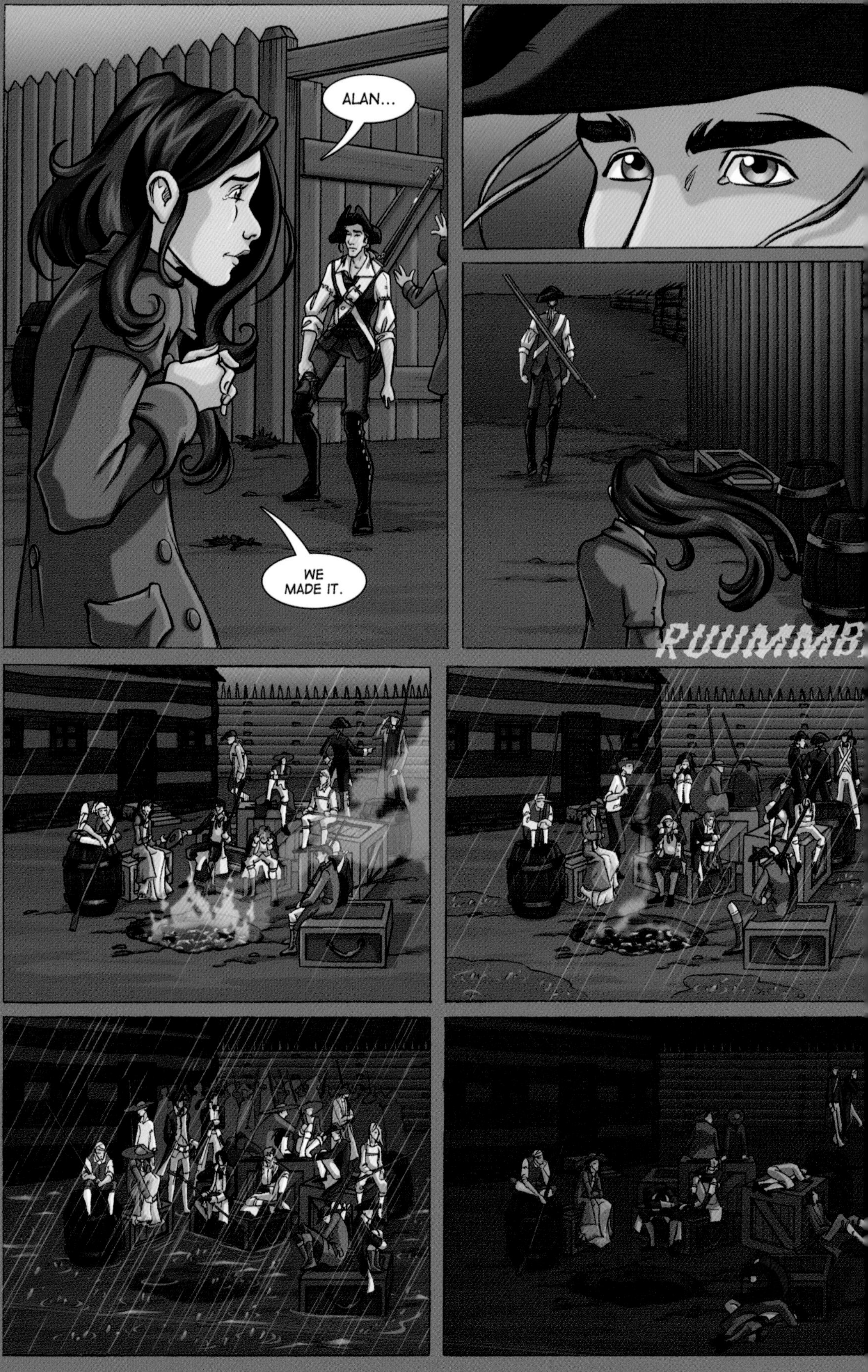
ALAN...
WE MADE IT.
RUUMMB

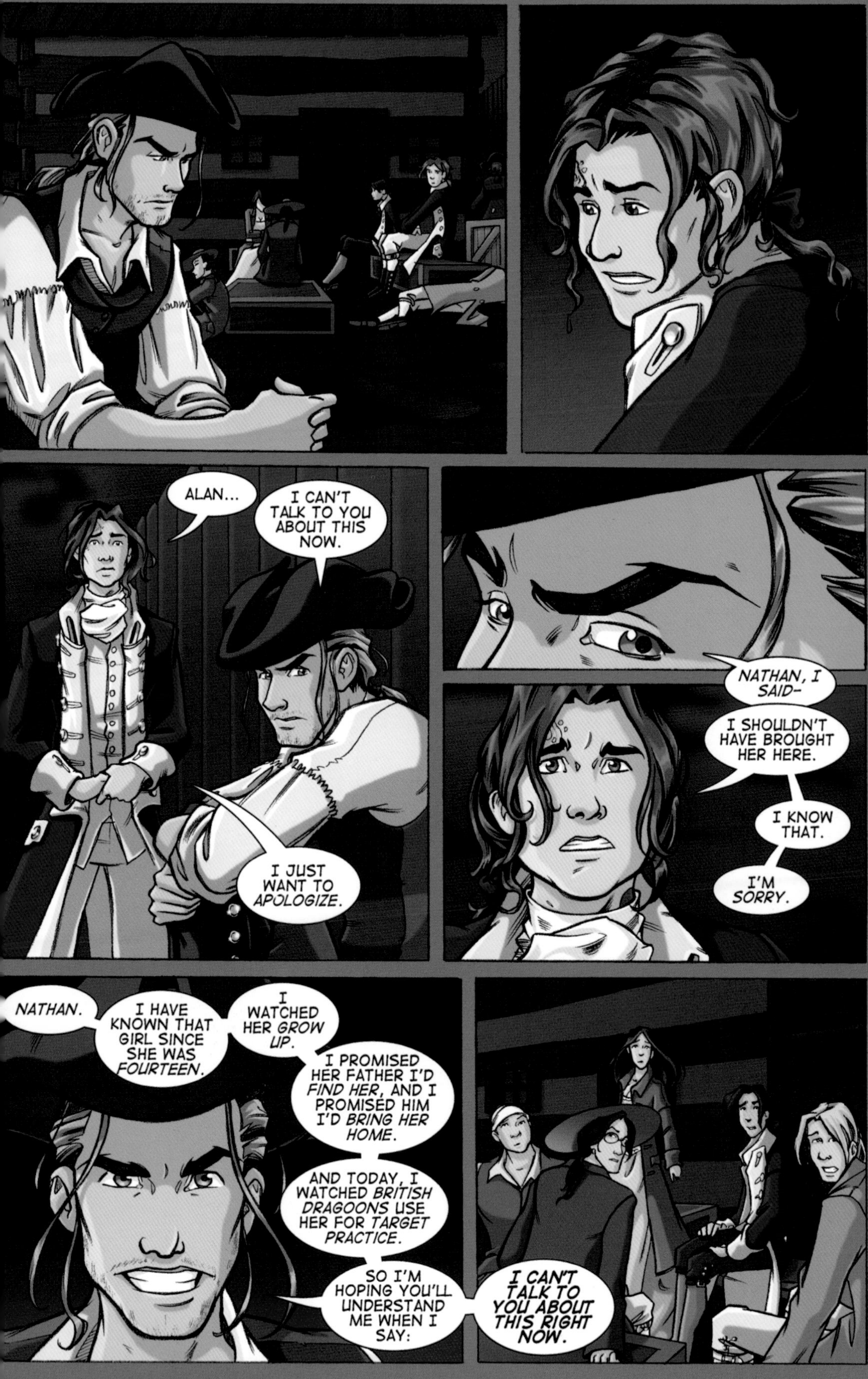
ALAN...
I CAN'T TALK TO YOU ABOUT THIS NOW.
I JUST WANT TO APOLOGIZE.
NATHAN, I SAID-
I SHOULDN'T HAVE BROUGHT HER HERE.
I KNOW THAT.
I'M SORRY.
NATHAN.
I HAVE KNOWN THAT GIRL SINCE SHE WAS FOURTEEN.
I WATCHED HER GROW UP.
I PROMISED HER FATHER I'D FIND HER, AND I PROMISED HIM I'D BRING HER HOME.
AND TODAY, I WATCHED BRITISH DRAGOONS USE HER FOR TARGET PRACTICE.
SO I'M HOPING YOU'LL UNDERSTAND ME WHEN I SAY:
I CAN'T TALK TO YOU ABOUT THIS RIGHT NOW.

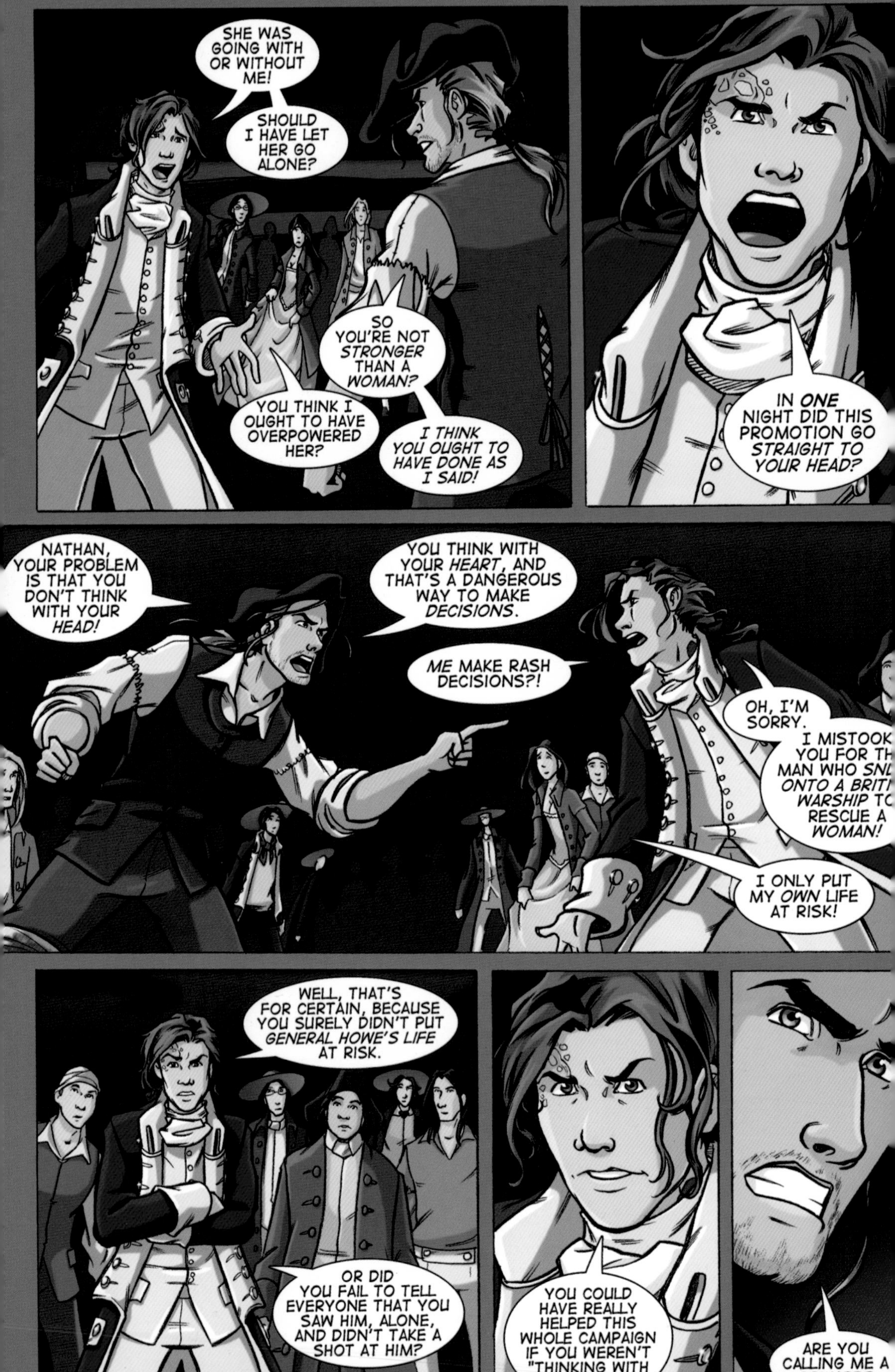
SHE WAS GOING WITH OR WITHOUT ME!
SHOULD I HAVE LET HER GO ALONE?
SO YOU'RE NOT *STRONGER* THAN A *WOMAN?*
YOU THINK I OUGHT TO HAVE OVERPOWERED HER?
I THINK YOU OUGHT TO HAVE DONE AS I SAID!
IN *ONE* NIGHT DID THIS PROMOTION GO *STRAIGHT TO YOUR HEAD?*
NATHAN, YOUR PROBLEM IS THAT YOU DON'T THINK WITH YOUR *HEAD!*
YOU THINK WITH YOUR *HEART*, AND THAT'S A DANGEROUS WAY TO MAKE *DECISIONS*.
ME MAKE RASH DECISIONS?!
OH, I'M SORRY.
I ONLY PUT MY *OWN* LIFE AT RISK!
WELL, THAT'S FOR CERTAIN, BECAUSE YOU SURELY DIDN'T PUT *GENERAL HOWE'S LIFE* AT RISK.
OR DID YOU FAIL TO TELL EVERYONE THAT YOU SAW HIM, ALONE, AND DIDN'T TAKE A SHOT AT HIM?
YOU COULD HAVE REALLY HELPED THIS WHOLE CAMPAIGN IF YOU WEREN'T "THINKING WITH YOUR HEART."
ARE YOU CALLING ME A COWARD?

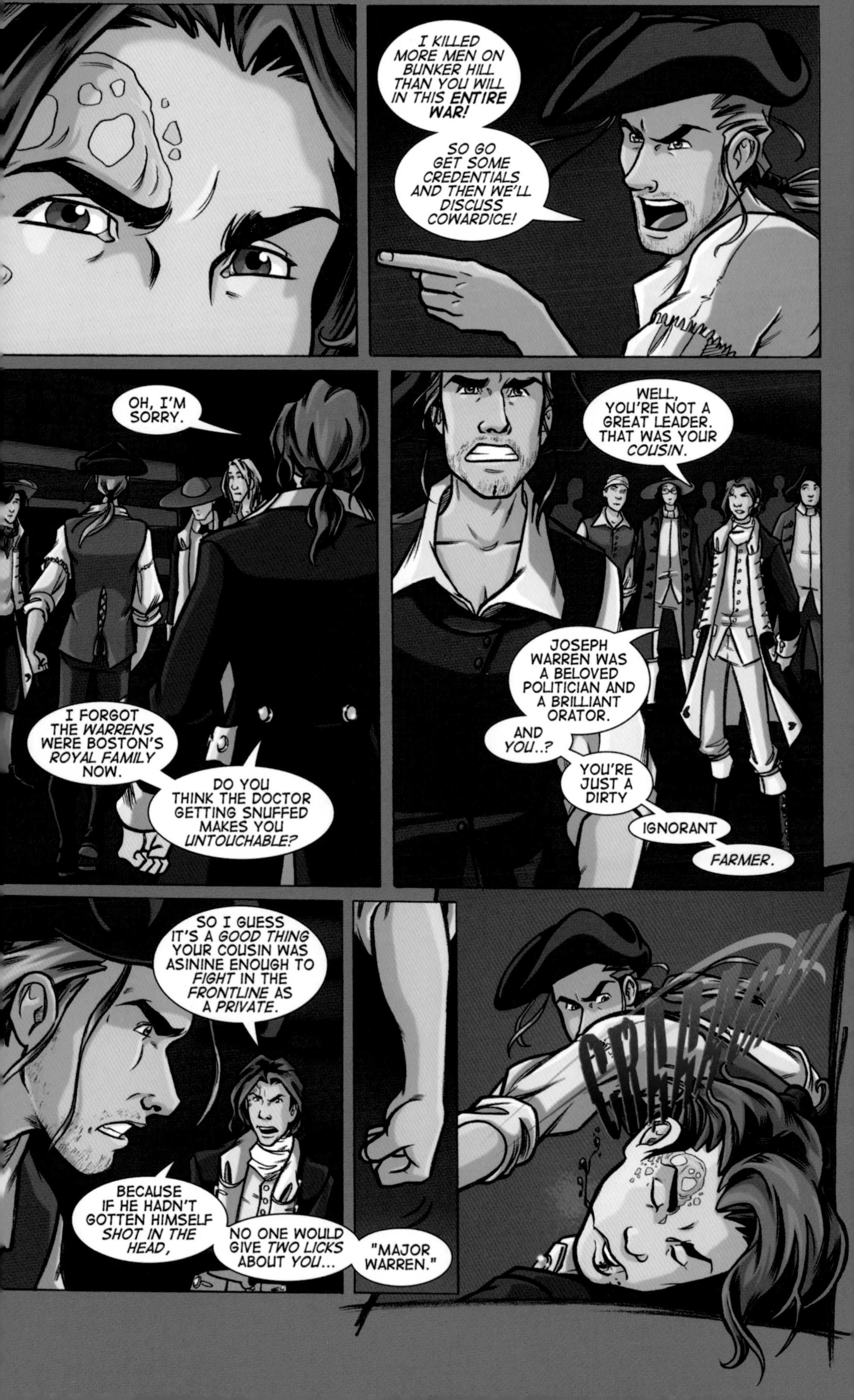

I KILLED MORE MEN ON BUNKER HILL THAN YOU WILL IN THIS ENTIRE WAR!
SO GO GET SOME CREDENTIALS AND THEN WE'LL DISCUSS COWARDICE!
OH, I'M SORRY.
I FORGOT THE WARRENS WERE BOSTON'S ROYAL FAMILY NOW.
DO YOU THINK THE DOCTOR GETTING SNUFFED MAKES YOU UNTOUCHABLE?
WELL, YOU'RE NOT A GREAT LEADER. THAT WAS YOUR COUSIN.
JOSEPH WARREN WAS A BELOVED POLITICIAN AND A BRILLIANT ORATOR.
AND YOU..?
YOU'RE JUST A DIRTY
IGNORANT
FARMER.
SO I GUESS IT'S A GOOD THING YOUR COUSIN WAS ASININE ENOUGH TO FIGHT IN THE FRONTLINE AS A PRIVATE.
BECAUSE IF HE HADN'T GOTTEN HIMSELF SHOT IN THE HEAD,
NO ONE WOULD GIVE TWO LICKS ABOUT YOU...
"MAJOR WARREN."

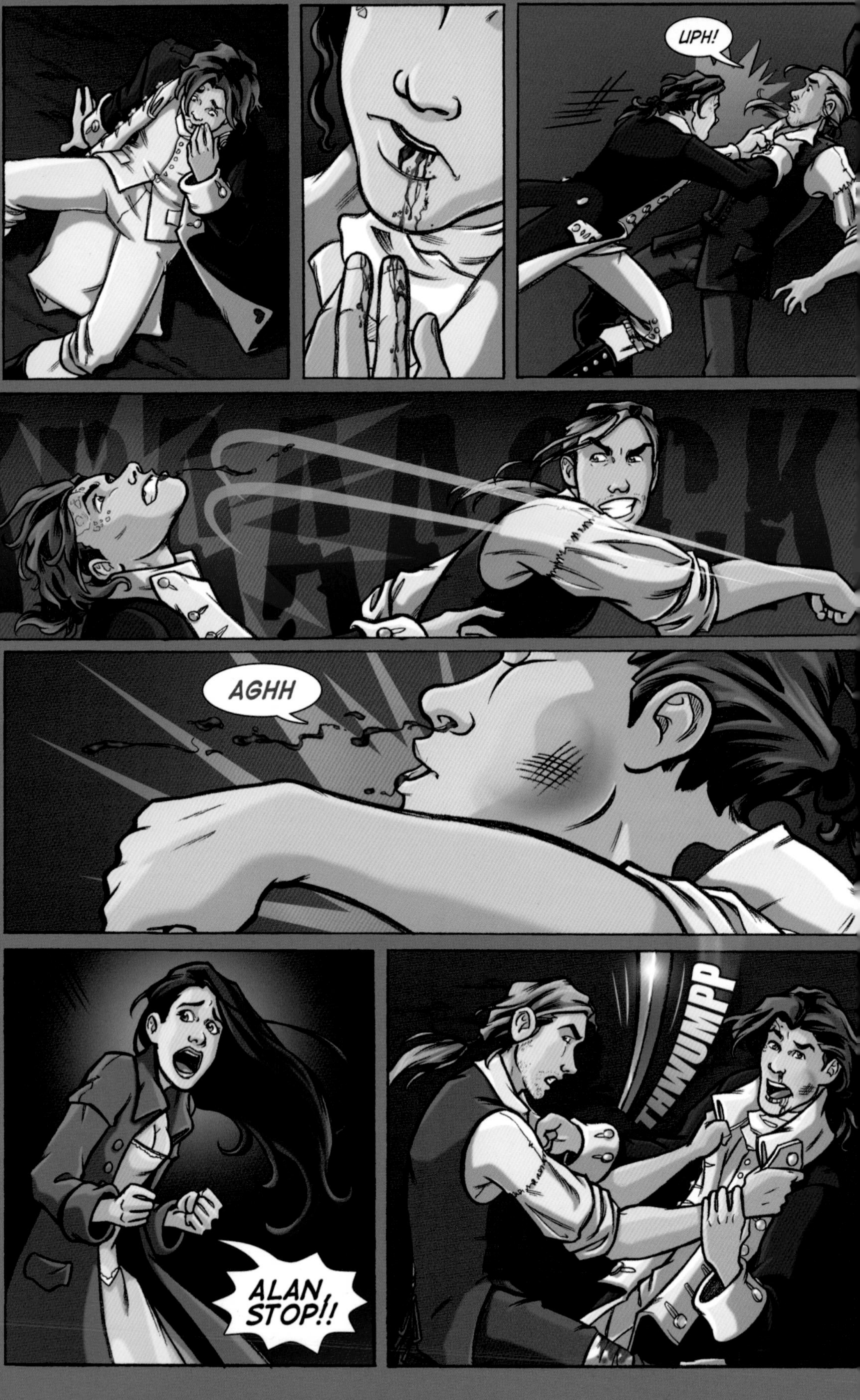
UPH!
AGHH
ALAN STOP!!
THWUMPP

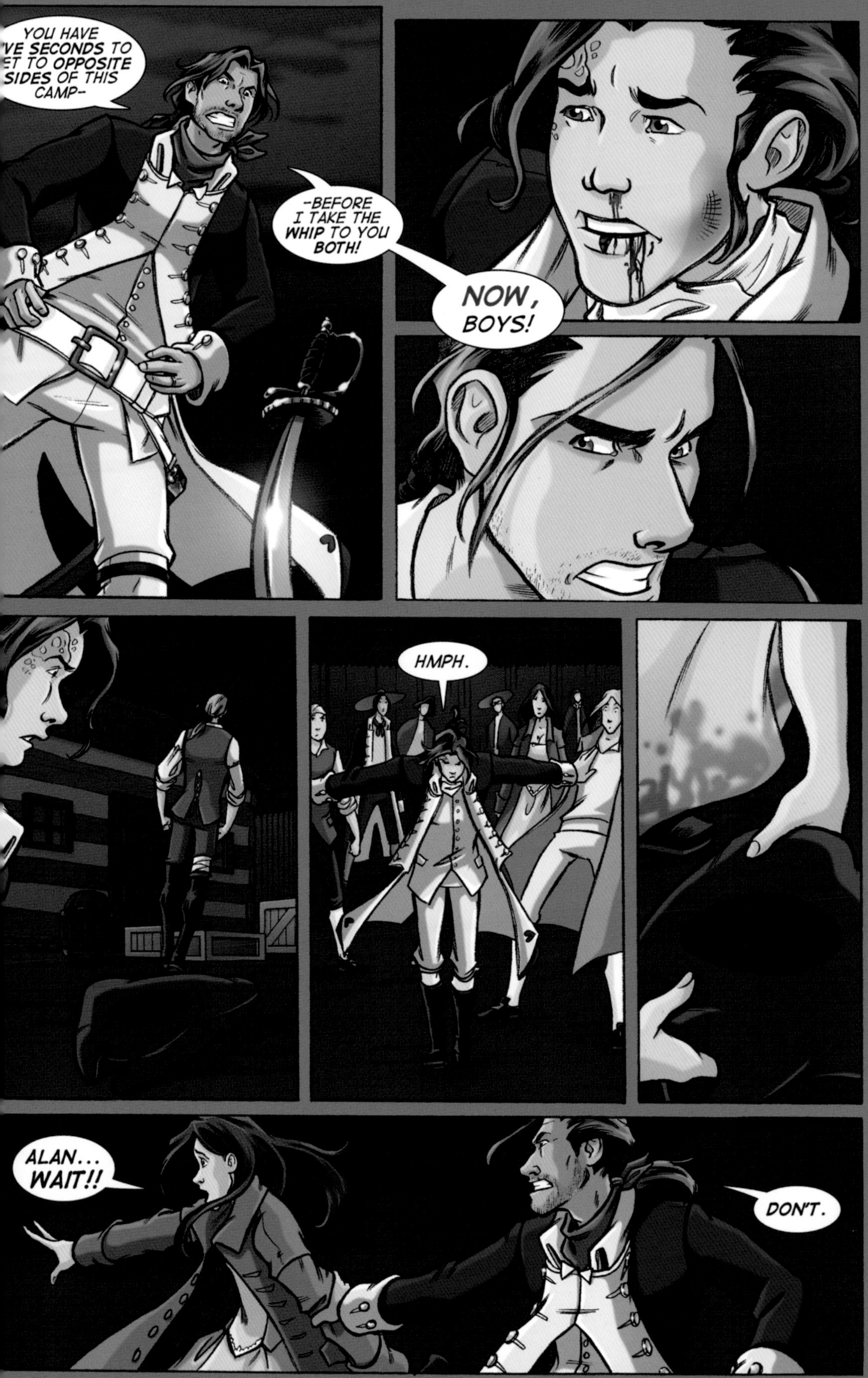
YOU HAVE 'VE SECONDS TO ET TO OPPOSITE SIDES OF THIS CAMP–
–BEFORE I TAKE THE WHIP TO YOU BOTH!
NOW, BOYS!
HMPH.
ALAN... WAIT!!
DON'T.

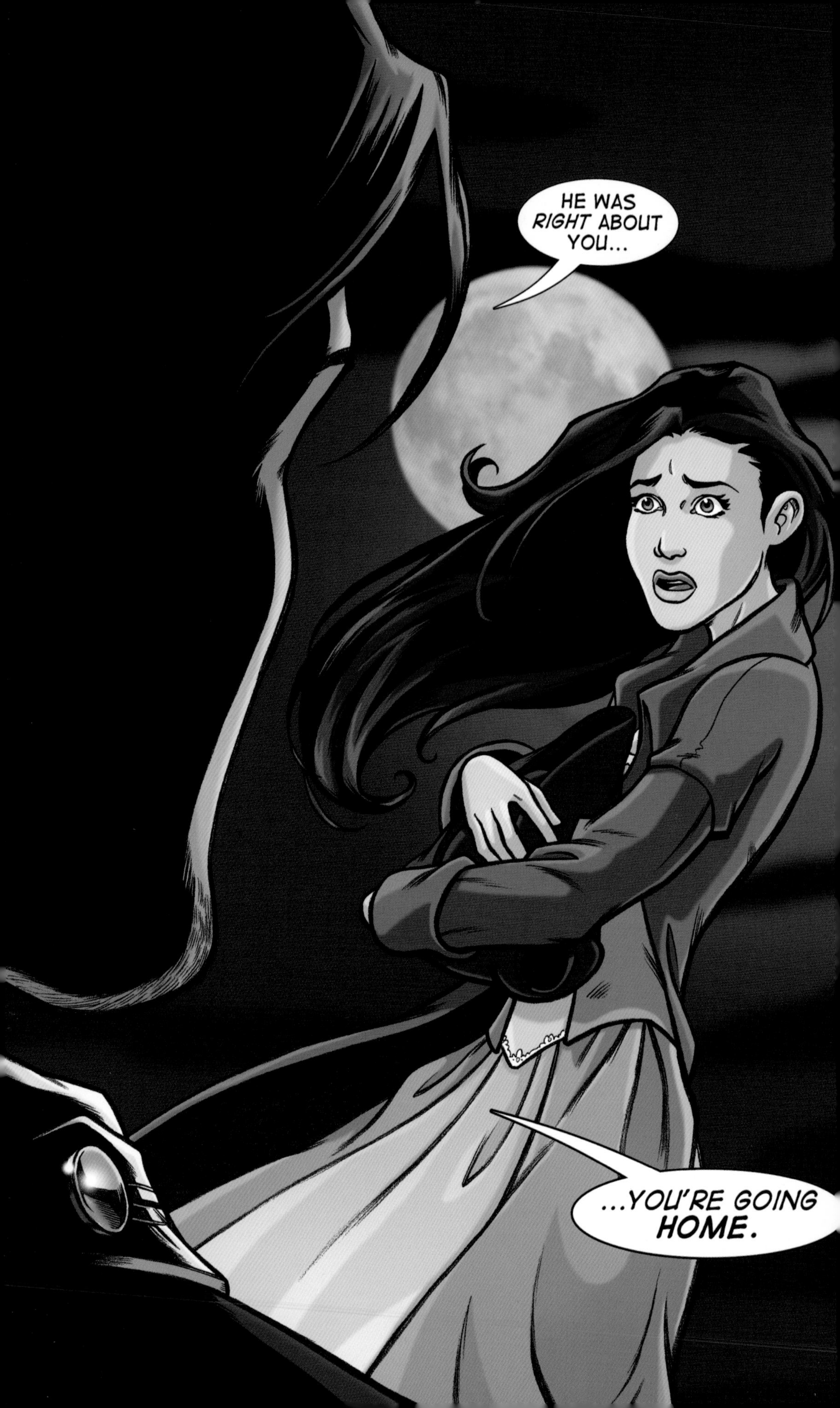
HE WAS RIGHT ABOUT YOU...
...YOU'RE GOING HOME.

Chapter Six

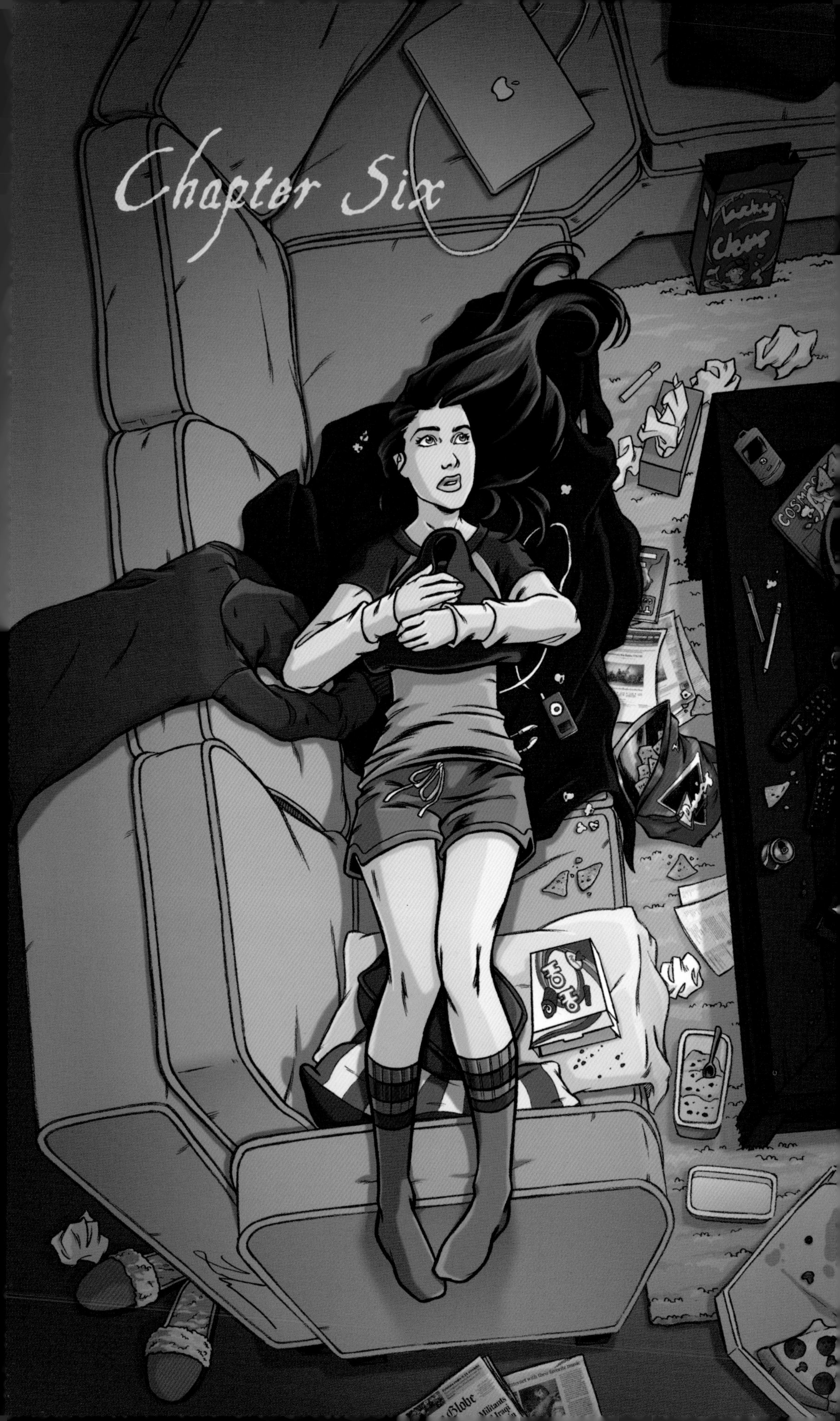

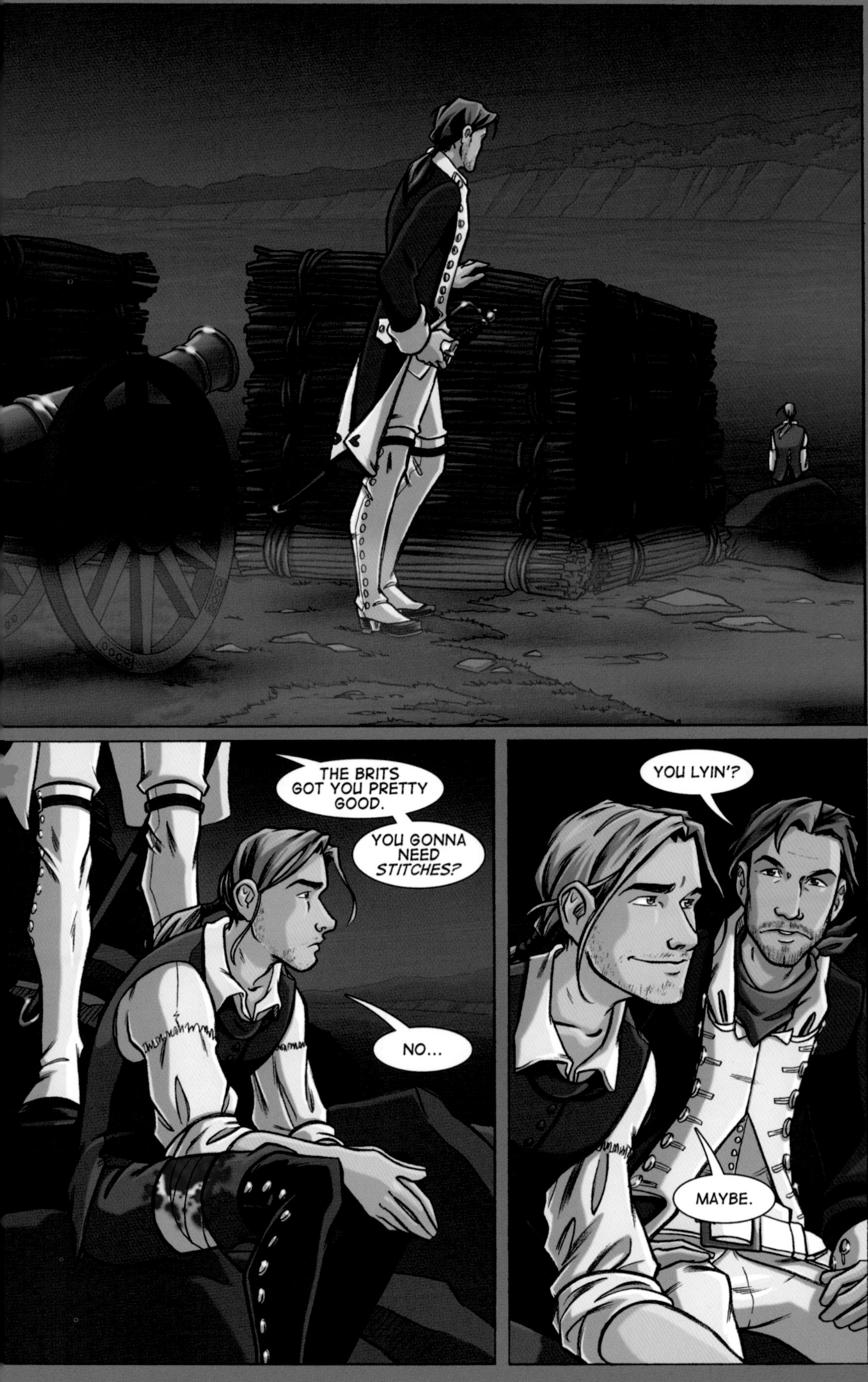
THE BRITS GOT YOU PRETTY GOOD.
YOU GONNA NEED *STITCHES?*
NO...
YOU LYIN'?
MAYBE.

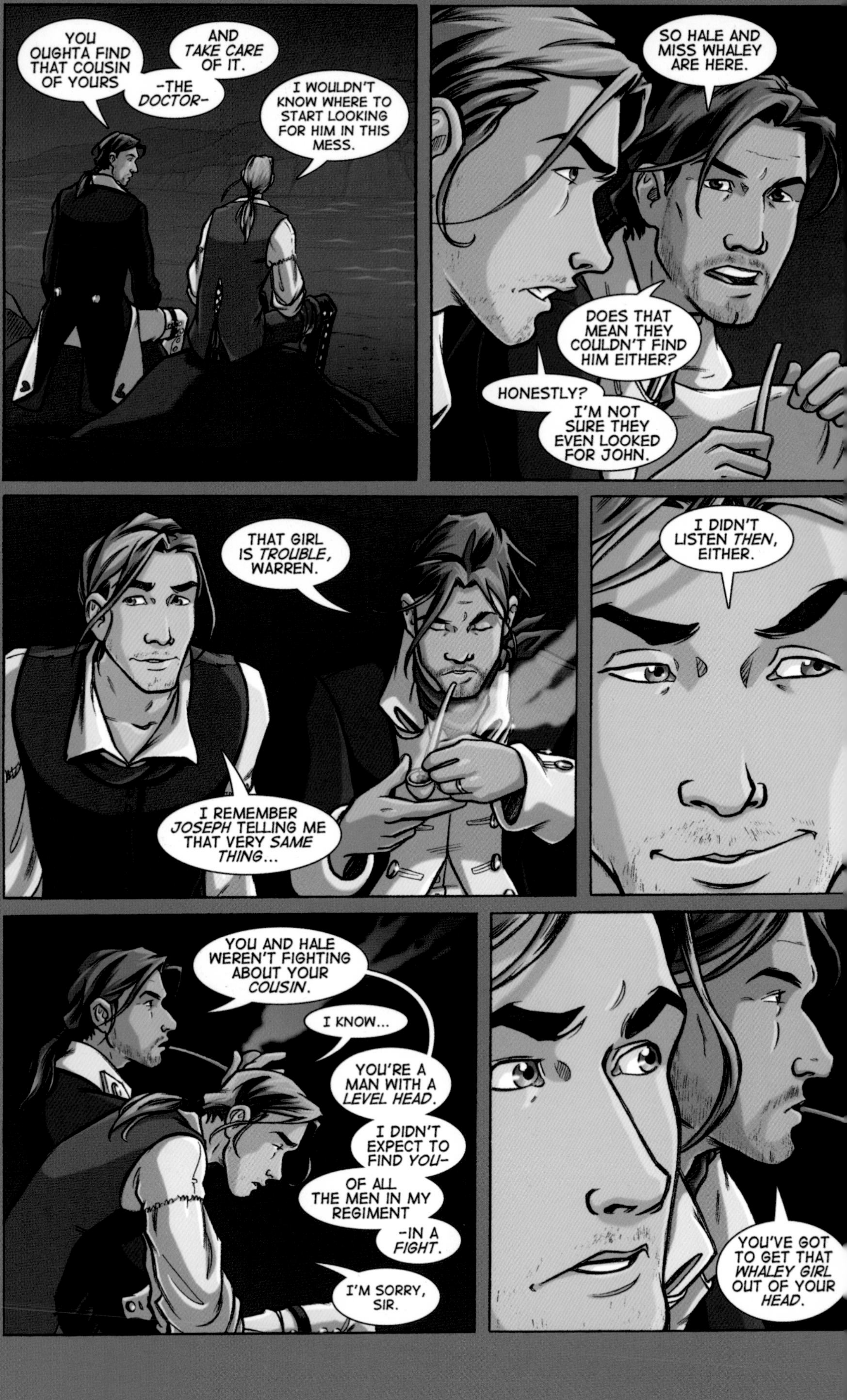
YOU OUGHTA FIND THAT COUSIN OF YOURS
-THE DOCTOR-
AND TAKE CARE OF IT.
I WOULDN'T KNOW WHERE TO START LOOKING FOR HIM IN THIS MESS.
SO HALE AND MISS WHALEY ARE HERE.
DOES THAT MEAN THEY COULDN'T FIND HIM EITHER?
HONESTLY?
I'M NOT SURE THEY EVEN LOOKED FOR JOHN.
THAT GIRL IS TROUBLE, WARREN.
I REMEMBER JOSEPH TELLING ME THAT VERY SAME THING...
I DIDN'T LISTEN THEN, EITHER.
YOU AND HALE WEREN'T FIGHTING ABOUT YOUR COUSIN.
I KNOW...
YOU'RE A MAN WITH A LEVEL HEAD.
I DIDN'T EXPECT TO FIND YOU-
OF ALL THE MEN IN MY REGIMENT
-IN A FIGHT.
I'M SORRY, SIR.
YOU'VE GOT TO GET THAT WHALEY GIRL OUT OF YOUR HEAD.

AND THERE ARE TWO WAYS TO GO ABOUT IT, SO FAR AS I CAN FIGURE.

FIRST, YOU CAN SEND HER HOME, LET HER GET MARRIED, AND FORGET ALL ABOUT HER.

CAN YOU DO THAT?

...NO.

I DIDN'T THINK SO.

SO YOU'RE JUST GOING TO HAVE TO *MARRY HER* YOURSELF.

EXCUSE ME?!

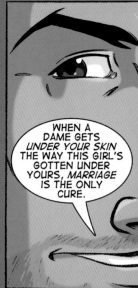

WHEN A DAME GETS *UNDER YOUR SKIN* THE WAY THIS GIRL'S GOTTEN UNDER YOURS, *MARRIAGE* IS THE ONLY CURE.

HA!

DO YOU SPEAK FROM EXPERIENCE?

I STILL *LOVE* MY WIFE...

BUT *LIVIN'* WITH A WOMAN GETS RID OF THAT CRAZY, WILY FEELING THAT'S GOT *YOU* ON A ROPE.

WELL, I'D MUCH LIKE A *CURE*, SIR.

BUT I'M AFRAID MISS WHALEY DOESN'T *REMEMBER* ME.

MORE *UNLIKELY* THINGS HAVE HAPPENED.

SHE SEEMS *AWFULLY* FOND OF YOU.

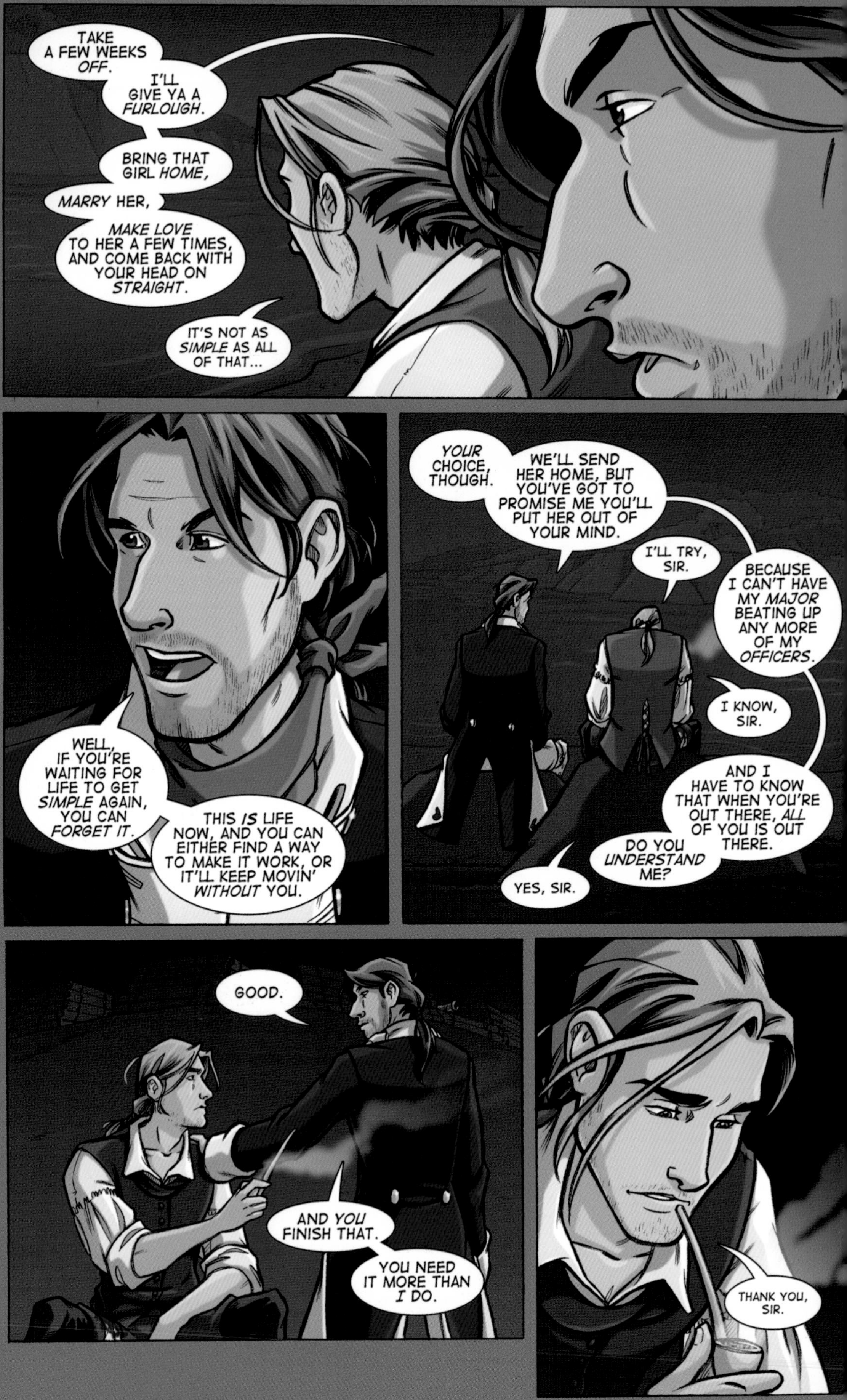
TAKE A FEW WEEKS OFF.
I'LL GIVE YA A FURLOUGH.
BRING THAT GIRL HOME,
MARRY HER,
MAKE LOVE TO HER A FEW TIMES, AND COME BACK WITH YOUR HEAD ON STRAIGHT.
IT'S NOT AS SIMPLE AS ALL OF THAT...
WELL, IF YOU'RE WAITING FOR LIFE TO GET SIMPLE AGAIN, YOU CAN FORGET IT.
THIS IS LIFE NOW, AND YOU CAN EITHER FIND A WAY TO MAKE IT WORK, OR IT'LL KEEP MOVIN' WITHOUT YOU.
YOUR CHOICE, THOUGH.
WE'LL SEND HER HOME, BUT YOU'VE GOT TO PROMISE ME YOU'LL PUT HER OUT OF YOUR MIND.
I'LL TRY, SIR.
BECAUSE I CAN'T HAVE MY MAJOR BEATING UP ANY MORE OF MY OFFICERS.
I KNOW, SIR.
AND I HAVE TO KNOW THAT WHEN YOU'RE OUT THERE, ALL OF YOU IS OUT THERE.
DO YOU UNDERSTAND ME?
YES, SIR.
GOOD.
AND YOU FINISH THAT.
YOU NEED IT MORE THAN I DO.
THANK YOU, SIR.

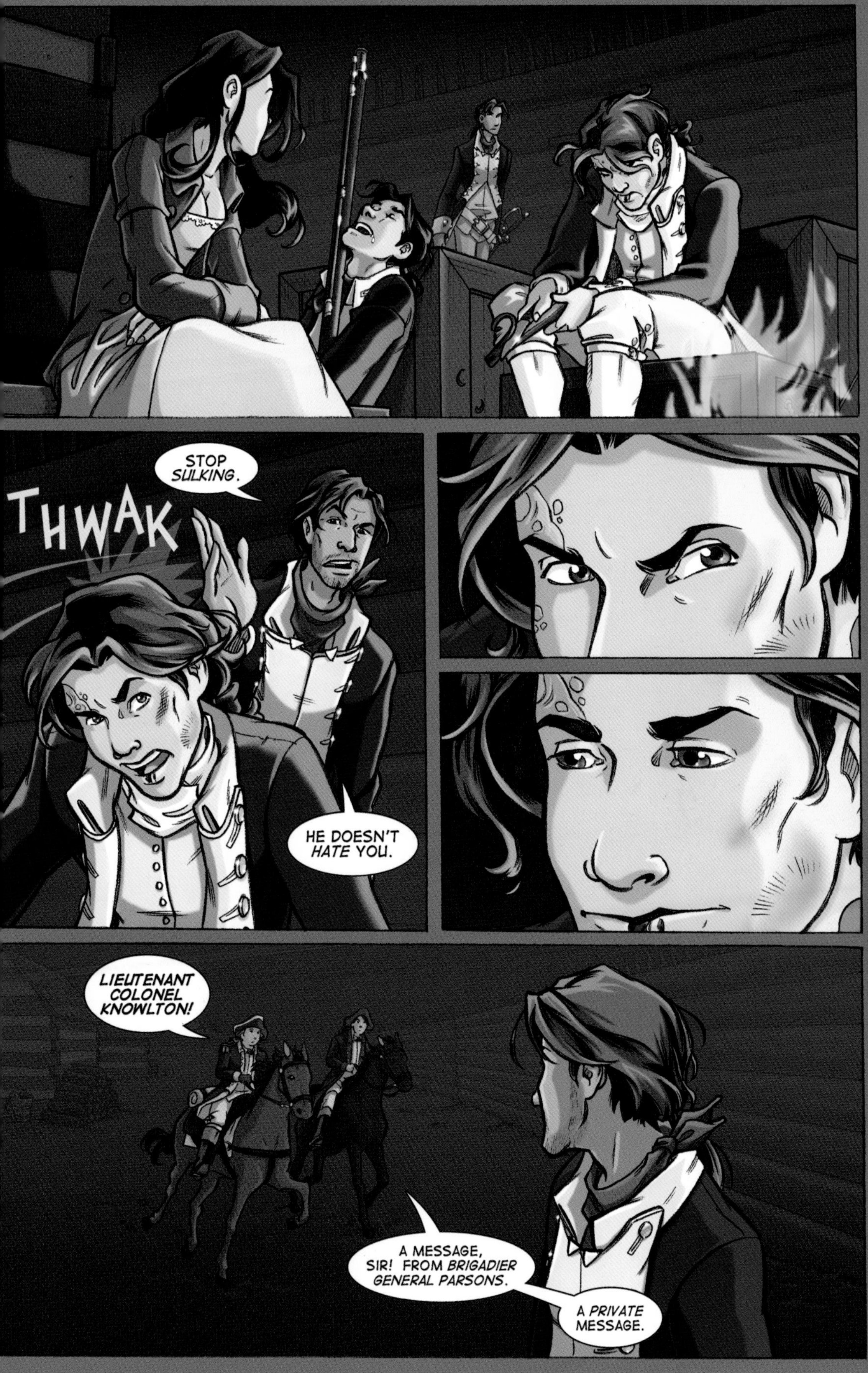
STOP SULKING.
THWAK
HE DOESN'T *HATE* YOU.
LIEUTENANT COLONEL KNOWLTON!
A MESSAGE, SIR! FROM *BRIGADIER GENERAL PARSONS*.
A *PRIVATE* MESSAGE.

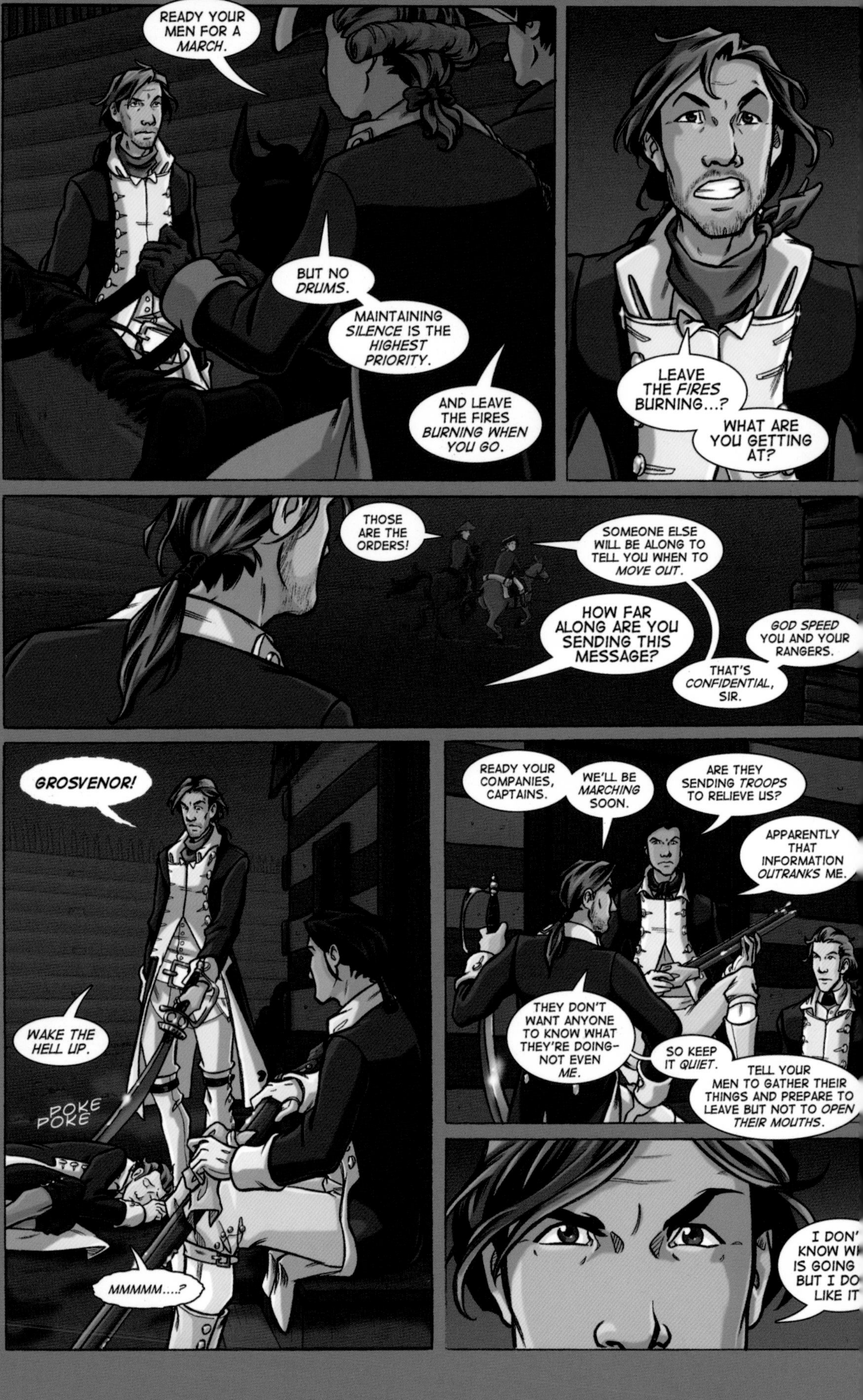
READY YOUR MEN FOR A MARCH.
BUT NO DRUMS.
MAINTAINING SILENCE IS THE HIGHEST PRIORITY.
AND LEAVE THE FIRES BURNING WHEN YOU GO.
LEAVE THE FIRES BURNING...?
WHAT ARE YOU GETTING AT?
THOSE ARE THE ORDERS!
SOMEONE ELSE WILL BE ALONG TO TELL YOU WHEN TO MOVE OUT.
HOW FAR ALONG ARE YOU SENDING THIS MESSAGE?
THAT'S CONFIDENTIAL, SIR.
GOD SPEED YOU AND YOUR RANGERS.
GROSVENOR!
WAKE THE HELL UP.
POKE POKE
MMMMM....?
READY YOUR COMPANIES, CAPTAINS.
WE'LL BE MARCHING SOON.
ARE THEY SENDING TROOPS TO RELIEVE US?
APPARENTLY THAT INFORMATION OUTRANKS ME.
THEY DON'T WANT ANYONE TO KNOW WHAT THEY'RE DOING- NOT EVEN ME.
SO KEEP IT QUIET.
TELL YOUR MEN TO GATHER THEIR THINGS AND PREPARE TO LEAVE BUT NOT TO OPEN THEIR MOUTHS.
I DON' KNOW W IS GOING BUT I DO LIKE IT

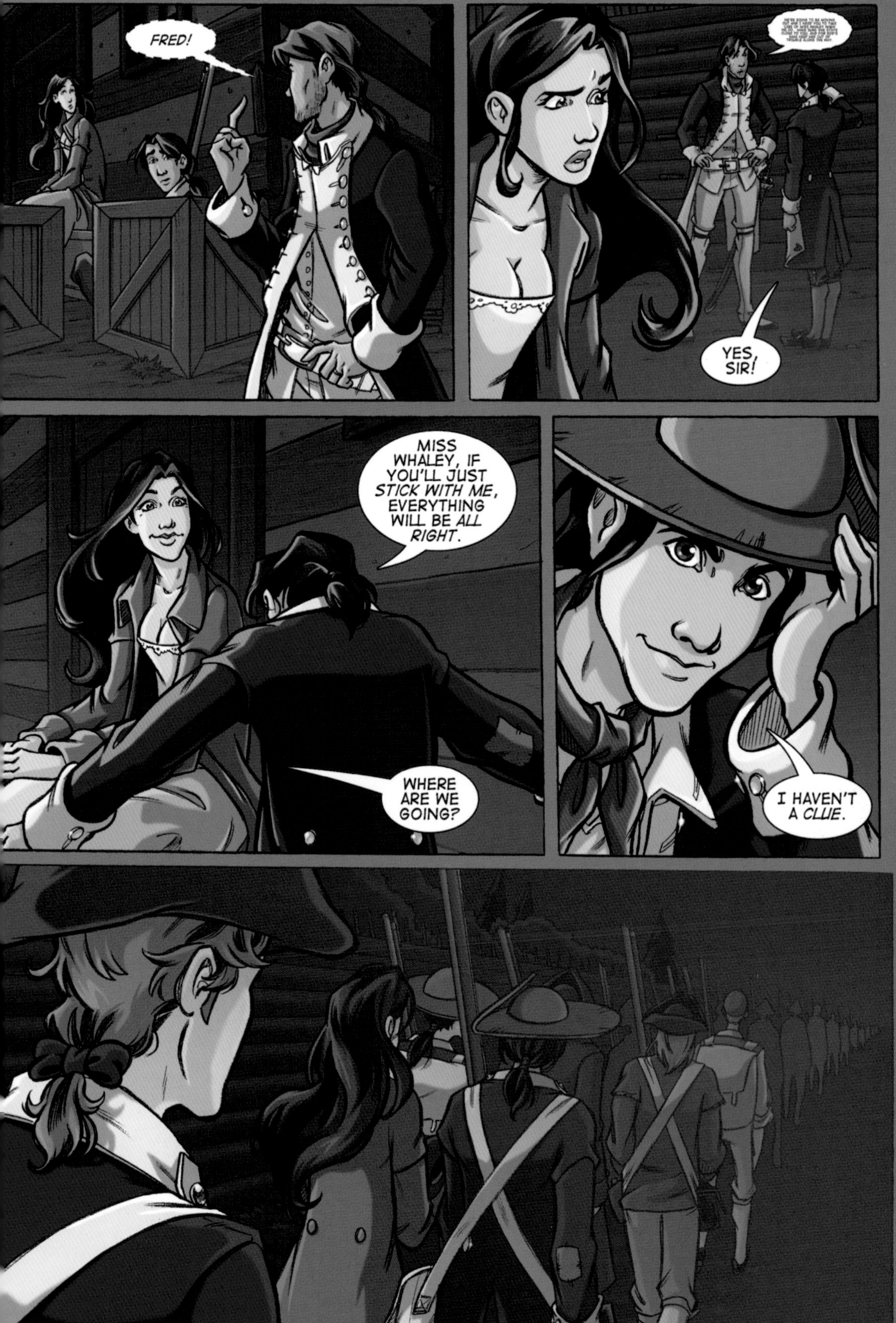

FRED!
YES, SIR!
MISS WHALEY, IF YOU'LL JUST *STICK WITH ME*, EVERYTHING WILL BE *ALL RIGHT*.
WHERE ARE WE GOING?
I HAVEN'T A *CLUE*.

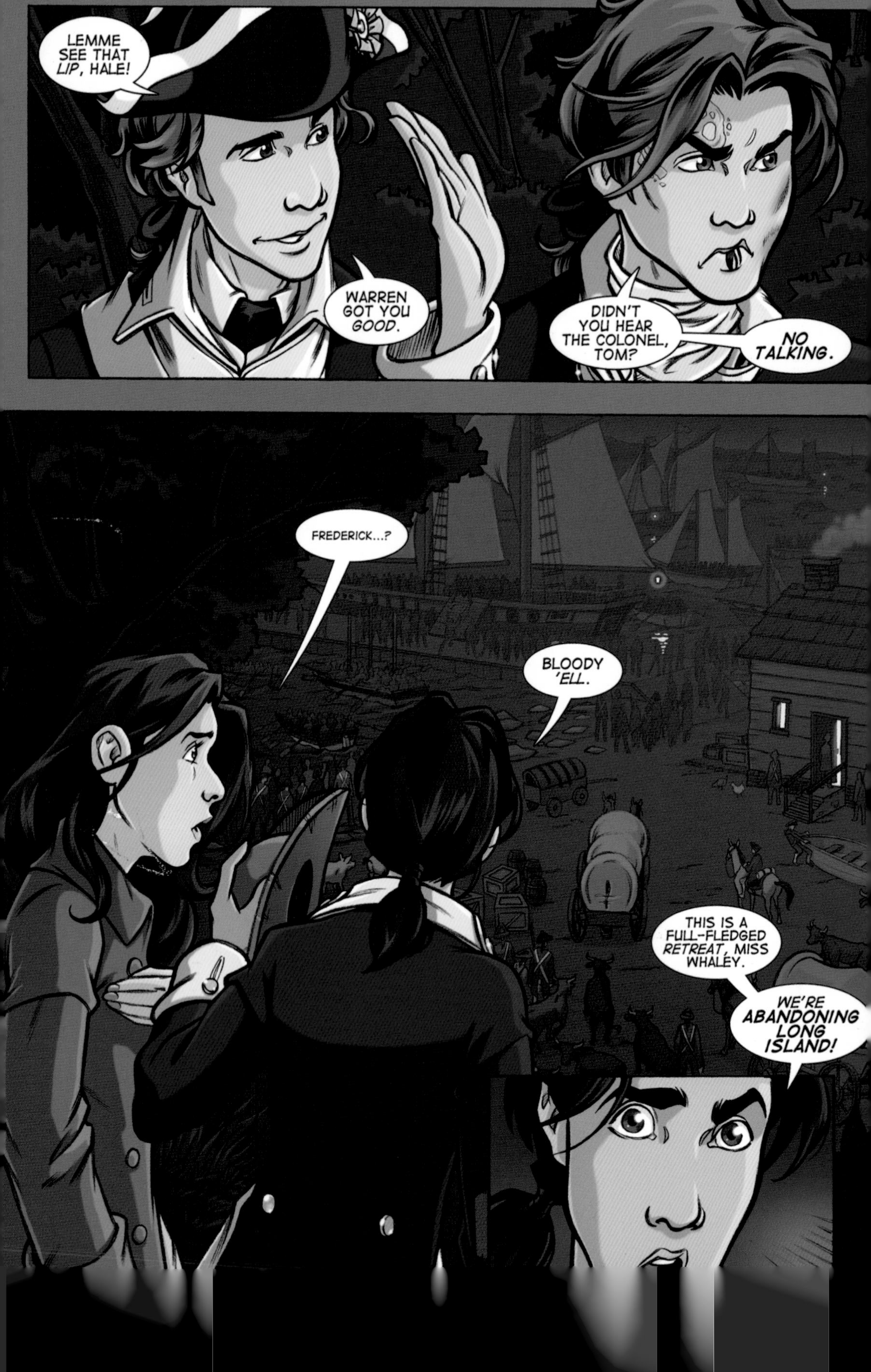
LEMME SEE THAT *LIP*, HALE!
WARREN GOT YOU *GOOD*.
DIDN'T YOU HEAR THE COLONEL, TOM?
NO TALKING.
FREDERICK...?
BLOODY *'ELL*.
THIS IS A FULL-FLEDGED *RETREAT*, MISS WHALEY.
WE'RE ABANDONING LONG ISLAND!

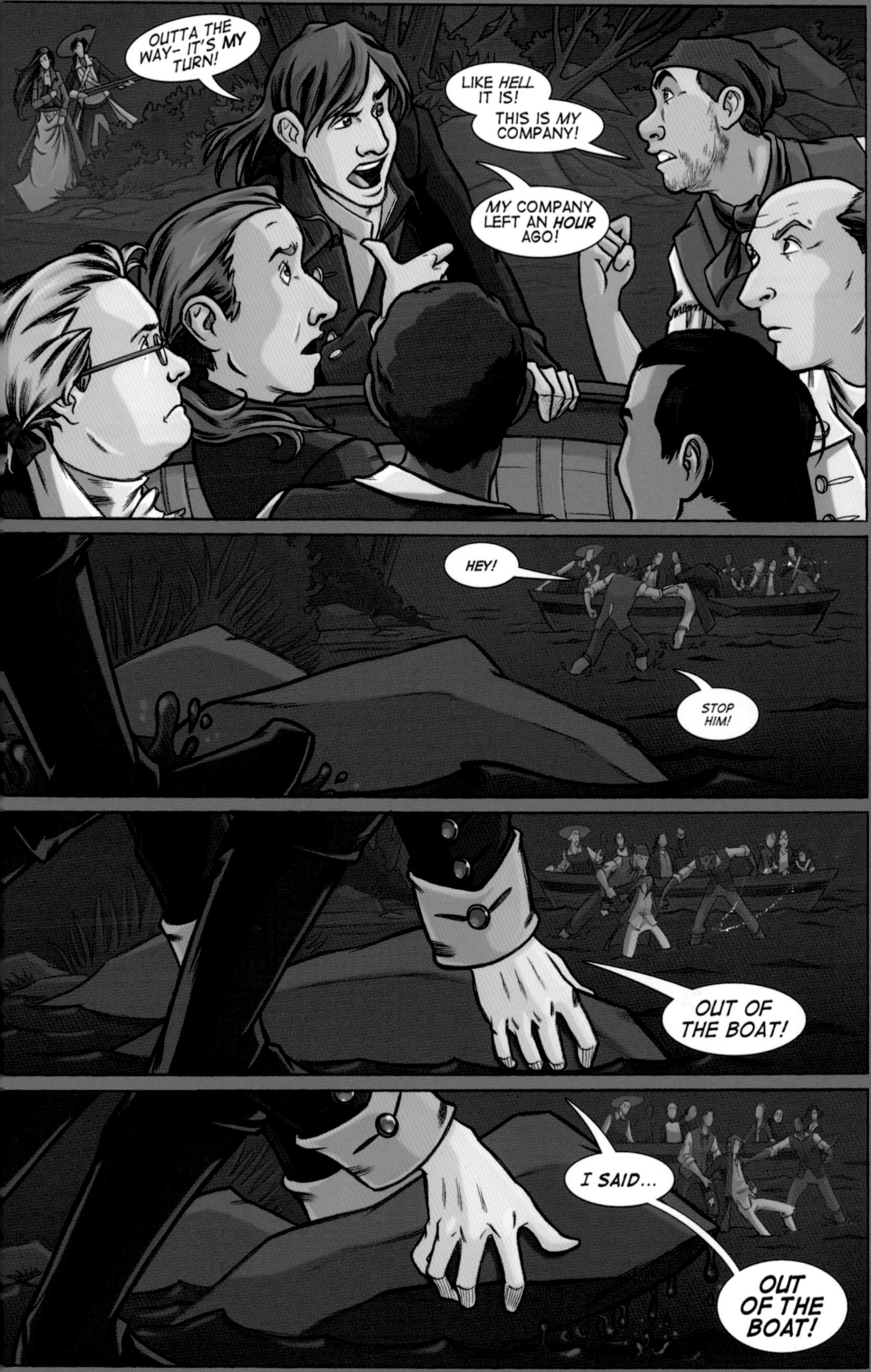
OUTTA THE WAY- IT'S MY TURN!
LIKE HELL IT IS! THIS IS MY COMPANY!
MY COMPANY LEFT AN HOUR AGO!
HEY!
STOP HIM!
OUT OF THE BOAT!
I SAID...
OUT OF THE BOAT!

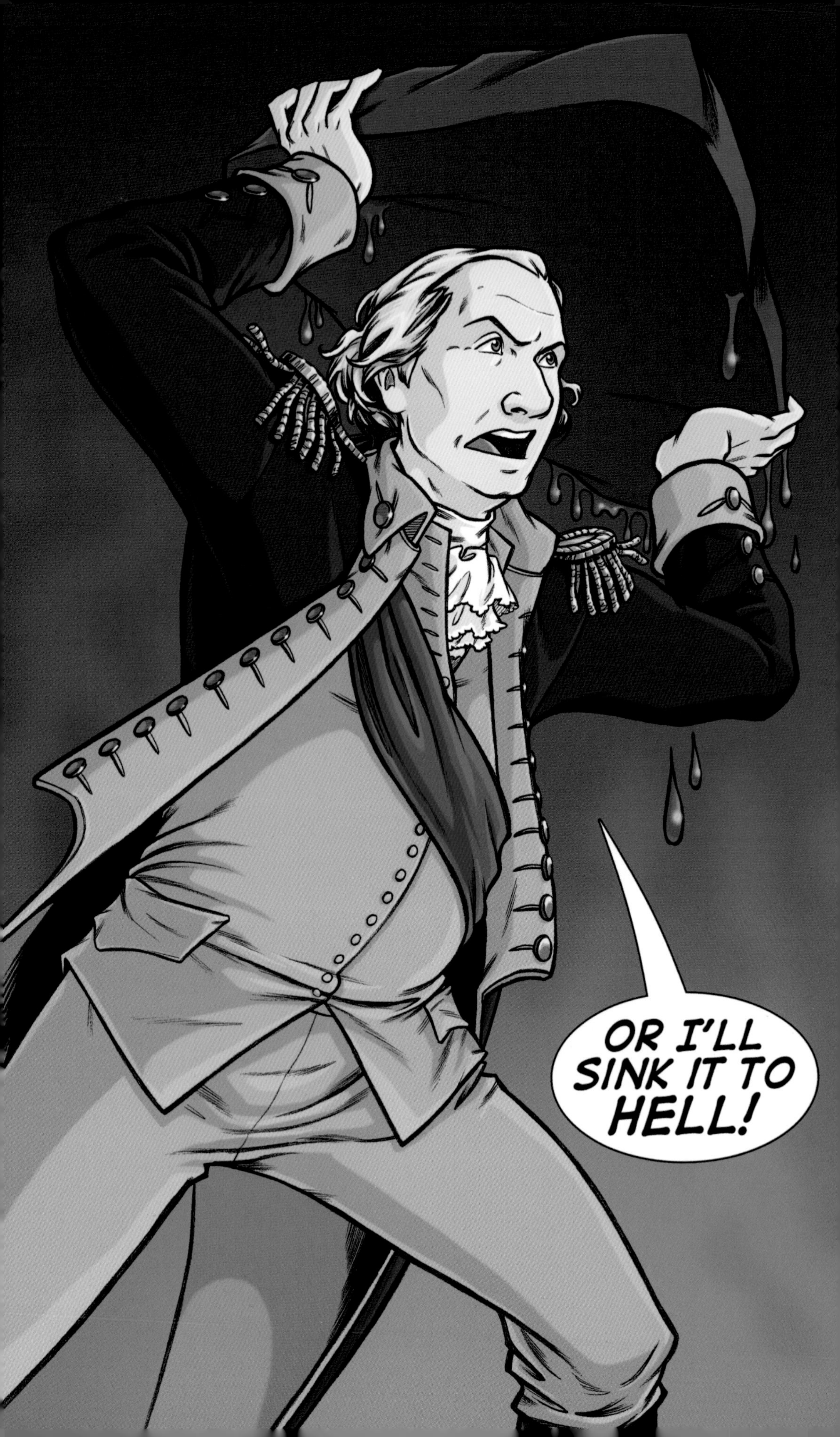
OR I'LL SINK IT TO HELL!

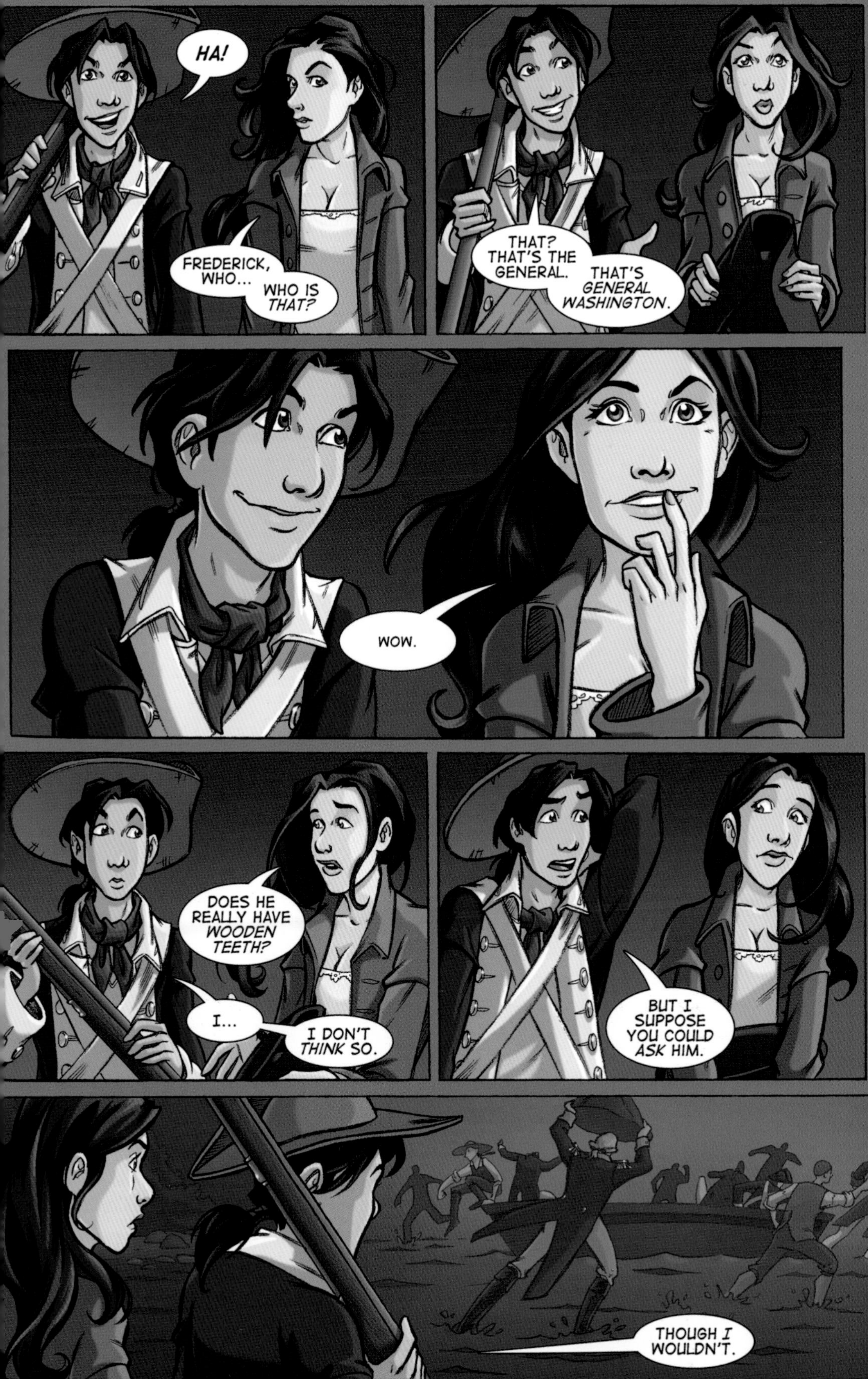
HA!
FREDERICK, WHO...
WHO IS THAT?
THAT? THAT'S THE GENERAL.
THAT'S GENERAL WASHINGTON.
WOW.
DOES HE REALLY HAVE WOODEN TEETH?
I...
I DON'T THINK SO.
BUT I SUPPOSE YOU COULD ASK HIM.
THOUGH I WOULDN'T.

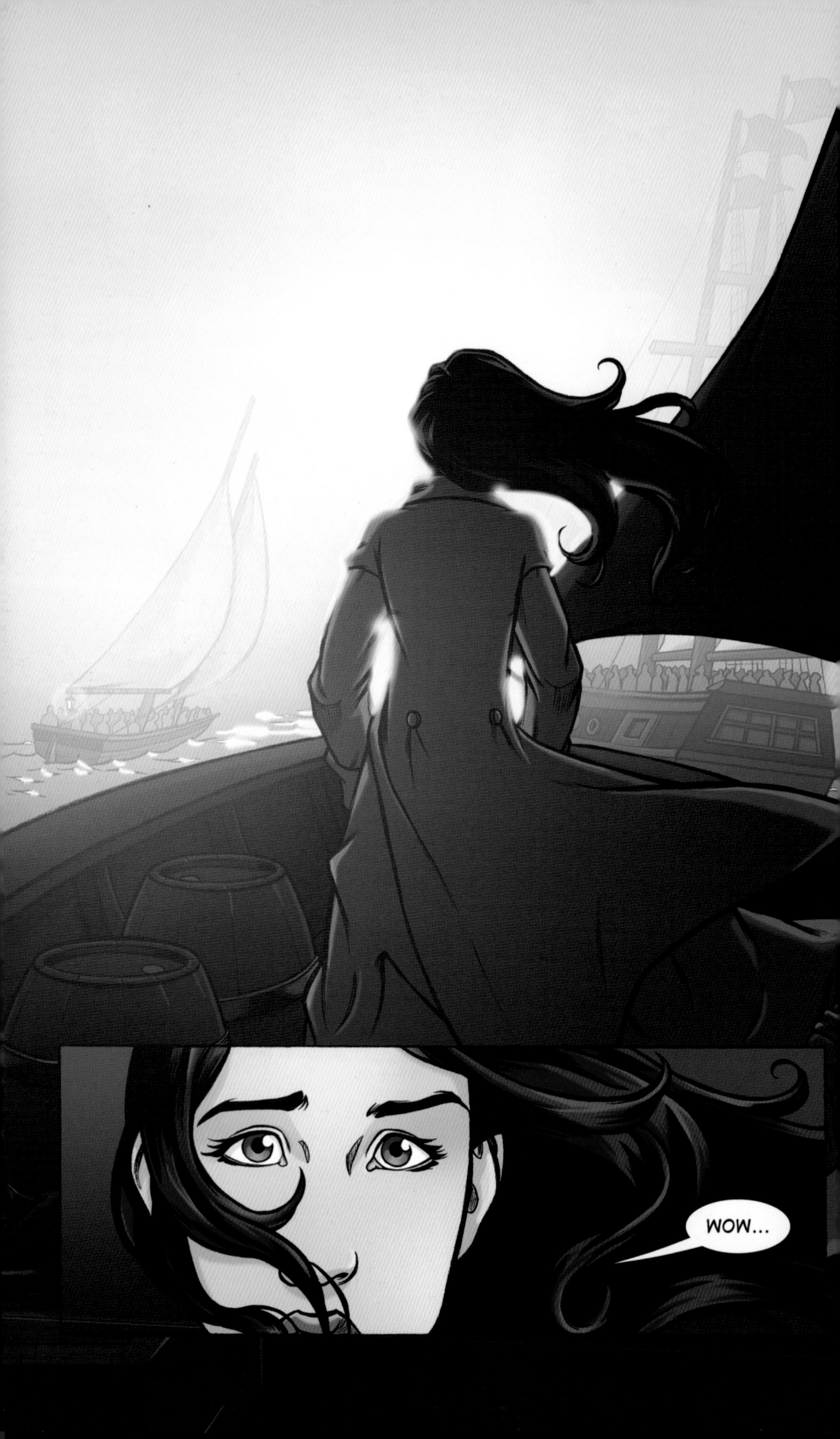
WOW...

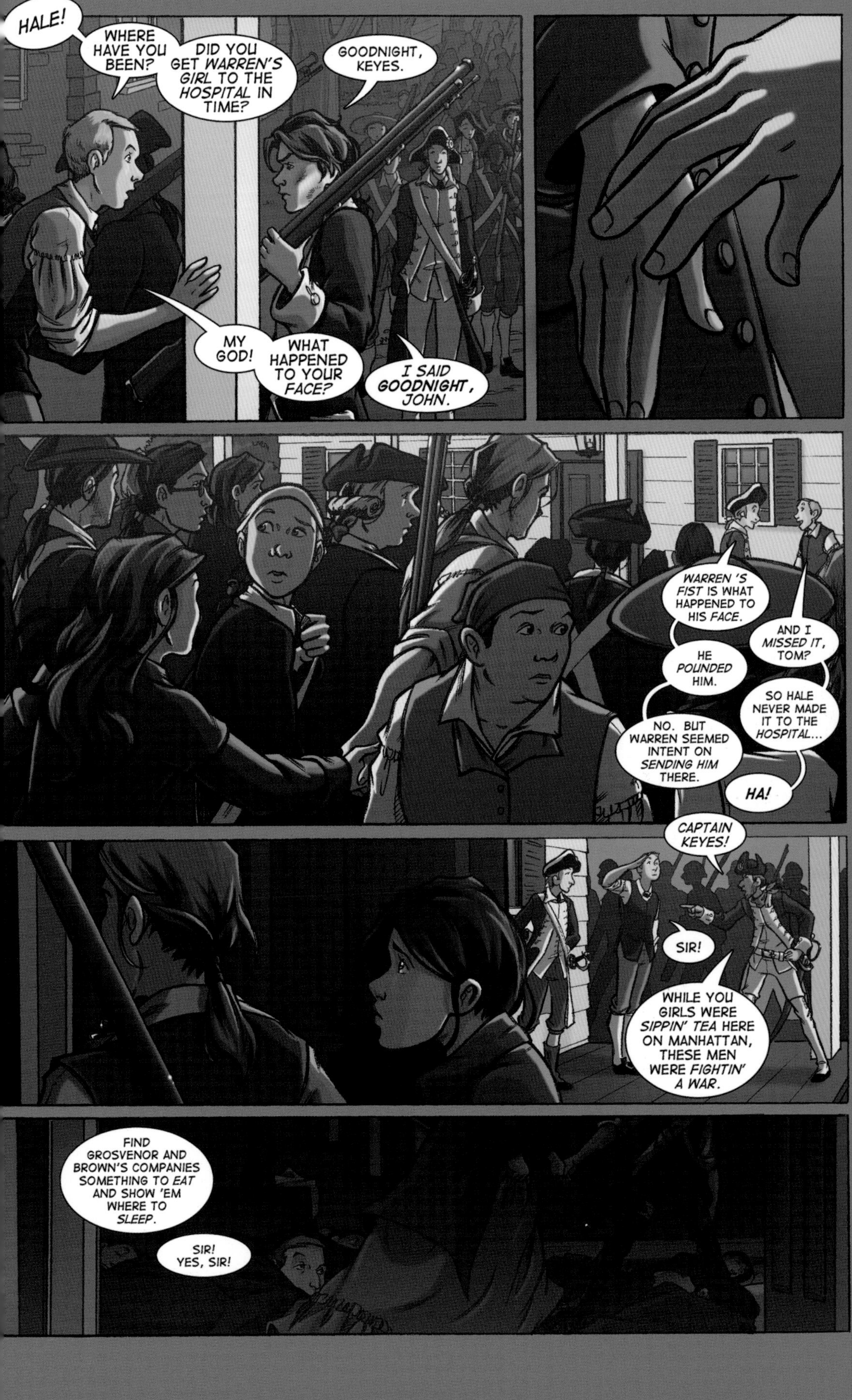
HALE!
WHERE HAVE YOU BEEN?
DID YOU GET WARREN'S GIRL TO THE HOSPITAL IN TIME?
GOODNIGHT, KEYES.
MY GOD!
WHAT HAPPENED TO YOUR FACE?
I SAID GOODNIGHT, JOHN.
WARREN 'S FIST IS WHAT HAPPENED TO HIS FACE.
HE POUNDED HIM.
AND I MISSED IT, TOM?
NO. BUT WARREN SEEMED INTENT ON SENDING HIM THERE.
SO HALE NEVER MADE IT TO THE HOSPITAL...
HA!
CAPTAIN KEYES!
SIR!
WHILE YOU GIRLS WERE SIPPIN' TEA HERE ON MANHATTAN, THESE MEN WERE FIGHTIN' A WAR.
FIND GROSVENOR AND BROWN'S COMPANIES SOMETHING TO EAT AND SHOW 'EM WHERE TO SLEEP.
SIR! YES, SIR!

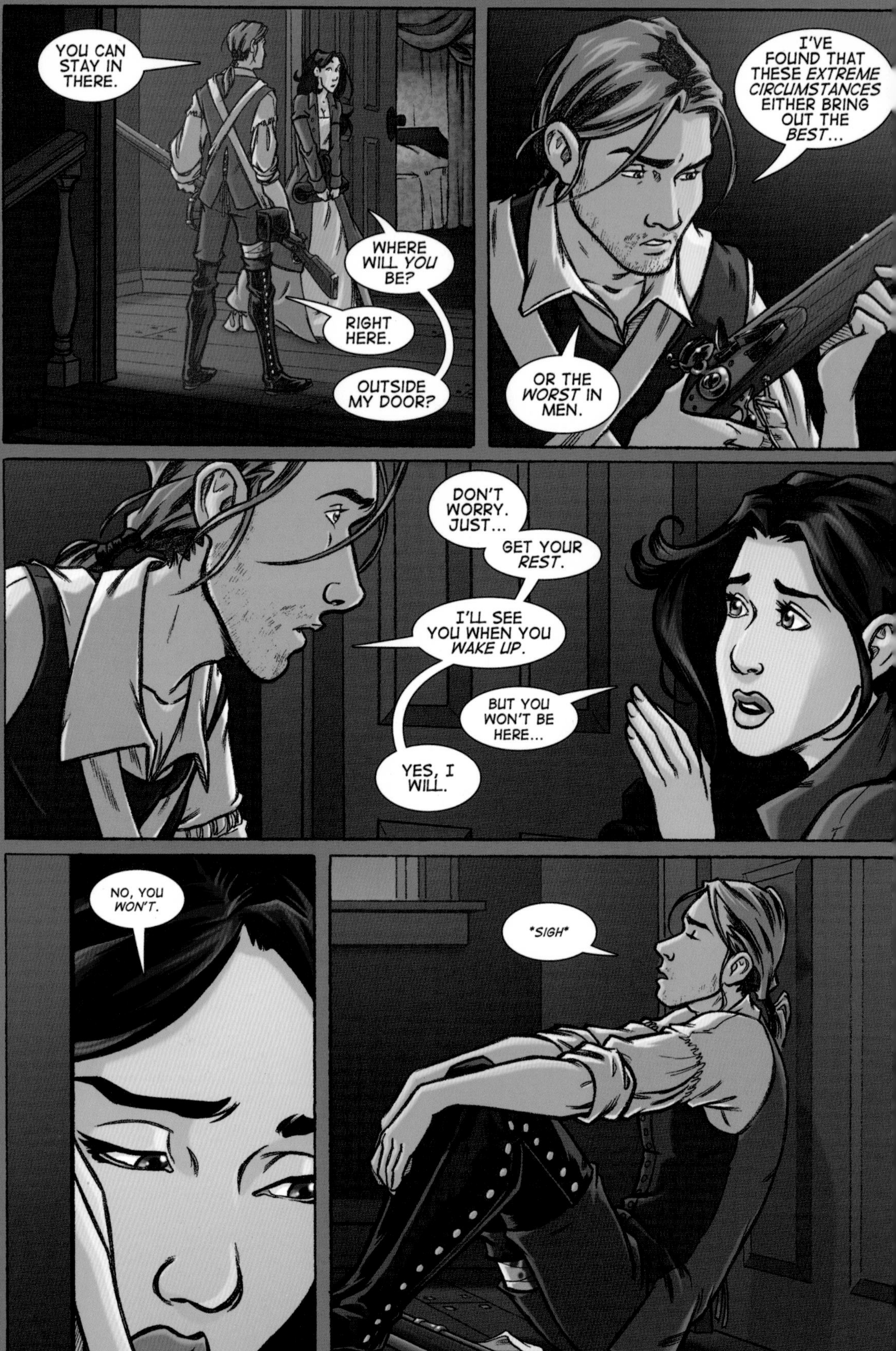
YOU CAN STAY IN THERE.
WHERE WILL *YOU* BE?
RIGHT HERE.
OUTSIDE MY DOOR?
I'VE FOUND THAT THESE *EXTREME CIRCUMSTANCES* EITHER BRING OUT THE *BEST*...
OR THE *WORST* IN MEN.
DON'T WORRY. JUST...
GET YOUR *REST*.
I'LL SEE YOU WHEN YOU *WAKE UP*.
BUT YOU WON'T BE HERE...
YES, I WILL.
NO, YOU *WON'T*.
SIGH

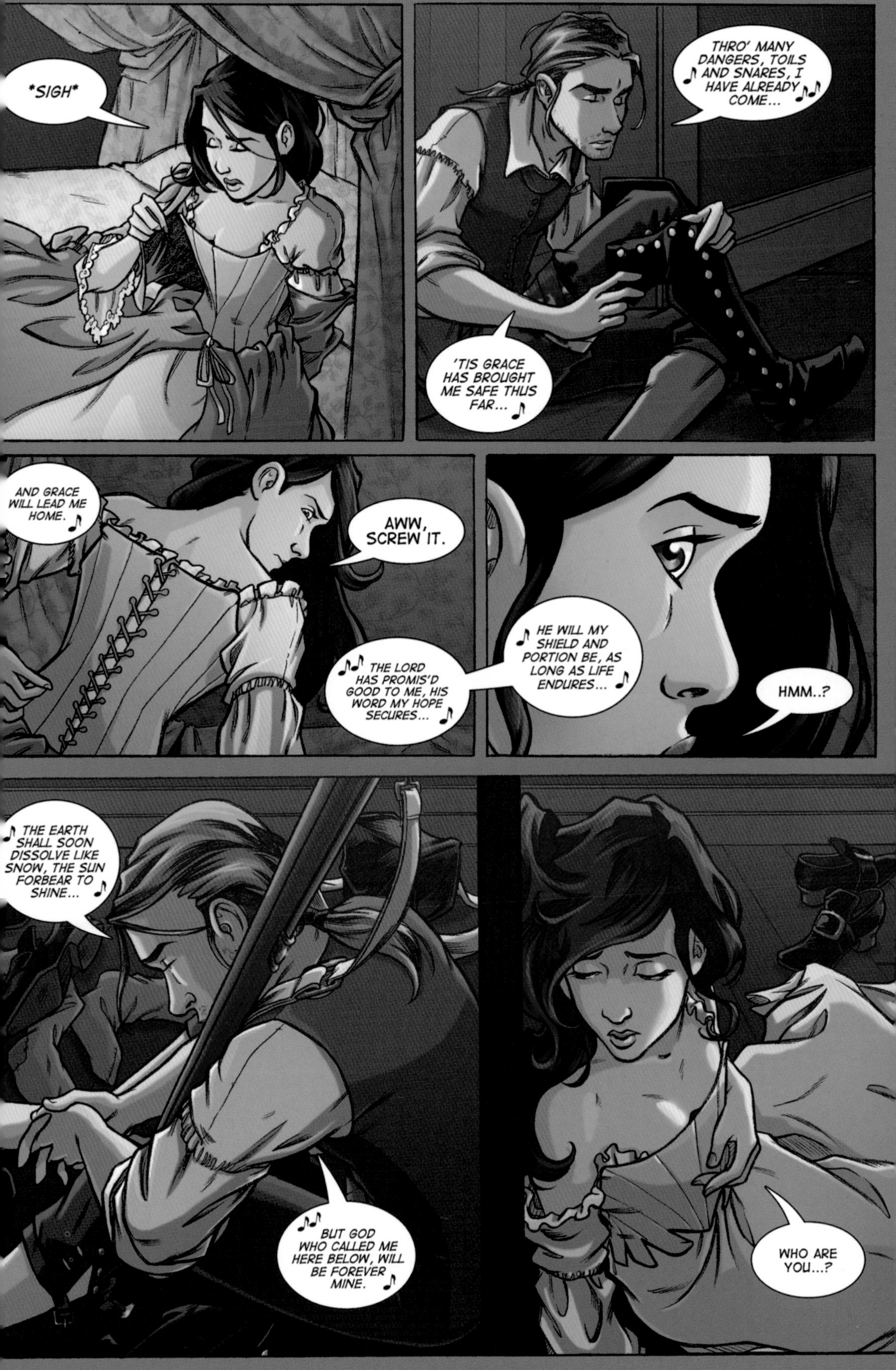
SIGH
THRO' MANY DANGERS, TOILS AND SNARES, I HAVE ALREADY COME...
'TIS GRACE HAS BROUGHT ME SAFE THUS FAR...
AND GRACE WILL LEAD ME HOME.
AWW, SCREW IT.
THE LORD HAS PROMIS'D GOOD TO ME, HIS WORD MY HOPE SECURES...
HE WILL MY SHIELD AND PORTION BE, AS LONG AS LIFE ENDURES...
HMM..?
THE EARTH SHALL SOON DISSOLVE LIKE SNOW, THE SUN FORBEAR TO SHINE...
BUT GOD WHO CALLED ME HERE BELOW, WILL BE FOREVER MINE.
WHO ARE YOU...?

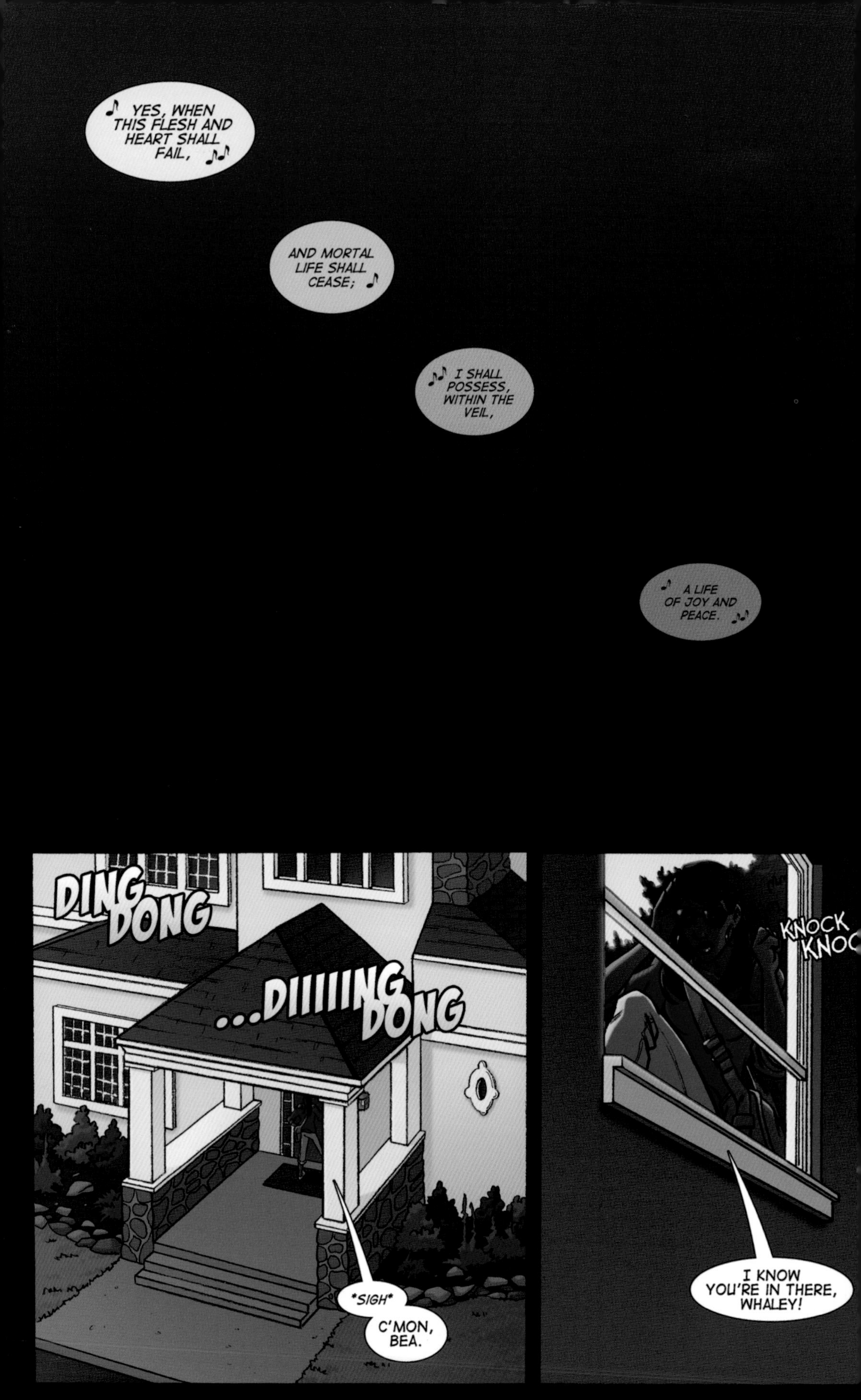
YES, WHEN THIS FLESH AND HEART SHALL FAIL,
AND MORTAL LIFE SHALL CEASE;
I SHALL POSSESS, WITHIN THE VEIL,
A LIFE OF JOY AND PEACE.
DING DONG
...DIIIIING DONG
SIGH
C'MON, BEA.
KNOCK KNOC
I KNOW YOU'RE IN THERE, WHALEY!

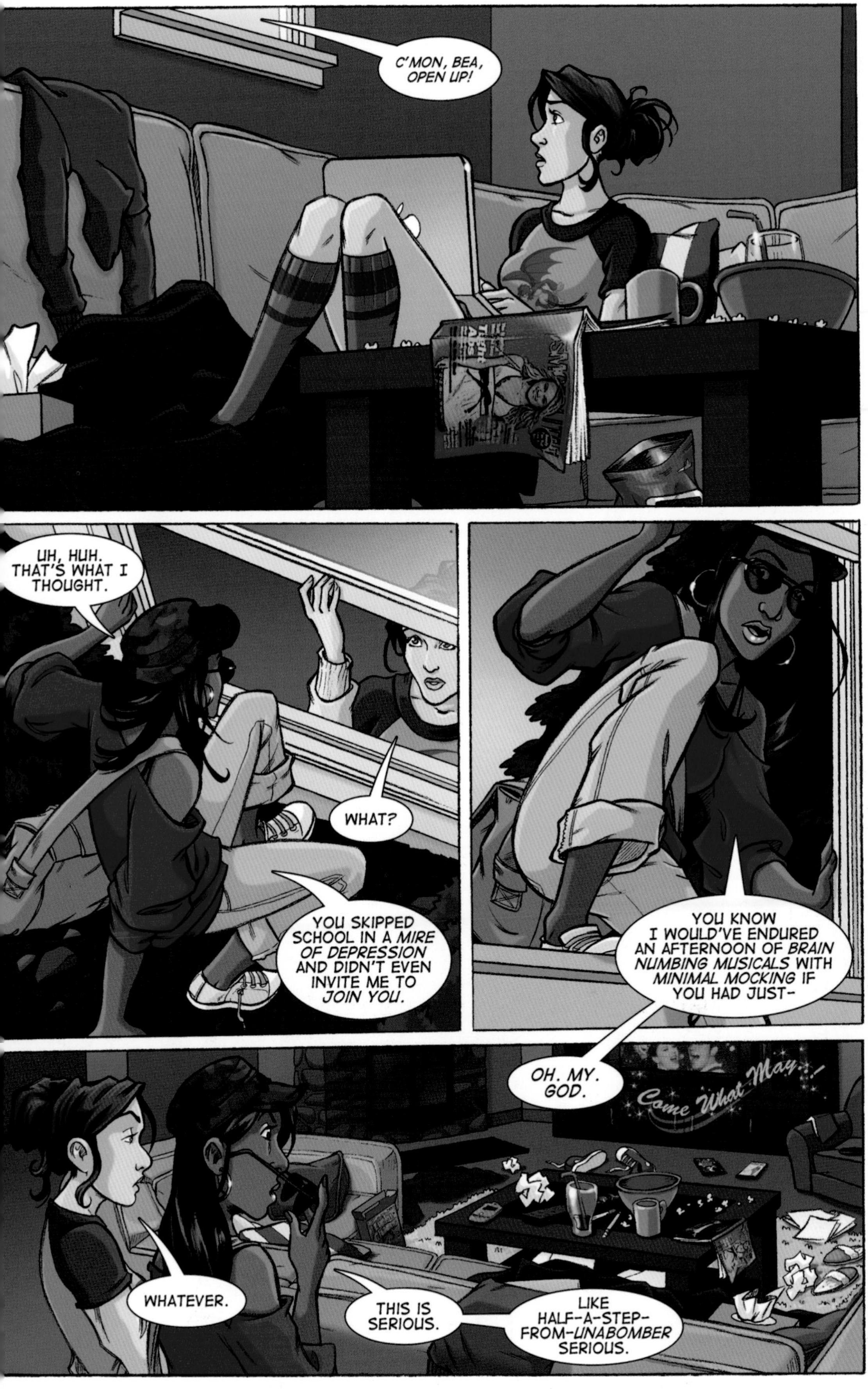

C'MON, BEA, OPEN UP!
UH, HUH. THAT'S WHAT I THOUGHT.
WHAT?
YOU SKIPPED SCHOOL IN A *MIRE OF DEPRESSION* AND DIDN'T EVEN INVITE ME TO *JOIN YOU*.
YOU KNOW I WOULD'VE ENDURED AN AFTERNOON OF *BRAIN NUMBING MUSICALS* WITH *MINIMAL MOCKING* IF YOU HAD JUST-
OH. MY. GOD.
Come What May...!
WHATEVER.
THIS IS SERIOUS.
LIKE HALF-A-STEP-FROM-*UNABOMBER* SERIOUS.

MULLIGAN DOES NOT DESERVE THIS LEVEL OF WALLOWING!

WHAT?

LIZ TOLD ME EVERYTHING THAT HAPPENED AT THE MUSEUM LAST NIGHT SINCE YOU DIDN'T CALL ME LIKE YOU *PROMISED*.

I SORT OF HAD OTHER THINGS ON MY MIND.

RING RING

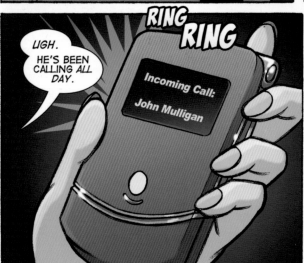

RING RING

UGH. HE'S BEEN CALLING *ALL* DAY.

Incoming Call:

John Mulligan

I GET THAT JOHN MULLIGAN IS A FIRST-CLASS LOSER, BUT I DON'T THINK HE DESERVES *THIS* MUCH ATTENTION.

I'M NOT UPSET ABOUT WHAT JOHN DID. I WAS OVER IT LIKE *FIVE MINUTES* AFTER IT HAPPENED.

YVETTE...

IF I TELL YOU SOMETHING, YOU HAVE TO *PROMISE* TO *BELIEVE* ME.

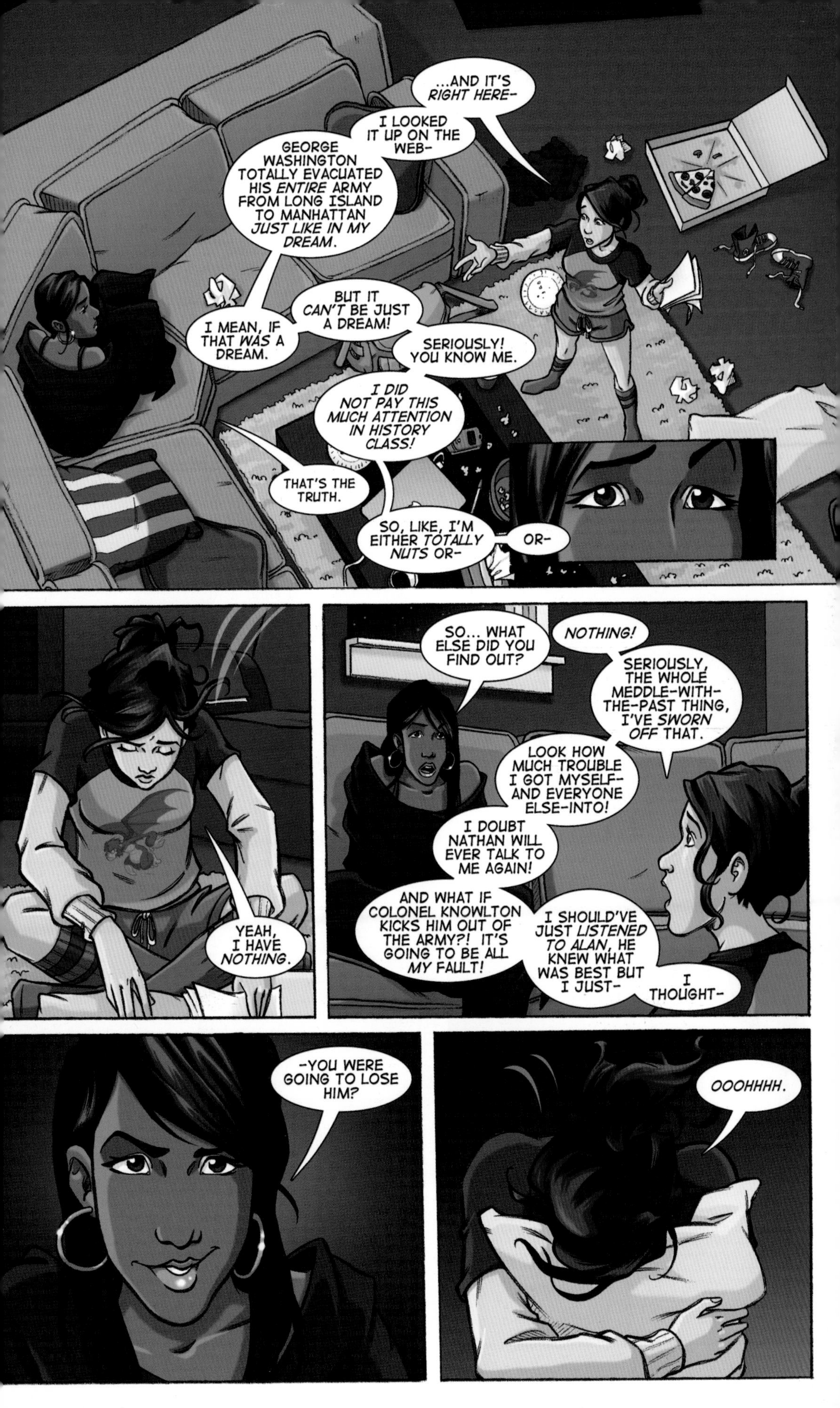
...AND IT'S *RIGHT HERE*-
I LOOKED IT UP ON THE WEB-
GEORGE WASHINGTON TOTALLY EVACUATED HIS *ENTIRE* ARMY FROM LONG ISLAND TO MANHATTAN *JUST LIKE IN MY DREAM*.
I MEAN, IF THAT *WAS* A DREAM.
BUT IT *CAN'T* BE JUST A DREAM!
SERIOUSLY! YOU KNOW ME.
I DID NOT PAY THIS MUCH ATTENTION IN HISTORY CLASS!
THAT'S THE TRUTH.
SO, LIKE, I'M EITHER *TOTALLY NUTS* OR-
OR-
YEAH, I HAVE *NOTHING*.
SO... WHAT ELSE DID YOU FIND OUT?
NOTHING!
SERIOUSLY, THE WHOLE MEDDLE-WITH-THE-PAST THING, I'VE *SWORN OFF* THAT.
LOOK HOW MUCH TROUBLE I GOT MYSELF- AND EVERYONE ELSE-INTO!
I DOUBT NATHAN WILL EVER TALK TO ME AGAIN!
AND WHAT IF COLONEL KNOWLTON KICKS HIM OUT OF THE ARMY?! IT'S GOING TO BE ALL *MY* FAULT!
I SHOULD'VE JUST *LISTENED TO ALAN*, HE KNEW WHAT WAS BEST BUT I JUST-
I THOUGHT-
-YOU WERE GOING TO LOSE HIM?
OOOHHHH.

GOD, THAT IS SO ROMANTIC!

IT'S LIKE SOMETHING OUT OF A MOVIE!

YES. *EXACTLY* LIKE THE MOVIES.

EXCEPT THAT THE CANNON BALLS CAN ACTUALLY KILL YOU.

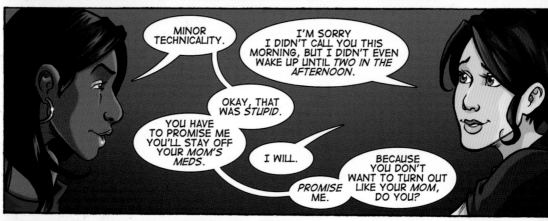

MINOR TECHNICALITY.

I'M SORRY I DIDN'T CALL YOU THIS MORNING, BUT I DIDN'T EVEN WAKE UP UNTIL *TWO IN THE AFTERNOON.*

OKAY, THAT WAS *STUPID.*

YOU HAVE TO PROMISE ME YOU'LL STAY OFF YOUR *MOM'S* MEDS.

I WILL.

PROMISE ME.

BECAUSE YOU DON'T WANT TO TURN OUT LIKE YOUR *MOM,* DO YOU?

ALL RIGHT, ALL RIGHT!

I PROMISE!

AND NO MORE MEDDLING WITH HISTORY, EITHER!

I'M DONE WITH *DRUGS* AND *HISTORY MUSEUMS* AND *INTERNET SEARCHES* FOR GOOD!

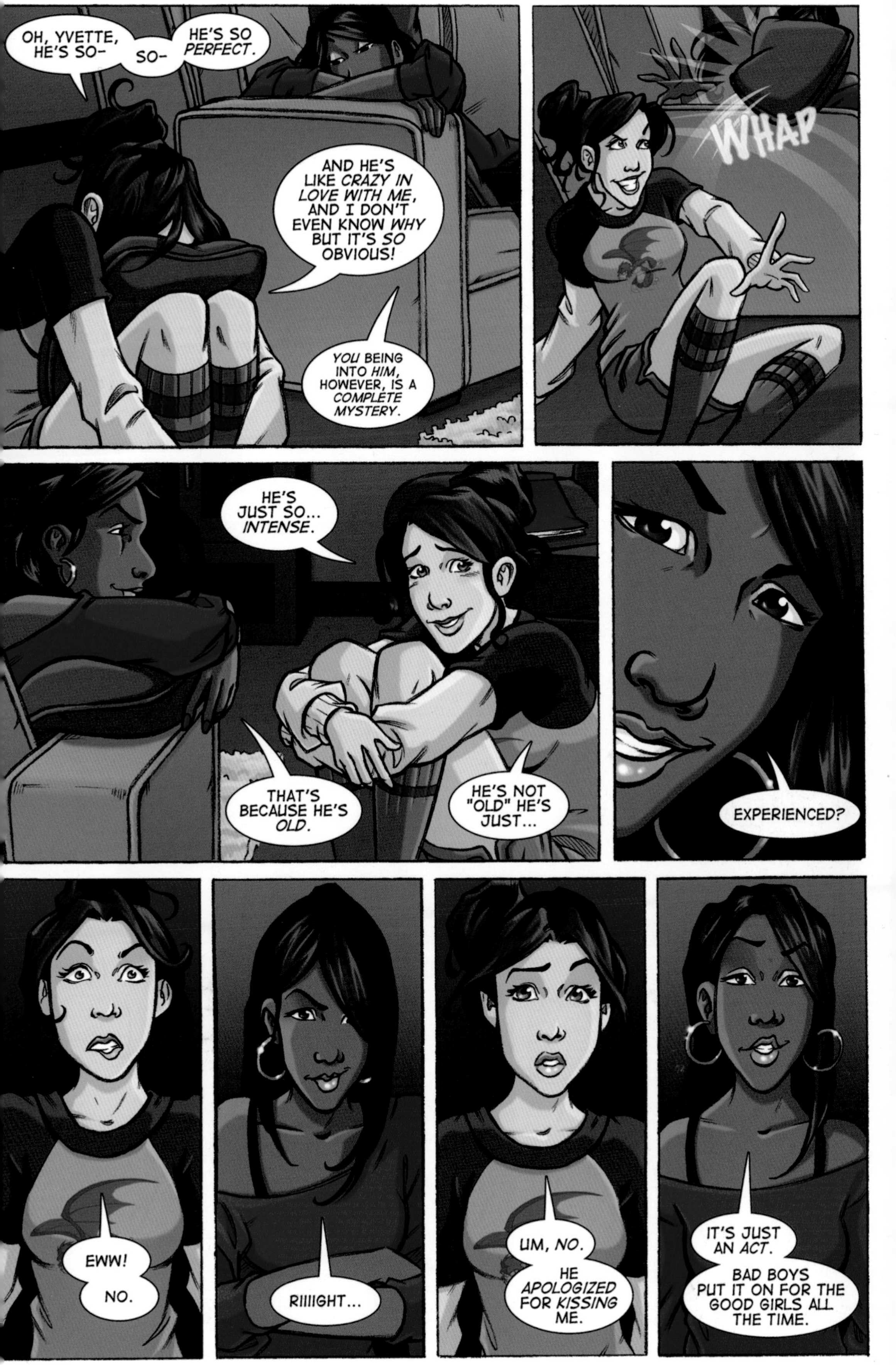
OH, YVETTE, HE'S SO-
SO-
HE'S SO *PERFECT*.
AND HE'S LIKE *CRAZY IN LOVE WITH ME*, AND I DON'T EVEN KNOW *WHY* BUT IT'S *SO* OBVIOUS!
YOU BEING INTO *HIM*, HOWEVER, IS A *COMPLETE MYSTERY*.
WHAP
HE'S JUST SO... *INTENSE*.
THAT'S BECAUSE HE'S *OLD*.
HE'S NOT "OLD" HE'S JUST...
EXPERIENCED?
EWW!
NO.
RIIIIGHT...
UM, *NO*.
HE *APOLOGIZED* FOR *KISSING* ME.
IT'S JUST AN *ACT*.
BAD BOYS PUT IT ON FOR THE GOOD GIRLS ALL THE TIME.

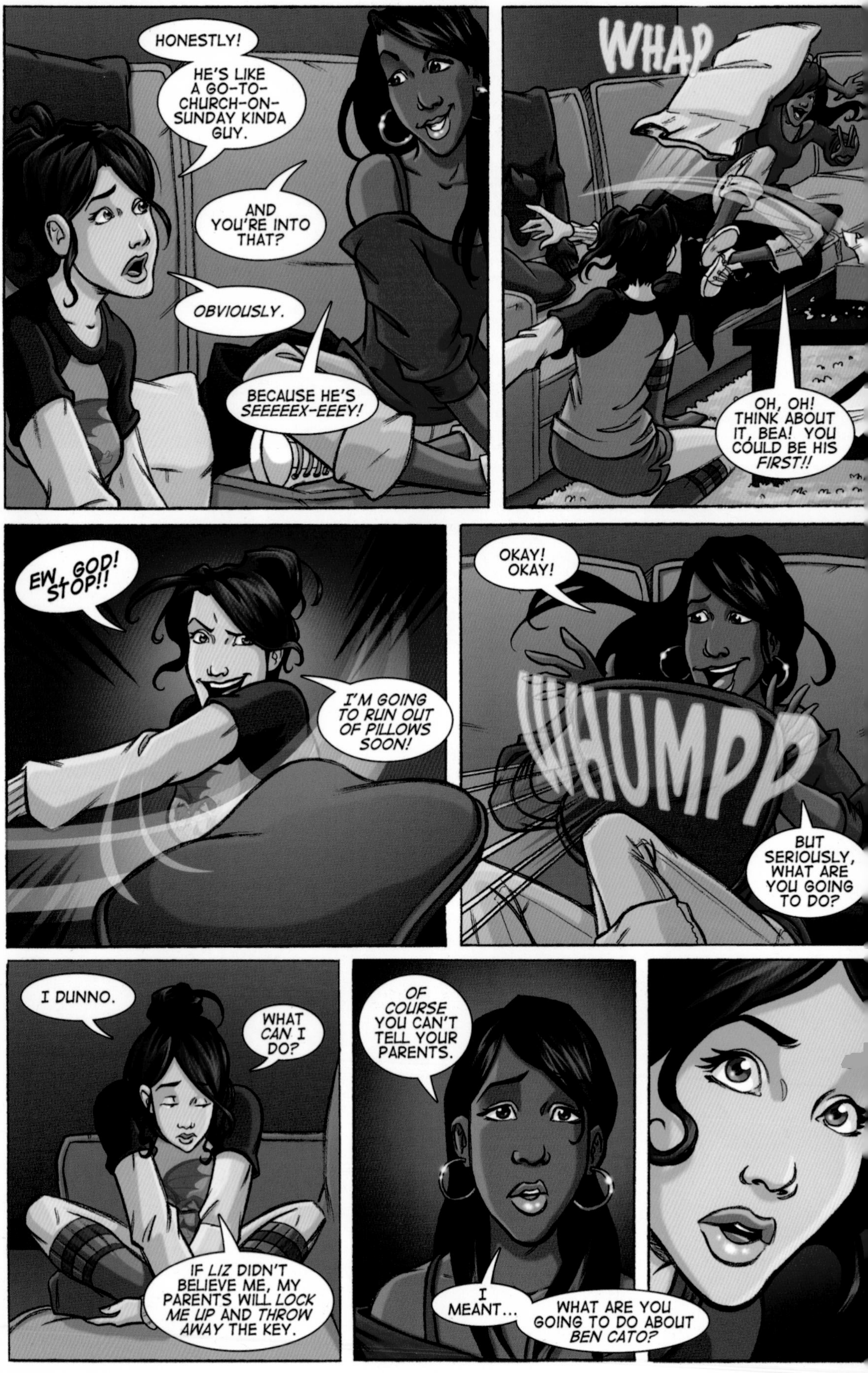
HONESTLY!
HE'S LIKE A GO-TO-CHURCH-ON-SUNDAY KINDA GUY.
AND YOU'RE INTO THAT?
OBVIOUSLY.
BECAUSE HE'S SEEEEEX-EEEY!
WHAP
OH, OH! THINK ABOUT IT, BEA! YOU COULD BE HIS FIRST!!
EW, GOD! STOP!!
I'M GOING TO RUN OUT OF PILLOWS SOON!
OKAY! OKAY!
WHUMPP
BUT SERIOUSLY, WHAT ARE YOU GOING TO DO?
I DUNNO.
WHAT CAN I DO?
IF LIZ DIDN'T BELIEVE ME, MY PARENTS WILL LOCK ME UP AND THROW AWAY THE KEY.
OF COURSE YOU CAN'T TELL YOUR PARENTS.
I MEANT...
WHAT ARE YOU GOING TO DO ABOUT BEN CATO?

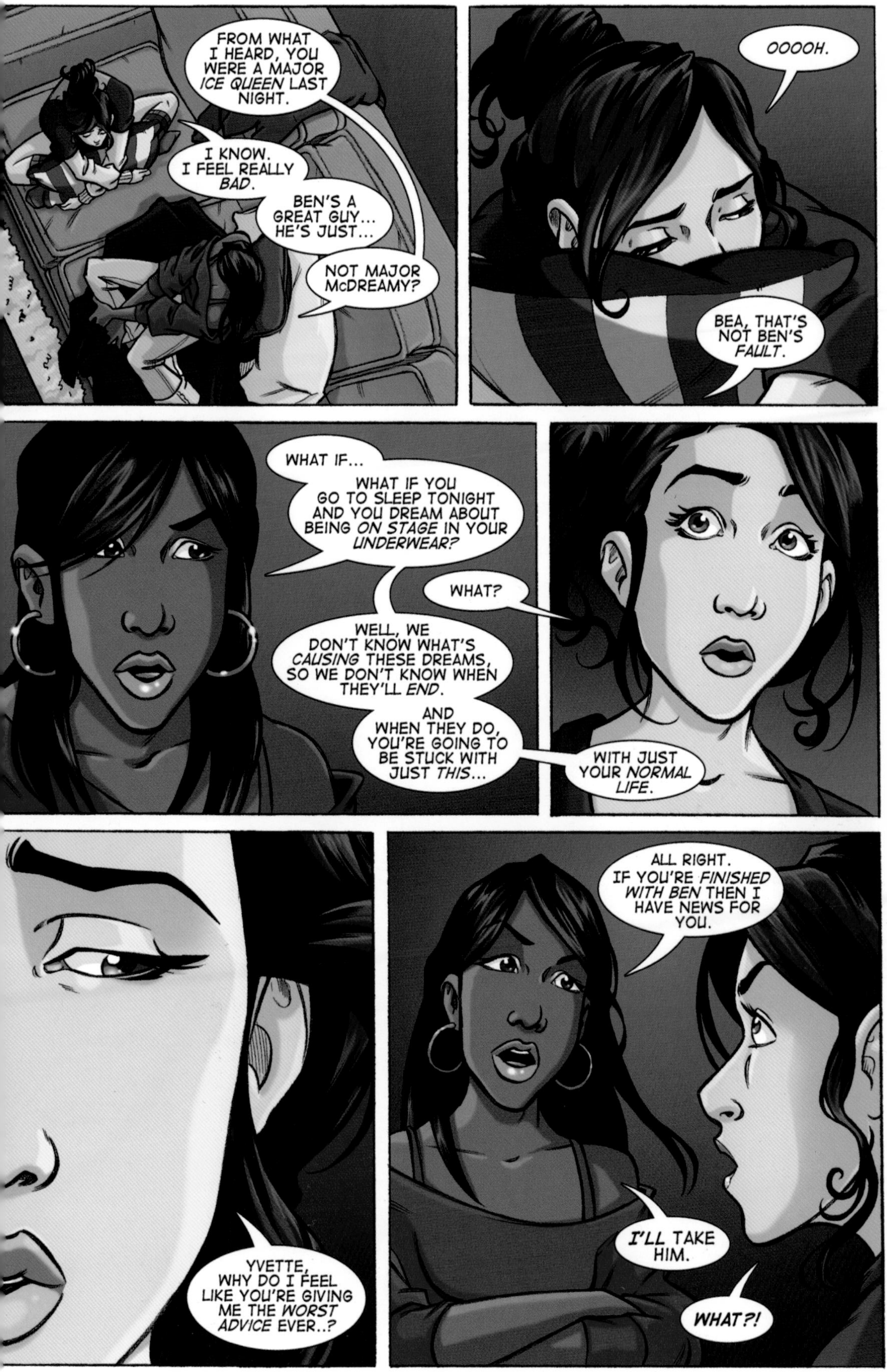
FROM WHAT I HEARD, YOU WERE A MAJOR *ICE QUEEN* LAST NIGHT.
I KNOW. I FEEL REALLY *BAD*.
BEN'S A GREAT GUY... HE'S JUST...
NOT MAJOR McDREAMY?
OOOOH.
BEA, THAT'S NOT BEN'S *FAULT*.
WHAT IF...
WHAT IF YOU GO TO SLEEP TONIGHT AND YOU DREAM ABOUT BEING *ON STAGE* IN YOUR *UNDERWEAR?*
WHAT?
WELL, WE DON'T KNOW WHAT'S *CAUSING* THESE DREAMS, SO WE DON'T KNOW WHEN THEY'LL *END*.
AND WHEN THEY DO, YOU'RE GOING TO BE STUCK WITH JUST *THIS*...
WITH JUST YOUR *NORMAL LIFE*.
YVETTE, WHY DO I FEEL LIKE YOU'RE GIVING ME THE *WORST ADVICE* EVER..?
ALL RIGHT. IF YOU'RE *FINISHED WITH BEN* THEN I HAVE NEWS FOR YOU.
I'LL TAKE HIM.
WHAT?!

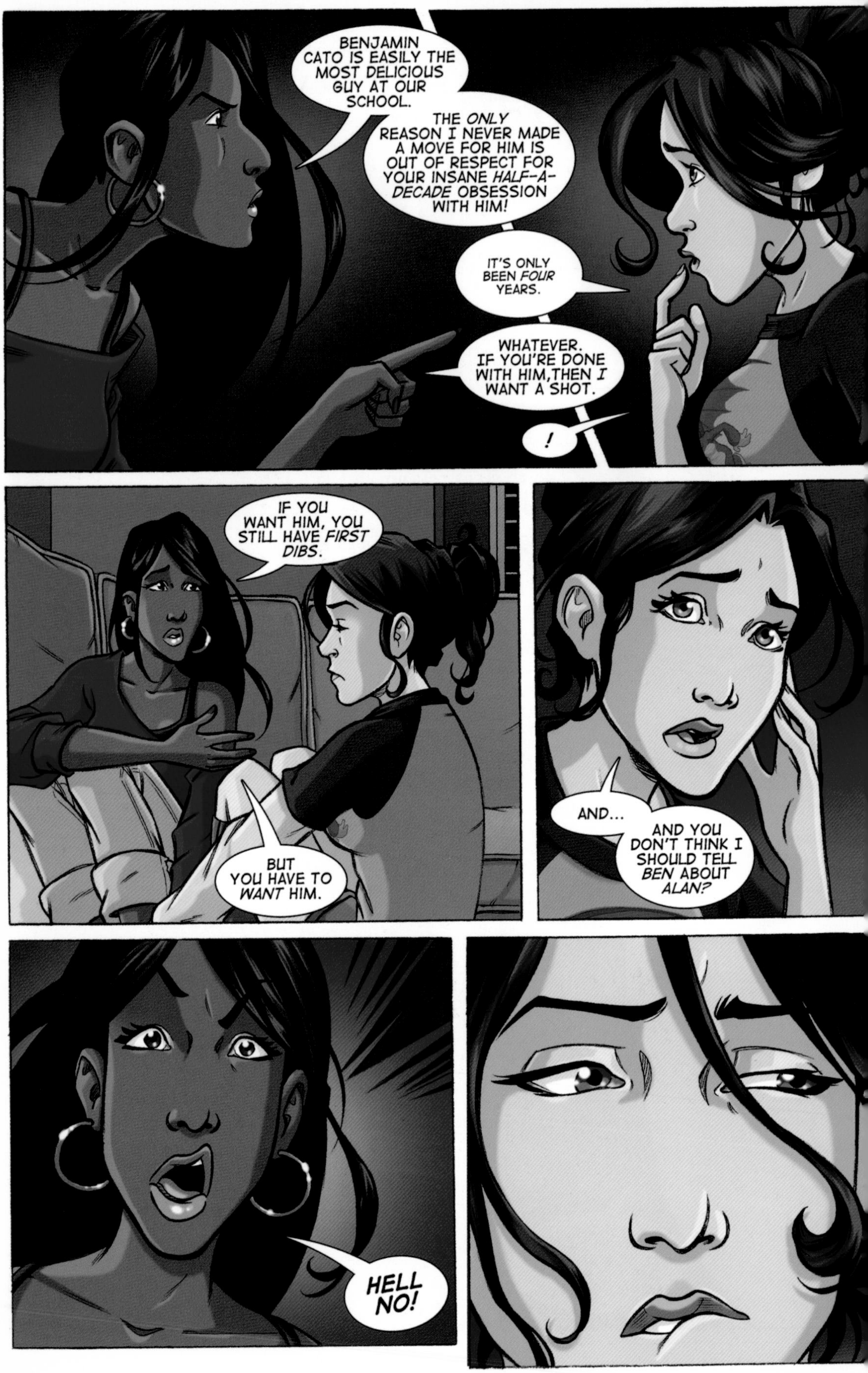
BENJAMIN CATO IS EASILY THE MOST DELICIOUS GUY AT OUR SCHOOL.
THE *ONLY* REASON I NEVER MADE A MOVE FOR HIM IS OUT OF RESPECT FOR YOUR INSANE *HALF-A-DECADE* OBSESSION WITH HIM!
IT'S ONLY BEEN *FOUR* YEARS.
WHATEVER. IF YOU'RE DONE WITH HIM,THEN *I* WANT A SHOT.
!
IF YOU WANT HIM, YOU STILL HAVE *FIRST DIBS*.
BUT YOU HAVE TO *WANT* HIM.
AND...
AND YOU DON'T THINK I SHOULD TELL *BEN* ABOUT *ALAN?*
HELL NO!

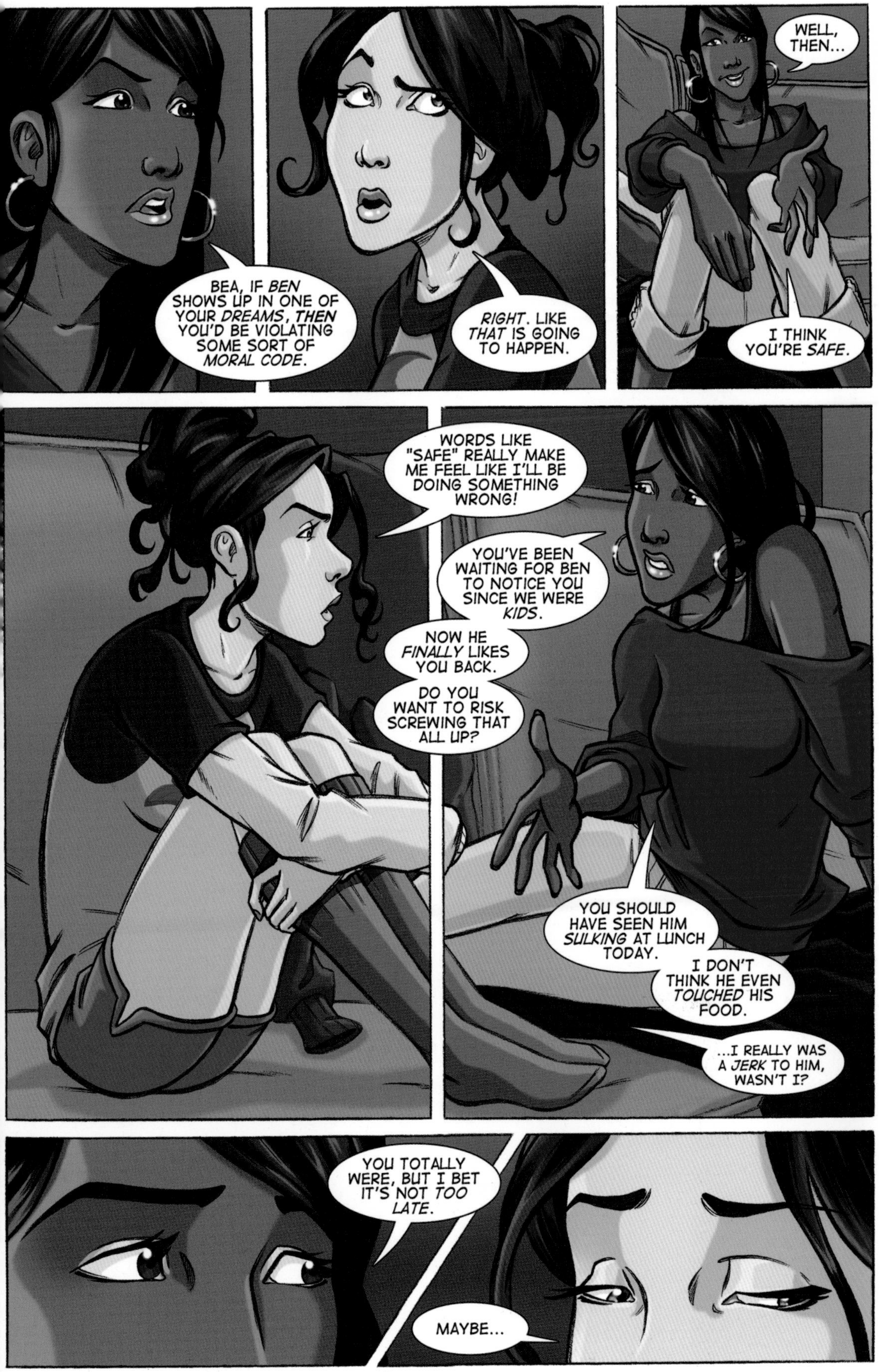
BEA, IF *BEN* SHOWS UP IN ONE OF YOUR *DREAMS*, *THEN* YOU'D BE VIOLATING SOME SORT OF *MORAL CODE*.
RIGHT. LIKE *THAT* IS GOING TO HAPPEN.
WELL, THEN...
I THINK YOU'RE *SAFE*.
WORDS LIKE "SAFE" REALLY MAKE ME FEEL LIKE I'LL BE DOING SOMETHING WRONG!
YOU'VE BEEN WAITING FOR BEN TO NOTICE YOU SINCE WE WERE *KIDS*.
NOW HE *FINALLY* LIKES YOU BACK.
DO YOU WANT TO RISK SCREWING THAT ALL UP?
YOU SHOULD HAVE SEEN HIM *SULKING* AT LUNCH TODAY.
I DON'T THINK HE EVEN *TOUCHED* HIS FOOD.
...I REALLY WAS A *JERK* TO HIM, WASN'T I?
YOU TOTALLY WERE, BUT I BET IT'S NOT *TOO LATE*.
MAYBE...

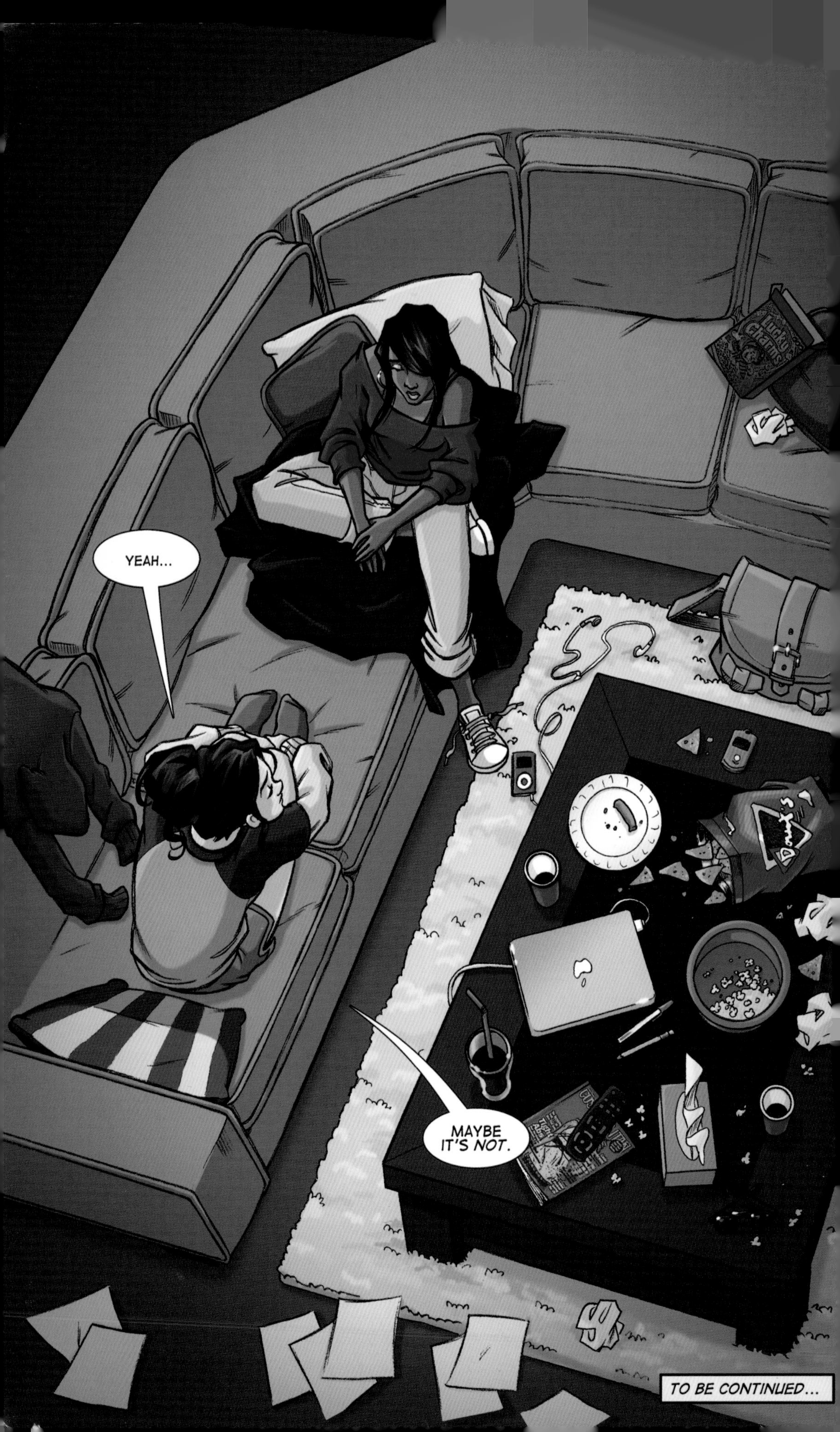
YEAH...
MAYBE IT'S *NOT*.
TO BE CONTINUED...

ART GALLERY BY
JENNY FRISON

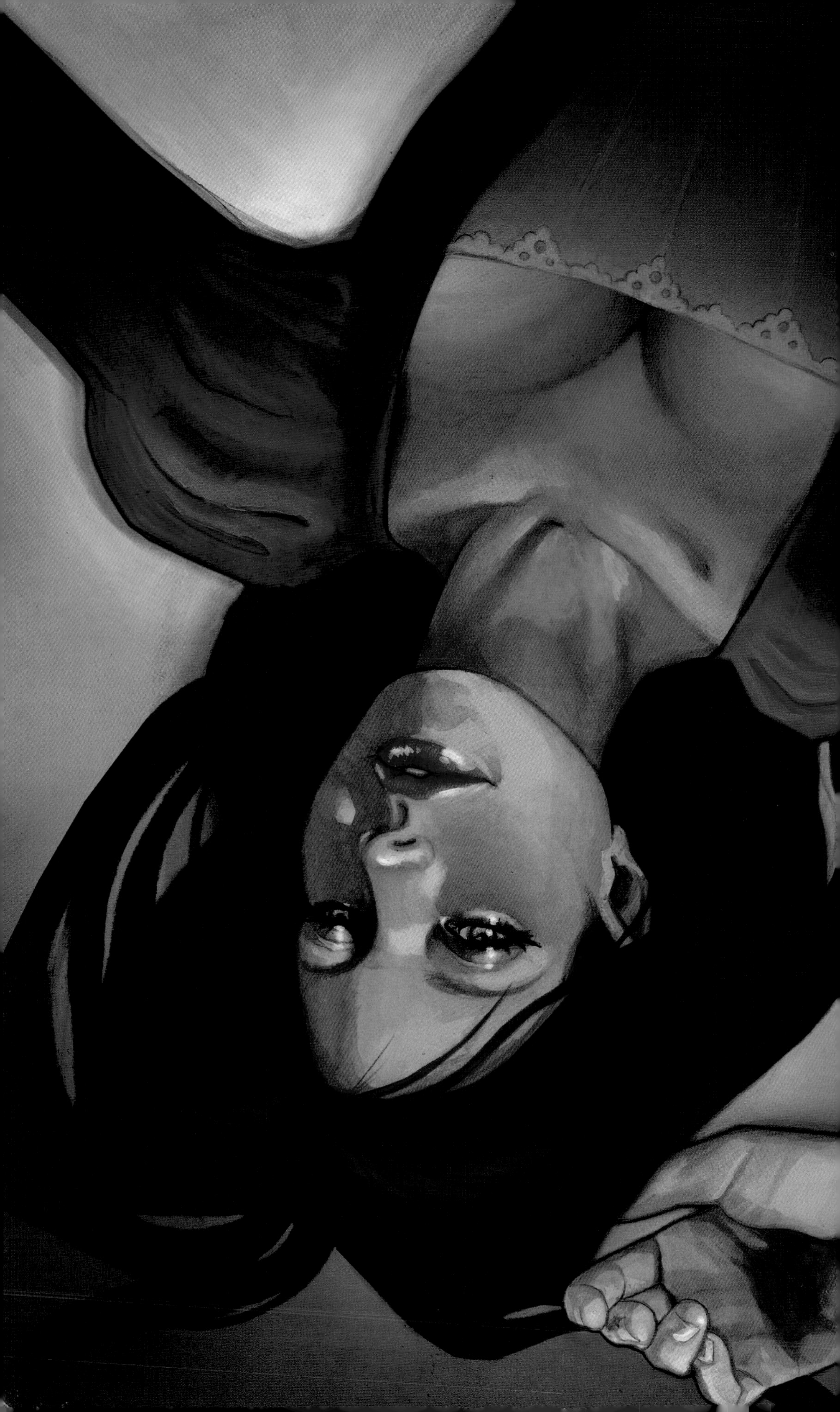

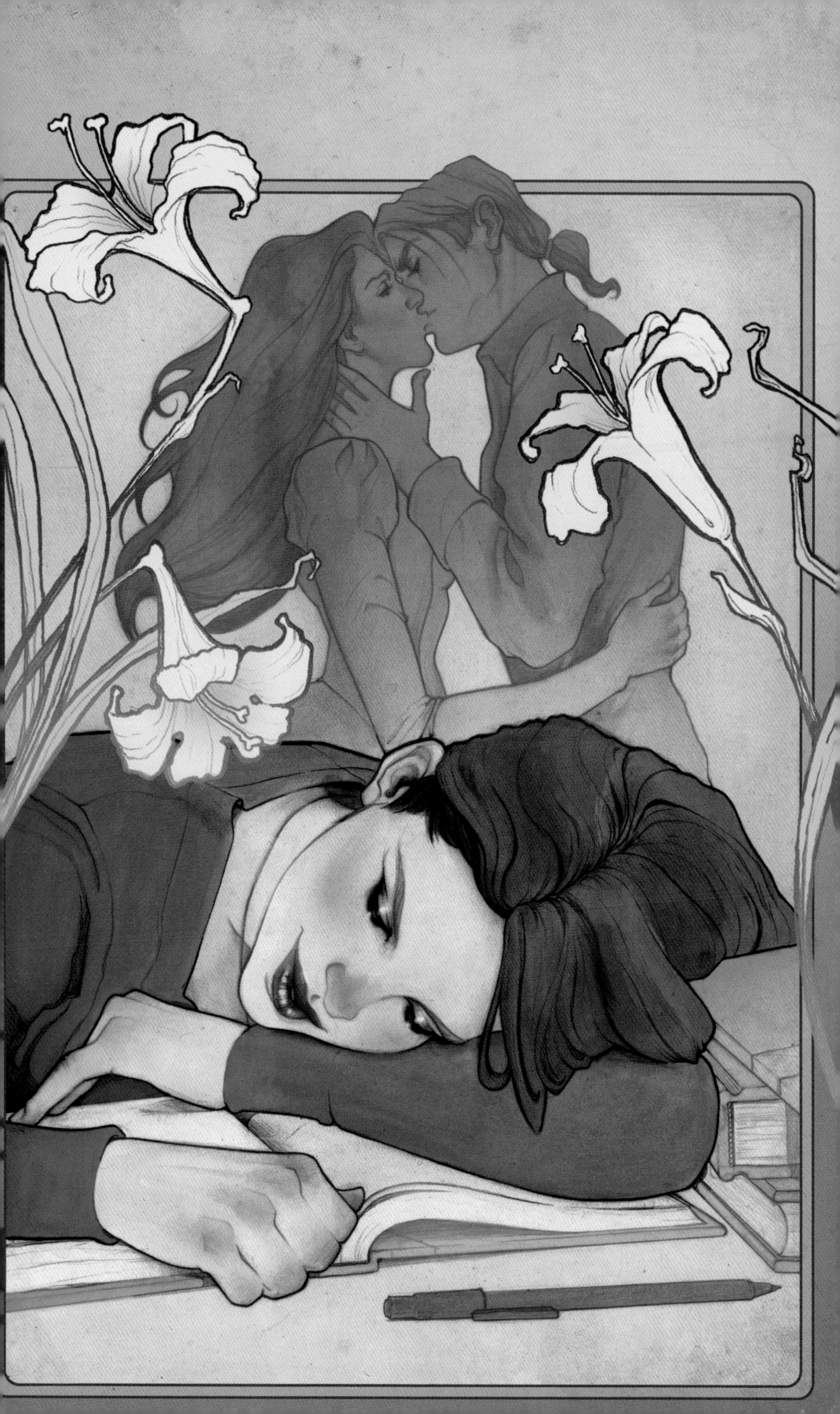

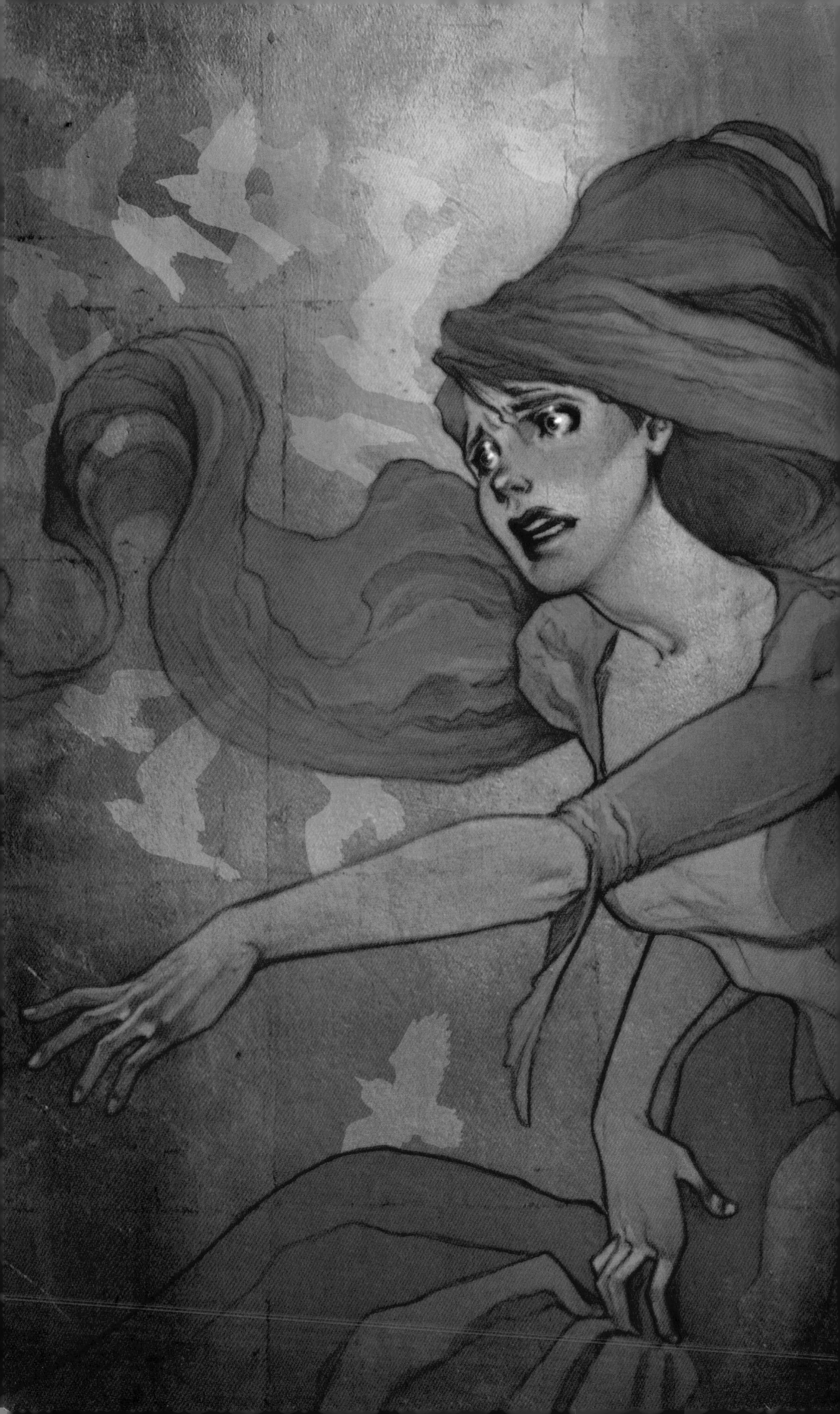

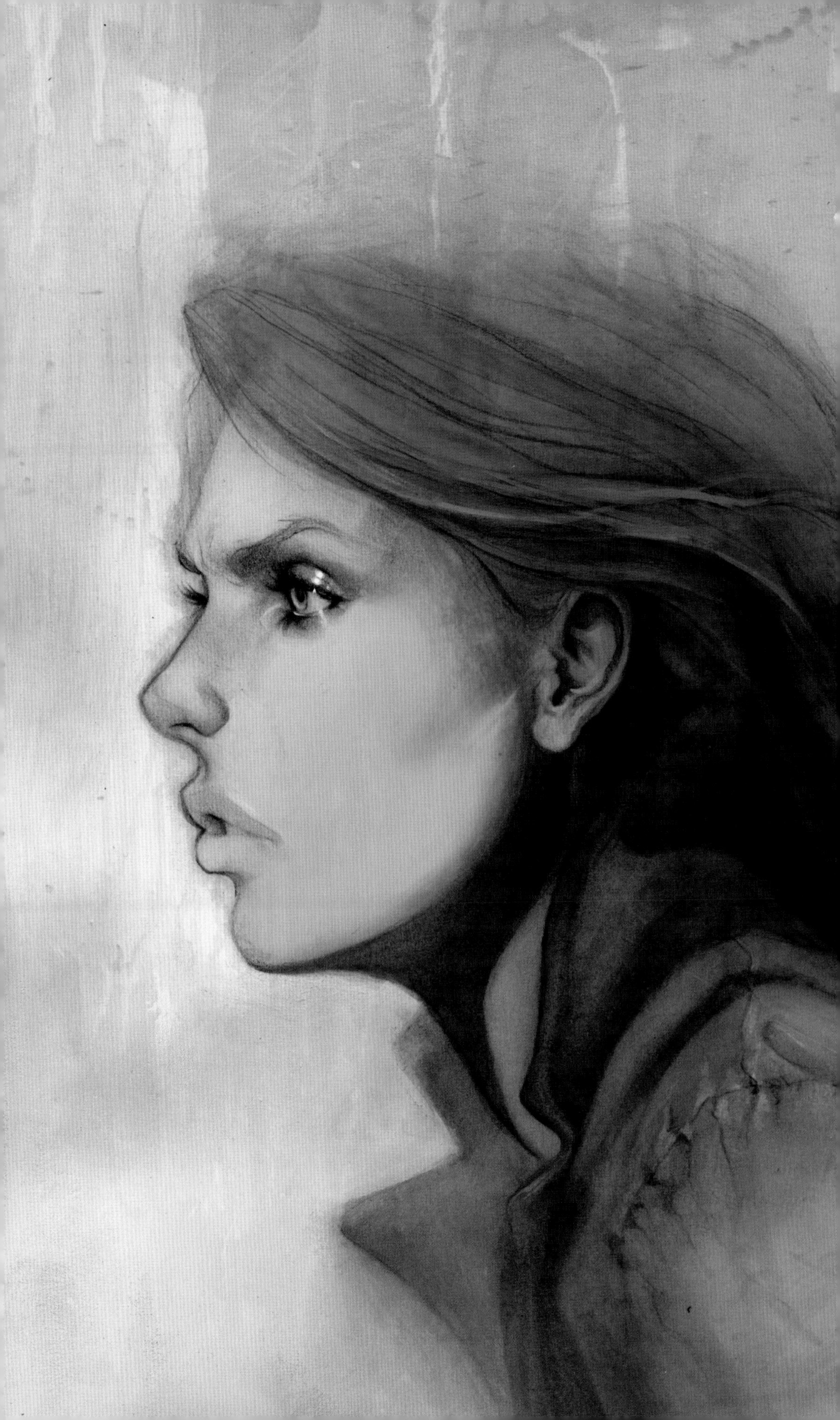

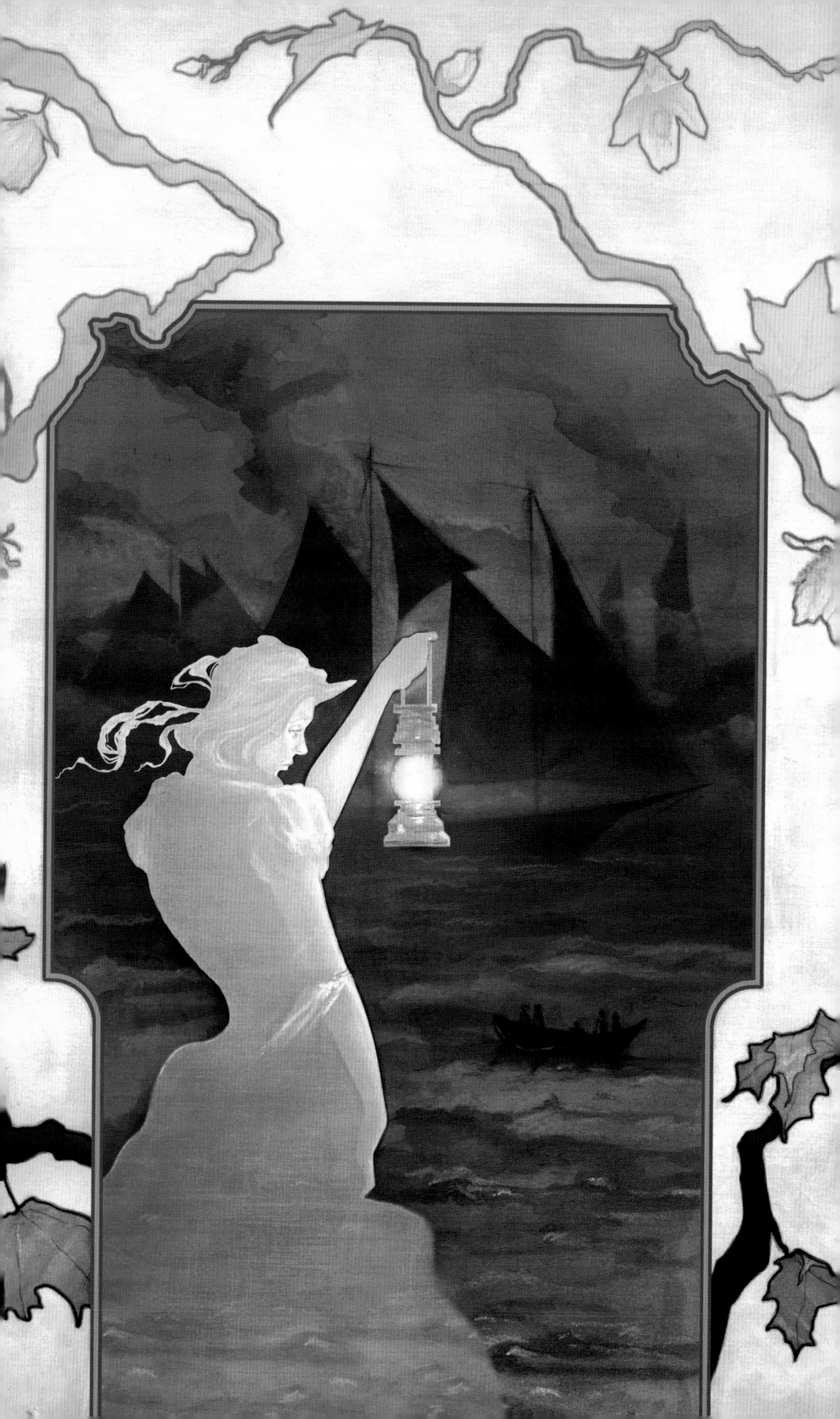

The Dreamer

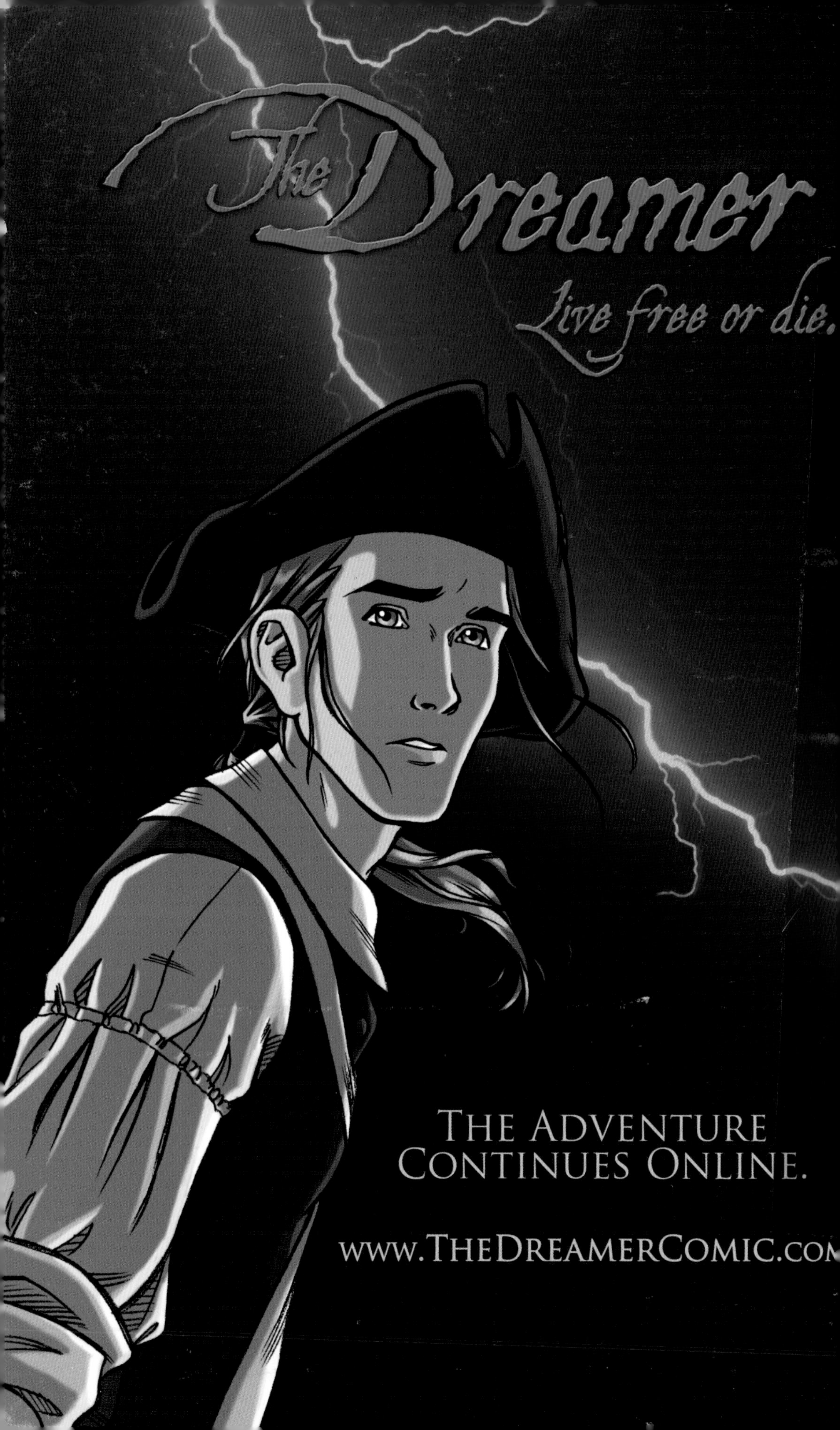
The Dreamer
Live free or die.
THE ADVENTURE
CONTINUES ONLINE.
WWW.THEDREAMERCOMIC.COM